CAPTOR'S KISS

"Are you looking for your father to ride to your rescue?" Gabel asked, leaning against the wall.

Ainslee gave him a brief look of disgust. "I am looking for your weak points, my cocksure knight, so that I may return to conquer your lands and give you a wee taste of captivity."

"I am all atremble." He took her hand in his, slowly drew it to his lips, and brushed a kiss over her knuckles. "Yet, what man could protest imprisonment by such fine blue eyes?"

It was nonsense, Ainslee knew, but she smiled and even felt her heart flutter. The tone of his deep voice stroked her. She tensed only briefly, when he reached out to thread his long fingers through her hair. She was not so naive that she was unable to recognize an attempt at seduction, but she did not feel any inclination to rebuff him.

"Ye talk a great deal of pretty foolishness," she murmured, making no attempt to elude him when he gently caged her body between his and the wall.

"Foolishness? Nay. 'Tis but the pure truth."

Ainslee shuddered when he brushed his lips over her forehead. They were soft and warm, and their touch clouded her mind. She knew he was going to kiss her. Warmth rushed through her body, pushing away all remnants of the chill caused by the brisk weather. She clutched at the front of his thick tunic, desperately needing the support when he slowly began to deepen the kiss. She clung more tightly to him, pressing her body closer to his as she fully succumbed to the power of his kiss . . .

Books by Hannah Howell

Published by Zebra Books

HANNAH HOWELL

MY VALIANT KNIGHT

ZEBRA BOOKS
KENSINGTON PUBLISHING CORP.
http://www.kensingtonbooks.com

ZEBRA BOOKS are published by

Kensington Publishing Corp.
850 Third Avenue
New York, NY 10022

All Kensington titles, imprints, and distributed lines are available at special quantity discounts for bulk purchases for sales
promotion, premiums, fund-raising, educational, or institu-
tional use.

Special book excerpts or customized printings can also be
created to fit specific needs. For details, write or phone the
office of the Kensington Special Sales Manager: Attn. Special
Sales Department. Kensington Publishing Corp., 850 Third
Avenue, New York, NY 10022. Phone: 1-800-221-2647.

ISBN 0-8217-7964-8

First Printing: January 1996
10 9 8 7 6

Printed in the United States of America

One

Scottish Highlands—1210

"The cast of that sky warns of a storm brewing, Ronald," Ainslee MacNairn said as she scowled up at the rapidly darkening sky.

"Aye, mistress," agreed her gray-haired riding companion. "Methinks we had best ride back to Kengarvey."

Ainslee smiled at him. "Are ye afeart of a wee fall tempest?"

"Nay, lass, and weel ye ken it. Howbeit, we have wandered far afield, and I am afeart of the Scots or the Normans. They would think it a fine thing if they got their hands on you. They would savor the chance to do a bit of bargaining or exact some revenge, or a wee taste of both. And with ye being such a comely lass, I dinna need to tell you how our enemies would seek their revenge through you."

As she turned her mount back toward the sturdy fortress she called home, Ainslee cursed softly and tightened the hood of her voluminous cloak over her dark red hair. "Will there never come a day when I can ride free of the fear of all our neighbors, Ronald? We are at odds with one and all of the nearest clans, at odds with the Normans our good king has set just o'er the river, and at odds with the people in the lowlands. Do ye ne'er grow tired of all the fighting and the dying?"

"Aye, but 'tis the way of the world, lass. Someone is always thinking to conquer us. Someone is always coveting our lands. There is always some dispute, someone claiming a grievance or insult. And there will always be the English, the Normans, or the neighboring clans to contend with. If it isna a raid, 'tis a fueding."

"Weel, I grow heartily sick of it all. I often wish to leave this place so badly I ache with it."

"Ye will soon be wed, and then ye will leave. Ye will, howbeit, forgive an old mon for hoping that that day doesna come too soon, as I have had the care of you since I set you on your first pony, and I will sorely miss you."

"Thank you, but it doesna appear too promising that I shall be wed and carried away to a better place, so I shouldna worry overmuch. I am eighteen, Ronald, and nothing has yet been arranged for me. By the time I was six, my sisters were wedded to men from our neighboring clans in the vain hope of increasing our laird's power. My father clearly feels that I am too thin and too ugly to make a good bargain with."

"Ye talk nonsense, lass." He shifted his stiff left leg to a more comfortable angle, and then idly rubbed the scarred spot on his left hand where he had lost three fingers. "Ye arena too thin. Under that heavy cloak is a form many a mon would be eager to curl up with. Aye, 'tis slim and limber, but ye have all the curves a mon wants. Ye have slim hips, but they are rounded enough to promise a mon the children he craves. Ye have fine red hair shot with gold, and eyes as blue as a loch on a fine summer's day. I could flatter ye more, but ye are blushing like fire now."

"Ye speak verra directly, Ronald."

"Someone must, if ye are to shed the foolish thought that ye arena bonny enough for any mon."

She smiled faintly as she slid her delicate, long-fingered hands up and down the reins she held. "Mayhaps I am not unpleasing to a mon's eye, but I am not what a mon searches for in a wife."

Ronald's weathered face creased into a grimace as he softly

cursed. " 'Tis true that, as the youngest of all your siblings by near to seven years, ye have grown to womanhood alone. Your friends and teachers have been those of us who serve the castle and the MacNairns. Your sisters were wed and gone, and your brothers were busy learning the ways of men. I was the one given the honor of raising you, and I fear I didna do it verra weel."

"Ye did verra weel indeed, Ronald. I learned a great deal from you."

"Aye, to ride as weel as any mon, wield a sword adequately, and be nigh on deadly with a knife. A bow is no stranger to those wee hands either, and ye have set many a beast of the forest on the tables of Kengarvey. Ye can read and write and even cipher a little, since ye blackmailed your brother Colin into teaching you when he returned from the monastery. Howbeit, ye have only a meager skill with a needle, unless ye are stitching a wound. Ah, but ye can play the lute and sing sweet enough to make even this hardened old mon weep. In truth, I dinna ken all ye can do or what skills ye have gathered in your unfettered life, but ye would make any mon a fine wife, one who can stand beside him and not cower behind him."

Ainslee smiled and shook her head. "That isna what a mon wants, Ronald, and weel ye ken it. A mon wants a wife who will kneel before him, heed his every command with blind, smiling obedience, and never, never complain. I dinna think that will change be the mon a Sassanach, a Scot, or one of those Normans our king so assiduously courts." She frowned when she realized that Ronald was no longer listening to her. "What is wrong?"

"Dinna ye hear that, Ainslee?" he asked as he stood erect in his saddle and looked around.

After listening carefully, Ainslee tensed and nodded. "Aye, I hear it. 'Tis the sound of horsemen, and they are coming up hard from behind us." She glanced down at the motley, huge gray wolfhound that trotted beside her and saw the fur bristle down his back. "Ugly hears it too, and by the mean look he now carries, 'tis not our own people who now approach."

Ronald signaled her with one sharp movement of his hand. She spurred her horse into a gallop at the same moment he did, and they raced toward Kengarvey. At the crest of the next rise, she saw a band of Normans clear the thick wood behind them. A cry cut through the chill fall air, announcing the dire fact that the Normans had espied her and Ronald. The chase was on. She could only hope that their enemy would be slowed by the weight of their armor, for there was a lot of distance between them and the safety of Kengarvey.

Gabel de Amalville shifted wearily in his saddle. He hated leading forays into the wild area of the Highlands. At times he wished he could slaughter the whole ragged collection of clans and reivers, sweeping the entire area clean for miles around. Even if he was allowed such freedom, he doubted he would succeed, however, for the troublemakers he sought were hard to catch. One glance at the twenty heavily armed men who rode with him told Gabel that they were as ill-pleased with the duty as he was.

"Gabel, look there," cried his cousin Justice Luten, tearing him from his disgruntled thoughts. "We have flushed out a pair."

"So we have, cousin, and, if we do not stop them, they will alert Kengarvey."

Gabel spurred his horse into a full gallop, and his knights were quick to follow. The pair of riders they sought were just disappearing over a small rise. They looked to be a young rider with an old man for an escort. It was not to Gabel's liking to put such people to the sword, but he steeled himself for the distasteful chore. If Kengarvey was forewarned, his journey there would be for nothing, as he could never storm the alerted keep. It was not until the distance between him and the fleeing

Scots was closed slightly that Gabel had the disturbing thought that one of the riders could be a woman.

He hastily shook away that idea. It was inconceivable that any woman could ride so well, or do so while riding astride such a powerful mount. The rider appeared completely unafraid of the speed of the horse and controlled the animal with an astounding skill. All of that told him that his prey could not possibly be a woman, yet his eyes continued to tell him that it was. He wanted the heavy dark cloak the rider wore to fly open, so that he could have a clearer view and end the confusion he suffered. Then, suddenly, Kengarvey rose into view and he reined in, too stunned to chase his prey even though they also reined to an abrupt halt. Kengarvey was in flames, and the harsh sounds of battle were easy to hear.

" 'Tis the MacFibh clan," cried Justice. "I recognize the banner. They have set upon the castle."

"Aye. It would appear that the castle was as weakly defended as we were told it was," agreed Gabel. "Watch our game, cousin. They now find themselves between two enemies. There is no way to guess how they will move next."

Even as he spoke the riders turned. Gabel shared the surprise of his men when the pair suddenly rode straight across their flank, racing back toward the shelter of the forest. His men loosed a few arrows, even as a cry went up from the MacFibhs and they sent a messenger out. Gabel wanted to race after the fleeing MacNairns, but was forced to wait.

"If 'tis the MacNairn ye seek," said the Scot as he reined to a halt before Gabel, "ye are too late. The bastard has fled with his four sons. The battle nears an end here. Those who arena dead or dying have fled, and the keep burns."

"Then we shall face MacNairn on another day. Hie, men, I want those two," Gabel cried to his men, even as he turned and spurred his mount after the two fleeing toward the forest.

Gabel was acting on impulse and intuition. Instinct told him that the pair of riders now barely in sight were of some importance. There was a chance that the MacFibhs were wrong, and not all of MacNairn's sons had fled at his side. If his instincts proved correct, he could demand a hefty ransom for the boy's return, a ransom that might well force MacNairn to at least confine his troublemaking to his own lands and those of his immediate neighbors like the MacFibhs. Gabel knew that this attack would not be enough to end MacNairn's reign. Kengarvey had been put to the torch numerous times over the years, and MacNairn had always risen from the ashes.

Any sort of truce with MacNairn would be a balm of sorts for the king, Gabel decided, and it was very important that he placate the king. Not only had he sworn allegiance to the Scottish king, but he was very comfortable in the keep and on the lands that pledge had gained him. Now that his elder brother had sired a third son, Gabel knew he had little chance of inheriting the English lands William I had given to their great-grandfather, Charles de Amalville.

The grant of lands from the Scottish king David was vitally important to Gabel, for he had no desire to live and die leaving nothing to the sons he craved. Neither did he wish to waste away his life as a mercenary, or join the priesthood. His time of personal service to David was nearly at an end, and, if he satisfied the king, the lands would be his. It had worked for others. If he could end the troubles stirred up by the MacNairns, he could then rest awhile, supporting the king by less demanding means. He could finally marry and begin his family.

Even now his manor was being prepared for a wife. Gabel decided it was not truly vain to be so confident that he would find one with ease. Women had never shied from him. Many a man had also indicated a wish to have him become part of their family. All he needed was the land, and the two riders now disappearing into the wood could well help him secure that largesse.

Minutes after they entered the forest, Gabel and his men had to slow their pace because of the thickness of the trees. When they lost sight of their quarry, Gabel ordered his men to halt. Justice dismounted and studied the ground. As he moved along, his mount trailing behind him, Gabel and the others gave their horses a well-deserved rest. Gabel refused to accept that he had lost the race. If Justice could find the trail, then they could catch their prey where the pair had gone to ground.

"One of them took an arrow, Gabel," Justice called. "The trail of blood is clearer than any of the hoofprints."

"Then they shall soon need to halt. Let us dismount and follow on foot for a pace," Gabel said as he slid out of his saddle. "Our horses need to rest. My backside could do with a respite from the saddle as well."

"See here, Gabel, they turn westward by this tree." Justice pointed at the gruesome markings when Gabel moved to stand beside him. "This bloody trail tells me that, whichever one of them is wounded, he will not be able to stay in his saddle for very much longer. Even now he must be growing very weak from loss of blood."

"Then we shall have them."

Ainslee turned to speak to Ronald about stopping at the small brook they crept by, and gasped. Ronald was as white as the cleanest linen. Even as she reached out to him, he swayed and slipped off his horse. Swallowing a cry of alarm, Ainslee flung herself from her saddle and rushed to his side. She cursed when she saw the arrow wound in his right leg.

"Why did ye keep silent about this?" she demanded. "Aye, but ye have lost a great deal of blood. The arrow?"

"I pulled it free, lass," he replied, his voice little more than a hoarse whisper as he clung to consciousness with grim determination. "Ne'ermind tending to me. Flee this place, ere those Normans catch you."

"And leave ye here to be captured, killed, or bleed to death? Never."

She fetched the small bag she always hung from her saddle.

Ronald had taught her to travel prepared for any trouble, no matter how short a journey. Since she had been a small child, there had always been Ronald and his small bag of assorted necessities. As she had aged, she had begun to assemble her own. In it were scraps of linen to bind his wound, and a mixture of herbs to use as a salve. All she needed to fetch was the water to clean his injury.

"Curse ye twice over, ye fool lass," Ronald muttered as Ainslee removed her mantle, folded it, and placed it beneath his head. "Will ye favor me by fleeing, while ye still can?" He started to curse fluently when she ignored him.

Ainslee knew what concerned Ronald the most. Without her mantle and its concealing hood, her sex was no longer a secret. She also knew that her now uncovered hair, free of braids and any other restraint, could act as a beacon to their enemies. Ronald was her only concern for the moment, however. If fate brought the Normans to her, then she would deal with them as best she could.

She gently bathed his wound and tried not to show her fear for him. He had bled freely, and that could prove dangerous. As she applied a paste of herbs, she prayed that the wound would not fester. Poor Ronald was crippled enough. He did not need his right leg becoming as stiff as his left. She bound the wound, then sat back on her heels, pondering what she could do next, for herself as well as for Ronald. He could not remount to flee with her. Their horses badly needed a rest as well, and even her gray wolfhound had collapsed beside them, his sides heaving.

After a moment's thought, she decided they had to take a risk, stay where they were and try to recoup their strength. They had taken a torturous route through the thick wood as they fled the Normans. It should follow that the Normans would find it very difficult to locate them. The Normans did not know the forest as well as she and Ronald did.

Not able to completely trust to luck and fate, however, Ainslee collected her and Ronald's swords. She knew it was a futile gesture, if the whole force stumbled upon them. Even more than two would be more than she and Ronald could deal with. Nevertheless, she also collected her bow and arrows and checked that her knives were in place. She was not one to swerve from a fight, nor did she mean to surrender meekly. If she and Ronald were fated to die, she intended to take a few of the cursed Normans with her.

"Lass, flee while ye still can," Ronald ordered in a fading voice.

"Nay, Ronald. Ye wouldna leave me, would ye?" She sat down next to him.

"That be different, and weel ye ken it. No mon with any sense of honor or a drop of courage in his veins would leave a wee lassie to defend herself against a foe."

"I can defend myself near as weel as any mon, and *weel ye ken it,* as ye yourself taught me such skills. Skills no mon will expect a woman to have." She smiled faintly. "I shall be a great surprise to those Norman dogs."

"Aye, ye will at that," grumbled Ronald. "Lass, ye are no fool. Canna ye see what those Norman swine will do to ye, if they catch ye? Ye, more than any other woman, must ken how a fighting mon's thoughts turn when he sets his hands on a lass."

"Aye, I do. I suspicion that the devils will think on raping me," she replied with a hard won calm. "Howbeit, if I see that fate has deemed that to be my lot, I shall kill myself."

"Nay," he cried, shock giving him a brief surge of strength. " 'Tis a mortal sin to take your own life, to die by your own hand. Ye could ne'er be buried in consecrated ground."

She shrugged and decided it would be best to divert his attention from that dark subject. "I believe the Normans may consider asking a ransom from my kinsmen for me. In truth, 'tis a very great possibility."

"Aye, a verra big one. Ye may weel be right in that, lass."

"Why, thank ye kindly, Ronald." She grinned, and he managed a weak one in return. "Now, ye are to rest," she ordered him in a stern tone of voice. "I can keep watch for our pursuers. Ye need to regain your strength, at least enough of it to continue on. Although, where we shall go is a great puzzle to me. My father and brothers have been most successful in assuring that we are surrounded by enemies."

As he closed his eyes, Ronald murmured, "We shall find some safe place and stay there a wee while, lass." He sighed. "My weakness is forcing me to obey your insolent command to rest. Dinna fret, sweeting. We will find a safe haven to crouch in, until we can learn the fate of your family."

Within moments, the only sounds Ainslee heard were the trickling of the brook and the chattering song of the many birds secluded within the trees. She sat cross-legged, as close to Ronald as she dared to without risking waking him, and laid her weapons across her lap. Ears trained for any sound of approaching danger, she tensely waited. Fear was a knotting coldness inside of her, but even that would not shake her from Ronald's side. He was her friend, her only friend, as well as her teacher, and had been more of a father to her than the man from whose seed she had sprung.

A soft sigh fluttered from between her lips, and she ran her hand along the sword resting in her lap. It would be a completely futile gesture to take up her sword against a knight trained and battle hardened. She hated futile gestures, yet knew she would do it, if she was forced to. Ainslee knew she could never simply sit quietly by and let her enemies do whatever they wished to Ronald and to her. She had spoken the truth when she had told Ronald that, if the Normans tried to sate their lusts on her unwilling body, she would kill herself. It was yet another futile gesture, but it carried the satisfaction of depriving the Normans of their brutal sport. The moment they tried to rape her, she would make certain that they held only a corpse.

The mere thought of rape caused a flood of fearful memories she had never successfully purged from her mind. She could still feel the bone-chilling cold of the dark, soggy hole her desperate mother had thrust her into, when the battle with one of the MacNairns's many enemies had turned against them. The piercing screams of her mother and the other women still rang in her ears. The sight that had greeted her young eyes when she had finally crawled out of that hole was still seared into her mind. It had all been more than a child of five could bear, and it had stilled her tongue for two years, before Ronald's loving care had freed her of terror's grip. Their enemies had taken their pleasure of every unfortunate woman who had fallen into their grasp, and then cut their throats. They had not bothered to cut her mother's slender white throat, for their ravenous lusts had killed her. Ainslee swore that that cruel fate would never befall her.

"Shall we give up the chase, Gabel?" asked Justice. " 'Tis almost as if our quarry has been swallowed up by these accursed trees."

"Soon," replied Gabel. "We had best look for some water and make camp nearby it. 'Tis far too late to journey back now." He scowled up at the rapidly darkening sky. "I but pray that we may find shelter as well, ere that brewing storm bursts over our heads."

"There is a surfeit of rocky hillside about this area. We may find a cave or, at least, a suitable ledge to huddle beneath." Justice abruptly halted and everyone immediately did the same. "Can you hear that, cousin?" he asked Gabel.

"Aye. Your sharp ears do not deceive you, Justice. 'Tis the sweet beckoning sound of water."

"And the sound comes from just beyond that thick grouping of trees. Do we leave our horses here?"

Gabel nodded. " 'Twould be wise. Our game may well have gone to ground here. Michael," he called to his other cousin, "you and Andre keep our horses still and quiet. The rest of us shall approach the stream as silently as we can. Shed any armor that may make noise, thus give you away," he ordered the rest of his men. " 'Twill not increase the danger to yourselves, for our prey wore no armor."

In moments Gabel and his men began a stealthy, annoyingly slow approach toward the sound of water. Stripped to their braies and deerhide boots, they made no sound at all. Gabel did not wish to battle with his quarry, just to capture the pair. Instinct told him that the ones he sought were not simple peasants. When he reached the edge of the clearing the brook trickled through, he came to a sudden halt, stilled by disbelief over the sight which greeted his widening eyes.

Two

Ainslee tensed, abruptly yanked from her dark memories of the past. She heard nothing, yet every muscle in her body was taut with a sense of danger. Her eyes widened and her heartbeat increased to a painful speed when she saw the men step out of the disguising shadows of the deep wood into the clearing. There was no time to use her bow. She might loose one arrow, but then they would be upon her. Slowly, she rose to her feet and took a protective stance over Ronald, her sword held securely and threateningly in her small hands.

Gabel stared at the girl and, realizing he was gaping, quickly closed his mouth. She was taut and prepared to do battle, her thick red hair sweeping around her slim shoulders, stirred to life by the increasing wind. Like some wild thing cornered, she faced them with the bravado of desperation.

He slowly looked over every slender, well-shaped inch of her. Her tunic was of a light gray hue and fit snugly over her strong slim arms. The bliand was of a bright woolen plaid, and the three-quarter-length overtunic was slit up both sides and laced tightly onto her shapely form. He expected that beneath that feminine attire, she wore long loose trousers of a heavy linen and hose of an equally thick cloth. That and the soft leather boots which reached to her knees and were held in place by cross gaitering were why, when he had seen her riding, he had thought that she was a he. Gabel briefly wondered if she wore a man's braies as well. Since she wore such heavy clothes beneath her gown, he suspected that she was also far more slender than she appeared.

His attention was drawn back to her hair, and he understood why she had worn a snug hood. No braids held the thick dark red hair in check, the fading light picking out the strands of gold in its depths. Her hair was like some glorious beacon, hanging beyond her waist in heavy waves, and he was not surprised when the sight stirred his blood. He doubted that any man could view such beauty and remain cold. As his desire quickly surged to a crippling height, Gabel looked at his men. They clearly felt as stunned and as moved as he did. The situation needed to be smoothed over and swiftly.

"M'lady," Gabel called to the girl in a light, friendly voice as he stepped to the fore of his men. "You cannot believe that you can take us all."

"Nay, my fine knight, I am not such a fool," she replied as she crouched into a fighting stance. "Howbeit, I shall leave ye sorely aware that ye have faced a MacNairn."

"Sweet heaven," murmured Justice as he edged closer to Gabel. "That bastard MacNairn breeds some very fine women."

"So, you believe she is that laird's spawn?" Gabel did not even glance at his cousin, his gaze fixed unwaveringly on the girl.

"Aye, Gabel. She wears the MacNairn brooch at her shoulder. You could see that for yourself, if you would but tear your eyes from her hair."

"Glorious, is it not? I have a craving to wrap myself in its thick waves. I will see if I can hold her gaze upon me, whilst you edge up to her from the left. Tread warily, cousin. She may well be able to wield that sword with some skill. It looks to have been made specifically to fit her small hands." Gabel smiled at the girl as Justice inched away. "There is no need for bloodshed, m'lady. We do not seek to harm you."

"Oh?" Ainslee briefly glanced at his men. "Ye brought a score or more fighting men with you so that we might exchange court gossip? Stay back," she hissed when she saw him edge toward her, Ugly's low growl of warning a confirmation of her suspicion that the man tried to sneak up on her. "Watch Ronald," she ordered the dog, and the animal adopted an unmovable stance by the unconscious Scot.

"Do not urge your beast to the attack, m'lady, for my men will quickly cut him down." Gabel knew he had judged her right when her eyes widened; she glanced nervously at the dog and then glared at him. The animal was trained to command, and eager to protect her and the man. It meant she had spent time and affection on the grotesque beast. "Give over, m'lady, and you will come to no harm."

Ainslee studied him closely and realized that she wanted to believe him, but she suddenly did not trust her own instincts. The man was too handsome, and she was far too aware of that despite the tense confrontation they were engaged in. He was taller than most of his men, his long body lean and muscular. Since he wore only his braies and boots, she could see that his complexion was naturally dark, not browned by the sun. His somewhat angular features could not really be called handsome, but they intrigued the eye and demanded respect. An aquiline nose was framed by well-defined, high cheekbones and led to a firm, slightly thin-lipped mouth. Straight dark brows crowned rich deep brown eyes so heavily lashed that Ainslee was certain they had caused some women to suffer sharp pangs of envy. His jaw was firm, implying a strength she had no doubt he possessed in full measure. His broad chest was smooth and hairless, a hint of dark curls finally appearing just below his navel and lightly dusting what little showed of his long, well-shaped legs. Both her mind and her body found the man far too intriguing, and she fought hard against that ill-timed interest.

She made a sharp, scornful noise in response to his claim that she would come to no harm. "Do ye mean to escort me home then, Norman?"

"I mean to hold you to ransom," Gabel replied.

There was such a strong tone of honesty in his voice that Ainslee almost submitted, but she suddenly espied one of the Normans stealthily approaching her from the side. Swiftly, not allowing herself time to consider what she was doing, she pulled her dagger from beneath the wide girdle at her waist, and hurled it at the man. Confident that her weapon had found its mark, she fixed all of her attention on the man facing her, for she knew there would be swift and lethal retribution.

"Justice," cried Gabel when his cousin yelped in pain. "Are you harmed?"

"Aye, but 'tis only a small wound in my shoulder," Justice replied.

Gabel scowled at the slim girl who stood before him, her sword at the ready. "You try me sorely, woman."

"Aye, but not enough, I am thinking," Ainslee replied, "for ye still cower out of reach of my sword, me frail, trembling knight."

He grit his teeth against the sting caused by the sneer in her melodious voice. "I will fight no woman."

"Then ye shall be a lot easier for me to kill," she said with a chilling sweetness even as she attacked him.

Gabel barely dodged the blade of her sword in time. His eyes widened as he raised his own sword in defense. Her swing had been a well-practiced one, not merely some blind thrust. The girl did possess some skill. His men fell silent and edged closer as he faced her, and Gabel knew they were intrigued by a battle between such an ill-matched pair. Gabel cursed as he realized he had been forced into a corner. He had to fight to protect himself, and could only hope that he could disarm the girl without hurting her.

The clang of steel against steel echoed loudly in the small clearing. The dog, caught between the command to guard the wounded man and his urge to protect his mistress, began to howl mournfully. The horses, infected by the dog's loud agitation, also grew noisily restless. Gabel was amazed by the girl's strength and skill. It took far longer than he had anticipated for her to begin to weaken, thus giving him the advantage he sought.

When he was finally able to knock the sword from her hands, she lunged to retrieve it. He kicked it out of her reach and she threw herself at his legs, knocking them out from beneath him. She fell upon him, yet another dagger in her hand. Gabel caught her by the wrist as she tried to thrust the point of her knife into his chest. He cursed as they rolled over the rough ground, and he struggled to disarm her. The knife finally dropped from her hand, and he quickly pinned her firmly beneath his body. He could see that she was panting as heavily as he was.

"Now, mistress, be that all of your weapons?" he asked, eager to pull away, for he was becoming all too aware of the tempting softness of her.

"Aye," she snapped, her angry tone weakened somewhat by her breathlessness. "So, ye can remove your hulking great weight."

He slowly got to his feet, watching her closely and keeping a firm grip on her slender wrist as he pulled her up. "Answer me true, mistress. Are you the daughter of the laird MacNairn?"

Ainslee nodded. "I am Ainslee of Kengarvey, the youngest daughter of Duggan MacNairn."

"Who is the man?"

"Ronald MacNairn, a cousin."

"Call off your dog," he ordered, and almost grinned when she did, for he found the animal's name humorously fitting. "Pascal," he called to a short, balding and stoutly built man. "Search the man and their horses for weapons. Gather whatever is at hand." He dragged Ainslee over to where one of his men was dressing Justice's wound. "Shall we survey your handiwork, Mistress MacNairn?"

Ainslee fought to hide all hint of emotion as she looked at the handsome young man's wounded shoulder. Her aim had been high, her knife piercing his smooth brown skin high on his left shoulder. Although it was not a mortal wound, it was clearly painful. Justice's features were taut and his face lacked color. She met Justice's dark gaze with a look of complete unconcern, contrary to the turmoil she felt. It upset her to cause anyone pain, although she never hesitated to strike if the need arose.

"Feeling remorse, m'lady?" pressed Gabel, frustrated by the lack of expression on her delicate face.

"Aye. 'Twas not one of my better throws," she replied in a too sweet tone. "May I see to my companion Ronald? His wound needs tending far more than this boy's pinprick." Just as she tried to pull away from the stern-faced man who held her, the man tending Justice began to cover the open wound with a piece of filthy cloth, neither washing or dressing the wound first. Ainslee knew she could not simply stand silent and allow that. "Ye great fool," she snapped, wrenching the dirty scrap from the startled man's hand. "Do ye wish to turn a minor wound into a fatal one? This cloth is not fit to wipe a dripping nose. Get me some water."

When the man looked at him, Gabel nodded, indicating that he should obey that sharp command. He cautiously released Ainslee's wrist when she tugged at it again, allowing her to fetch a small bag next to her cousin Ronald. He found it strangely reassuring to discover that she was not as unmoved by a man's pain as she tried to pretend. When, after washing Justice's wound, she poured a dark liquid over it that clearly pained his cousin, Gabel knelt by her side and snatched the flask she held.

"What is this?" he demanded, grimacing slightly as he sniffed it.

"Uisge-beatha—the water of life. A strong drink we brew. How long have ye been in Scotland?"

"Long enough, but I have wit enough to abstain from tasting any of the local poisons. Why pour it o'er his wound?"

" 'Tis said that it will aid the healing, and it appears to do so."

"Now what do you put on him?" he asked as she smeared a gruesome-looking paste over the wound.

Ainslee sat back on her heels, rinsing clean her hands before applying a bandage, and cast the man a look of pure annoyance. " 'Tis an herbal salve to aid his healing. When ye slither back into whate'er hole ye crawled out of, ye can wash it clean and stitch the wound, then apply some more."

As she wrapped a clean strip of cloth over Justice's injury, Gabel grinned at his cousin. "An ill-tempered wench, eh?"

"A prisoner canna be expected to be all that is courteous and cheerful," Ainslee said.

"You are no prisoner, mistress, but a hostage," Gabel replied.

"There is some difference?" The man nodded as she rose to her feet, and she added, "Weel, I fear it eludes me. I will tend to Ronald now."

Gabel watched her walk away, then ordered a man to fetch their horses and the other men before looking at Justice. "The lady has a sharp tongue. How fares your shoulder?"

"Whatever the girl did has served to ease the pain," Justice replied. " 'Tis naught to concern yourself with. I have had far worse than this, although it grieves me to have suffered it at the hands of such a tiny lady." He weakly returned Gabel's grin.

"A storm still brews," Gabel murmured aloud, scowling at the sky. "We must find some shelter soon."

"We must tell them where shelter lies," Ronald said as Ainslee helped him sit up.

"I care little if the Normans suffer a true battering by the weather," Ainslee muttered.

"Nor do I, but we are now in their grasp, and we shall suffer with them. We both ken that a Highland storm can be both fierce and dangerous. I dinna want us to sit out in it."

Ainslee sat beside Ronald as he called to the leader of the men and told the Norman where they could all find some shelter. She suffered from an uncomfortable mixture of anger and sadness. It puzzled her that she felt no fear. A twinge of self-disgust rippled over her as she wondered if that lack was because she found the Norman knight far too handsome for her own good.

She quickly shook aside that thought. He could easily have killed her, yet had clearly made an effort not to hurt her. She also could have been well used by him and his men by now, yet not one man had made a lustful advance toward her. Ainslee was not fool enough to think that meant that her virtue was safe, but she was growing confident that she would not be used as some communal whore. That bone-chilling fear was rapidly fading. Somehow she had realized that from the start. When she recalled her decision to take her own life if she was threatened by rape, she grimaced in self-mockery. When the Norman stepped up to her, she could tell by his dark expression that she had not succeeded in hiding all of her thoughts.

"Why do you look so forlorn, mistress?" he asked.

" 'Tis merely that I have had to confront my own cowardice," she replied as she stood up and walked to her horse.

Gabel kept pace with her and shook his head. "You are no coward, mistress. No man here would question your bravery. You faced me with all the courage any man could hope to show."

She knew he was speaking the highest flattery, but it did little to raise her spirits. "I am alive."

"It would have been more courageous to die?"

"Mayhaps. At least in death my honor would remain untouched. I made a vow, ye see. If dishonor threatened, I would take my own life. Instead I but talk myself out of feeling threatened. I dinna have the courage to honor my own vow."

"Dishonor does not threaten."

"Nay? And whose word am I to put my trust in? I ken ye not."

Gabel flushed a little as he realized he had neglected to introduce himself. "I am Sir Gabel de Amalville, and the man you skewered is my cousin and sergeant-at-arms, Sir Justice Luten. And I should not need to remind you that suicide is a mortal sin. You would be denied a resting place in consecrated ground."

"The MacNairns have been excommunicated. I dinna think I can rest in consecrated ground anyway."

"If your father would cease his lawless ways, that would quickly change."

"My father was born into a lawless land, and a lawless man seeded him. I dinna think some French guest of our king will cause Duggan MacNairn to change his ways."

"I am no guest, but an anointed knight of the king, and will soon hold my own lands."

Before Ainslee could reply, a low rumble rolled across the sky. " 'Tis a pleasant conversation, m'laird, but I fear it must end, or we shall never find shelter ere that storm begins."

She swung up into her saddle, scowling down at him when he grasped the reins as she reached for them. A quick glance toward the others revealed Ronald and Justice being settled on hastily prepared litters, despite their protests that they did not need such coddling. Ronald could not escape now, and she could not leave him behind. He was a poor man, and her father would never ransom him. Ronald could be in grave danger once the Normans discovered how worthless a hostage he was. She looked back at Gabel and knew he did not really trust her to stay with them once he released the reins.

"Mayhaps you should ride with me," Gabel said, his tone indicating that was an order not a request.

"I willna try to escape. Ye hold my dearest friend," she replied.

"Who would undoubtedly cheer if you should manage to slip my grasp."

"Undoubtedly. Howbeit, I didna heed his urgings to flee ere ye stumbled upon us, and I willna leave him now. Aye, especially not now that I have seen how poorly ye tend the wounded." He opened his mouth to protest, but she halted his words by adding, "So, if ye willna allow me to ride alone, then I think ye should ride with me."

"Nay, I *willna* allow you to ride about alone," he drawled.

She ignored his mocking of her speech, despite how it irritated her. "Then ride with me. I ken the way we must go, and my mount is verra surefooted."

"Your companion told me how to find the place."

"Then ye will be able to see if I try to lead you in the wrong direction." When he swung up behind her, she glanced at the brown arms encircling her waist, then at the strong, bare thigh touching hers. "I pray ye havena lost your clothes, Sir de Amalville, for ye will be in sore need of them when the rain starts."

He chuckled, then called to his men to follow, and Ainslee immediately decided that riding two in the saddle with this man had not been a good idea. His warm breath stroked her hair, and the feel of it stirred something to life deep inside of her. As they rode, his legs brushed against hers, increasing that newborn feeling, until she recognized it for what it was— lust. Her body was responding to the proximity of his with alarming haste, greed, and ill judgement.

She inwardly cursed. It was a poor time for her womanly desires to spring to life. Gabel de Amalville now held her prisoner. He had said that she would not be dishonored, but they had been speaking of rape. He had not sworn not to seduce her and, if he sensed her interest, he could well try and lure her to his bed. The feelings now running through her body told her that he could probably succeed. It would not taint his honor if she went to his bed willingly. Since she had never felt attracted to a man before, she did not know how to control the wanting she now suffered, and now was a very poor time to try and learn such lessons.

A moment later she silently scolded herself for being vain. She had not spent very many moments of her life fighting off the unwanted attentions of men. There was no reason this man should crave what no other man had. The cajoling voice in her head gently reminding her that she had had little contact with men aside from those within her own family, did not ease her self-castigation by much.

The chill touch of rain on her face yanked her from her musings, and she frowned up at the sky. "I dinna believe the rain will be kind and wait until we reach the shelter we seek."

Gabel also scowled up at the sky. "We are not far from it, if your companion spoke the truth."

"He did. Ronald has no desire to weather a Highland storm in the open." She glanced down at his leg, and smiled faintly when she noticed the bumps raised on his skin by the increasingly cold wind and the damp. "Ye will soon sorely regret your lack of covering."

"You are most concerned about my state of undress, mistress. Does it trouble you?"

"Only in that I have no wish to nurse even more Normans."

"A little wetting will not cause me to fall ill. It will but wash away the dust."

"A warm, French rain may weel be so refreshing, Sir Gabel. Howbeit, this is a Highland rain, and 'tis late in the year. This rain will push the cold through your flesh to your verra bones."

"Then nudge your mount to a greater speed. The hill we plan to hide in is but a short trot from here."

"My horse shouldna be made to endure such a trial. He is unused to carrying such weight."

"This huge beast could carry two fully armed knights upon his strong back and little notice it." Gabel patted the animal's side.

"Aye, when he hasna already been ridden for hours and forced to flee a pack of French reivers."

"I am no reiver. Once we are in our shelter, sitting round a warm fire, we will talk. You will soon learn that I am no reiver, once you come to know me."

That was the very last thing Ainslee wished to do. It was proving difficult to ignore the allure of his body and handsome face. He was dangerously attractive. She dreaded thinking of how much that allure could deepen if she began to know the man, to respect or even like him. As she reined in by the mouth of the cave they sought, Ainslee prepared herself to face an ordeal—fending off Sir Gabel's attempts to charm her, to make her forget that she was a prisoner, and lead her to falsely believe that she could ever be anything more.

Three

"My cousin needs no more tending, mistress," Gabel said as he stepped up next to Ainslee.

Ainslee gave a slight start, then cursed the tension that caused her to be so obviously uneasy. She had been purposely avoiding Sir Gabel from the moment they had entered the cave, barely escaping the sudden downpour of rain. The last thing she wished to do was to sit near him around a fire, talking and learning all about him. There was a look on his handsome face which told her that he suspected that she was trying to elude him, and she inwardly grimaced, silently cursing herself for a coward.

"I was stitching his wound. It needed closing," she murmured, and struggled against flushing guiltily beneath the sardonic look he cast her way.

"You could have sewn together a full court gown by now, m'lady." He grasped her by the arm and tugged her over to the fire. "You must warm yourself and partake of some of our food and wine."

"I should look to see how Ronald fares," she protested, pulling lightly against his grip.

"The man fares no worse than he did when you last crouched by his side. Sit," he ordered, nudging her down by the fire.

Ainslee sat, but rebelled enough to glare at the chuckling men who also shared the fire's warmth. It annoyed her when her anger only amused them more. She said nothing as she accepted, with ill grace, the bread and cheese offered to her. The cautioning voice in her head, which warned her against scorning her good luck in being captured by such apparently kind and good-humored men, was one she easily ignored. If these men were so kind and honorable, they would release her and Ronald.

"The fare is not to your liking?" Gabel smiled faintly when she glowered at him even as she accepted a second thick slice of bread.

" 'Tis rather fine food to take upon a raid," she said between bites.

"This was no raid, but a righteous vengeance sought by an angry king." When she simply continued to stare at him with open anger, he continued, "I always carry good food and drink with me when I begin a foray. It does not last long, of a certain, but I see no need to waste time foraging, simply because I do not carry adequate or palatable supplies. Foraging, taking whatever is at hand to feed my men, troubles me some as well, for 'tis too often the poor who suffer."

"A laudable sentiment, m'laird, but it doesna stop you, does it?"

"Nay, my ill-tempered lady, it does not. My men must eat."

She took a long drink from the wineskin he held out to her, then made a soft scornful noise as she wiped her mouth with the back of her hand. "Your men could eat well, aye, better and more often, if ye stayed at home."

Since he could understand the testiness she revealed, Gabel found it an easy thing to ignore. "That is impossible, and I believe you may have the wit to realize that."

"How kind of ye to say so," she muttered, and fought to ignore the charm of his brief smile.

"I am a knight who has pledged himself and his sword to the king. I do not believe the king asked for my pledge so that I could skulk inside of my castle walls and do naught."

It did not improve Ainslee's mood at all to find herself agreeing with him. If she was to hold onto her anger, he had to be boorish, irritating, even dimwitted. Instead, he spoke calmly and with a quiet reason she could not fault. He answered her sullen remarks with an almost friendly courtesy. Protecting herself against that somber, subtle charm was not going to be easy. In fact, when she met his dark gaze and realized that he was speaking to her in a way few men would speak to a woman, nearly as an equal and as if she actually had some wits, she knew he could easily prove to be impossible to resist. Ainslee struggled to hide the alarm which suddenly swamped her.

"Ainslee has the ring of an English name," Gabel said, breaking into her thoughts.

"Nay, it doesna," she snapped.

"Aye, it does, and I now recall it being said that MacNairn's wife had some English blood."

"If she did, 'twas swiftly subdued by her good, hale Scots blood."

"Of course."

"The food and wine were good," she said, as she cautiously rose to her feet, tensed to resist any attempt to restrain her. "And I thank ye kindly for it. I am weary and will bed down next to Ronald now."

"I noticed that you had spread a blanket at his side."

"He may have need of me in the night."

Gabel briefly scowled toward the mouth of the cave. "Do you expect this storm to last throughout the night?"

"Aye, if 'tis a small one. Good sleep, sirs." She bowed slightly to the men and went to curl up next to Ronald and Ugly.

"An odd young woman," murmured Michael Surtane as he sidled closer to his cousin Gabel after Ainslee left.

"Odd?" Gabel asked, ignoring his cousin's intent stare.

"She acts like no lady I have ever met before."

"I was not in Scotland long before I learned one cannot judge the women here as one does the ladies in France or England."

"I was thinking of the Scottish lasses I have met when I spoke. She is not like them either."

Gabel laughed softly. "I concede, cousin. Aye, m'lady Mac-Nairn is not like any other lady you or I know. Methinks she has had an unusual raising."

"True. One must not forget who her father is."

"Nay, there is a harsh truth and a wise warning." He frowned at Ainslee, her slim form nearly hidden by the shadows at the back of the cave, and inwardly sighed, a little astonished at the sudden confusion of emotion he was afflicted with. " 'Tis strange, but I do not sense any of Duggan MacNairn's taint within her. 'Tis as if the man has had little or nothing to do with her."

Michael nodded, glancing briefly at Ainslee before returning to his close study of his cousin. "I noticed that you had a sharp interest in her."

"She is intriguing. The girl has skills more suited to a man, and I believe there is a keen wit behind those fine blue eyes."

"And under that heavy, glorious hair you are so bewitched by."

"Ah, I begin to see what may concern you, cousin. Do not fear. I am not so bewitched that I forget who and what she is—a MacNairn and a prisoner for ransom." Gabel smiled with a mixture of amusement and curiosity when his cousin frowned. "You look as if you have suffered some disappointment."

"Nay." Michael grimaced and ran his fingers through his dark hair, then laughed softly. "You have ever been the one with the coolest blood, and we owe our lives to it. 'Tis but, well, just once I should like to see you beguiled by a lovely face, and Mistress MacNairn has the fairest face I have seen in many a year."

"That she has. Howbeit, I learned at a young age that 'tis dangerous to allow a fair face to beguile me. Such foolishness nearly cost me my life once, and it did end the life of my good friend. If I had not been so blinded by Lady Eleanor's fair face, I would have seen the treachery she worked."

"Gabel, that was nearly ten years ago. You were but a boy, untried and easily led," Michael complained as he poked a stick into the waning fire.

"And I learned my lesson well. As you said—you owe your lives to it."

"Well, aye, but 'twould make the rest of us feel better if you stumbled in your perfection a time or two."

Gabel laughed and clapped his cousin on the back before moving to seek his own bed. "I have never been perfect, Michael. You know that as well as any can. I have simply taken to heart a lesson painfully learned—cool blood and following one's head, not one's heart or passions, is the best way to stay alive. Wake me if the storm wanes, or if I am needed to stand a watch."

"Do you think there may be some trouble?"

"In this weather? Nay. Howbeit, keep a watch, for one must always be wary in this land."

As Gabel settled himself on his meager bed of blanket and rock near the right side of the cave, he fought the urge to look over at Ainslee, and failed miserably. Even as he shifted his weary body until her slight form was in view, he cursed himself as a weak fool. He had indulged in a false boast when he had not argued Michael's opinion that he was ever cold-blooded and clearheaded, but he did not wish to expose what lay beneath his armor and somber facade. If his own men knew of the turmoil within him, of the constant battle he fought to make calm thought overwhelm discordant emotion, they would undoubtedly question his ability to command.

From the moment he had set eyes on Ainslee MacNairn, he knew he faced one of his toughest battles with himself. Standing there in all her belligerent glory, she had accomplished what no woman had done for years—stirred a deep, immediate, and fierce emotional response within him. Gabel both savored it and feared it. He had never felt so alive, so eager to face the hours, days, and weeks stretching out before him.

What he had glimpsed of her character so far had intrigued,

surprised, and excited him. That was something he considered to be very dangerous, and not simply because she was a Mac-Nairn, the daughter of a man he had sworn to defeat, and his prisoner. Lady Eleanor DesRoches had shown him the folly of trusting in his emotions. Older and more worldly, she had used the lust and blind love of the boy he was to try and aid her true paramour, a man who wished to destroy the de Amalvilles and coveted all they owned. His friend Paul had tried to warn him, but he had been deaf to the truth. It had taken her attempt to end his life before Gabel had felt his naive trust crumble and harden into a wary cynicism he fought hard to cling to. A flame-haired Scottish lass with fine blue eyes was not a good reason to cast aside that hard-won control.

And what good could come of such an infatuation anyway? he asked himself as he forced his eyes closed. Even if Ainslee MacNairn was not a prisoner and one of the enemy's spawn, she was wild, clearly untutored in the proper ways of a lady. She would still be highly unsuitable for him, and would never be able to fit into the life he had so carefully planned for himself. Such a free-spirited woman would indeed make a very poor wife.

But she would make an exciting lover, a voice whispered in his head, and Gabel found himself staring at Ainslee again. He cursed and tightly shut his eyes. The thought was a tempting one, but he girded himself against its allure. Gabel was no monk, but he struggled to remain honorable in all his dealings with women. Taking a wellborn young lady as his woman, fully intending to cast her aside when he found the wife he searched for, was not the act of an honorable man. As he struggled to banish all thought of an impassioned and willing Ainslee from his mind, Gabel hoped that her father would be swift in ransoming her.

A scream echoing in the cave yanked Gabel from his hard-won sleep. He grasped his sword from its place close by his side and staggered to his feet. A quick glance at his men showed that they, too, were in an unsteady state of groggy awareness.

"M'laird," called Ronald, drawing a rapidly waking Gabel's attention his way.

Gabel looked at the aging Scot, who was struggling to sit up, and immediately noticed that Ainslee was no longer curled up at the man's side. He whirled to face the mouth of the cave and saw one of his men fighting to hold onto Ainslee. Just as he moved to go to the man's aid, Ronald's wavering voice drew his attention back.

"She is but caught in a dream," Ronald said.

"She does not try to escape?"

"Only from the dark memories that sometimes haunt her sleep. She can be difficult to rouse, m'laird," Ronald advised as Gabel strode toward the guard who clearly did not know how to control a blindly frantic Ainslee. "Ye may have to shake her free of the dream's grip, or e'en slap her."

Once at the side of the struggling pair, Gabel knew that Ronald was right. There was a look of stark terror on Ainslee's small face and no sign of recognition in her wide blue eyes when he called out her name. She was babbling something about her mother, her accent so thick he could barely understand her. What caused Gabel to feel the cold touch of alarm, however, was that Ainslee's voice was that of a very young child.

"Ainslee," he snapped as he yanked her out of the other man's arms and shook her. "Wake up!"

"I must get out of the hole. *Maman* needs my help." Ainslee pushed at Gabel's chest in a vain attempt to break free of his hold. "Canna ye hear the women screaming?"

"No one is screaming but you. Come to your senses, woman. 'Tis but a dream which afrights you."

"Nay! *Maman* is screaming." When Gabel finished shaking her for a second time, Ainslee slumped against his chest. "I was too small to help, but I am bigger now." Ainslee frowned, confused by her own words as the tight grip of her nightmare began to ease. "Nay, that isna right. *Maman* is dead. I canna change that."

"Nay, you cannot." Gabel felt her body grow lax and he tightened his grip on her, fighting to ignore how good it felt to hold her in his arms. "One cannot go back and change another's fate."

"But 'twas such a pitiful fate, so painful, so horrifying. I can still see all the blood," she whispered. "I couldna clean it away. I tried, but I was just a bairn. I closed her eyes so that the sun wouldna burn them."

Relieved to hear her voice returning to normal, Gabel gently urged Ainslee toward the fire. He glanced at Ronald, who nodded and laid back down. One sweeping look at his men was enough to send them back to their posts or their beds. Instinct told him that Ainslee would be embarrassed, although he was a little confused as to how he could feel so certain about that.

"I should return to my bed," Ainslee muttered even as Gabel made her sit down by the fire.

"Drink this," he quietly ordered as he sat down next to her and handed her his wineskin.

Slowly recovering from the chilling horror of her memories, Ainslee found the strength to give Gabel a cross look as she took a drink of the sweet wine. She struggled against a sense of deep embarrassment over revealing her weakness and fear before Gabel and his men. Ainslee also knew that many men would consider her mother's death a shameful one, even though none of the women killed that day had asked for the horror they had suffered through. One reason she never spoke of her mother's death was to try and prevent anyone from thinking poorly of the woman, of her honor, courage, or morals. Such undeserved scorn infuriated her, especially since she knew that such men could never be swayed from their unfair condemnation by any argument she might choose to make.

"Do ye think this wine can dull the sharp edge of my dreams?" she asked in a near whisper.

"Mayhaps for the rest of this night," Gabel replied. "I but wish I had some potion which could steal such dark memories from your mind for all time. You watched your own mother die?"

"Nay, I listened to her. Aye, and to all of the other women cursed enough to be captured."

"You *listened?*" Gabel did not want to contemplate what such horror could do to a child.

"Aye. My mother hid me in a dark hole, covering it with debris. She told me to stay there and make no sound. I wasna the most obedient child e'er born," she smiled crookedly for one brief moment, "but that time I did exactly what I was told to. I huddled there in the dark until all was quiet, and then I crept out to see the brutal destruction men can so easily wreak upon the innocents."

Gabel inwardly winced beneath her look of condemnation. "I cannot claim that my men and I are free of any such crimes, but none of us has ever cruelly slaughtered a woman." He sighed and shook his dark head. "I have been amongst warriors who have, and in battles where such crimes were committed. Since I cannot claim to have stopped such dishonorable acts, I must claim some of the guilt. Where was your father?"

"Running for his life and saving his sons."

"And leaving his wife and daughter to face a battle-maddened enemy?"

"My father prizes his sons most highly. As he has ofttime said, daughters can only gain a mon a wee bit through a good marriage, and a mon can always find himself a new wife. He has buried two wives since my mother died. Since neither woman provided him with a live son, I believe he has cursed us all to hell's fires and plans to wed no more."

"So, you have lost three mothers."

"Nay, only one. My father's other two wives were no more than shadows flitting through the halls of Kengarvey. They had no use or love for me. I kenned that and left them be. After my mother was murdered I was given into Ronald's care, and there I have remained."

It was hard for Gabel to understand such a bleak childhood. His family had its troubles, but he had never felt unwanted. Despite all the rivalries and arguments, he enjoyed a true bond with his family, the near and the distant relations. Judging from the way Ainslee spoke, the only member of her closest family who had cared for her had died years ago, leaving only Ronald, a man most people would consider little more than a servant.

He studied her as she took another sip of wine, pleased to see the color returning to her ashen cheeks. It was not difficult to see the child within the woman. Ainslee MacNairn must have been a very engaging child, yet she had been tossed aside by her father like leavings from the table. Only briefly did Gabel question the truth of her sad story. Her terror had been too real, and she spoke of her bleak life as if she had accepted it and certainly did not expect any pity.

"Your man Ronald did his duty well," Gabel said.

"Aye, although it is certain that many folk wouldna think so." Ainslee smiled faintly and glanced toward her sleeping mentor. "Ronald taught me all of his skills, gave freely of all his knowledge, but 'tis not the sort of skill or knowledge a wellborn lass should have."

"In this rough land it probably serves you well."

"Verra weel except in gaining a husband." Ainslee briefly wondered why she spoke so freely, then decided she was simply too tired to guard her tongue. And, since theirs was to be a short acquaintance, she also decided that what Gabel learned about her life was of little consequence. "A mon first looks to gain land, coin, or power. Then he looks for such skills as fine needle-work and courtly manners. After all, a wife is but a tool for gain and the breeding of sons. Aye, I may produce sons, for my mother bore four living ones, but I canna say that I would bring a mon much gain. Nay, especially not with my father causing such trouble and making so many enemies."

Everything she said was true, and the reasoning was both

common and practical. It was the reasoning Gabel himself used in his search for a wife, yet he inwardly winced. There was no condemnation or anger in her voice, but simply speaking of such methods aloud made them sound callous and mercenary. Gabel did not like to think that he shared such ungallant ideas, but, he also knew most people would consider him the greatest of fools if he did not consider lineage, fertility, breeding, and gain when he sought out a wife. He also realized he was being ridiculously contrary when he mused that a man would have to be a fool not to consider Ainslee for a wife, despite all she lacked.

"A man must look to his future," Gabel murmured.

Ainslee wondered why the man sounded defensive, even apologetic. Gabel de Amalville was a man of good birth and knowledge. Such men choose their wives carefully. It was not only accepted, but expected of anyone in his privileged position. Ainslee decided she was so tired she was hearing things in his voice that were not there.

"I believe my fears have waned now, Sir Gabel," she said as she rose to her feet. "I will return to my bed. I pray I willna disturb everyone's rest again this night."

"There is no need to apologize for something you cannot help," he said. "Few of us can boast that we are free of the night's terrors."

"Mayhaps, but I shall endeavor to cease dragging all about me into the midst of mine. Good sleep, Sir Gabel."

"Good sleep," he replied as he watched her return to her bed at Ronald's side.

As she wrapped herself in her blanket, Ainslee fought the strong urge to look back at Gabel. Waking from her nightmare to find herself in Gabel's arms had been quite a shock. Even more so when she had recognized how much his touch and deep soothing voice had contributed to the easing of her fears. That was not something she wished him to discover.

Especially not now when he kens most everything else about you, she thought with a strong hint of self-disgust. Her decision not to control her words suddenly felt like a grave error, and not only because of all Gabel had learned about her. His responses had revealed a few things about him, that he could be a gentle man for one thing. Ainslee did not want to know about the man's good qualities. She was going to have enough difficulty controlling her attraction to the man. She sighed and yet again prayed that her father did not prove obstinate about ransoming her.

Four

"Twill be a fine, sun-kissed day," said Gabel, gazing up at the sky.

Ainslee glared at his broad back and heartily wished that there was some way to ride behind him safely without having to wrap her arms about his waist. That brought her very close to his strong body, and the warmth such nearness engendered within her irritated her. The fact that he had taken possession of the reins of her horse irritated her as well. Even the beautiful weather annoyed her. She was being taken away for ransom. The storm of last night should still be raging in heavenly protest. That her horse had so amiably accepted a new rider's commands seemed to her to be a particularly cruel blow. She glanced down at Ugly, who trotted along beside them, and wondered when he, too, would desert her.

"You do not find the sun's warmth pleasing?" Gabel asked, glancing briefly over his shoulder at her.

"Can ye not tell that from my smile?" she snapped.

"From that grimace of clenched teeth? Nay. Your restlessness in the night has left you in a foul temper."

" 'Tisna my restlessness which causes my ill humor."

"And will m'lady grace me with the knowledge of what does cause her to be such poor company?"

Certain she could hear a tremor of laughter in his voice, Ainslee fought the urge to punch him squarely between his broad shoulders. "Mayhaps I find it annoying to have Normans creeping about my lands taking whatever they covet—lands, keeps, honors, women, *and* horses." She cursed under her breath, sure that she could see his shoulders shake with amusement.

Gabel stroked the neck of her horse. "A fine, strong steed. Mayhaps too strong for a woman."

"Did ye see me have any difficulty with him?"

"Nay. You ride with great skill."

His flattery only soothed her bad temper a little. "I suggest ye dinna get too comfortable on his back. My father will soon ransom me, and I shall take my horse with me when I leave."

"There are many men who would consider such a fine animal as the spoils of victory."

"Ah, but 'tis ofttimes said that Sir Gabel de Amalville is not like other men."

She was a little surprised when Gabel laughed aloud, a hearty, open laugh. A quick look at the men riding with them revealed several openly amazed expressions, as well as some looks of intense curiosity directed her way. Her tone of voice had been so sweetly flattering she had expected some amusement from Gabel, but not so much. What troubled her was how that deep, pleasant laugh caused a tingling warmth to curl around her insides. This further indication of her total lack of control over her own errant feelings heightened her sour mood, pushing aside the brief flash of good feeling inspired by his laughter.

"Did you think that sudden piece of honey-sweet cajolery would alter my decision about anything?" he asked, grinning at her over his shoulder.

For what felt like an embarrassingly long time, Ainslee was unable to speak. The playful smile that lightened his dark face seemed to push all the air from her lungs and shape it into a hard knot in her throat. As she struggled to clear away that obstruction, she prayed she did not look as spellstruck by his smile as she felt.

" 'Twas worthy of a try," she finally said, hoping he could not hear the hint of huskiness in her voice.

"I shall have to watch you closely."

Ainslee's reply died on her tongue when she idly glanced to the side. There was no mistaking the swift yet silent advance of armed men. It was not only their stealthy approach that warned Ainslee of danger. From all she had heard in the last few months, from all the whispered tales of horror in the kitchens and stables, she knew what now approached them was the newest scourge to darken her land.

"I think you had best watch the men on your right more closely, m'lord," she said.

Even as Gabel looked around, the men ceased all attempts to be stealthy, screamed out an ear-splitting mix of war cries, and charged. "Who in Mary's sweet name are they?"

"Outlaws, men cast out of their clans, towns, and homes. Men far past due for a good hanging, and a few of the notorious Graemes. Ye had best act soon. They are swift."

In a heartbeat Gabel assessed the vulnerability of his men and made his decision. Unprepared for the attack and dragging two wounded men plus one girl, they were left with few choices. He snapped out orders to his men even as he spurred Ainslee's strong mount into a gallop. While Gabel and the greater part of his force made a loud show of fleeing, the two men dragging the litters carrying Justice and Ronald hurried into the disguising shadows of the forest on their left. Three men slipped after them to guard their backs.

As he rode, drawing the outlaws after him on their swift mounts, Gabel cursed fluently. He detested fleeing like some coward, but he had to pull the attackers away from the weaker members of their group. He wished he had had the time to send Ainslee off with the wounded. Gabel also cursed the distraction he had allowed to creep into his mind, stealing his usual keen sense of danger. He should have been paying attention to the treacherous country he rode through, not the weather and not the tiny female clinging to him.

"If ye turn a wee bit westward right now, ye will reach a rocky rise where ye might make a stand against this swine,"

Ainslee yelled, trying to be heard above the pounding of the horses' hooves.

Gabel did as she suggested and immediately wondered why. Instinct had directed him, but he had to question how good that instinct was. What would a young wellborn woman know of the proper place to try and defend oneself? A moment later he knew his instinct had been right. He did not even have to order his men to make for the rocky knoll. They quickly recognized its worth as a temporary fortress.

Ainslee cried out softly as she was pushed from the saddle the moment they reached the top of the hill. She barely stopped herself from hitting the ground hard enough to hurt herself. Even as she struggled to steady herself, Gabel shoved her back amongst the horses, then turned with his men to meet the attack.

As Ainslee huddled amongst the fretting horses, her panting wolfhound collapsing at her side, she watched the outlaw force reign to an abrupt halt at the base of the hill. She prayed that they would decide that an attack would be too dangerous and flee, but doubted that her prayers would be answered. Such men had so little to lose, they would undoubtedly try an attack at least once. She did not want any of Gabel's men to be hurt, then briefly worried that she might be betraying her family with such sentiments. After a moment's thought she decided she was no traitor to the MacNairns. It was not wrong to wish no one would be injured or killed and, at this precise moment, the Normans were all that stood between her and the ruthless criminals at the foot of the rocks.

"M'lady, did you say you know who these men are?" asked Gabel as he waited for the attack he knew was to come.

"Only through the tales of their many crimes," she replied. "They are murderers, thieves, rapists, and traitors; many thrust into banishment by their own kinsmen."

"So these are not men who will wish to treaty with us."

"Nay. The only thing anyone might wish to say to them is to wish them a swift and early plummet into the fires of hell.

Of course, I confess that my knowledge comes only from what has been whispered about by others."

"Why have I heard nothing about them?"

"They have only just begun to spread fear and death over this land. Someone must have appeared to band them all together." She silently echoed Gabel's hissed curses. "Do ye think they will attack?"

"Aye. Howbeit, although there are more of them, we hold the high ground. They cannot win."

It was a proud boast, yet Ainslee found she could not scorn it. She suspected his confidence in himself and his men was well earned. As the two forces stared at each other—tense, glaring and exchanging taunts—Ainslee looked for her weapons. Gabel and his men might well be capable of fending off any attack the marauders made, but the chances were good that the outlaws would overrun the hilltop for one brief time. Ainslee did not want to stand there helpless and unarmed when that happened. The increasing noise from the men told Ainslee she did not have much time left. She recognized the bellowed taunts for what they were—a prelude to an attack.

When she found the saddlepack holding her weapons she breathed a hearty sigh of relief. The outlaws were banging their swords against their shields, stirring their blood in preparation for the charge. She took out her bow and quiver of arrows, briefly scorning the men for refusing to use such a weapon, clinging to their swords as if their were badges of honor. Gabel had only brought two archers with him on his foray, and had then sent them off with the wounded. Tucking her daggers away and sheathing her sword, she moved to a spot that still sheltered her near the horses, yet allowed her to see clearly in all directions. She just hoped that the attack would come before Gabel or one of his men could notice that she was armed, and take away her weapons.

Even though she had fully expected the attack, Ainslee felt a sharp thrill of fear when the final war cry was sounded by the outlaws, and they raced up the rock-strewn hillside. She stood up, drawing her sword. Ugly stood beside her, tensed, snarling, and prepared to defend her. The first clash of swords made her wince, and she steadied herself to feel nothing as men screamed in pain.

As she had feared, the outlaws soon swarmed over the top of the hill. They hoped to use their greater numbers to win the fight against the Normans. It was immediately apparent that that tactic was going to fail. Not all of the outlaws had the stomach to face battle-hardened knights. Now was the perfect time to use the bow and arrow, but it still appeared that only she possessed that weapon and, to use it, she would have to tell Gabel that she was now armed, if only so that she might get a clear shot at their enemies. Declaring that she had obtained her weapons was the surest way to lose them. A few well-aimed arrows would have neatly thinned the horde scrambling up the hill. Instead the men met face-to-face, sword to sword. Men, Ainslee mused with a soft snort of disgust, could behave quite foolishly at times. Men thought that the most important things in a battle were honor, bravery, and victory. She felt the most important thing was surviving.

Ainslee tried to remain alert, constantly struggling to keep a close watch on all sides, but her gaze continued to linger on Gabel. The sight of him tore her apart with fierce conflicting emotions. She thought he looked magnificent as he battled his enemies, even as she trembled with fear for his life. That she could feel so strongly about the man who held her for ransom was both astounding and irritating.

A sound from her right yanked Ainslee from her confusing thoughts. One of the outlaws had pushed through the tight battle line of Normans and stumbled over to face her. A grim smile curved his bloodied mouth. He had not come through the line unscathed, but clearly believed that she was not to be feared. Ainslee braced herself, crouched into a fighting position, and prepared to prove him wrong. As she raised her sword to meet his blow, the force of the clashing weapons ripping through her muscles, she wondered if she had been a little too confident. Ugly sent up a howl as he trotted around them, eager to help her, but trained not to interfere in such a fight unless commanded to. Ainslee felt her fear ease somewhat. If and when the time was right, she only needed the strength to utter one command, and her enemy would discover himself attacked from two sides.

Gabel cut down the man before him. The outlaw's scream had barely gurgled to a halt when Gabel heard the wolfhound's agitated barking. He ordered his men to stand fast, not to chase the now retreating Scots for fear of a trap, and turned to see what danger Ainslee had gotten herself entangled in. A vile curse was all he could utter when he saw her fighting with one of the outlaws, a burly man who far outweighed her and stood head and shoulders above her.

"She is armed again," said Michael as he stepped up next to Gabel.

"Aye. The foolish woman thinks she is a man." A quick glance around revealed that the battle was as good as over, and Gabel cautiously moved toward Ainslee. " 'Tis clear that we did not secure her weapons well enough."

"I can understand her need to face the enemy with a sturdy weapon in her hand. 'Twould not be to my liking to stand helpless when these dogs attacked, my only defense being to hide or flee."

" 'Tis the defense most women are content with. Do not try to soothe my anger. We will gain nothing if the foolish girl gets herself killed."

Gabel ignored his young cousin's knowing glance. The ransom was indeed the very last thing he was concerned about at the moment, but he had no intention of confessing to that. He began to circle the ill-matched combatants, hoping he could find some way to nudge Ainslee aside and end the battle himself. She would soon tire, and he realized he was terrified of the possibility of seeing her wounded or killed.

"Curse the girl," he muttered. "If I draw any closer, I could easily cause her death rather than save her."

Before Michael could reply, the man Ainslee faced stumbled. Ainslee did not hesitate to take advantage of her enemy's sudden vulnerability. The death stroke she inflicted was swift and clean. The Scot fell with barely a sound. She stood, her sword still slick with blood, and stared down at the man she had just killed.

"Ainslee," Gabel called as he tentatively approached her, unsettled by her ashen complexion and the look of stunned horror on her small face. She spun around, facing him with sword in hand. "Do you mean to skewer me as well?" he asked, holding his hands out in a gesture of peace.

" 'Twould free me," she said, her voice thick and husky.

"Nay, 'twould get you killed, right here, right now."

"Your men would hesitate to kill a woman."

"Not if that woman's sword was sticking out of my chest."

A sigh shuddered through her slim body as she handed him her sword, watching morosely as he cleaned the blade. "I probably would have cut your throat, not impaled you."

When Michael stepped up beside her, Ainslee meekly handed him the rest of her weapons, hesitating only briefly before giving him her second dagger. Her stomach clenched painfully, but she was unable to fully quell the nausea churning inside of her. She had never killed a man before. It was possible that one of the arrows she had loosed at an enemy had found its mark, but she had never stared into a man's eyes as her sword plunged into his flesh, spilling his life out onto the ground. She felt weak, sickened, and horrified.

"You have ne'er taken a man's life before?" asked Gabel, signaling Michael to remove the body.

"Nay." Ainslee shrugged. "Not that I can recall. Certainly not face-to-face."

" 'Tis always hard the first time."

"Why? He was trying to kill me. I should feel nothing, no regret, no mercy."

"It will take time for that truth to settle into your heart. Just continue to repeat it and soon you will accept it. The man gave you but three choices—flee, which was impossible; hide, another poor choice in such a small place; or kill him before he killed you." He took her by the arm. "Come, we had best leave this place."

"The battle is over?" she asked as she looked around.

"Aye. The dogs left alive have fled with their tails atween their legs."

"Ye didna pursue them?"

"Nay. I think it best if we just leave this place. That may not be all of them. To follow could put us into the midst of a trap. I did not come here to battle outlaws and outcasts. That would only gain me the pleasure of having seen justice done, for I am sure that each one of those men is long overdue for a hanging."

"*Long* overdue." After he mounted her horse, she allowed him to pull her up behind him. "Do ye think that the others, your men who fled with Ronald, are safe?"

He nodded as he urged her horse down the rocky hillside. "We will not meet with them again before nightfall. This battle has delayed us, and I fear we will need to camp the night. If all had gone well, we would have been upon my lands by now."

She rested against his back and struggled to banish the image of the dead man from her mind. It would not be easy. Ainslee feared she would be forever haunted by the look of surprise upon the man's face as she had killed him, by the way all the life had seeped out of his eyes. She needed to talk to Ronald. He had always been there for her when she was troubled. She prayed Gabel was right, that Ronald was safe and would be waiting for them somewhere along the road.

Ainslee muttered a curse when she was lightly shaken. Soft, deep, male laughter further pulled her out of her sleep. Blinking and rubbing her eyes, Ainslee sat up straighter, looked around her and frowned. She fixed her gaze on the strong arms wrapped around her waist.

"How did I get here? I was riding behind you," she muttered, rubbing her temples as she tried to clear the fog of sleep from her mind.

"Aye, but you fell asleep," Gabel replied as he reined the horse to a stop.

"Did I fall from the saddle?"

"Almost. I stopped and had Michael move you."

" 'Tis odd that I canna recall that, that I didna wake up."

"You roused enough to thank him most sweetly." Gabel dismounted and lifted her down. "We will camp here for the night and will reach my lands in the morning."

"Is Ronald here?" Ainslee asked, wriggling free of Gable's light hold and looking around.

"Aye. He and the men were waiting here for us. He is off to your left by the line of trees."

Gabel watched her run to her companion's side and was startled by the pang of jealousy he felt. With each moment he spent in her company, matters grew more and more complicated. As his men set up camp and began to prepare a meal, Gabel walked over to Justice and sat down.

"How do you fare today, Cousin?" he asked the younger man as he offered Justice a drink from his wineskin.

"Too well to be imprisoned upon this litter," Justice grumbled.

"You will only be on it for a short while longer, and then you may lie upon a soft bed to recover."

"Gabel," Justice began in protest.

"Do not try and tell me that you are hale and ready to fight at my side. You are still pale, and you wince each time you move. Unless we face a battle where even your weakened sword arm is needed, 'tis but foolishness for you to ignore your wound. Do not let vanity slow your healing, mayhaps even leave you forever weakened in that arm."

Justice cursed softly and slumped against the rough trunk of the tree he had been set near. " 'Tis not the wound which troubles me," he admitted in a faintly sulky voice, "but that I gained it at the hands of a woman. A tiny, red-haired Scottish lass has cut me down as if I was no more than some virginal page." He glared at Gabel when the man laughed. "I see no humor in this. You need not add to the laughter I will have to endure."

"Do not fear that your pride will take a bruising. 'Twill soon be known by all at Bellefleur that Lady MacNairn is no weak, pretty child. She killed a man today in a sword fight." He nodded when Justice gaped at him in surprise. "She armed herself, and one of those outlaws was fool enough to think her an easy kill." Gabel looked to where Ainslee sat close beside Ronald. "She found her first killing hard to bear, but I believe she has the will to overcome that."

"Aye, that is one very willful woman. The ladies at Bellefleur will find her a puzzle. No doubt of that." Justice studied his cousin for a moment before adding, "A woman so brave and skilled would be a good wife for a man trying to grasp a foothold in this wild land."

"Do not try and choose my wife for me, Cousin," Gabel said, smiling faintly at Justice to soften the reprimand. "I have decided upon the sort of wife I must have, and, beguiling and stirring to the blood as Ainslee MacNairn is, she is not what I seek. She is but a pawn in a game of treaty." Gabel avoided Justice's stare, certain that his lack of conviction in his own words would show in his face. "That lovely girl is one tiny, enchanting packet of trouble, which we must be rid of as swiftly as we can."

"Ease your mind, lassie," Ronald soothed Ainslee after she told him all that had happened to her upon the rocky hill. "That mon would have killed ye without a thought."

"I ken it." She looked Ronald over carefully, relieved to see that fleeing from the outlaws had not served to worsen his condition. "Ye appear to have survived your flight through the forest."

"Aye. The lads did their best to travel gently yet swiftly. My only regret is that their care is spent in taking me to Bellefleur and not to Kengarvey."

"Bellefleur?"

"Aye. That is the name of Sir Gabel's keep."

"Bellefleur, eh? It doesna sound a verra strong name for a knight's fortress. I wonder how he came to choose that name."

"Methinks ye might *wonder* about that mon far more than might be wise."

Although she flushed slightly under Ronald's steady, knowing gaze, Ainslee nodded. There was no reason to hide anything from him. "I fear I might indeed, but I shouldna fret yourself o'er it, my friend."

"Nay? We could find ourselves held at Bellefleur for a verra long time."

Ainslee recognized the danger of that as well, but just smiled and patted Ronald's hand. "Sir Gabel is an honorable mon, and I am a woman full grown. If anything happens betwixt us, 'twill rest upon our own heads."

She smiled ruefully when Ronald muttered a curse, and wished she felt as brave as she sounded. If Gabel de Amalville had any interest in her as a woman, a long stay at Bellefleur could prove to be very dangerous indeed. However, Ronald could not help her this time. Whatever did or did not develop between herself and Gabel was a matter only she could deal with. All she could do was pray that she had the wit and the strength to do so without endangering them or her own heart.

Five

Bellefleur rose from a dark bed of rock, strong and majestic. As Ainslee reached the crest of a small hill and saw Gabel's keep, she hesitated. King David was rewarding the Norman very well indeed. Even from a distance the keep bespoke wealth and refinement, neither of which her family had ever attained. The imposing stone fortress was a huge symbol of the massive gap between Sir Gabel de Amalville and herself. All the other differences and complications, from Gabel's holding her for ransom to her unusual upbringing, could be explained away, pushed aside and ignored. There was no deluding herself about the large, sturdy symbol of power and prestige she was looking at. Bellefleur made Kengarvey look like the meanest of crofter's huts.

"Have you grown weary, Mistress Ainslee?" asked Gabel as he rode up beside her.

"Nay," she replied and started walking again, hurrying a little to catch up with Ronald, whose litter she had been walking next to. "I but needed to pause for a moment before climbing the rest of this mountain." She ignored his grin and frowned at how comfortably he sat astride her ash gray gelding. "I still believe that *my* horse needs a respite from carrying two people."

"A mount as strong as this would not be troubled by the addition of your small weight." He stroked the horse's strong neck. "What do you call the animal?"

"Malcolm," she replied with little grace, certain that the man planned to keep her horse.

"Malcolm?" Gabel laughed softly and shook his head. "Why call a destrier Malcolm?"

"Why not? 'Tis a good name."

"A very good name, just an odd one for a horse."

"I suppose you think I ought to have named him Blood-spiller or Skullcrusher."

Gabel just smiled and did not respond to her petulance. "What do you think of my Bellefleur?"

"It looks a strong place, something much needed in this land." She eyed him with a curiosity she made no effort to hide. "And why should a knight call his fortress by such a pretty name?"

"My cousin Elaine named it." Gabel made a good-humored grimace. "I promised her whatever she wished for the day she turned thirteen. She decided she wanted to name my lands. Bellefleur is not such a poor choice."

"Nay." Ainslee briefly contemplated the sort of names a young girl could have thought of, and laughed softly. "It could have been far worse."

After politely inquiring about Ronald's health and comfort, Gabel rode to the front of his men. Ainslee made a brief effort to ignore him, then gave into the strong urge to watch him. He rode well, and she reluctantly admitted that he looked very good on the back of Malcolm. She liked her horse and had fought hard to wrest the animal from her family's greedy hands, but realized that, if Gabel liked and wanted the beast, she would accept the loss. The horse would certainly live a better life at such a fine keep. She doubted that Bellefleur suffered from the lean winters which often plagued Kengarvey, long cold days when even feed for the horses was scarce.

She sighed as she walked toward Bellefleur. Despite her best efforts not to, she had slipped into the occasional reverie about a future with Gabel de Amalville. Bellefleur showed her just how big a piece of nonsense such imaginings were. Her bloodline could not be faulted, but her father's and grandfather's actions had stolen all of the other qualifications she needed to make such a good marriage. The lawless ways of the MacNairns over the last fifty years or more had stolen all prestige, power, and riches from the clan. Seeing Bellefleur made it achingly clear that Gabel would gain absolutely nothing from wedding a woman like her. Ainslee doubted that the man would even allow himself to consider the possibility, however briefly.

"Dinna look so mournful, lassie," Ronald said, drawing Ainslee's attention his way. "If we must be held prisoners, we have fallen into the right hands. We need not fear these men."

"Not even if my father refuses to ransom us?" Ainslee asked, not wanting to consider such a possibility, but knowing her father well enough to know that such a possibility existed.

"Nay, not even then. And I dinna think that will happen."

"Ronald, my father—"

"—is a lawless bastard—aye. Despite his countless faults, he willna leave us to rot with the Normans. He will fear to blacken the MacNairn name. True, the fool hasna the sense to realize near all he has done in his cursed life has thoroughly blackened our name, but leaving his daughter to rot in the hands of his enemies is one thing he willna do. What troubles me is the gnawing fear that he willna abide by any treaty or bargain made to free us."

"I have worried about the same thing, then scolded myself for thinking so poorly of my own father."

" 'Tis no fault of yours, lassie. When a mon acts as your father has over the years, he earns the doubt of even his closest kin." Ronald reached up to briefly clasp her hand. "Just heed this—if your father means to trick or betray Sir Gabel, he will give no thought to your weel-being. 'Tis a hard truth for ye to face, but ye must face it square. Kenning how treacherous your father can be may be all that saves your life."

Ainslee lightly squeezed his hand before releasing it. "Ye are right. 'Tis hard to admit one's own father canna be trusted, not even to keep his child safe from harm, but I accepted that distasteful truth a long time ago. I but suffer from the occasional twinge of guilt o'er thinking it. What troubles me is the feeling that I ought to warn Sir Gabel."

"The mon kens what your father is, sweeting."

"True, yet, Sir Gabel is an honorable mon, I think. An honorable mon isna often weel-armed against a mon like Duggan MacNairn. The betrayals my father can commit wouldna be easy for a mon like de Amalville to guess at."

"Weel, ye must follow what your heart tells you. If the time comes when ye can see that your father means to pull some trickery, to break a bond of honor, and Sir Gabel doesna see it, ye can speak out without fear of being a traitor. It canna hurt to let Sir Gabel see that at least one of the MacNairns understands the meaning of honor."

As they rode through the huge, iron-studded gates of Bellefleur, Ainslee began to feel painfully conspicuous. She knew that her clothes had suffered badly from their travel, and that she was probably dirty as well. There had been little opportunity to wash off all the travel dust clinging to her. When two women rushed up to Gabel to cry welcome and embrace him, Ainslee felt even worse. The women were adorned in lovely gowns of a soft, flowing material. Ainslee felt as if she wore rags. It was pinched vanity which caused her such discomfort and she knew it, but she was unable to push it aside. All she could think about was what Gabel must think when he looked at the lovely darkhaired women greeting him, and then looked at her.

Before the women could ask any questions, Gabel instructed two men to take Ronald to a room and make him comfortable. Ainslee tried to follow Ronald, but Gabel grabbed her by the arm and tugged her into the great hall, ushering the two blatantly curious women in ahead of him. Ainslee was gently pushed into the seat on his right and waited in tense silence as the two pages hastily served them a light repast of sweet wine, bread, and cheese. By the time Gabel introduced her to his aunt Marie and her daughter Elaine, Ainslee's stomach was so knotted with nerves she could barely eat.

"You should have sent word that you were bringing guests," Marie gently scolded Gabel.

Gabel slouched comfortably in his high-backed oak chair, sipped wine from an etched silver goblet, and smiled at his petite aunt. "Lady MacNairn's addition to our party was quite unexpected. Aye, she is a guest, but, then too, she is not."

"You confuse me, nephew."

"I wish the Lady Ainslee and her companion to be treated as our honored guests, but they are also to remain under guard. They are being held for ransom. You look quite shocked, Aunt. 'Tis not as if such a happenstance was rare."

"True, but you have never dealt with anyone in such a manner."

"A mere whim of fate. No one has fallen into my hands is all."

"Ransoming is quite common in Scotland, m'lady," Ainslee said, then wondered crossly why she felt any need to defend Gabel's actions.

"You have been ransomed before?" asked Elaine, her brown eyes wide with a mixture of horror and fascination.

"Weel, nay. My brother George was held once," Ainslee replied.

"You must have been terrified. Gabel, how could you be so cruel?"

"Oh, I kenned that he wouldna hurt me," Ainslee assured the girl.

"And just when did you *ken* that?" Gabel asked. "Was it before or after you tried to cut my heart out?"

Ainslee intended to ignore him, but then Elaine cried, "You tried to kill Gabel?"

"When he and his men first appeared I did attempt to defend myself," Ainslee said, briefly casting an annoyed look at a faintly smiling Gabel. "I saw no gain in simply standing there and awaiting my fate."

"You must have been very frightened. And, mayhaps, you still are, for you eat very little."

"My appetite is somewhat dulled for I am weary and havena had the time or the chance to clean away the dust of my travels." She had to bite back a smile when Gabel's aunt looked at him with a hint of outrage and sternness.

"Gabel," Marie said, tapping her nephew's arm with her finger. "Have you no manners? The poor child must be shown to a room immediately. Come, Elaine, you and I shall see that a bath is prepared, and we shall search out some clean clothing for our guest." As Marie stood up, tugging her daughter up beside her, she added, "Lady MacNairn may stay in the bedchamber Lady Surtelle stayed in last month!"

"You enjoyed seeing me scolded like some errant boy," drawled Gabel as soon as his aunt and cousin left the great hall.

Ainslee smiled sweetly at him. "Aye, I did."

"Then I had best take you to your quarters ere my aunt returns and provides you with even more enjoyment." He stood and held out his hand to her.

"Ye appear to have a multitude of cousins residing with you." Ainslee hesitated only a moment before allowing him to take her by the hand and help her to her feet. Refusing to touch him would certainly make him suspicious, and she did not want him to guess how much even his light touch affected her.

Gabel nodded as he led her out of the great hall and up the narrow curving steps to the bedchambers. "I have a large family and, at this time, there is a greater chance of advancement here in Scotland or even in England. Then there are the ones such as my aunt who was left a widow and, through the sly work of her husband's kinsmen, lost all her lands and money. One must care for one's family. Those my brothers cannot care for are sent here and some, such as my poor aunt, feel a true need to leave France." He looked down at her as he stopped before a thick, iron-banded door. "Do you not shelter your kinsmen?"

"There arena many who wish to be sheltered at Kengarvey. In truth, most of our kinsmen arena speaking to us, and stay as far from us as they are able. They dinna wish to be dragged down with my father. 'Tis evident that they were wise to separate themselves for the king himself has now decided that my father must be punished. 'Tis why ye were riding to Kengarvey."

"Aye. I have made no secret of my purpose," he said as he opened the door to the bedchamber.

"Weel, I pray ye willna think ill of me if I am not so forthcoming."

"Ah, you fear you may tell me something that I could use against your father."

"Aye. I dinna like the way my father acts, am even ashamed of all of the wrongs he has committed, but he is my father. To help ye defeat him would be a great betrayal of my own blood."

"I understand. I would not ask such a thing of you. I hope you find these quarters comfortable. You are free to move about as you please within the walls of Bellefleur, but 'twould be unwise to attempt escape."

It was politely said, but Ainslee could hear the cold steel beneath his courteous warning. She smiled and entered the room, inwardly wincing when he shut the heavy door behind her. The bedchamber was far more elegant and comfortable than any she had ever slept in. Heavy tapestries warmed the stone walls. Sheepskins cut the chill of the floor. She was drawn to the fireplace that covered the wall opposite the bed, entranced by the luxury she had only heard tales of. After she warmed her hands at the small fire burning there, she sat on the large bed, not surprised to find that the thick mattress was stuffed with feathers and not the coarse hay she was accustomed to. Gabel de Amalville may have been landless, but he had clearly had a very full purse when he arrived in Scotland. She did not know any Scotsman, save perhaps the king himself, who could afford such luxuries as chimneys and feather mattresses.

A soft rap at the door pulled her out of her morose thoughts concerning this further proof of the vast differences between her and Gabel. She opened the heavy door and caught a quick glimpse of young Michael standing guard, before the maids scurried in with her bath. Yet another luxury she was unused to, she thought crossly as she watched the wooden tub set before the fire and filled with hot water. She weakly thanked the maids when they handed her scented soap, warmed drying clothes and clean clothes of a quality she could never afford. Only one of the maids was less than friendly and courteous. From what the others said as they hurried the glaring young woman from the room, Ainslee realized the maid was enamored of Gabel's cousin Justice.

The moment she was alone, Ainslee shed her dirty clothes. "Ye have a true skill, Ainslee MacNairn," she muttered to herself as she eased her body into the hot water. "Not many can make an enemy ere they even meet them." As she began to enjoy the rare pleasure of a hot bath, Ainslee hoped Justice would recover quickly and soothe the maid's temper.

Gabel smiled faintly when he stepped into Justice's room and a blushing young maid scurried away. "I came to see how you fare, but 'tis clear that you are rapidly recovering," he drawled as he shut the door and walked over to the bed.

Justice grinned as he sat up, leaning insolently against the thick newly fluffed pillows. "I am well tended."

"Obviously." Gabel helped himself to a tankard of cider from the flagon set on a table next to Justice's bed, and then sat down on the edge of the bed. "I have secured our prisoners."

"So you have, if one can call giving them the best chambers in Bellefleur *securing* them."

"They have shown no sign of being troublesome. And, I see no need of locking a crippled old man and a *wee lass* in my dungeons. They are also being closely watched."

"*And* m'lady MacNairn has such a fine, bright pelt of hair, 'twould be a true shame to see its luster dulled by the dungeons." Justice grinned at his cousin.

"There is that to consider," drawled Gabel, but, after a brief smile, he frowned in thought. "Do you think I err in treating them with such courtesy?"

"Nay," Justice replied after a moment of thought. "Once the girl surrendered herself and her companion, she has been little trouble. There is also one thing I am very certain of, something which strengthens my belief that you may not even need the guard."

"And what is that?"

"That girl will never leave without her companion, and Ronald MacNairn will not be hale enough for a race back to Kengarvey for many a week."

"Ah, of course, the wondrous Ronald." Gabel looked at Justice with curiosity when the man laughed. "And what do you find so amusing?"

"You sounded almost jealous, Cousin," Justice replied, accepting the tankard of cider Gabel served him with a short nod of thanks.

Gabel looked toward the arrow slot which served as the small bedchamber's window, averting his face from Justice's keen eyes so that his cousin could not possibly read his expression. He *was* jealous of Ronald, deeply so, and found that both embarrassing and troubling. As they had traveled from Kengarvey to Bellefleur, Gabel had closely watched the rapport between Ainslee and Ronald, the way she tenderly cared for the man's wounds and how Ronald fretted over her, as well as the way the pair talked to each other, openly with an unhidden affection. With every mile they rode, he had grown to dislike it more and more. He had even caught himself vying for Ainslee's attention like some lovesick boy.

If Justice discovered that, Gabel mused, the man would tease him unmercifully. Worse, Justice might even feel inclined to indulge in a little matchmaking. Although he had only known Ainslee for two days, Gabel knew he was going to have difficulty fighting the allure Ainslee MacNairn held for him. He did not need Justice trying to push him and Ainslee into each other's arms. He was going to have to be careful, and make

Justice believe that, if he felt anything at all, it was a base lust. That was something he and Justice could occasionally chuckle over and then forget.

" 'Tis but stung vanity," Gabel replied, and smiled crookedly at Justice. " 'Tis not easy to seduce a lass or convince her of my greatness when she spends all of her time nursing some old man."

Justice laughed and shook his head. "For shame, cousin. You should not be considering seduction when you are in the midst of a search for a wife to grace Bellefleur."

"Aye, a wife." Gabel was disappointed, yet not really surprised when the thought of searching for a suitable wife no longer held any interest for him. "Aunt Marie told me that Lady Margaret Fraser will be arriving at Bellefleur in a few days. Her father hopes to convince me that his daughter will make me a good wife."

" 'Tis not a good time to conduct a courtship. Knowing all we do about Duggan MacNairn, I cannot believe this ransoming will be an easy business."

"Nay. I expect trouble. Howbeit, 'tis too late to stop Fraser. He has already begun his journey here, and we do not know what route he travels."

Justice nodded. "So we must do as best we can. For your sake, I pray that there is no trouble."

"You can not pray for that any harder than I do."

It was not easy, but Ainslee ignored Michael as she made her way up onto the thick encircling walls of Bellefleur. The young man clung to her like a shadow on a sunny day. He had been standing outside her room when, clean and refreshed from her bath, she had gone to see how Ronald fared. Assured that her dear friend was not suffering, and still surprised over the high quality of the quarters he had been given, she had left to find a faintly smiling Michael outside that room as well. She knew he was now at her heels, but she refused to look at him.

Standing at the ramparts, she took a deep breath of the crisp fall air. It was nearly dark, the days already growing noticeably shorter. Ainslee knew that, if her father hesitated to ransom her, she could easily be a captive at Bellefleur for the length of the winter. When she saw Gabel approach her, she knew that a lengthy stay could prove dangerous. Just the sight of his big, strong form caused a skip in her heartbeat. She hated to think of how that infatuation could mature, if she spent too much time in his company.

"Are you looking for your father to ride to your rescue?" Gabel asked, leaning against the wall and subtlely waving Michael away.

Ainslee gave him a brief look of disgust. "I am looking for your weak points, my cocksure knight, so that I may return to conquer your lands and give you a wee taste of captivity."

"I am all atremble." He took her hand in his, slowly drew it to his lips, and brushed a kiss over her knuckles. "Yet, what man could protest imprisonment by such fine blue eyes?"

It was nonsense, Ainslee knew it, but she smiled and even felt her heart flutter. The tone of his deep voice stroked her. She tensed only briefly when he reached out to thread his long fingers through her hair. She was not so naive that she was unable to recognize an attempt at seduction, but she did not feel any inclination to rebuff him. Although she knew there was little chance of his ploys leading to anything more than a turn in his bed for the duration of her stay at Bellefleur, she discovered that she was still curious and highly aroused by his actions.

"Ye talk a great deal of pretty foolishness," she murmured, making no attempt to elude him when he gently caged her body between his and the wall.

"Foolishness? Nay. 'Tis but the pure truth. You do have very lovely blue eyes and hair that leaves a man speechless, there being no words to adequately describe such beauty."

Ainslee shuddered when he brushed his lips over her forehead. They were soft and warm, and their touch clouded her mind. She knew he was going to kiss her. Despite a multitude of self-scoldings about rampant vanity and the folly of it, Ainslee had suspected that he wanted to kiss her since shortly after they met. It might be wise and proper to sternly rebuff his advances, but she knew she was going to consign right and proper to the winds. She was far too curious, had thought about kissing him often enough to want to know what it would feel like. When he touched his lips to hers, she leaned into him, wordlessly conveying her willingness.

Warmth rushed through her body, pushing away all remnants of the chill caused by the brisk weather. She clutched at the front of his thick tunic, desperately needing the support when he slowly began to deepen the kiss. A tremor went through her when he invaded her mouth with his tongue. Each stroke of his tongue within her mouth increased the sense of hunger swamping her. She clung more tightly to him, pressing her body closer to his as, for a moment, she fully succumbed to the power of his kiss. Then, as he smoothed his hands over her back, a flicker of alarm broke through passion's haze. The need in her was too strong, the desire too hot and fast.

It was not easy, but Ainslee pushed Gabel away. She took a few deep unsteady breaths and, her voice so thick and husky she barely recognized it as her own, she said, "I believe I will return to my chambers now. 'Tis a very fine room, though 'tis still a prison." Afraid she was in danger of babbling, she sidled around him and headed toward the narrow steps which led down from the walls. "Howbeit, prison or not, it does seem the safest place for me to be right now." Without waiting for him to respond, she fled.

Gabel smiled as he watched her flee. It was wrong to try and seduce her, yet he found it easy to push aside all twinges of guilt. That one kiss had shown him a glimpse of a passion so fierce and rich he could not simply ignore it, no matter how fleeting it may be. He knew Ainslee would now try to hide from him, and he would allow her that escape for a while, but he knew nothing would stop him from taking up the chase again—soon.

Six

As quietly as she could, Ainslee began to creep down the stairs. For the first time since Michael had been ordered to guard her four days ago, she had caught him napping. It only surprised her a little, as she had worked very hard to ensure that the young man got no sleep during the night. She had done everything from noisily moving the heavy furniture in her bedchamber—thus stirring up his suspicions about what she was doing—to using the garderobe so often he had to think she was ill. Her games had left her exhausted as well, but they had succeeded in freeing her of her constant shadow for the first time since her arrival at Bellefleur.

She glanced over her shoulder to make certain Michael was not following her. When she looked back down the stairs, she cursed and abruptly stopped. Another few steps and she would have walked right into Gabel. He stood at the foot of the stairs, hands on his trim hips, watching her with unveiled suspicion.

"And where are you creeping away to, m'lady?" asked Gabel. "Escaping?"

"Oh, aye. I thought I would rush boldly from the keep and bound through the gates," she replied, leaning against the tapestry-draped wall flanking one side of the narrow, winding stairs. "I feel assured I can do so without any of your score or more fighting men espying me. And 'twould be but a small challenge to outrun all your war-horses."

"A restless night clearly makes your tongue even sharper. 'Tis not a good day to be so clever. A few of us are not in the kindest of humors, after being roused from our beds in the middle of the night."

Ainslee ignored his remark, but inwardly grimaced with guilt. At one time during the long night she had feigned having a nightmare. It had seemed like a clever way to keep Michael from getting any rest until a concerned Gabel, his aunt, and young Elaine had also stumbled into the room. Lady Marie and her daughter had been all that was kind, but a gleam of suspicion had quickly entered Gabel's sleep-softened eyes. Gabel had seen her caught in the throes of a real nightmare, and she knew she was not skilled enough to imitate it properly, especially since she woke from her nightmares with little memory of what she had said or how she had acted. She would never admit to such a deception, however.

"Many pardons for being such a troublesome guest. Mayhaps it would be best if ye sent me back to Kengarvey."

"I think not," he replied with a crooked smile. "What I will do is select a second guard for you, so that you can no longer weary the man so much so that he becomes less alert."

"As ye wish, m'laird," she said, but silently cursed. Until Ronald was well she had not planned to try and escape, but now her little game to elude Michael could well have cost her any chance to flee. "I was about to go for a wee walk," she murmured as she cautiously continued down the stairs, ignoring his wide grin as she nudged her way by him.

"I insist upon joining you, m'lady," he said as he hooked his arm through hers, tightening his grip when she tried to slip free, and ignoring the glare she sent him. "I should think you would be interested in what your father has replied to my ransom demands."

"I am surprised ye would feel ye could repeat his reply to a lady," Ainslee drawled.

She was not really sure she wanted to know what her irascible father had said. There were two ways he could respond to a ransom demand for her—with anger and numerous attempts to delay paying, or by telling Gabel to do as he pleased with her. Ronald believed her father would never simply cast her to the wolves, but she was not so confident of that. Her father had no love for her, and, since no match had ever been arranged for her, she was beginning to think he had no use for her either.

Gabel laughed, but the thought of her father's callousness killed his humor as quickly as her wry comment had roused it. The laird's reply to the ransom demand revealed that Duggan MacNairn cared nothing at all for his daughter or her servant. There was only one captive the man had inquired about—the horse. Gabel hoped Ainslee was not too fond of the beast, for he had decided to keep it just to spit in MacNairn's eye. It was a somewhat childish gesture, but eminently satisfying. His concern at the moment, however, was to tell Ainslee what response her father had made, yet not hurt her feelings. One glance into her wide eyes told him that he was probably trying to protect her from a truth she was already well aware of.

"Your father's language was somewhat belligerent." Gabel ignored her soft snort of derision over his politely vague reply. "He is attempting to negotiate your price."

"If he refused to buy me back, ye need not fret about telling me so. I have long understood that I am not dear to my father's heart. I canna be hurt by a truth I have already learned," she lied, and prayed her appearance of outward calm could not be penetrated by Gabel's piercing look.

"Are you certain you want the full truth?" he asked, stopping to face her.

"Aye, 'tis always best."

"Sometimes it can be cruel." Gabel wondered if he could diminish her loyalties with the truth. It might well stop her from enacting any dangerous attempts to escape just to save her father's pride and coin.

"The truth is still best. Aye, I would never tell a friend that the gown she wears makes her look like a grazing cow, nor that she dances like a goat with three legs, but, on most occasions, the truth does more good than harm."

"Then have the truth. Most of your father's reply was a pro-fane rant against ransoms, empty-headed daughters, and ambitious Normans. He feels you are at fault for this, you and your companion. The only one whose welfare was inquired after was your horse. Your father also told me that he can only afford to pay a pittance, a sum so small 'tis an insult to me as well as to you."

That did hurt, and did so more deeply than Ainslee felt it ought to. Hiding her pain, she gave Gabel a brief smile and stepped around him. "That does sound like my father."

Gabel fell into step beside her as she walked toward the narrow steps which led up the walls of Bellefleur. He wished he could see her eyes. It was hard to believe that she could be quite so nonchalant about her father's cruelty as she pretended to be.

"I have sent a messenger to him today," he said, as he followed her up the steps, his gaze fixed upon the gentle sway of her slim hips. "I told him what I have just told you—that his offer is an insult. Since he ignored my mention of the king's wishes for a cessation of his lawless ways, I have repeated them, and I warned him of the consequences of thinking himself beyond his king's reach."

"My father isna a mon who considers the consequences of anything he does."

"Are there no wiser heads at Kengarvey?"

"Aye, and they grace the pikes upon the walls of Kengarvey. My father's reply to any advice is a blind fury at the one offering it. No one speaks out now, no matter how great a folly their laird commits. After all, one might survive Duggan MacNairn's mistakes, but one never survives the urge to advise him."

"I am surprised that anyone remains at Kengarvey."

"Some have no other choice. Also, Kengarvey is their home. Even if they must endure a fool for a laird, they stay out of love for Kengarvey." She sighed as she stared out over the walls of Bellefleur. "Kengarvey isna as fine as this keep, neither as sturdily built nor as comfortable, but 'tis home and, for many, 'tis the only home they have ever kenned. There are fools there as weel, dim-witted ones who think my father is the bravest of men. They admire the way he spits in the eye of anyone who tries to rule him."

Leaning against the cool stone wall at her side, Gabel asked quietly, "Even his king?"

"Do ye wish me to talk my father into a charge of treason?"

"Such a charge already hangs o'er his head and, if he does not soon swear the allegiance asked of him, he will find out that the king he scorns can be a formidable enemy."

Ainslee shuddered at the thought of the fate her father tempted. The penalty for treason was death, a long, gruesome death. It would not be only her father who suffered it either. Most certainly he was placing his precious sons at risk, and could even be endangering her and her sisters. She could not defend her father's actions, but she decided it was past time to begin weighing her every word. By neither word nor action would she help Gabel or the king brand her father a traitor. Although her father had done nothing to earn such loyalty, it could easily prove to be a matter of self-preservation.

"My father but plays the ransom game, Sir Gabel," she replied. "Verra few people bow to the first ransom demand made."

"I cannot believe you truly think that."

"What ye believe about me and my thoughts, sir, doesna really matter." She returned to staring out at the countryside and tensed when he moved closer to her, his body brushing against hers all along one side as he lightly stroked her hair.

"But it does matter. I do not know you well, Ainslee Mac-Nairn, but I did feel that you were an honest woman."

"I have told ye no lies."

"Nay, but you have told me few truths either."

"Weel, here is a truth. Someone approaches and 'tisna my kinsmen."

He tensed, stared at the riders moving toward Bellefleur at

a slow, steady pace, and moved away. Ainslee felt the chill of
his leaving immediately, and knew it was not just from the
removal of his warm body. He had retreated from her in every
way. She looked more closely at the riders, trying to discern
the reason for his almost complete withdrawal. In the midst
of the riders was a small horse-drawn cart. Within the cart sat
several women, one of them clearly a wellborn lady. Ainslee
recognized the party as the Frasers, one of her father's many
enemies and the most ardent.

There were two reasons for the Frasers to travel to Bellefleur. One was to ally themselves with Gabel against her father,
but the wellborn women of the clan did not often join such a
venture, especially not at this time of the year. The other was
to attempt to bind the two families together through a marriage.
Ainslee had the sinking feeling that the lady in the cart was
going to be offered as a possible bride for Gabel.

Ainslee was torn between fury and disgust. She had har-
bored no illusions about Gabel's attempts to seduce her, although the depth of her hurt indicated that she might not have
been as free of romantic self-deception as she had thought.
For Gabel to try and draw her into his bed even as he courted
a bride was not only infuriatingly arrogant of him, it was
deeply insulting. If she was right and this was a candidate for
a bride entering through the heavy gates of Bellefleur, then it
was indisputable proof that Gabel de Amalville had a very low
opinion of her. He really did see her as no more than someone
to dally with then cast aside, as no more than some common
hedgerow whore, for it was evident that he did not treat every
wellborn Scottish lady the same.

"I believe I will return to my bedchamber," she said as she
headed down the steps, desperate to get away from him for
fear he would read the turmoil she suffered in her eyes.

"You do not wish to meet the Frasers?" Gabel asked as he
quickly followed her.

Ainslee wondered what would happen if she pushed the fool
off the walls. She could not believe he wanted to introduce his

intended leman to his intended bride. "This particular Fraser loathes my clan. I dinna believe he would be pleased to see me."

Despite her best efforts to reach the safety of her bedchamber before Colin Fraser or his people saw her, Ainslee found herself trapped in the bailey as her clan's deadliest enemies arrived. She tried to hide behind Gabel as he shook hands with Lord Fraser and greeted the man's daughter, a dark buxom beauty named Margaret. Ainslee knew her pathetic attempt to hide until she could flee to her room had failed when Lord Fraser glared at her.

"What is one of those MacNairns doing here?" Fraser demanded.

"She is a prisoner," Gabel replied. "I am discussing her ransom with her father even now."

"Ye let a prisoner walk about freely? Especially one of those treacherous MacNairns? Ye should lock the bitch in chains, or ye will soon find a knife sticking in your back."

"At least MacNairns dinna smile sweetly at a mon whilst using lies, the law, and the king to rid ourselves of him," Ainslee snapped, glaring right back at the burly man.

"Your father has never obeyed a law in his whole miserable life, so 'tis sure he wouldna ken what ones to use to his advantage. And he certainly canna even go near the king or he will swiftly be hanged for the thieving dog he is."

"Enough," Gabel said and, seeing an abashed, sleepy-eyed Michael walking toward him, nudged a glowering Ainslee toward her youthful guard.

Although it caused the bile of fury to sting the back of her throat, Ainslee bit back the final insult she was prepared to hurl at Fraser. The look of contempt Margaret Fraser gave her only made that silence harder to maintain. Ainslee ached to hit the woman, but allowed Michael to drag her away. Watching Gabel soothe his guests and flirt with a suddenly coquettish Margaret was not something she wished to be subjected to anyway. She did wonder how much the circumstances of her captivity would now change.

* * *

"Ye will ne'er believe who is stomping about these halls," Ainslee announced as she strode into Ronald's bedchamber later.

"Colin Fraser and his hell-bound daughter Margaret," Ronald replied as he pushed himself up until he could rest against the pillows Ainslee hastily plumped at his back.

"Ye ken who Margaret Fraser is?" Ainslee poured him a tankard of mead, then sat on the edge of his bed.

"Only through rumor, lassie. I have ne'er met the woman meself."

"Weel, what does rumor have to say about her?"

"That she has a hearty dose of her father's blood. 'Tis said she is even better at intrigue than he is. The Frasers are the kind of sly, ambitious courtiers who make the king's court such a dangerous place. They are as bad as your father, but with the wit to hide their outlawry and treachery behind a cloak of courtly manners and legality."

"Old Colin wasna so courtly when he saw me." She smiled faintly when Ronald laughed. "His daughter looked at me as if I were some nasty bit of muck staining her embroidered slippers. I canna believe Gabel would want to marry such a woman."

"Do ye think a wedding is planned?"

"Margaret is certainly planning one. I dinna think any betrothal has yet been agreed to, however. Gabel didna speak to the Frasers as if they were already his kinsmen. Margaret is here to be chosen."

Ronald shook his head, then finished off his mead. "An alliance there would certainly be ill news for us."

"From what ye have said, it wouldna be verra good for Gabel or Bellefleur either. 'Tis foolish, I shouldna fret o'er what fate may befall my captors. By all rights, I should wish them all the ill fate and God may deal them."

"Nay, sweet lass. Ye have too good a heart." Ronald briefly patted her hand, then winked at her. "And I ken that ye have cast a favorable eye at young Gabel de Amalville."

" 'Tis not my eye he wishes me to cast upon him." As Ronald laughed, Ainslee puzzled over the strong yet even mix of jealousy and concern which assailed her. "The mon tries to seduce me until he sees his possible bride trot into view. I ought to cast him to the wolves and take gleeful pleasure in watching them tear the blind fool apart. Howbeit, as ye say, I have too good a heart and, mayhaps, too empty a head. If these Frasers are as treacherous as ye say—"

"Mightily so. And, if but half the whispers about bonny Margaret are true, she is the most poisonous of adders. From what talk I have heard about these halls, de Amalville has gained great favor with our king."

"And thus becomes someone who is in the way of others who aspire to that place of honor."

Ronald nodded as he set his empty tankard aside. "De Amalville is our captor. He means to bring your father into the king's fold, or put an end to the trouble he causes. Howbeit, he is also an honorable mon, who would prefer a treaty to a battle, and who treats us most kindly. He deserves better than to be betrayed and brought low by an ambitious mon and his equally sly daughter."

"Ye are quite right," Ainslee agreed as she stood up and walked to the door.

"And what do ye plan to do?"

"Just watch," she assured him as she paused by the door.

"Just watch for what?"

"First, to see if Gabel has the wit to see deception in such a bonny face. I will also watch to see if the Frasers are deserving of all that they are accused of. If they are, it might not serve us to aid Gabel, but 'twill certainly benefit us to ruin whatever plots the Frasers may have devised."

"Aye, it will. Your father isna a good mon, but he makes no effort to hide what he is. He isna beyond betraying people or acting treacherously, but, if ye have any wit at all, ye ken where ye stand with him."

"Carefully and with a close eye on your back." She exchanged a brief grin with Ronald. "I ken what ye are saying, Ronald. Fraser is no better than my father. In truth, he is worse, for he plays at being the best of gentlemen. I will be careful."

"Good, for if the Frasers suspect that ye are aware of their deceptions, ye will find yourself in grave danger."

Ainslee did not tell Ronald, but she suspected she might already be in danger. She had at first dismissed Margaret Fraser's look of angry contempt, as that of a woman who thought far too highly of herself. If even part of the rumors whispered about Margaret were true, however, that look could well be a warning she should not ignore. Her biggest problem might not be Margaret Fraser, however. If the Frasers did plot against Gabel, it could require more skill than she possessed to convince Gabel that he was being taken for a fool.

"Why was our little flame-haired guest not at the table this eve?" asked Justice as Gabel helped him back to his bedchamber, the simple act of dining in the great hall weakening him.

Gabel told his cousin what had happened when the Frasers and Ainslee had first met in the bailey. "I felt time was needed for tempers to cool, and both sides to grow accustomed to the other's presence."

"It might be for the best. That MacNairn girl has a temper to match the fire in her hair." Justice smiled weakly and allowed Gabel to undress him.

"And a tongue as sharp as her sword's blade."

"True. And, I think I allowed my pride to force me from my bed too soon." He groaned softly as he settled down in his bed, half-reclining against the full pillows. "I should have stayed here. I would have saved the bruises to my poor vanity caused by needing your aid to leave the table."

"You did not look that poorly, cousin." Gabel sat on the edge of the bed and poured them each a tankard of sharp cider from the decanter on the bedside table. "I did not come to your aid because you looked too weak, but because it gave me the chance to flee the company of the Frasers."

"That does not promise a successful bond between the de Amalvilles and the Frasers."

"It *would* be a good match. Both sides would gain."

"Do you wish to hear my opinion of old Colin Fraser and his dark beauty of a daughter?"

"Aye, I believe I would."

"Then you shall have it, and I pray you will not be offended. They are wellbred, powerful and rich, the match would please the king, and Margaret Fraser is the fairest yet of all the women who have sought you as a husband. Many men would be eager to get her into their bed. And yet," Justice shrugged gently, favoring his wounded shoulder, "I do not believe I trust her. I know of a certain that I do not trust her father."

Gabel nodded and frowned into his drink for a moment. "That pair makes me uneasy as well."

"Mayhaps the words Lady Ainslee spat at Fraser were not simply a slander one exchanges with an old foe."

"I wondered the same. Howbeit, I do not believe I should ask Ainslee about the character of a woman I am considering taking as my bride. When Ainslee first saw the Frasers approaching, there was a look in her fine eyes which told me that she had guessed exactly why Lady Margaret journeyed to Bellefleur." Gabel shook his head and muttered a curse. "I should not have kissed the girl. 'Twas but an attempt at seduction, and 'tis ill of me to seduce one wellborn lass whilst trying to find another to be my bride."

" 'Tis indeed ill done of you, but I believe I would have found you to be the strangest of men if you had not at least tried. Lady Ainslee is too fair to ignore. And, as I have not seen any sign of injury upon you, I must assume that Lady Ainslee did not fight the embrace."

"Nay, she did not fight me. I think she may even have forgiven me that first transgression. Howbeit, I was attempting to steal another kiss when the Frasers arrived."

"Sweet heavens, Gabel. That was callous. 'Twas certainly a poor choice of time."

"A very poor choice of time. Howbeit, offending Ainslee is the least of my worries just now. I may have just welcomed a nest of adders into my home."

Ainslee cursed as she watched Gabel climb up to the wall and walk toward her. The fact that she had been right, that Margaret Fraser was there to be considered as a suitable wife, did not please her at all. For once in her life she would have been quite happy to be wrong. That Gabel would try to seduce her with one hand, while courting a bride with the other, still offended and hurt her. However, the worst sin he had committed today, and the one she had come up on the walls to sulk over, was not allowing her to join everyone in the great hall for the evening meal. She knew it was absurd to be so hurt over that, for she was a prisoner and should not be dining with the family of her captor anyway. Ainslee knew what truly stung, and that was that she was being pushed aside, hidden away like some embarrassing relation the moment Lady Margaret Fraser rode into Bellefleur.

"Is this to become your pouting room, m'lady?" Gabel asked as he leaned against the wall at her side.

"And why should ye think I am pouting? What could I have to pout about?" She frowned when he held up his hand to stop her words and then laughed softly.

"Please, m'lady, do not list all the wrongs you feel have been inflicted upon you. I do not wish to wile away the entire night begging your pardon."

She ignored that piece of foolishness and asked bluntly, "Why am I suddenly banished to my room instead of taking my meal in the great hall?"

"Is that why you are skulking along my walls and pouting?"

"I am *not* pouting. And, considering the treatment I have received since I was brought to Bellefleur, 'tis not unreasonable to ask why matters have so abruptly changed." She tensed when he reached out to stroke her long thick braid, shocked and insulted that he would even think of trying to seduce her again.

"After the way Lord Fraser and you acted when you met earlier today, I felt it would be wise to keep you apart until both of you had had time to calm yourselves. 'Twas too easy to envision you and him trying to stab each other with your eating knives." He slipped his arm around her shoulders and pulled her close, brushing his lips over her forehead as he asked, "Why do you hate Fraser so?"

"Because it was Fraser and his men who killed my mother." For a moment she relaxed in his hold, her desire for him sweeping over her. Then she remembered Lady Margaret Fraser and, more important, the reason the woman was at Bellefleur. "I think it would be wise if ye saved this play for the woman ye are courting, m'laird," Ainslee said as she broke free of his grasp.

Before Gabel could make any reply, Ainslee hurried away. Halfway up the stairs leading to her bedchamber, she was confronted by Lady Margaret Fraser. The hard, cold look in the woman's eyes told Ainslee that the woman had been watching her and Gabel upon the walls.

"I shouldna try to play that game if I were you," Lady Margaret warned.

"And what game is that?" asked Ainslee, instinctively tensing for an attack when Lady Margaret made a sound very similar to a soft snarl.

"Ye try to capture Lord de Amalville for your own. I canna believe a mon of his ilk would stoop to wed a MacNairn."

"Then why trouble yourself to warn me?"

"Men have been kenned to do foolish things. Heed me, MacNairn, I willna stand by and be pushed aside by you. I will ne'er allow you to savor a victory o'er me."

Lady Margaret pushed past Ainslee and strode away. The chill of the woman's hissed threat caused Ainslee to shudder as she hurried to her bedchamber. The room was intended to be her prison cell, but, more and more, it began to look like the only safe haven within the walls of Bellefleur.

Seven

A chill tore up Ainslee's spine. She wrapped her heavy cloak more tightly around herself, and looked around the shadowed bailey. For the two days since Lady Margaret had threatened her, Ainslee had been playing a dangerous game, but she began to think it was far more dangerous than she had realized. She had ceased trying to completely elude Gabel, although she had been successful in not getting caught alone with the man, and had even begun to flirt with him, something she was not sure she did with any great skill. The looks of fury Lady Margaret had sent her way had been satisfying, even amusing. Ainslee decided her humor may have been seriously misplaced.

She looked around again and still saw nothing of her constant guard. The plump, jovial Vincent now shared the guard duty with Michael, and should have been plodding along behind her. He had been at his post when she had left her bedchamber, and she was sure he had started to follow her. Somewhere between her bedchamber and the bailey, the man had disappeared, and Ainslee had a good idea of where he had gone or, more precisely, of who had led him astray. Lady Margaret's maid had been flirting outrageously with both Michael and Vincent. Michael had found the maid's lascivious attentions amusing, but Vincent had clearly been aroused. Ainslee was certain that the man had finally succumbed and slipped away with the woman. What troubled her was why Lady Margaret's maid should be luring her guards away.

"And, whatever reason Lady Margaret has for wishing me

to be left alone, it canna be a good one," she muttered, deciding to limit her walk to one complete circle of the keep.

It was pride forcing her to meander around the bailey as had become her habit, despite the fact that all of her instincts warned her of danger. The wise thing to do would be to hurry back inside and place herself amongst Gabel's people. Lady Margaret would never try to harm her with Gabel or his kinsmen close at hand. Ainslee kept walking and prayed that she was simply allowing her mistrust of Lady Margaret make her see daggers in every shadow.

A soft scraping noise above her roused Ainslee from her musings, and she paused to look up. She saw only the faintest of movements at one of the few wider windows of the keep, but a wave of alarm swept through her. Ainslee flattened herself against the cold, damp wall of the keep. An instant later a huge stone plunged down from the window above, passing so close to her that it brushed against her skirts.

Although she heard another sound from above, Ainslee resisted the urge to look. It was undoubtedly the person who had tossed the rock down, but, to see clearly, Ainslee would have to step away from the wall, and she did not dare risk it. For a long time she remained pressed to the wall, staring at the rock. It had required a great deal of effort and stealth to carry such a large stone into the keep and heave it out of the window. It had also been intended to land on her, undoubtedly to kill her. Ainslee knew that Lady Margaret had planned the attack just as surely as she knew it would be impossible to prove. What truly frightened her was the cold determination to kill her that was revealed by such an attack.

Staying close to the wall and continuously glancing upward, Ainslee made her way back to the entrance of the keep. She no longer cared if it looked like the most ignominious of retreats. Pride would have to sacrifice itself to the need to survive. She also needed to rethink all her plans for thwarting Lady Margaret's plan to be Gabel's bride. This attempt at murder revealed how important it was to stop that marriage, but it also showed that a woman like Lady Margaret would not be stopped by such simple games as flirting with Gabel.

Once inside of the keep, Ainslee paused to take a deep, steadying breath. She tossed her cape to a young maid who was hurrying over to greet her, and strode toward the great hall. Straightening her shoulders, steeling herself for the first real meeting with the Frasers since their arrival, Ainslee stepped into the great hall. It did not really surprise her to find Lady Margaret seated at the lord's table with Gabel and her father. It certainly did not mean that the woman was innocent. Lady Margaret would not dirty her white hands enacting such a murder. She simply ordered it done. What brief flicker of doubt Ainslee suffered about her conclusions vanished when Lady Margaret looked at her. The woman's expression was briefly one of complete surprise, and then it hardened into fury.

"Lady Ainslee," called Gabel, smiling and waving her toward the table. "Come and join me. I sent a page to your chambers, but he said you were not there."

"I went for a wee wander about the bailey," she replied as she approached the table.

"And where is Vincent?"

"Do I need my guard in this place where I am surrounded by de Amalvilles and their allies?"

"Of course not," Gabel murmured, glancing toward the door and back at Ainslee, then frowning. "Come, sit here," he said, indicating the seat to his left.

Ainslee hesitated, for that seat put her next to Lord Fraser. She suspected that some of the rage flushing the man's craggy face was due to the fact that Gabel was offering her a seat which placed her higher at the table than him. Assuring herself that nothing could happen to her at the head table with the lord of the manor close at hand, she moved to sit down.

"Ye treat your prisoners most kindly, Sir Gabel," said Lord Fraser, his tone of voice cordial, but his eyes revealing his distaste as Ainslee sat down and a page hurried over to serve her.

"This particular prisoner is a lady of good birth, sir," Gabel replied. "And she has offered me no trouble. I see no reason to treat her otherwise."

"And how does your father intend to gather your ransom, m'lady?" Fraser asked Ainslee. "Steal it from his neighbors as he has ever done?"

Before Ainslee could reply, Gabel set his tankard down with a distinct rap and said, "I have decreed that Lady Ainslee be treated as my guest, Lord Fraser. I had not realized that custom now allowed one guest to insult another at the host's own table."

"It does not, m'lord. Forgive me. I allow old animosities to rob me of my manners."

Ainslee knew some reaction was expected of her, and she nodded in reply to Lord Fraser's insincere apology. The words she wished to say were hard to swallow, stinging her throat as she choked them back. If she was to show Gabel how sly and untrustworthy the Frasers were, she had to behave better than they did. She began to think that was going to be the hardest thing she had ever done, for every time she looked at the Frasers, she could hear her mother's screams.

"You are looking somewhat tousled, Ainslee," Gabel said as he idly tidied her hair. "Has the wind grown strong?"

"Nay." Ainslee wondered if Gabel was aware of how inappropriately he was acting as he neatened her lightly braided hair and spoke to her so informally. The Frasers had noticed and clearly detested the casual familiarity Gabel was showing. "I fear I must tell ye some distressing news—your fine keep appears to be crumbling." Ainslee watched Lady Margaret narrow her eyes in warning.

"Crumbling?"

"Aye. I nearly had my head crushed by a falling rock." She fought to hide her astonishment when Gabel paled slightly and looked her over carefully.

"You were not injured?"

"Nay. A sound warned me of the approaching danger. It but brushed by my skirts."

"I will have the mason survey the keep on the morrow."

Ainslee just smiled and began to eat. She knew the mason would find nothing wrong, and hoped that would rouse a suspicion or two in Gabel's mind. The look of hatred Lady Margaret sent her way when Gabel was not watching the woman told Ainslee that Lady Margaret feared the very same thing.

Despite Gabel's genial company, Ainslee found the meal an ordeal. Lady Marie and Elaine were seated on the other side of the Frasers, so it was difficult to converse with them. At times the looks the Frasers sent her way were so fierce, Ainslee felt the urge to huddle closer to Gabel. She was just about to leave, needing a respite from their oppressive company, when the Frasers excused themselves and left the hall. Ainslee had her goblet refilled with heady cider, and took a long drink to calm her nerves and ease the knot in her belly.

"I know that was difficult for you," Gabel said, watching Ainslee closely. "I thank you for setting aside the anger you feel for the Frasers."

"I didna set it aside," Ainslee replied. "I swallowed it and 'tis certain that, if the Frasers are to be your guests for the duration of my stay, I shall return to Kengarvey with a belly so rotted I will ne'er eat in comfort again." She frowned when Gabel briefly smiled. "Ye find my distress amusing?"

"Nay, not at all. 'Tis but the way you describe it. You have a true gift with words, m'lady."

"A part of me wishes to say thank ye, but another part of me wonders why, for I am not sure that your words were flattering."

"Oh, aye, they were."

"Then thank ye."

Before Gabel could say anymore, an earsplitting scream cut through the murmurs of conversation in the great hall. Gabel leapt from his chair and raced to the hall outside the doors, Ainslee and a few of his men close on his heels. The sight which greeted them caused Ainslee to curse and push to the fore of the small crowd. Lady Margaret clung to the thick stone posts framing the bottom of the stairs, looking disheveled and terrified. Her father stood beside her, sword in hand. Facing the pair was a snarling Ugly.

"This beast attacked us," bellowed Lord Fraser. "I want it killed."

"Nay," cried Ainslee as she hurried over to Ugly, knelt by his side, and patted the dog, all the while mumbling soothing nonsense to still his agitation.

"He tried to kill me," said Margaret, placing her hand over her heart and slumping against the post as if she were about to faint. "I was but walking upon the stairs when the beast lunged at me."

"What did ye do to him?"

"Naught. The animal simply attacked me."

"Ugly would never attack someone without reason, or without a direct command from me."

Ainslee could feel the slight tremor still coursing through her calming pet. Ugly was not angry, he was afraid. The Frasers had clearly done something to the dog to rouse his ferocity. Cornered and threatened, the animal had prepared to strike back, as any animal would. Ainslee knew what game was being played now. Since Margaret's attempt at murder had failed, the woman was striking back like some spoiled child, trying to hurt Ainslee by hurting her pet. All Ainslee could do was pray that Gabel would hesitate to kill her pet. If he fully believed the Frasers's claim of a vicious, unprovoked attack, Ugly would be slain, and Ainslee knew she would be unable to stop it.

Gabel frowned, glancing from Ainslee, who still hugged her now docile dog, to the Frasers, who had relaxed their poses of terror. He found it hard to believe that the wolfhound had attacked the Frasers. The dog had shown no sign of being vicious, was in fact extremely well trained. It was why he had allowed the animal to roam freely around Bellefleur. His people had quickly accepted the dog. A glance at the men who had followed him to the door showed that they had their doubts about the Frasers's claim as well. Gabel thrust his fingers through his hair and struggled to think of some compromise.

"Mayhaps ye commanded the dog to attack me," said Lady Margaret.

"Dinna be a fool," snapped Ainslee. "I have just suffered in your company for an hour or more. Ugly may be a clever dog, but even he canna be given an order and told to follow it later. Ye canna have dealt much with dogs if ye think I could tell him to sit here and, when the Frasers finally stroll into view, attack them." A soft snicker from several of Gabel's men told Ainslee that she had made an argument the Frasers would find very hard to dispute.

"Then the dog has simply taken a dislike to us."

" 'Tis clear that Ugly is an animal possessing great discernment."

It was also clear to Gabel that Ainslee and Lady Margaret would argue over the matter for a long time if he did not interrupt. "Enough," he ordered. "I believe the answer is to confine the dog whilst the Frasers are my guests." He reached to grasp the neatly braided leather collar around the animal's neck, and looked at Ainslee when she did not immediately release her pet.

"Ugly has ne'er been caged," she murmured, briefly glaring at a smug Lady Margaret before looking beseechingly at Gabel. " 'Twill upset him."

" 'Tis better that he is upset than that he is killed."

"Ye wouldna kill him, would ye?"

"*I* would not, but someone has now declared him a threat," he replied in a voice too soft for the others to overhear. "Give him o'er, Ainslee. The man who tends to my dogs will be good to him."

After giving her dog a brief hug, Ainslee released him. She watched morosely as Gable had one of the men lead Ugly away, drawing a little comfort from the kind way the man treated the dog. As she stood up and brushed off her skirts, she glowered at Lady Margaret, sickened by the way the woman cooed her gratitude to Gabel. When she noticed the faintly sardonic look upon Gabel's face, she began to relax. Lady Margaret's need to spite her may well have worked against the woman. Since Gabel did not believe Margaret's claim that the dog had attacked, he had to wonder why the woman made it, and that could well rouse his suspicions against the Frasers.

"I believe I will retire to my room now," Ainslee said, cutting through Lady Margaret's cloying flattery of Gabel.

"Ainslee," Gabel called, pulling slightly away from a clinging Lady Margaret.

She ignored him and started up the stairs. "Mayhaps Ugly can spend part of his confinement locked in my room or in Ronald's. 'Twould calm him if he could spend some time with us."

"Aye—mayhaps."

After a quick look at Lady Margaret, Ainslee added, "And I am to be the only one who feeds him. 'Twill stop him from becoming too much a member of your pack and keep him from feeling abandoned."

"As you wish."

Gabel divided his attention between a clutching Margaret and a retreating Ainslee. He was sorry to see Ainslee disappear. She had donned a soft blue gown the ladies of Bellefleur had given her, and the way it flattered her eyes and coloring made her more of a pleasure to look at than usual. He also had the feeling that some dangerous game was being played right beneath his nose, but he had yet to sniff it out. It was doubtful that Ainslee would confess anything to him, but he wanted the opportunity to question her. As he escorted Lady Margaret to her bedchamber, he found himself wondering how he could rid himself of his guests without offending them.

* * *

"Are ye sure your beastie is safe, lassie?" Ronald asked as he watched Ainslee pace his room.

"As sure as I can be." She stopped, leaned against the ornately turned bedpost at the foot of his bed, and sighed. "She went after my dog out of pure spite, Ronald."

"Because ye didna have the grace to die beneath that rock."

"Exactly. I wouldna be surprised if she still tries to kill Ugly. 'Tis why I have demanded that I be the only one who feeds him. Gabel appeared to have accepted my reasons for that and agreed."

"Mayhaps he suspects something."

"He may weel do so. Lady Margaret may weel have erred in trying to claim Ugly was a vicious dog, given to unprovoked attacks. Neither Gabel nor his men really believed that. Ugly has become the pet of Bellefleur, with even the kitchen maids slipping him a wee treat now and again."

"Then it could weel serve a good purpose. The beast willna suffer."

"Nay, I ken it. I ne'er realized how difficult it can be to rouse a person's suspicions about someone without actually saying anything. 'Twould be much easier to just sit the mon down and tell him what I think and ken about those cursed Frasers." She shook her head. "I did tell him that it was Fraser and his men who killed my mother, but he has said nothing about that."

"What can he say? Sadly, folk die in battle. Aye, the lad may condemn the murder of innocents in the heat of battle, but too many of his ilk have done the same for him to now condemn Fraser for it." He frowned. "Sir Gabel doesna think ye had the dog turn on the Frasers, does he?"

Ainslee grimaced and shrugged. "He may have considered it at first, but, nay, I dinna think so. I was seated next to him in the great hall. E'en he must ken that, whilst ye can make a dog hunt someone down and ye can e'en make the animal kill a mon, 'tis impossible to make a dog lie in wait for hours to attack one particular person. Gabel had to do something to placate his guests. I must find consolation in the fact that he didna order the dog killed. 'Twas what Fraser was demanding."

"The bastard. Weel, my wounds will soon be healed enough for me to leave my bed, and ye willna have to wander through this nest of adders all alone."

"Dinna try to move too soon out of fear for me. I am weel enough."

"They tried to kill you," Ronald protested.

"Aye, and failed. I am now alerted to their deadly intentions and will be even more careful. Soon my father must ransom us and we can leave this place. Now, I have wearied ye enough with all my complaints—"

"Ye ken that I am always ready to listen," Ronald assured her.

"Aye, I ken it." She moved to his side and kissed his cheek before walking to the door. "I will be fine. Dinna fret o'er me."

"Nay? I canna help doing so when I recall that 'twas the Frasers who slaughtered your poor mother."

"The Frasers will discover that I have a goodly share of the MacNairn blood mixed with that of my mother. I willna be such an easy kill."

Gabel stood by the narrow window in Justice's room and scowled down at the dog pens next to the stable. Ugly sat in the middle of the pen howling softly but mournfully, the other dogs huddling in the far corners of the pen. Ugly was so much bigger and stronger than his dogs, there had been little fighting when the animal had been tossed in with the pack. Nevertheless, Gabel had to fight the urge to go down and release the animal. He inwardly grimaced as he admitted to himself that he wished to do that not for the animal's sake, but for Ainslee's. Her pet's unhappiness was going to distress her, and he badly wanted to avoid that.

" 'Tis nonsense, you know," Justice murmured as he stepped

up next to Gabel and peered out at the dog. "That dog has been raised with a gentle, loving hand. He is a fighter, but he would not attack without reason."

"I believe that as well, although I did have a moment's doubt. Ainslee and the Frasers hate each other. I did briefly wonder if Ainslee had tried to make the dog hurt them. Howbeit, why would the Frasers wish to harm a dog? It makes no sense."

"Nay? You just said that the Frasers hate Ainslee MacNairn. Ainslee loves that dog."

"And, so, if you hurt the dog, you hurt Ainslee? 'Tis a child's spiteful act. Lord Fraser and his daughter are full grown and high-ranked members of the king's court."

"So you think them above such nonsense?" Justice laughed and shook his head. "Only a saint is above the occasional act of spite, cousin, and the Frasers will ne'er gain sainthood. I was not surprised when I heard the tale. Since you have spent more time in the Frasers's company than I, I wonder why you are so puzzled by the deed."

Gabel sighed and leaned against the wall. "I am not. In truth, I am now ashamed of my brief suspicion about Ainslee. What troubles me is the conviction that this incident is but a small part of something else. Something is happening between Ainslee and the Frasers, I am certain of it, yet I cannot guess what it is, and none of them has allowed even the smallest hint to escape them."

"Then why are you so certain?"

"There is a feeling in the air, as if I am being buffeted by conspiracies and treacheries whirling about me, ones not aimed at me directly, but which will concern me. 'Tis as if I have been dragged into a dance I do not know the steps of. I believe the Frasers are the most guilty, yet Ainslee plays some game as well. At times I feel that she tries to make me see something, but I know not what."

"Then ask her."

"And you believe she will simply tell me all?"

"Not without some coercion, but I do believe the girl cannot lie. She can twist her words and dance about the truth, but I truly think that she will not lie." Justice pointed down at the dog pens. "And, if you hurry, you may have a chance to get a few of the answers you seek."

Gabel stared down at the dog pens, watching as Ainslee fed her dog some scraps. He shared Justice's opinion that Ainslee would not outright lie to him. As he turned and started out of the room, he just hoped he could abide whatever truth he might pull out of her.

Eight

"There, my poor wee laddie," Ainslee cooed as she fed Ugly a scrap of meat through the slats of the pen.

"Poor—mayhaps. Wee—never," murmured Gabel as he stepped up behind her.

Ainslee gave a soft cry of surprise, for she had not heard his approach, then cast him a brief glare of annoyance over her shoulder, before returning all of her attention to Ugly. The way Gabel stood so closely behind her quickly began to unsettle her. She was too keenly aware of his presence, of his warmth at her back. It annoyed her that, despite his spending most of his day with another woman, her interest in him had only grown stronger. She still wanted him, still dreamt of him, and still ached for his kisses. It was, she decided, all rather pathetic. Her only comfort was in the fact that he had no knowledge of her weaknesses.

"He has been treated as weel as any bairn," she said, squeezing her fingers through the slats to scratch her dog's ears. "He doesna understand why he canna run free."

"As I said, I believe that, if he runs free now, he will die." Gabel slipped his arms about her tiny waist, and rested his chin on the top of her head. "The Frasers see your dog as a threat."

"And ye canna stop them from doing as they please?" She inwardly cursed the hint of huskiness in her voice caused by the warmth his touch stirred within her.

"Stop them from protecting themselves? Nay. I could deny

that your dog was a threat, but, in truth, most people would wonder why I troubled myself over a dog. The king would see any complaint as a foolish waste of his time."

"And because the dog is mine, 'twill be thought by many that the Frasers were right to kill him," Ainslee said quietly, ruefully acknowledging that the MacNairn name was enough to condemn her or any of her own.

"I fear so." Gabel touched a kiss to the back of her ear, smiling faintly when she trembled in his arms. "Why would the Frasers falsely accuse your dog?"

"They hate dogs." As he teased her ear with warm, gentle kisses, Ainslee closed her eyes and leaned back into his hold.

"Clever, Ainslee, but not an answer good enough to silence my questions."

"Why trouble me with questions anyhow? What does it all matter?"

"Something is going on at Bellefleur, something between you and the Frasers."

"Do ye think we plot against you?"

Ainslee turned around to face him. She had hoped that that move would end his kissing and the confusing heat stirred by his body pressing so close to hers. The respite she gained was only brief, for he placed his hands against the sturdy pen on either side of her, caging her body between his and the dogs' cage. She shuddered when he touched a kiss to her cheek, slowly drawing his body closer to hers until they brushed against each other. She clenched her hands into tight fists as she fought the urge to reach out to him and pull him hard up against her. All her needs and desires were descending upon her with a vengeance and a strength she was finding impossible to fight. The clarity of mind she needed to fend off his questions was swiftly retreating.

"Nay," he murmured against the curve of her neck. "I do not believe either of you are much concerned with me, but there are definitely plots afoot. They whirl about me so strongly, I can feel the breeze. I realize that there is an old animosity between you and the Frasers—"

A brief flicker of sanity cut through the haze of desire clouding Ainslee's mind, and she leaned away from him. "Animosity? Such a gentle word for what lies between me and the Frasers. They killed my mother, dinna forget that. And, even before my clan became so lawless, the Frasers and the MacNairns opposed each other. 'Tis not animosity, m'lord, but clear, hard loathing. Ye are probably the first in a hundred hundred years to see Frasers and MacNairns within the same keep. In any other place, one of us would have cut the other's throat by now."

"Are you certain that such a murder is not being plotted even now?"

"*I* dinna plot to murder anyone."

There was a look in his eyes which told her that he had caught the distinct inflection in her words, but he said nothing. She clung to the slats of the pen as he edged closer, brushing soft kisses over her throat. Ainslee knew she ought to push him away, but she simply tilted her head back to allow him access.

She knew Gabel just sought to placate his desires. Lady Margaret's presence was all the proof she needed that Gabel de Amalville would not even consider the possibility of marrying her. He just wanted a lover for a little while. Ainslee already knew that she wanted far more than passion from him. Common sense told her to shove him aside, loudly proclaim her outrage and leave, for the passion he offered would cost her dearly. That passion was hard to resist, however. The fact that she had almost been killed and that even her dog's life was in danger made her hesitate to do what was considered right and honorable. The threat to her life still loomed. She dreaded the thought of dying unloved, even if that love was the fleeting sort born of lust.

While logic and passion still wrestled in her mind, Gabel pulled her hard against him. He brushed his lips over hers, teasing them apart and then easing his tongue into her mouth. Ainslee flung her arms around his neck and decided that she would let passion rule her actions. There would be a price to pay for her recklessness, but, as he started to stroke the inside of her mouth, she decided she was more than willing to pay it.

Gabel hoisted her up in his arms and pressed her even closer to him. When she wrapped her slim legs around his waist, he groaned. Holding her as she clung to him, and moving his attentions to her ear so that he could keep her enflamed yet still see where he was going, he strode to the stable. He went to a secluded, hay-strewn corner, sheltered from the cold and prying eyes. Even as he worked to stifle any protest she might consider making with kisses and heated flattery, he shed his cloak and tossed it over the hay. He gently urged her down onto the rough bed and then settled himself between her legs in an enticing mockery of the intimate embrace he craved.

Ainslee gasped as his body came to rest against hers. She could feel the hard proof of his need pressed firmly against her. Knowing she could stir Gabel so worked to heighten her own need. As he smothered her throat with hot kisses and slowly unlaced her bodice, she curled her legs around his trim hips and pressed him even closer. She echoed his hoarse groan, an ache flaring out from that point of contact and rushing throughout her body.

Still reeling from that feeling, she offered no resistance as he tugged off her tunic. It was not until he began to slide her chemise up her body that she awoke to the fact that she would soon be sprawled beneath Gabel dressed only in her braies. She struggled to regain some glimmer of sanity and crossed her arms over her chest. Gabel was oblivious to her silent and somewhat weak gesture of protest, however. He sat astride her staring down at her braies with a mixture of surprise and amusement.

"You wear braies," he muttered even as he pulled off his tunic and tossed it aside.

"What a clever mon ye are, m'lord." The sting she had intended to put behind her words was greatly reduced by the soft huskiness in her voice.

Gabel laughed and bent to kiss her as he unlaced his shirt. "I have ne'er known a woman to wear braies." He took off his shirt, rolled it up, and placed it beneath her head.

"Ronald insisted that I wear them. He said that it was one more shield, one more thing to cause a mon to hesitate and thus allow me a chance to get away."

"And are you going to try and get away from me?"

"I should," she whispered as she gave into temptation and smoothed her hands over his broad chest, savoring the way he trembled beneath her touch. "I should strike ye sharply, push ye aside, and flee to my bedchamber, honor and maidenhead still intact."

"I have no plans to steal your honor, sweet Ainslee."

"Nay? Ye mean to bed me, to use me to sate your desires."

He touched a kiss to her frowning mouth as he eased her chemise off of her faintly trembling body. "I do not mean to *use* you, Ainslee MacNairn. I mean to enjoy you, savor you, and please you. Do you deny what flames between us?"

She shivered as he threw her chemise aside and crouched over her. The way he stared at her as he slid his big hands down to her braies made it hard to breathe. There was no ignoring or denying the passion darkening his eyes. Desire had put a light flush upon his high cheekbones and tightened his lean features. The knowledge that that passion was for her was a heady thing. He shared her hunger and her need, even if he did not share any of the deeper feelings she was afflicted with. Ainslee only briefly wished that she had the strength of will to leave his arms. She wanted him too much, wanted desperately to taste the passion he offered her. She gasped with pleasure and thrust her fingers through his thick long hair, when he touched a kiss to the tip of her breasts.

"Tell me, Ainslee. Do you deny the passion which gnaws at us?"

"Nay," she whispered, trembling as he pulled off her braies. "Howbeit, I should still refuse it."

"As should I, but I fear I have no strength to do so," he muttered, hastily shedding the last of his clothing as he looked over every inch of her slim, pale body.

" 'Tis good to hear that I am not the only weak soul here."

When Gabel tossed aside the last of his clothes and crouched over her again, Ainslee felt a touch of alarm ripple through her desire. He was a big man, and she was suddenly all too aware of how small and slender she was. Their passion matched, but she was no longer so certain that their bodies would. When he eased his body down onto hers and their flesh met, such a wave of desire tore through her body, it pushed aside all of her concerns. He felt good, and he made her feel very, very good. Ainslee suddenly did not care about anything else.

"Are you going to push me aside, fair Ainslee?" he whispered against her lips.

"Nay, ye rutting Norman bastard, I canna, and I think ye ken it weel," she replied, her words harsh, but her tone of voice soft and welcoming.

"Nay. I but prayed that I was not the only one crippled by this aching need."

Ainslee knew exactly what he referred to. The passion was so strong, the need so great, she simply did not care about such things as consequences. She greeted his fierce kiss with a hunger to equal his. As his kisses moved to her throat, she ran her hands over his back and down his sides, the warm tautness of his skin a delight to touch.

A soft cry escaped her when Gabel's kisses reached her breasts. He stroked the aching tips with his tongue and she arched against him, burrowing her fingers into his hair to hold him in place. As he drew one hardened nipple deep into his mouth, a tremor tore through her body, the strength of feeling his caress invoked causing her to shake. She grew feverish in her movements as he moved his hands over her body, finding every sensitive spot upon her skin. Gabel kept her fever raging with his touch, his kisses, and the heated words he whispered against her skin.

Only once did shocked modesty cut into her blind desire. Gabel slowly covered her inner thighs with kisses, then lightly touched one to the aching place between them. Ainslee gasped and flinched away from him, but Gabel gave her passion no time to fade. He quickly returned to the caresses and kisses that had fired her blood, banishing all the cooling effects of her shock.

When Gabel loomed over her, she looked at him. Before she could find the voice to ask him why he had stopped kissing and stroking her, she felt him press into her. She stared at his taut features as he eased their bodies together, breathless with anticipation. A sharp pain caused her to gasp, and she clutched at his shoulders. Even though desire still held her tightly in its grip, the pain dimming it only briefly, Ainslee suddenly felt clearheaded. She was intensely aware of their entwined bodies, of the feeling of being joined with Gabel, and even the rhythms of his breathing. With a deep sigh of pleasure, she curled her body around his and pulled him closer.

A groan shuddered through Gabel, and he came alive in her arms. Ainslee felt her body quickly learn to parry his every thrust. The desire that had flooded her body began to collect low in her belly in a hot knot. It grew to a strength that was almost painful, then burst, spreading over her with such force that she cried out his name. A small part of her was aware of Gabel tightly gripping her hips and driving deep within her as he shuddered and groaned. She blindly wrapped her arms around him when he collapsed against her.

It was a long time before Ainslee regained her senses. She was wondering what to say or do, when Gabel left her arms. Chilled, she tugged his cloak over her, suddenly painfully aware of her nudity. When he returned with a damp rag, she blushed as he bathed away the stains of her lost innocence. She was still unable to look at him when he laid down beside her and tugged her into his arms. The warmth of his body and the way he stroked her hair smoothed away her embarrassment, but she was still unsure of what to do next.

"Do you now regret what we have done?" Gabel asked, Ainslee's continued silence beginning to make him uneasy.

"Oh, nay," she assured him, finally looking at him and briefly touching his cheek. "I should regret it, of course, and now loudly bemoan my loss of honor, but, to speak truthfully, 'twas great fun."

"Fun?" Gabel laughed and kissed her, delighted by her response. "I have ne'er heard a woman call it fun."

"Oh? And ye have had your skills judged often, have ye?"

"Not as often as you may think. You did not expect a man of six and twenty to be a virgin, did you?"

She smiled, her brief flare of jealousy quickly passing. He spoke pleasantly, simply stating a fact she could not dispute, and not admonishing her. Ainslee also knew that, although Gabel might find a hint of jealousy amusing, even flattering, too much could become deadly to whatever they might share. There was no future for them, and so tearing herself apart over his past or future lovers was extremely foolish of her. She idly ran her foot over his calf and wondered how much more they might share before she had to leave Bellefleur. Ainslee hoped to gather up a multitude of memories to take back to her bleak life at Kengarvey. She dared not ask, however, knowing that any demands at all could easily push Gabel away, and that was the last thing she wanted to do.

"Nay, I didna think ye were as innocent as I," she said. "I ken the ways of men better than I do the ways of women, but vanity briefly made me wish to be something more than just one out of many."

"Oh, you are certainly that, Ainslee MacNairn." He gently kissed her.

"I canna bear the uncertainty any longer," she burst out. "What am I to do now?"

Gabel grinned and took her hand in his, kissing her palm.

"We could stay here or we could slip away to my bed or even yours. Did you think I would now dress and stride away?"

"Weel, nay, but I wasna sure who was supposed to do what."

"There is a chill in the air," he said as he sat up, pulling her up with him. " 'Twill be more comfortable if we return to the keep." As he handed her her clothing, he added, "We can slip away from here without being seen, so you need not fear that everyone will soon be whispering about you."

"Not even my guard?" Ainslee briefly feared that her constant guard had been lurking outside of the stable for the whole time.

"I sent the man away when I first came out to join you by the dog pen." He glanced at her as they both began to dress. "I still puzzle over why you were wandering about alone earlier this evening."

"Alone? Why should ye think that I was alone?"

"Because, if your guard had been with you as he should have been, he would have told me of your trouble with that falling stone. Vincent knew nothing of it."

"I eluded him for a wee while, is all."

"Nay, I think not, although you should be commended for trying so hard to save a fool from a much deserved punishment. Vincent is a fool, but he is an honest one. He confessed to being distracted. So, Paul now shares the guarding of you with Michael."

"And what will happen to Vincent?" Although she knew it was a grave crime for a guard to neglect his duty, she did not wish to see Vincent pay too dearly. He had simply been a pawn in Lady Margaret's deadly game.

"He will be mucking out the stables for a fortnight. A sore blow to a knight's pride. When he returns to his post as one of my men-at-arms, I am certain he will be more diligent."

Ainslee nodded as Gabel helped her don her cloak and led her out of the stables. It was demeaning to be reduced from a man-at-arms to a stableboy, but, if she had been any real danger to Bellefleur, Vincent's distraction could have cost his lord very dearly. What Ainslee did not know, and dared not ask about, was if Gabel had taken any special note of whose maid had led the guard astray. If he had, he would have to ask why, and the answers might make him suitably suspicious of the Frasers. She prayed Gabel was asking himself a lot of questions.

As they reached the head of the stairs, Gabel hesitated only a moment before leading her to her bedchamber. Ainslee was briefly distracted by a soft noise, like the faint click of a door latch, but she could see no one. A chill rippled down her spine, and she huddled a little closer to Gabel. When they entered her bedchamber, she was momentarily concerned that Gabel would now leave her, but he smiled, then shut and latched the heavy door. Ainslee laughed softly and tossed aside her cape. She sat down on the bed and, with opened arms, silently invited him to join her. To her delight, he also laughed and strode over to the bed, gently tumbling her down onto it. Their love affair was destined to be a short one, but Ainslee intended it to be full and memorable.

"What ails ye, daughter?" grumbled Lord Fraser as his daughter shut her bedchamber door and angrily paced the room, pausing only to kick out at a piece of furniture.

"That MacNairn whore has taken Sir Gabel to her bed," Margaret snapped, and threw a heavy tankard against the wall.

"Are ye certain?" Lord Fraser rescued the dented tankard and filled it with mead before sitting down on her bed.

"They just slipped by my door, wrapped in each other's arms. They hadna even brushed the hay off of their clothes. 'Tis clear that they have been rutting in the stables like animals."

"That doesna mean that he will now take her to wife. She is a MacNairn. Not only has her father blackened the name, but she has no dowry—no lands, no coin, no power. A pitiful poor choice for a bride."

"Men have made pitiful poor choices before." She leaned against the bedpost and crossed her arms over her chest as she scowled at the door. "And 'tis a sore blow to my pride to have that MacNairn whelp bedding the mon I intend to wed. She must pay for that insult."

"Ye have only had one plan to rid Bellefleur of the lass, and that failed."

She glared at her father. " 'Twas a good plan, but I have fools surrounding me. I must see to this myself. I begin to think it might not be wise to kill her here."

"Where else can ye kill her? Ye canna wait until she returns to Kengarvey."

"Nay, I canna. Howbeit, it should surprise no one at Bellefleur if the whore disappears. After all, prisoners escape all the time."

Nine

Ainslee stretched, reached out, and sighed when she found the other side of the bed empty. Gabel had quietly slipped away before dawn, just as he had said he would. She knew it was for the best. Such discretion would save her some embarrassment. Nevertheless, she regretted the need for such subterfuge. It would have been far nicer to wake up to the morning wrapped warmly in his arms, with no need to worry about what people saw or thought. The need to creep about stole some of the beauty from their lovemaking.

She crossed her arms beneath her head and stared up at the ceiling. There was an aching in her body as a result of her first bout of lovemaking, but it was a discomfort made bearable by sweet memory. Everything she had ever been taught told her what she had done and what she intended to keep on doing was wrong, but her emotions told her it was right. Ronald would never condemn her for what she did, for her attempt to grasp at some happiness for herself, and his was the only opinion that mattered to her.

Curling up on her side, she decided it was too early to get out of bed. The sun had not even risen yet. Gabel's leaving must have disturbed her and caused her to wake up, for she was still very tired. A cool breeze briefly touched the back of her neck, and she tugged the coverlet more tightly around herself. She then frowned, certain that she had heard a footfall, but, even as she turned to look, a blinding pain burst inside of her head.

* * *

"Careful, fools," hissed Lady Margaret as she hurriedly looked over the unconscious Ainslee's wound. "We dinna wish to leave bloodstains behind." Assured that Ainslee was not bleeding, she signaled the two burly men with her to wrap Ainslee up in the blanket. "Get her out of here, and be careful not to be seen. I will follow as soon as I have gathered up her clothes."

"Why do we need to take her clothes?" asked the pox-marked, dark-haired man who tossed Ainslee over his broad shoulder.

"Because, my idiot cousin, she is to have escaped. No one will believe that she has fled into the night barefooted and dressed only in a thin nightrail. Go, Ian," she ordered her cousin, "and be sure that your hulking companion keeps a close watch upon your back."

Lady Margaret cursed softly as she stuffed Ainslee's clothes into a saddlepack. She wished she had more clever allies than her cousin and his friend. They were the only ones who could ride away from Bellefleur without rousing too much curiosity, however. No one would question two Fraser men-at-arms riding away to rejoin Lord Fraser's son. Ainslee's blanket-shrouded form could easily be explained away as part of the travellers' baggage.

The first tint of sunrise was coloring the sky before Lady Margaret watched her cousin and his companion ride away. She was not too concerned about being seen up and about at such an early hour. No one at Bellefleur knew her well enough to dispute her claim that she had risen to be certain that her cousin carried a gift and a message from her to her brother. Rubbing her hands together to warm them, she hurried back into the keep, already anticipating the uproar, when it was discovered that Ainslee MacNairn had escaped.

* * *

A groan escaped Ainslee as she felt her body hit something hard. Cursing, she sat up, wavering slightly as a fierce dizziness overwhelmed her. She wondered dazedly how she had gone from her soft warm bed to a crumpled blanket on the hard, frost-tinged ground. Two pairs of dirt encrusted boots entered her line of vision and, rubbing her temples in a vain attempt to stop the throbbing in her head, she slowly looked up at the two men standing before her. She recognized one as Ian Fraser and felt a spasm of alarm. There was only one reason for her to be smuggled out of Bellefleur before dawn and dumped miles from anywhere. She was about to be murdered.

"Where have ye brought me to?" she demanded, hiding her fear and watching the two men closely.

" 'Tis a wild place south of Bellefleur," replied Ian. "Near to five hours ride to the south."

"Ah, so ye arena intending to return me to Kengarvey."

"Nay. Me cousin has taken a fierce dislike to you, Ainslee MacNairn. Now, de Amalville is a stranger here and doesna ken much about Margaret, but I wager *ye* ken what happens to ones she takes a dislike to."

"Aye, she sends hulking idiot cousins out to get the blood on their hands."

"I wouldst dull that sharp tongue of yours, woman. I hold your life in me hands," he snapped, flushing with anger.

"Nay, ye hold the means of my murder, is all. Ye havena the courage to return to that hell-born cousin of yours and tell her that ye left me alive. So, why dinna ye and that mute, witless hulk with you just do as ye have been commanded to, and then skulk off to whatever hole ye slithered out of."

To her surprise it was not Ian Fraser who lunged at her, but his companion. Her goading had served its purpose, however, by instigating a blind attack. Ainslee grunted with pain as the man fell upon her and wrapped his thick hands around her throat. She groped for his dagger, even as she fought for breath and against the urge to pull at his choking hands. When her fingers closed around the hilt of his knife, she nearly cried out her relief. Using the man's body to hide what she was doing from Fraser, she stabbed her attacker between the ribs, driving the well-honed blade of the dagger into his heart. Even as he grunted and slumped against her, she pushed him aside. In one swift, graceful move, she took the man's sword and stood up to face a stunned Ian Fraser, armed and ready for battle.

When the man reached for his sword, she tensed, hoping she had the strength to wield the heavy sword well enough and long enough to stay alive. Ian did not draw his sword, however. He stared at his dead friend, then at a grim-faced Ainslee, and back again several times. Her heart skipped with hope when he cursed and rushed to his horse.

Ainslee did not ease her fighting stance until Fraser was long out of sight. She slumped to the ground, weak with relief and some disbelief that she had fended off two strong men. Fortunately for her, they had been both stupid and cowardly. It was several moments before she realized that she was far from safe. She was out in the middle of a harsh cold land wearing only a nightrail, and with no chance of getting any supplies, for they were on the back of the horses Fraser had taken with him.

She grimaced as she looked at the man she had killed. Now that the threat to her life had passed, she was nauseated by what she had been forced to do. She fought that sickness, firmly telling herself that there were far more important things to do—such as survive.

It made bile sting the back of her throat, but she began to strip the dead man of everything she could use. She cut a length of material from his heavy cloak and her blanket, and wrapped them around her feet to protect them from the cold. Grimacing with distaste, she took his hose, cutting them to fit and using the strips to tie them to her legs. She used his sword scabbard to tie the cape around herself, and stole the Fraser brooch he wore to pin the blanket around her shoulders. The man had attacked so brashly and so quickly, he still had his wineskin slung over his shoulders, and she helped herself to that as well. Shaking her head over how odd she must look, she surveyed the land around her.

After several moments of studying the area, Ainslee reluctantly confessed that she had no idea of where she was. Ian Fraser had said she was south of Bellefleur, which put her a little too close to the lawless lands between England and Scotland for her liking. It also put her farther from Kengarvey than from Bellefleur.

Ainslee closed her eyes, clenched her fists so tightly her nails scored her palms, and then took several deep breaths. She needed to decide what to do with her head and her instincts, and not her heart. Returning to Bellefleur might well be the wisest thing to do, but she wanted the decision to be one well-thought-out and not born of emotion. This was the time to think of clan loyalties, and not of her desire for Gabel de Amalville.

Even on a straight unhindered course, Kengarvey was more than twice the distance from her as was Bellefleur. She had no suitable clothing, no horse, no weapons made specifically for her small hands, and no food, only one half-full wineskin. Between her and Kengarvey lay days of rough travel. She looked up at the sky and frowned. It was nearly midday, yet there was little light. The sky was a dull threatening gray. It was certain that the weather would soon hinder any travel. Whether it was rain or snow, she was not adequately dressed to endure it. Ronald was still a captive and, if she could succeed in returning to Kengarvey, her father would never ransom the man.

Opening her eyes, she straightened her shoulders and started walking in the direction of Bellefleur. She prayed that Ian Fraser had spoken truthfully when he had told her that they had ridden south for five hours. If she kept up a steady pace, did not get lost, met no outlaws or wild animals, and the weather did not grow too fierce, she could reach Bellefleur sometime before the midnight hour. She smiled faintly as she thought of the reactions of Lady Margaret and Gabel. Seeing that would almost be worth the arduous journey ahead of her.

"Gabel, Ainslee is nowhere to be found," Michael announced as he strode into Justice's room, where Gabel shared a morning meal with his cousin.

"What do you mean?" Gabel demanded, finishing off his tankard of cider and standing up from where he sat on the edge of Justice's bed.

"I mean what I just said. Ainslee MacNairn is not at Bellefleur. I took up my post outside her door as always, and I did wonder why Paul was not there."

"I sent him away last night," Gabel muttered, talking mostly to himself as he began to pace the room. "Where could the girl have gone? She was sleeping when I left, and that was but two hours or so before you would have taken up your post."

Gabel stopped pacing as he realized what he had just said, and slowly turned to face his cousins. He met their knowing grins with a stern frown, but neither flinched. It was clear that they had guessed where he had spent the night. Justice could easily have watched him take Ainslee into the stable, and Michael would have grown suspicious when he did not find Paul guarding her door. It evidently took a great deal more than tiptoeing around to assure discretion, he thought crossly.

"I was attempting to keep the matter secret," he said.

"A secret at Bellefleur?" Michael laughed, but, seeing that Gabel did not share his good humor, quickly sobered. "Mayhaps that is why she has disappeared?"

"The girl was willing," Gabel said.

"I did not suggest otherwise. Howbeit, I would wager that she was also virginal." Michael shrugged. "What a virgin willingly gives up in the night, she may sorely regret in the morning."

"Do you think she has fled back to Kengarvey?"

"Where else can she be? Call for another search, if you wish, but I assure you that no corner of Bellefleur has been missed. She is gone. A number of her clothes are gone as well."

" 'Tis hard to believe that she would flee without Ronald or that dog of hers," said Justice.

"Ronald, of course," Gabel cried and strode to the door. "He may know something."

It was over an hour before Gabel accepted Ronald's claims of ignorance and believed in the man's show of concern for Ainslee. He realized that the only answer to Ainslee's disappearance, one that he found painful to confront, was that she had escaped, and that she may have done so to flee from him. As he gathered up a small force of men to search for her, he grew angry. Ainslee had used him, had bedded him in order to dull his guard that she could easily slip away. The pain he felt over her desertion began to harden into fury as he slowly began to believe that he had allowed a tiny, red-haired, Scottish lass to make a fool out of him.

As he started to lead his men out of Bellefleur, Justice trotted up beside him and Gabel scowled at his young cousin. "You should not be here."

"I am healed enough to ride about looking for a tiny female," Justice replied.

"The weather could turn poorly, and that could go hard on you."

"If the weather turns against us, then I will turn back."

"Why are you so determined to go on this search?"

"She is a tiny woman wandering about a dangerous land with no horse and none of her weapons. She did not even take her dog which, to my mind, is very strange. 'Tis but gallantry which prods me."

Gabel snorted softly in derision as they rode through the gates. "You but find excuses to leave your bedchamber. 'Tis boredom which prods you."

Justice laughed and nodded. "Aye, there is some truth in

that." He grew serious and studied his cousin closely. "I also have a strange feeling about all of this. True, wellborn virgins can sorely regret the loss of their maidenheads, and some even act most oddly come the morning. Howbeit, Ainslee MacNairn does not act like any lady I have met, so why should she act like one now? Why not at least take the dog? It would have been easy for her to slip the beast free. No one guards the dogs. And, Gabel, what of Ronald? Everything she has done until now has shown that she would ne'er leave the man behind, yet suddenly, she walks away without even telling him? Nay, cousin, I find this all very troubling and confusing."

After a moment's thought, Gabel nodded. When he had realized that Ainslee had not even said farethewell to Ronald, he too had begun to be puzzled, but at that time his anger had clouded his thoughts. His suspicions still lingered, for he did not dare trust her too completely, but now he was willing to at least listen to her—if they got her back to Bellefleur.

Ainslee stumbled down the small rise and cursed as she scraped her legs on the rocky ground. She was tired, cold, and her head ached so badly she had trouble seeing clearly at times. It was nearly sunset and, if she had judged her distances and directions correctly, that meant she was barely half the way to Bellefleur. That thought was so debilitating, she wanted to sit down and weep.

There was a dampness in the chilling air that told her the storm which had hung in the sky all day was about to unleash itself, and she feared it would be snow. Since she did not really know where she was, she did not know where she could find shelter, and that frightened her a little. If the snow was a gentle one, she could continue on, but there was always the chance that it could be a fierce storm, the sort that could leave livestock and people buried until the spring thaw.

"Enough," she snapped at herself. "Ye have quite enough trouble to deal with without scaring yourself to death, fool."

She paused to study her clothes, then sat down and cut a few strips of cloth from her blanket cape. Her hands were chilled to the bone and she needed to warm them. Ainslee hoped that the strips of blanket wrapped around her cold fingers would be enough to keep them from getting a dangerous chill.

"I am going to kill Lady Margaret Fraser when I get back," she swore in a low, hard voice as she started walking again. "I am going to kill her verra slowly, too."

As she carefully crossed over a low, swiftly running brook, she cursed the encroaching darkness. She still was not sure where she was, and finding her way through a strange land in the dark was not going to be easy. Ainslee prayed she had covered more distance than she realized, for she was definitely going to be slowed down.

Gabel had to know that she was not at Bellefleur by now, and she wondered what he was thinking, then grumbled a curse. Gabel de Amalville was probably thinking she had fled his embrace or, worse, used his lusts against him to enable herself the freedom to escape. He had no reason to trust a MacNairn, and she had begun to suspect that he had no great trust in women. He was probably out looking for her, and thinking some very unkind things about her. That would certainly please Lady Margaret, and the thought that that woman might benefit from her crimes gave Ainslee a little burst of strength. When she got back to Bellefleur, she would no longer play any games, no longer wait for Gabel to see the truth for himself, she would expose Lady Margaret Fraser for the devious, deadly adder she was.

A light flurry of snow dampened Gabel's face, and he cursed. It was almost dark, but they still had enough light to search for a little longer; however, the coming of snow ended all hope of continuing. It was time to head back to Bellefleur and not just for Justice's health. There was no telling how fierce the storm might become, and they needed what time they might have left to reach the safety and warmth of his keep. He was angry at the weather, angry at the dark, and, most of all, angry that he had failed to recapture Ainslee, if only so that he could have a few answers to all the questions crowding his mind.

"We must turn back," he announced to his men, and politely ignored the relief they could not hide. He forced a smile of greeting for Justice, who rode up beside him. "You do not look poorly."

"Nay. An easy ride looking for someone was not enough to weaken me, although I shall be pleased to get in out of the cold and damp," Justice said.

"I do not understand how she has eluded us. Aye, she is but one small lass on foot and thus could easily hide, but we should have seen some sign of her."

"That is something that troubles many of the men. There is no trail. There was nothing to reveal that she even left Bellefleur, except that she is not there."

"Well, Ainslee has many skills one would not believe a woman would have."

"That she does, but there ought to be at least a footprint, a broken twig, something. There is nothing. 'Tis as if she floated away from Bellefleur and, clever lass that she is, even I do not believe she can fly."

"If she is not at Bellefleur, then she has to be heading to Kengarvey."

"One would think so." Justice shrugged. "Yet, it greatly disturbs me that we have seen no sign of her passage. None of your men-at-arms saw her leave. None of your crofters has seen any sign that someone has passed by them."

Gabel frowned and rubbed his chin as he thought for a moment. "Do you think she may have gone in the wrong direction?"

"I have already considered that, and whilst you were glaring at the ground and cursing all women, I took the freedom to send two of your men off to look south, east, and west."

"And they found no sign of her?"

"They have not returned to report any, so I must assume that they found none and now wait for us at Bellefleur."

"Curse the girl, where is she? She will be caught out in this poor weather, and that can be very dangerous. Even if she is headed straight to Kengarvey, she will not reach there before the storm reaches its full strength." Gabel realized that, despite his lingering anger, he was now worried about Ainslee. "I think I need to sit and think. You are right, something is very strange about this whole matter. I heard she was gone and immediately assumed she had escaped. Mayhaps that was a swift, harsh judgement brought about by my own mistrusts. I simply do not know, and that leaves us to ride about in circles."

"Aye, and mayhaps we should look at what else could have driven her from Bellefleur, or if there are other reasons and causes of her disappearance."

"Do you think some harm has been done to her?"

"Who can say, but I think you might consider the fact that the Frasers have made no secret of their hatred of the Mac-Nairns," Justice reminded him. "They might have decided that striking at the MacNairns was worth abusing the hospitality of their host."

"I never considered that," Gabel whispered, and cursed his own stupidity. "I must tread warily in finding out what, if anything, they had to do with this. They are powerful and well favored at the king's court. It would do us no good to offend them or accuse them, without the sort of proof that cannot be denied or ignored."

The possibility that Ainslee had been hurt or even murdered sent a chill down Gabel's spine. He much preferred being angry, even hurt, that she had left him or even tricked him. If any harm had come to her at the hands of the Frasers, he would have to shoulder some of the blame. He had had his suspicions about his guests, and they had made no secret of how much they loathed Ainslee, yet he had done nothing to protect her from them. Suddenly, instead of cursing her as yet another treacherous female, Gabel found himself hoping that Ainslee had indeed used his desire for her to gain a chance of escape. At least she would be safe.

It was not until late that evening that Gabel got an opportunity to subtly question the Frasers. He joined his guests in the great hall for a late meal. As he studied Lady Margaret Fraser and her father, Gabel realized that he did not find it hard to believe that they would hurt a small woman who had done them no real harm.

"I hear that ye had little success in finding that MacNairn womon," Lady Margaret said as she had a page refill her tankard with ale.

"Nay, none at all," replied Gabel. " 'Tis as if the girl flew away."

"What do ye mean?"

"She has left no sign of her passing, not a footprint, not even a scent for the dogs."

"Ye sent the dogs out?"

"Only to try and find the start of her trail. I am not one to set the dogs on anyone. I thought it would help us, but they found nothing. Even her own hound could not track her."

Gabel admitted to himself that Ugly's inability to find his mistress's scent had been the most alarming of his failures to find her. He watched Margaret closely as he spoke, but he saw no hint of guilt, or of a fear that he might discover what she and her father had done. Neither did he see any sign of concern or, more curiously, surprise. He had just told her that one tiny Scottish lady had fled the crowded, well-guarded Bellefleur leaving no trace of her passage, and that even the dogs could not sniff her out. This was at least worthy of an expression of astonishment, but Margaret did not blink an eye. It was as if she knew there would be no sign. Gabel told himself not to let his old mistrust of women now lead him to rashly suspect Margaret, but his growing suspicion could not be stifled.

"Weel, the MacNairns have always been a stealthy lot with a true skill at sneaking about."

"Mayhaps. We only found the trail your cousin and his friend left behind. 'Tis odd, but they rode south. I thought they went to join your brother at the king's court, which is north of here." Lord Fraser looked up a little sharply, but Gabel saw no response in Margaret's expression except for a slow closing of her eyes, and then one, brief narrow-eyed glance.

"I suspect they have journeyed to visit their whores ere they become entangled in my brother's work, and the whore my cousin Ian favors lives a few miles south of here," Margaret replied, smiling sweetly at Gabel. "If my cousin arrives at court late, my brother will soon discipline him for his laxity."

"As he should," Gabel murmured, but his suspicions hardened. Even if the Frasers did not have a hand in Ainslee's disappearance, they knew where she was. He was increasingly sure of that. "I but find it all a little puzzling that she would flee without telling her man Ronald anything, and without even trying to take her dog with her."

"Weel, servants canna be trusted to keep a confidence and why should the woman care about that dog? She can get another one."

Gable shrugged, not arguing her opinions, but finding the swift explanations and the intensity behind them interesting. Margaret was working hard to keep her eyes averted, thus sheltering her expression. If the woman had something to do with Ainslee's disappearance, she was probably beginning to think that she may have made a few serious mistakes. Gabel wished she would add some revealing slip of the tongue to that list of errors, but he began to doubt that he would ever be able to get Margaret or her father to say anything that would implicate them in any crime. That left him with nothing more than suspicions, guesses, and possibilities. Gabel cursed inwardly. He needed far more than that. Ainslee's life could easily depend upon it.

"I worry the matter too much," he said and took a sip of his wine.

"Aye. Ye will see. When that thief MacNairn replies to your last ransom demand, it will be to tell you that he need pay you naught, for his daughter is safe at home."

"I hope you are correct, Lady Margaret. I wished to collect a ransom for the girl; I did not wish any harm to come to her, either from someone within Bellefleur or because of my own neglect. If I discover that she has been purposely harmed, I will see that the crime is punished." He smiled sweetly at her, his expression indicating that he did not mean her, but the looks that briefly passed over her and her father's faces told Gabel that they had heard and understood the threat.

"M'lord," cried a page as he hurried up to the table. "I think you had better come with me. Sir Justice says there is something beyond the walls that you will be most interested in."

Ten

A vicious curse broke from Ainslee's wind-chilled lips as she stumbled and her painfully cold hands became buried in the icy snow. Out of habit she looked around to make sure that no one had heard her, then cursed again. She was the only unfortunate to be out in the freezing cold and snow. No matter how foul and blasphemous she spoke, no one was there to admonish her.

Ainslee stood up and vainly tried to brush the snow from her hands and her clothes. It was a useless gesture for she was already soaked through to the skin, but she hoped that, if she could not see herself covered in snow, she might be able to convince herself that she was not as cold as she was. As she plodded on, she wondered what she had done in her short life to deserve such a punishment. It seemed grossly unfair that the devious, murderous Lady Margaret was warm and comfortable inside of Bellefleur, while she was in danger of freezing to death. Even if she did not die in the snow itself, Ainslee was beginning to fear that she was returning to Bellefleur only to fall ill with a fever and die.

She was tired and she ached to lie down, but she knew the danger of that. To give into the urge to sleep was to welcome death. What kept her trudging on now was not only the desperate need to make Margaret pay for her crime, but also the intensifying craving to see Gabel and Ronald one more time. If she was going to die, she did not want to do it out in the middle of nowhere with no chance of saying farewell to her friend and her lover. There were things she wanted to say to both men, things she would never be able to say if she lost her life beneath the icy white covering the ground.

Just as she began to think she did not even have enough stubbornness left to keep moving, a dark shape formed ahead of her in the snow. Afraid to believe her eyes, she stumbled forward until the shape became more distinct. When she recognized it as Bellefleur, she wanted to weep with relief, but, even if she could produce the tears, she was sure they would freeze upon her cheeks.

"Now all I have to pray for is that some guard upon the walls does not mistake me for an enemy or a possible meal and cut me down," she muttered as she struggled to move faster through the deepening snow.

Justice stared out at the figure stumbling through the snow and shook his head. When Gabel rushed up to his side upon the high walls of Bellefleur, Justice said nothing, simply pointed. He nodded when Gabel gaped out at the tiny shape moving clumsily across the snow, then cursed.

" 'Tis Ainslee?" Gabel whispered, shock and doubt turning his statement into an uncertain question.

"It appears to be," said Justice. "My first thought was to hurry out and get her, but I thought again."

"Why? She must be nearly frozen to death." Gabel scowled at his cousin when the younger man grabbed him by the arm and kept him from running down off the walls.

"She may be, but she is a MacNairn, one of a clan you have declared outlaws. I do not believe she would do so, but one cannot ignore the possibility that she is being used as a trap, as a lure meant to make us open our gates."

"She has not had time to get to Kengarvey, plot that clever a trap with her kinsmen, and return."

"Nay, I do not think so. 'Twas one of those things I felt you must decide."

"Alright. We will not open the gates widely, only enough to allow one thin girl in, and the men are to be prepared to respond swiftly and fully to any hint of attack." As Gabel hurried down the walls, he heard Justice relaying his orders to the other men.

Gabel eased open the gate and peered out. He could see no one beside Ainslee. As she approached, she stumbled every few steps. He ached to rush out and help her, but he stood fast. The need to cast aside all caution and run to her aid was born of emotion, and he had too many people to protect to act upon that. She fell against the edge of the door and he grabbed her by the arm, pulling her inside even as the two gatekeepers hurried to close the gates and bar them again.

He tugged her into the circle of light cast off by a torch stuck in the wall near the gate and studied her, as Justice ran up to them. She looked dangerously cold, and her attire was strange. When she moaned softly and collapsed against him, he picked her up in his arms.

"Did you become lost, Mistress MacNairn?" he said, his voice hard as he fought to hide his worry. "Kengarvey is still many miles to the north."

"I have walked as far as I can today, m'laird. I believe I would like to seek my bed now."

With a concerned Justice keeping pace, Gabel strode into Bellefleur. Her answer, gritted out from between chattering teeth, still told him nothing about what had happened. As he stepped into the hall, the brighter light there gave him a better look at Ainslee. It would be a while before she was recovered enough to question.

Ainslee struggled to lift her head from where she had rested it against Gabel's shoulder. The bright light briefly blinded her, but then she saw Margaret Fraser standing in the doorway leading to the great hall. She moved so abruptly that Gabel nearly dropped her, but Ainslee managed to free herself from his hold. When she tried to stand up, she swayed and he caught her by the arms, but she held firm, refusing to allow him to pick her up again.

"I am not as easy to kill as my mother," she said, staring right at Lady Margaret, who was too furious to hide her feelings.

"I fear the poor girl has been made delirious by her ordeal and now babbles," Lady Margaret replied, her voice cold even as she attempted to give Gabel a polite yet beseeching smile.

"Nay. Ye canna play that game anymore, Margaret. Ye should have stayed with boulders dropped from the windows, or mayhaps a touch of poison. Ye should have kenned that, if this grand scheme to be rid of me failed, ye had no way to explain or excuse it."

"Ye are talking like a madwoman."

Although it caused her raw hands to bleed, Ainslee took the Fraser brooch from her shoulder and tossed it at Margaret's feet. "Do ye recognize this, m'lady? I fear your dim-witted cousin Ian has lost the only friend he probably had."

"Ye have spilled Fraser blood? This is why she spits out such wild accusations and lies, m'lord," Margaret said to Gabel. "She tries to excuse her crimes."

"If I werena little more than a lump of ice, I would gladly spill a wee bit more Fraser blood by cutting your throat," Ainslee snapped and even attempted to take a step toward Margaret, crying out in frustration when Gabel again lifted her up in his arms. "Give me but a moment to warm myself, Gabel, and then I will make that sly whore pay."

"Hush, Ainslee," he ordered her, and then he looked coldly at Margaret. "Justice," he called to his cousin, "I would like you to keep company with the Frasers until I have tended to Ainslee, for I wish to talk to them." He waited long enough to see Justice and another man nudge Lady Margaret back into the great hall and then climbed the stairs to Ainslee's bedchamber. "We searched for you, but could find no trail."

"Ye were looking for the wrong trail, one made by me alone," Ainslee said. "Ye should have looked for the trail I ken her cousin and his friend left. Those fools were too stupid not to have left a verra clear trail." As her body warmed, she became aware of a great many pains and touched her fingers to her stinging mouth. When she saw the blood on her fingers, she cursed. "I think my lips have fallen off in the snow."

"Nay," he replied with a calm he did not feel. "I believe there are still a few pieces left beneath the blood."

A sharp, stinging pain began to creep over her body, and she moaned softly. "I think I am bleeding everywhere."

"I do not believe so, dearling. 'Tis just the blood moving through your veins again."

"I dinna think it is verra fair that becoming warm again should be such a painful thing."

Ainslee said nothing else as Gabel took her into her room and set her down on her bed. With occasional help from a maid, he stripped off her soaked clothing, bathed her, and wrapped her in a warm gown. He helped her sip a tankard of warmed mead, and then tucked her securely beneath the blankets. Once the pain in her body began to ease and all her injuries and raw skin were covered in salve and bandaged, she began to feel sleepy. For a moment she fought the feeling, still afraid to sleep, for it could be the first step toward death.

"You did not try to escape?" he asked, growing more and more certain that she had not, but wanting to hear her say so.

Her voice barely a whisper, and her words a little slurred as she tried not to move her lips much, Ainslee replied, "Gabel, I tell ye truly, my father willna pay for Ronald alone. He doesna like Ronald and considers him a worthless cripple. Making the mon my nursemaid wasna meant to be an honor, ye ken. Nay, unless Ronald returns with me, he willna return. If I left Ronald here and went to Kengarvey alone, I would never see the mon again. Kenning that, do ye really believe I would try to escape without him?"

"I did consider that odd."

"But, when ye found me gone, ye thought I had slipped

away so that I might deprive ye of your ransom and your chance to please the king."

It was faint, and Gabel suspected that was only because she was so exhausted, but the sting in her words made him flinch with guilt. "Aye, although I did still have a few questions."

"Did ye. Howbeit, ye had been smelling plots, and when I was gone ye felt that escape had been the plot ye had been sniffing out. Weel, I am sorry that I canna make it all that easy for ye." She winced, for the movement caused her pain, but she reached out to grasp his hand. "I willna say that I will ne'er try to flee, but I would ne'er leave Ronald behind. He, Ugly, and Malcolm are my family. Try to forget that I am one of the lawless MacNairns for but a moment, and look about ye, Gabel de Amalville. I am not the one plotting here."

"Is that what you have been trying to tell me for days?"

"Aye. I felt ye would ne'er heed the warnings of a MacNairn against a Fraser and hoped to make ye see their treacherous natures on your own. Weel, that game has twice nearly cost me my life. I believe I canna wait for ye to open your eyes any longer. I am too weary to say much now. Come back when I have rested, and I will tell ye more than ye may wish to ken about your guests. If ye dinna wish to wait that long, then go and speak to Ronald. Tell him that I have confessed to my little games and that I accept failure. In truth, he kens more about them than I do."

"I will. Rest, Ainslee," he said softly and brushed a kiss over her wind-reddened forehead. "I will send my aunt in to sit with you for a while," he added, and then smiled faintly, for she was already asleep.

As soon as he had fetched his aunt to nurse Ainslee, Gabel went to Ronald's room. The man's blatant relief that Ainslee had been found and his concern over her health only worked to confirm her assertions. Once Gabel gave Ronald her message, the man spoke freely about the Frasers. Gabel could not believe he had been so blind. He wanted to make them pay dearly for their attempts to murder Ainslee, but he knew that would be a mistake. At the moment the king would consider their only crime to be an abuse of his hospitality, for the Mac-Nairns were declared outlaws, and that gave anyone the right to do to them as they wished.

When Gabel finally entered the great hall to meet with the Frasers, he did not want to listen to any explanations they had devised, but he forced himself to do so. He heard them out, then coldly told them they were to leave Bellefleur as soon as the weather had improved. It did not surprise him when they both acted outraged. The Frasers could not afford to have him as an enemy, and would do most anything to sway his favor back to them.

"M'lord," Lady Margaret said as she drew near to him and lightly stroked his arm, ignoring the way he tensed and jerked away. "How can ye believe the lass's tales? She is a MacNairn. She obviously tried to escape, something went wrong, and she had to come back here, so she tries to turn your righteous anger away from herself."

"Then explain to me how she came by a Fraser's brooch, as well as the cloak and sword of one of your men?"

"She stole them ere she fled into the night."

"Nay, I think not. I think she got them when she was forced to fight for her life. Go. You are to leave as soon as travel is possible, and I suggest you keep out of my sight until that time comes."

Before Margaret could protest anymore, her father dragged her out of the great hall. Gabel sighed, poured himself a tankard of wine, and had a long drink. When Justice sat down beside him, he pushed the jug of wine toward his cousin.

"So, you believe Ainslee's claim?" asked Justice as he poured himself a drink.

"Aye. Although some of the clothes she was given are missing, she wears none of them. She was dressed in a man's cloak, her nightrail, and a blanket. Scraps of cloth were all she had for her feet and hands. Ainslee would never leave so ill prepared. Nay, I do not know exactly what happened out there, and will not know until Ainslee is recovered enough to tell me, but this was no attempt to escape."

"If she did not tell you exactly what happened, how can you be so sure the Frasers had a hand in it?"

"Because of all that Ronald told me about them. Ainslee had a Fraser brooch, so a Fraser had to be with her. Margaret's cousin and his friend left before dawn, just as we had thought Ainslee had. They obviously took her out of here. Neither of those men has, or had, the wit to plan such a trick, and we can be very sure that they were not trying to help her."

Justice shook his head. "They may well have put a lot of their prestige and power at risk. Mayhaps it was done for more reasons than an old hatred."

"What other reasons? They were not taking her to Kengarvey, so they could not have made some bargain with her, nor could they have been thinking of ransoming her themselves and making their own treaty with the MacNairns."

"The only thing the Frasers appear to want to do to the MacNairns is slaughter them to a man. Nay, I but wondered if Lady Margaret was aware of your interest in Ainslee. She does not seem to be the sort of woman who would tolerate a rival, especially if she considers that rival little more than a thieving peasant."

Gabel stared at his cousin for a full minute before cursing. "I do not wish to believe that, for it would mean that I allowed my own lusts to place Ainslee in danger of her life."

"I do not think it is all that simple," Justice said in a vain attempt to reassure him. "Howbeit, you must consider that possibility. I press it for, if that is the way of it, then you must now consider that Lady Margaret will not only see Lady Ainslee as a rival, but as someone who has beaten her."

"I knew that tiny red-haired girl would be trouble from the moment she faced me with that accursed sword in her hand," Gabel complained, not truly angry with Ainslee, for he knew none of this was her fault, but needing to vent his frustration. "I shall put a much heavier guard on her and on the old man.

Those Frasers have already shown that they are not above striking down the ones Ainslee loves simply because she loves them. And have that monstrously ugly dog of hers brought into her room." He smiled faintly as Justice laughed, bowed mockingly, then hurried away to get the dog, and select a few men for guard duty on the MacNairns.

Groaning softly, for he detested such intrigues, Gabel finished his drink and went to Ainslee's room. He intended to keep a watchful eye on Ainslee himself, and he doubted that anyone at Bellefleur would be surprised or shocked at that. It was a decision based mostly on emotion, but, after what had happened today, he began to wonder if he was wrong to so completely ignore what his emotions told him. He had been fighting them so fiercely and questioning his every move so thoroughly to be certain it was not an emotional one, that he had missed a great deal of what had been going on directly beneath his nose.

His aunt smiled at him as he slipped into Ainslee's bedchamber and, as he quietly approached the bed, he asked, "How does she fare?"

"She sleeps," Marie replied. "Her breathing appears to be untroubled, and she has grown warm, yet not feverishly so."

"I am pleased to hear that, for I was concerned that she might catch a fever." He helped his aunt from the stool she was sitting on next to the bed and began to urge her toward the door. "Go to your bed, Aunt. I will watch o'er her now."

"But she may have need of a woman's touch," Marie protested, even as Gabel pushed her out of the door.

"If she asks for it, I can call for you or for one of the dozen or more maids scurrying about Bellefleur. Sleep well, Aunt," he said, kissing her cheek and then shutting the door.

Gabel poured himself a tankard of mead from the jug by the bed, then made himself comfortable at the end of the bed, his gaze fixed firmly upon a sleeping Ainslee. He was a little discomforted by how pleased he was to see her alive and apparently surviving her ordeal unscathed. It revealed far more depth to what he felt for her than the lust he readily admitted to. That was dangerous. The wise thing to do would be to distance himself from her, but, looking at her face and smiling crookedly, he knew he would not do that.

It was amusing in a sad way, but everything which attracted him to Ainslee was exactly what made it impossible for him to keep her around. That and the fact that she was a MacNairn. It became clearer every day that Ainslee had not been tainted by the poison infecting her father and his father before him, but the name was now a burden. It sounded callous to think that way, but Gabel knew he had to be callous. A lot of people depended upon him, and he could not do anything that might risk the position he had already attained, or hurt any future gains he might make. He wished he had more freedom to do as he pleased, but he did not, and he could not allow his feelings for Ainslee make him act as if he did.

She groaned softly, drawing his attention to her eyes as they slowly opened. He was not surprised to see her awake, as her stomach had been loudly protesting its emptiness for several moments. Even as she stared at him, her sleep-clouded eyes beginning to clear, her stomach grumbled again. Gabel smiled when her eyes widened and she placed a hand over her stomach.

"Was that me?" she said, her voice husky with exhaustion.

"Aye. I have been serenaded by it for a while. There is some bread and cheese next to your bed." He frowned when she just looked at it. "Do you need some help?"

"Nay." She eased herself up into a sitting position, looked down at the nightrail she wore, and then looked at him. "I was too tired to reproach ye for your inappropriate assistance in removing my clothes, so shall I say it now?"

"I believe you just said it. Have something to eat ere we are both deafened by your growling belly."

She helped herself to some bread and cheese, a little surprised at how weak she felt, yet relieved that she had not sickened from her ordeal. " 'Tis rather loud. I have had naught to eat since last night. A few sips of sour wine makes for a poor meal."

"Ainslee, I want you to tell me exactly what happened."

She eyed him warily as she ate. "Are ye sure ye want to hear it? Or am I just going to be wasting breath and strength telling ye a tale that ye will cry a falsehood?"

"Nay, I will listen, and I think I can assure you that I will question none of it." He shrugged and smiled crookedly. "I did as you said and talked to Ronald. It was not difficult to guess what had happened then. Howbeit, I should like to hear it from you."

In between bites of food, she told him everything. He moved to check the bump on her head and she knew it was not to verify her claim, simply to assure himself that it was not a serious injury. She was pleased that he had finally seen the truth about the Frasers, but, as she finished eating and slumped against her pillows, she wished she could benefit from that. He would not now turn to her and look at her as a possible wife, so she tried to find some solace in the fact that she was being believed. It was not something that often happened to a MacNairn.

"You are a most surprising young woman, Ainslee Mac-Nairn," Gabel murmured.

"If I must continue to take lives to be surprising, I believe I should like to be verra dull indeed."

He sat down on the edge of the bed and took her hand in his in a gesture of comfort. "I am sorry that I remained blind to the troubles you faced. If I had seen more clearly who the Frasers really were and what they were doing, I could have saved you from that. I must also take some of the blame for Lady Margaret's attacks. If I had left you alone as any honorable man would have, she would not have been stirred to consider you a rival she needed to dispose of."

"I shouldna blame yourself. If I recall that night weel, I was a most willing partner."

Gabel grinned and touched a kiss to the palm of her bandaged hand. "You are most kind to try and relieve me of some of my guilt. The Frasers cannot be forced out into the storm, but they will be leaving as soon as it has ceased. I have also put a heavier guard on you and Ronald. Justice was to have brought that dog of yours in here, but I believe I heard my aunt direct him to take it to Ronald's room until we are sure you are not going to sicken from the chill you suffered."

"Aye, 'tis best. After he has been kept in a pen he might be a wee bit too happy to see me, and I am too tired to wrestle with him tonight. How long do ye think the Frasers might remain here?"

"I cannot say. I pray that the storm has ended come morning, but who can tell what whims the weather might follow. I wish I could punish them in some manner, but since the Mac-Nairns have been declared outlaws by the king himself—"

"The Frasers have committed no crime in trying to kill me," Ainslee said, and sighed with a mixture of weary resignation and anger. "A MacNairn is fair game for anyone. The worst the Frasers have done is to be poor guests."

"And that is nothing I can punish them for, except to ne'er allow them near me again and, mayhaps, make it well known what they did whilst they were here. Sadly, few people will have sympathy for you, but they will not like the devious way of the Frasers."

"That is something, I suppose." She yawned and slid down beneath her covers. " 'Tis a fine thing to be warm," she said with a faint smile, and then grimaced as she looked at her bandaged hands. "I fear I must look quite battered and dreadful. It feels as if the wind and the cold tore half my skin off."

"The salves will help, but, aye, you were quite raw. If you had been out in the storm for very much longer, I think you would have lost a few of those fingers and toes."

"Aye, and when the cold bites into one to that depth, it can also take your life." She shivered as she realized how close she had come to dying, then turned her attention to Gabel. "Watch the Frasers, Gabel."

"I am."

"Nay, I dinna mean just while they remain here, although I feel much better kenning that there are guards about. Nay, I mean from this day onward ye must watch the Frasers and watch them closely. Ye have done them no real wrong, but they have a most odd way of looking at rights and wrongs. Ye have caught them in their scheming and could taint their name, and ye have beaten them, taken away the prizes they sought—my death and ye as Margaret's husband. I believe ye have just been added to the verra long list of ones the Frasers consider enemies and a danger to them. Watch your back, my trusting knight, for even Margaret is capable of sticking a dagger in it."

"Why, Ainslee MacNairn, are you concerned for my well-being?" He grinned at her disgusted look and softly touched a kiss to her painfully chapped cheek.

"If my clan is to survive, my cocksure and too vain knight, a treaty must be struck with someone, and ye are the only one I have met thus far who would keep a bargain made with my father. 'Twould be quite costly for the MacNairns if ye died, 'tis all."

"Of course," he murmured. "Rest, Ainslee. You need it to recover." He laughed softly. "This was not the way I had envisioned this night."

Knowing he had thought to return to their lovemaking just as she had, she grinned sleepily. "I fear ye shall have to cool your fever for a wee while, m'laird. At least until we are certain that what little skin the cold left upon me is healed enough to stay there." As she felt the need to sleep pull at her, she reached out and touched his cheek. "I meant what I said, Gabel. Watch your back, for if ye are fool enough to forget that, and the Frasers stick a dagger in it, I shall return from wherever I am and kill ye myself."

"If it is possible for a man to be killed twice, then I believe you may just be the woman who could do it."

Ainslee laughed, a soft, brief sound, before she gave into

the urge to sleep. For a long while Gabel just stared at her, tenderly holding her bandaged hand. Although it would still leave him with far more problems than he wanted to deal with, he found himself hoping that Duggan MacNairn was as dishonorable and as heartless as he was rumored to be, and that the man refused to ransom his own daughter. Gabel then cursed himself for a selfish bastard who was trying to have everything he wanted—the treaty or an end to MacNairn, Ainslee, and the appropriate wife. Keeping Ainslee as his leman would hurt her, as would her father's refusal to ransom her, no matter how stoutly she claimed it did not, and Gabel knew he would do most anything to keep from hurting her. He knew he had lost the battle to keep his emotions tucked away, but he vowed that he would not let them rule him.

Eleven

"Stop fretting o'er those hands, lassie," Ronald scolded Ainslee as he entered her bedchamber to find her rubbing more salve onto her almost healed hands. "Ye will be rubbing them back to the raw, tattered state they were in a week ago."

Ainslee smiled crookedly as she watched her friend walk to the bed and sit down on the edge. Insisting that she needed to be protected, he had gotten out of bed the day after her ordeal. It had concerned her that he would further harm himself by trying to do too much too soon, but the Frasers left two days later. That had allowed Ronald to rest again, although he had not completely returned to his bed. His strength had returned more each day, however, and she began to feel confident that he would make a full recovery from his wounds.

She set aside the pot of salve, arranged herself more comfortably on the sheepskin before the fire, and idly scratched her sleeping dog's ears. Although she was very glad to see Ronald, a part of her was disappointed that it had not been Gabel at her door. Gabel had made no attempt to make love to her again. He had been affectionate, but had never ventured beyond a light caress or a gentle kiss. She was beginning to fear that he no longer wanted her, that their one night together had been all she would ever have. That thought made her want to weep, but she struggled to hide her worries and unhappiness from Ronald.

"Ye appear to be quite hale," she said.

Ronald nodded and helped himself to a tankard of mead. "It

tires me to be on my feet, yet, at the same time, it helps me regain my strength. Each day I need to return to my bed less and less." He silently offered her a tankard of the honey wine, and she shook her head. "I am glad to see how weel ye have recovered, and to see the backs of those Frasers." He frowned as he sipped his mead. "The parting wasna friendly. Young Sir Gabel had best watch his back around those Frasers."

"I think he is weel aware of that now. The mon might be too honorable to see all the treachery some people can brew, but he has wit enough to watch for it once he has been warned."

"Aye, he does. He spends a great deal of time with you, lassie."

"He does, but ye can get that glint out of your eyes, old friend. There willna be a match made there."

"And why not? The lad has bedded you—"

"Ronald!"

"I may be old, lassie, but I am nay blind nor deaf."

"People are talking about it?" she asked, dismay softening her voice, for she had hoped that, although it was no secret, it would not become the fruit of gossip.

"Dinna look so horrified. 'Tis no more than a word whispered here and there, a hint. I suspected what might happen between ye and that braw Norman, so I kenned what was meant. Truth, I dinna ken what makes the difference, but none here condemn ye or speak of the matter as if it be a sin and a shame. Ye can still hold your wee head up as ye walk these halls."

" 'Tis most likely the great love they hold for their laird." She smiled crookedly. "I have gained the feeling that many here believe the mon can do no wrong, that he is but a step away from beatification."

Ronald laughed and shook his head. "Aye, I have seen that as weel." He grew serious and studied her closely. "And how do ye feel about the lad?"

The way Ronald kept referring to Gabel as a lad made her

smile, but her good humor was fleeting. "I think ye ken how I feel."

"Ye love him."

"Aye, but it matters not."

"Nay? 'Tis why ye bedded down with him."

"I think it may be, although I wasna thinking much about love at the time." She briefly giggled at the way Ronald rolled his eyes. "I wanted him, and I am sorry if that causes ye any disappointment."

"Ye are a lass of strong feeling, Ainslee. I always kenned that, when your woman's heart was finally touched, ye would give all. Nay, ye can ne'er disappoint me. I am not so blind with a father's affection that I think all ye do is right, but ye need not fear that I will condemn ye for, mayhaps, loving unwisely."

"And that is just what I have done, I fear. Oh, aye, the mon is worth loving. There is no question of that. The lack of wisdom is in loving him when I kenned from the beginning that he would ne'er wed me or e'en love me back. Howbeit, my feelings couldna be tidily locked away and made to act as they should."

"Feelings ne'er can."

She tilted her head and looked at him with open curiosity. "Nay? I think Gabel locks his away verra tightly, and is e'er on the alert for their escape." She flopped down onto her back, crossed her hands beneath her head, and smiled fleetingly when Ugly groaned in his sleep and stretched out at her side. "Gabel doesna want to feel anything except lust. He likes the passion and is willing to let that have its way, but I think anything else gets firmly chained away."

"That isna a good way for a mon to live. If ye swallow such emotion too often, 'twill rot your belly. Are ye sure? Mayhaps he is but one of those men who canna show what he feels verra clearly, and canna find the words to speak about it."

"I am sure. His cousin Elaine told me a tale of betrayal that explains his manner verra weel. A woman he trusted, mayhaps loved, used him, tricked him, and his blindness to her true nature cost him the life of his closest friend, a companion since boyhood."

"Many a lad suffers a heart's sorrow—"

"I ken it, but do they also suffer the loss of a friend?"

"Weel, nay, but—"

"Ronald, he was but an untried boy. The woman was older, wiser, and steeped in treachery. She also worked to help her true lover murder the de Amalvilles and steal their wealth. She tried to kill Gabel, but his friend took the mortal wound instead. Gabel held him as he died. He kenned who had ordered the murder as weel. He was able to warn his kinsmen of the treachery afoot, but that couldna soothe the pain of kenning that his blindness had killed his dear friend and could weel have helped his enemy defeat his own family." She turned on her side to look at Ronald. "I think it was then that Gabel decided emotion was a dangerous thing, feelings could not be trusted, and, mayhaps, that love was the most dangerous emotion of all."

"He doesna seem to be a cold mon."

"Nay, and at times I believe that truly irritates him." She grinned when Ronald laughed. "I am soon to return to Kengarvey. There is no way Gabel can keep me here, even if he wanted to. The bargain must be made, for the king has demanded a treaty. I dinna have the time to try and heal his wounds, to try and make him trust in emotion again."

"And so ye must take whate'er ye can."

"I fear so. Howbeit, I begin to think that his passion was even more fleeting than I had thought, for he has not been in my bed since that night." She frowned when Ronald chuckled and shook his head. "Ye canna find that amusing?"

"Nay, not that if it were true, but it isna."

"Oh? Have ye the skill to ken what Gabel de Amalville thinks?"

"Dinna hone your tongue on me, lass," Ronald admonished her gently. "Tell me, did the lad stay the night with you?"

"Aye. Weel, he slipped away before the sun rose so that some discretion might be maintained." She failed to stop her blushes as she answered, but acted as if she was oblivious to them.

"If the mon found the bedding of ye to be a sad disappointment, he wouldna have stayed the night. And he wouldna have his men wondering why he is behaving so gallantly, and thus making his mood so sour."

Ainslee grimaced and blushed again at the thought of Gabel's men discussing them. "So, I *have* become the fodder of gossip."

"Nay, I swear ye havena. 'Tis but a few remarks made by those who have felt the keen edge of their laird's temper. They ken exactly why he is in such a black mood."

She sat up and smiled faintly. "Because he is doing something he doesna really like to do—staying away from me?"

"Exactly. Howbeit, lassie, ye can only be hurt by all of this. As ye say, ye must leave soon. Mayhap the parting will go easier if ye havena been sharing his bed. Mayhaps, if ye step away now, ye can begin to put aside your feelings for him, and ye willna be so sorely hurt when ye are taken back to Kengarvey."

"Nay, that willna work." She stood up, walked over to Ronald, and kissed his cheek, before helping herself to a small drink of mead. "I love that Norman oaf. Bedding him or not bedding him willna change that. Nay, nor will it change how it shall pain me to leave him, to ken that he will soon take another to wife. I must take what pleasure I can, whilst I can. I must try and drink my fill of all the good Gabel and I share, whilst I can. All I will have when I return to Kengarvey are my memories, and I plan to make so many that my heart and mind will be crowded with them."

Ronald stood up, flexing his stiff leg before he started toward her door. "I canna say I wouldna do the same." He paused before opening the door. "Doesna it anger ye that he willna wed ye, that he wouldna e'en consider ye as a bride?"

"At times," she confessed as she sat down on her bed. "Howbeit, I ken weel what I lack. I also understand that he canna think only of himself or of me when he chooses a bride. There are too many people depending on him. The MacNairns are outlaws, condemned and reviled by the king. It willna help Gabel's cause or his future if he claims one of us as his bride. Nay, 'twould be wondrous if he could love me enough to risk the king's anger or his future to take me as his wife, but e'en if that was possible, I dinna have the time to make it happen."

"Nay. Weel, take care, lassie. I canna shield ye from this pain."

She sighed and flopped down on the bed after he left. It was easy to talk so nobly, to display such acceptance and wisdom, but she was not sure she felt it, or believed everything she said. Leaving Gabel was going to tear her apart, and she dreaded it. She also knew that nothing she could do or say could prevent it. At times she thought she had made a terrible mistake in letting him make love to her, but then she would recall the beauty of it. How could she resist it, especially when she knew it was all she could ever have?

It was weak to let her emotions rule when her mind told her she gained nothing from it, that she would in fact lose a great deal. That made it easy to understand Gabel's resistance to any emotion. She did wish, however, that he would give her some sign, some word, that she would not be forgotten the moment she was back at Kengarvey. He would be haunting her memories for the rest of her life. It seemed only fair that she should haunt his at least for a week or so.

Gabel took a deep breath to calm himself, then spoke to the stableboy in a more controlled voice. The lad had only erred slightly, feeding a colt who had already been well fed was not a crime worth the anger he had nearly buffeted the boy with. There was an ache gnawing at his insides which kept him taut and ready to lash out at everyone and everything that crossed his path. He had had but a brief taste of the fierce passion he shared with Ainslee, and he wanted, needed, more.

Out of consideration for the ordeal she had been through and her injuries, he had stayed out of her bed, not wanting to press his attentions on her when she was still healing. It was gallant and the right thing to do, but he hated every minute of it. Gabel knew that some of his urgency came from the knowledge that she would not be at Bellefleur for very much longer. Each night they slept apart was one more night lost forever. He forced a smile, ruffled the boy's curls, and headed back into the keep. If he was fortunate, he could reach his bedchamber without meeting anyone. When, just inside the keep, he met Justice, he cursed. The grin on his young cousin's handsome face told him that Justice was aware of what ailed him, and intended to tease him about it.

"Aye," drawled Justice as Gabel slipped around him and started up the stairs. "I think it past time that you sought the bedchamber."

"I am going to my bedchamber to clean the stable dirt from my hands," Gabel replied, giving his cousin a repressive look that Justice gleefully ignored.

"Wrong bedchamber, if you intend to cure what ails you and what makes you most difficult to bear."

"Ware what you say, cousin. I am in no humor to hear e'en the tiniest insult."

"I would ne'er insult my most honorable cousin."

" 'Twas not me I referred to, and you know it well."

Justice leaned against the stair post and shook his head. "I am not sure why you are putting us all through this ordeal. 'Tis not as if the woman has refused you, or told you to leave her be."

"You cannot know what passes between me and Ainslee."

"Nay, not all of it. Howbeit, I am not some sweet page who has ne'er loved or lusted after a woman. I believe I also know Ainslee MacNairn. If she let you bed her once, 'tis not her who keeps you out of her bed now. You do. I but wonder why."

"Have you forgotten the ordeal she suffered through because of Lady Margaret's attempt to kill her?"

"Not at all. That was a week ago, cousin. The woman is healed now. In truth, except for her badly roughened and snow-burned skin, she was hale enough for what you crave by the very next day. You have claimed that she is not the same as the ladies we are accustomed to, that she is stronger, wilder, yet you treat her as the most delicate of flowers. I praise you for your gallantry, but I do wish you would put a swift end to it. Aye, as do most of your men, kinsmen, and maids."

"I am sorry if you have found me such poor company these last few days," Gabel snapped.

"Good. You should be. Half the maids and pages are hiding, and I should like to be able to assure them that you are not some changeling."

Gabel cursed and headed up the stairs, trying to ignore his cousin's laughter. He knew he had been short of temper in the last week, but he had not realized he had been as bad as Justice implied. Justice would not have been quite that insistently impudent without reason, however. Shaking his head over how poorly he was keeping his emotions chained, Gabel entered his bedchamber and began to clean away the dirt of a long day.

Once he was clean, Gabel hesitated only long enough to enjoy a goblet of wine, then he went straight to Ainslee's door. He pretended not to see the guard's relief when he waved the man away and entered Ainslee's room. When she sat up from where she had been gracelessly sprawled on the bed and gave him a tentative smile, he inwardly sighed, then shut and latched the door behind him.

"Ainslee, have you decided that that night in the stable was a mistake?" he asked.

"Nay." She blushed beneath the heated way he stared at her, and knew why he had come. "I never make mistakes," she murmured and gave him a sweet, welcoming smile.

" 'Tis to my advantage not to dispute that arrogance."

"Aye, very much so."

Ainslee's eyes widened when he strode to the bed, shedding his tunic and shirt as he walked. She shifted a little when he sat down on the edge of the bed and, still watching her with that tightly hungry expression, he yanked off his boots and hose. A soft cry of surprise escaped her when he tumbled her down on to the bed and sprawled on top of her. His intensity began to infect her, and she helped him as he pulled off the robe she wore. As he took her mouth in a hot, fierce kiss, she tugged off his braies. They both groaned as their flesh met.

In but a moment, Ainslee lost herself in the hurried frenzy of his lovemaking. His lips and hands were everywhere, causing her passion to spiral out of control. A sharp cry of welcome escaped her when he swiftly joined their bodies, but she gasped in dismay when he suddenly grew still. She slowly opened her eyes, confused and afraid, especially when she saw the expression on his flushed face. It was impossible to guess what his look meant.

"I have hurt you," he whispered in a hoarse, unsteady voice.

Relieved that he only feared that he had been too rough with her, Ainslee laughed and curled her body tightly around his, pulling him closer and echoing the tremor that ripped through his strong body. "Fool," she whispered with an affection she could not hide. "Has the great knight of Bellefleur suddenly forgotten how to wield his sword?" she teased, and laughed again when he grinned and began to move.

Passion soon stole away all her amusement. She clung to him as he rapidly satisfied the need she had ached with for days. When the culmination of her desire flooded her body, she cried out his name and told him of her love in Gaelic. The way he echoed her cries of ecstasy was music to her ears. She continued to keep her body wrapped around his as he collapsed in her arms and they lay entwined, struggling to regain their senses.

When he finally eased free of her hold, she stretched, feeling relaxed and content for the first time in days. She did not even flinch when he bathed her before returning to her embrace. This was neither the time nor the place for too much modesty.

"You have healed almost completely," he murmured against her skin, as he took her hand to his lips and kissed her palm.

"I wasna badly injured in my ordeal," she said, pleased to find that he did not feel her skin was now too rough.

"I was most relieved when the weather eased and I could rid Bellefleur of Lady Margaret and her skulking father. 'Twill be difficult to face them when next I go to court."

"Just be certain that ye do keep facing them, and ne'er give them a chance to creep up behind you," she warned.

"My back will always be well guarded." He held her close and nuzzled her thick, silken hair. "I stayed away too long."

"I began to think ye had changed your mind."

"About wanting you? Nay. I was being gallant."

"Ah, and now ye have ceased to be gallant?"

"Justice told me I was frightening the maids and the pages." He smiled when she laughed. "Gallantry was making me a most ill-tempered man, badly souring my temper. 'Twas lying abed alone at night and thinking too long on where I would rather be."

"Here?" she asked, lightly running her feet up and down his calves.

"Exactly here." He touched a kiss to the tip of each breast, murmuring his pleasure when they immediately hardened in invitation. "I will not leave here again."

Not until I am sent back to Kengarvey, Ainslee mused, then forced that thought from her mind. It made her sad, and this was no time to become mournful. She also feared such thoughts might prompt her to ask questions better left unasked. She knew exactly what Gabel wanted of her—a passionate, undemanding lover—and she was determined to be just that. While she was at Bellefleur she would revel in the passion they inspired in each other, ask no awkward questions, and make no demands. Since she would get none of the answers she wanted and he could never give her what she truly needed, there was no point in ruining the time they could share.

For a moment she grew angry, at Gabel and at herself. It seemed so weak to swallow all she wanted to say and to force herself to act in a certain way just to keep him happy. This was not her. To please him and to keep everything falsely blissful, she was playing the sweet supplicant, giving all and asking nothing. It annoyed her that Gabel did not seem to notice how odd it was for her to act that way. He may not have known her very long, but she was sure he had seen that she was not some sweet acquiescent girl.

As he nuzzled her breasts and she combed her fingers through his thick black hair, she fought down that anger. It was unfair. Gabel had not forced her down the path she was walking. She had chosen it herself, had made the decision all unaided and uncoerced to keep her mouth shut and pretend that she needed nothing more than what he offered. There was some comfort to be found in the knowledge that the passion they shared was a special thing. Despite her own innocence, she was sure that such a fierce desire did not come often, and she was also sure that Gabel fully shared it. She promised to remind herself of that the next time she grew angry with the situation.

"You have grown very quiet, Ainslee," he said as he touched a kiss to her cheek.

"Is there something ye wish to discuss?" she asked as she smoothed her hands down his back.

"Nay. It but seemed to be a most serious silence, and I wondered if anything troubled you."

"Nay. I just didna have anything to say. Weel, I was wondering about the Frasers," she said, considering it only a small lie, for she had thought about them earlier in the day. "I but hope that they dinna try to strike at my family because they are angry that they failed to kill me." She frowned when he smiled crookedly. "I didna think that was funny."

"Their attempts to murder you were certainly not funny."

He gently kissed her as he ran his hands up and down her body. "And an attack upon your family would not be very humorous either. 'Tis just the way you spoke of it. As I have said, you have a strange way with words, Ainslee MacNairn."

Gabel frowned as he flopped onto his back and gently pulled her into his arms. "I had not considered the possibility that the Frasers may try to vent their fury upon your family. 'Twould not be just you or your clansmen that it could harm. Such a thing would greatly hurt my attempts to gain some sort of truce and I have always believed that a treaty is preferable to a killing."

"Weel, killing the troublemaker would certainly solve the problems he stirs up."

"True, but a live ally is better than a dead enemy. The more allies one has, the less one needs to fear his enemies."

"Ah, there is some truth in that, I suppose."

Ainslee did not want her clan attacked, for many would lose their lives and not everyone at Kengarvey was guilty of scorning their king. She did not believe her father would ever be Gabel's ally, however. Duggan MacNairn did not have allies; he had people he loathed and people he robbed from. She did not think she ought to say so. If she spoke too much about how little Gabel could trust her family, he might well decide that there was no gain in even trying to treat with her father. She did not want to see any of her people killed and know that, if she had just kept silent, they might have lived, at least for a little while longer.

"Forgive me, Ainslee," Gabel said quietly, breaking into her thoughts.

"For what?" she asked as she straddled his body.

"For speaking of all the ill which could befall your clan. I often forget that you are a MacNairn."

"There are times when I should like to forget that too, but there is no discarding the blood in one's veins just because you do not like the mon who put it there."

Gabel forgot what he wanted to reply to that as Ainslee

brushed soft, warm kisses over his throat. She was perched upon his body in a way that had him aroused anew. Every movement of her lithe body against his increased his desire. He closed his eyes as she stroked him with her small hands and began to cover his chest with kisses. As coherently as he could, he urged her on in her boldness with flattery and praise, letting her know how good she was making him feel.

When her kisses reached his stomach, slipping ever lower, he curled his fingers in her soft hair, wanting to urge her on, yet afraid of shocking her so badly that she ceased her attentions completely. While he was still trying to decide, she brushed a kiss over his manhood and he groaned, jerking slightly from the pleasure that tore through him. She tensed and began to pull away, but he held her in place. He struggled to enjoy her unskilled but enflaming caresses for as long as he could, but soon realized that his passion was still too hot and new for such control. With a soft growl, he pulled her up his body. His hands on her slim hips, he directed her in the joining of their bodies.

To his delight, Ainslee needed little direction. Her movements quickly became smooth, her skill increasing with every thrust. Gabel watched her and, until passion forced his eyes closed, decided he had never seen anything so enticing.

Ainslee glanced up at Gabel as she lay curled up in his arms, lifting her head from his chest only enough to see him clearly. She wished to know that she had not been too bold. It seemed reasonable to her that, if he could kiss and caress her wherever he pleased, then she should be able to do the same to him. It was not until their pleasure left them sated, collapsed in each other's arms and trying to catch their breath, that she began to think that she may have overstepped. Men did not always want women to act upon their own.

"Now ye are the one who is, mayhaps, a wee bit too quiet," she murmured, smiling a little timidly when he looked at her.

"A man needs time to regain his breath after such strenuous lovemaking," he said, then smiled and kissed her forehead.

"Strenuous, was it?" She relaxed a little, for he did not sound as if she had shocked or offended him, nor was he looking at her as if she had behaved like some whore.

"Mightily so. I feel as if I have had all the strength drained from my body."

"Aha, so then ye are at my mercy."

"After what we just shared, I can think of few places I would rather be."

"Then ye dinna think I was too bold?" she asked, then inwardly cursed her inability to tame her tongue.

"Is that why you watch me so warily? Have you been waiting for me to berate you, or climb from this bed so shocked by your behavior that I must leave?"

"Ye need not make a jest of my concerns," she muttered, frowning when he grinned, but her stern expression did not dim his smile at all.

"I would never make jest of you, sweet Ainslee." He brushed the stray wisps of hair from her face. "Ah, but you are a confusing woman. You blush so prettily, yet make love so freely. You speak sharply and have the air of a prickly thistle, but when one peers into your heart, they find only thistledown." He laughed at her confused expression and hugged her. "Nay, I did not find you too bold. I find you a delight, a woman who can drive a man to madness, and one who heats my blood with but a smile. When I have recovered sufficiently from your newfound skills, I will show you just how deeply I appreciate that wildness in you which makes you do as you want."

Ainslee snuggled against him, murmuring her pleasure as he stroked her. She was not sure what his pretty words meant or how seriously she should take them, but they pleased her. There was a true delight behind his words and in his eyes. She sensed that she surprised him because no other woman had treated him so, and that also pleased her. If she was to linger in his mind, she had to be different from the others he had known. The way he was acting told her that she had taken the first step to making herself, if not the best lover he had ever had, at least one of the more memorable. It was small consolation when she wanted and needed his love, but she knew that one day she would be able to find great satisfaction in the knowledge. She might be able to accept that he would never love her and that, once she returned to Kengarvey, she would never see him again, but she did not think she would ever be able to accept being forgotten. All she prayed for now was the gift of time, time enough to truly establish herself within his mind.

Twelve

"There has been another reply from your father," Gabel announced as he strode into Ainslee's bedchamber.

Ainslee tensed, clutching her hair comb tightly. From where she sat on a sheepskin before the fire, she kept her gaze fixed upon Gabel's boots as he walked over to her. All the pleasure she had gained from her hot bath abruptly faded. Inwardly taking a deep breath to calm herself, she began to slowly pull the comb through her hair.

It had been a fortnight since the storm, and she had allowed herself to be lulled into a false sense of calm and happiness, spending her days within the safe, elegant Bellefleur and her nights curled up contentedly in Gabel's strong arms. The Frasers had gone, her dog roamed freely throughout the keep, Ronald was now completely healed, and she was blissfully wrapped in passion every time she and Gabel had some time alone. That had made it easy to push aside all of her doubts and concerns. Now her father had rudely intruded into her dream world. All she could do was hope that her father was going to continue to be stubborn, lengthening the negotiations, but something about Gabel's expression made her feel certain that that was not going to happen.

"Does my father want me back now?" she asked, feeling that she had a firm enough hand on her errant emotions to look at him again.

"Well, he still does not agree to all I ask, not fully," replied Gabel as he sat down next to her.

"So? What does he offer?"

"Too little."

"Gabel, what has my father said?"

"He will ransom you and says you may bring Ronald along as well, if you must, but that he will not pay anything for the man."

"Ungrateful bastard," Ainslee muttered, angered as always by her father's contempt for Ronald, a man who had always been a faithful, hardworking servant. "Many times I have wondered if my father scorns Ronald because he can never be the mon Ronald is."

" 'Tis possible. Some men find those who have the goodness they lack to be very irritating." Gabel smiled faintly when Ainslee laughed.

"When am I to be sent back to Kengarvey?" she asked in a soft voice, her humor fading swiftly as she tensed for his reply.

"We will leave here in three days' time and meet with your clan at the river."

Gabel inwardly cursed when she used her hair to hide her face and thus her expression. He wanted to know how she felt about leaving Bellefleur, about leaving him. It was unfair and he knew it, but that did not dim his need to know. He could not keep her. Although they shared a passion he had never tasted before and was not sure be would ever find again, he could not cast aside all his carefully laid plans and disregard all he believed was right for Bellefleur and his people just to hold onto it. Knowing that, it was wrong, even cruel, to try and make her expose her feelings for him, yet he realized that he ached to know what was in her heart and mind now that she was faced with the end of their time together.

"We have a few days left to spend together, Ainslee," he said, as he edged closer to her, took the comb from her hand, and began to comb her slightly damp hair.

"I ken it." She sighed and glanced at him. "I confess, I am surprised that my father has agreed so swiftly."

"I thought he had proved to be most stubborn."

"Nay, not truly. If he had wanted to, he could have played this game for months."

"That could have put your life in danger, at least as far as he could know."

"Nay, my father kens that I am safe here at Bellefleur. He learned all about you, Gabel, ere ye had lit your first hearth fire in your fine new keep. How do you think my father has survived for so long when so many ache to kill him?"

"Luck and skill," he replied as he set the comb aside and tugged her into his arms.

"Aye, there was some of that, to be sure." She leaned against him and stared into the fire. "He also kens that a mon's best defense is to learn what he can about his enemies, and he had no doubt that ye would soon join that vast number. If my father had put all of his wit and skill to a good cause, he could have become the greatest of men. Howbeit, both gifts have served only to make him the most elusive and deadliest of foes. As soon as I was of an age to ken what he was, I also kenned what he could have been. I think that is why I grow so angry at him at times."

He slid the robe she wore off of her shoulder and touched a kiss to her warm skin. "Mayhaps he saw that knowledge in your eyes, and 'tis why he so dislikes Ronald. Your father knew who you compared him to."

Ainslee frowned as she considered that possibility, then shrugged. "I find it most difficult to believe that my father was ever concerned about what I thought. Howbeit, pride may prompt it, for there was a strange incident once when I was but eleven that I have ne'er found a reason for. Ronald had taken ill and had sent me from his side for fear that I would catch whate'er it was that ailed him. That evening I dined in the great hall with my father and brothers for the first and last time in my memory. I ken that I watched my father as I ate, but I dinna believe I cast him any particular look which could have revealed the thoughts whirling about in my head, not all of which were kindly. Suddenly, he lunged at me and began to beat me, bellowing about teaching me some respect."

"Did he hurt you badly?"

"It felt so at the time. My brother Colin rescued me at some risk to himself when he began to fear that my father would kill me. I returned to Ronald and told him that, whate'er ailed him, it could not be as frightening nor as dangerous as being near my father."

Gabel said nothing, just held her and softly kissed her neck. He fought the surge of guilt sweeping over him as he thought of how he was about to return her to that life. But what choice did he have? Even if he decided that he did want to take her as his wife or she agreed to become his leman—something he could never ask her to do—he still had to go through with the ransoming. He was doing the king's work now, and could not cease simply because Ainslee might suffer a beating when she returned to her family. Few men would understand why that should even trouble him, for, while they might not agree with the beating of women and children, Ainslee's father had the right to do with her as he pleased. Gabel silently cursed again, and wondered for the hundredth time how and when he had allowed one tiny red-haired woman to so complicate his life and disorder his thoughts.

"So, in three days' time we will meet my most notorious sire at the river," she murmured.

"Aye," Gabel agreed, forcing a smile when she turned in his arms to face him directly. "I felt it would be wise to have the river between us."

She smoothed her hands over his chest and then began to unlace his tunic. " 'Twould be for the best to put the whole of Scotland between you and my father, but I ken that ye must draw closer than that." She smiled faintly when he laughed, but then grew serious, taking his face between her hands. "Beware my father, Gabel."

"Is it not strange for the daughter of the man to warn the one who seeks to punish him?"

"Aye, and it may e'en be a wee bit traitorous. Howbeit, I see no real wrong in simply warning an honorable mon that he is about to face one who, sadly, doesna have any honor left. Ye deal in the truth. My father could spout lies to a priest on the altar. If ye make a bond, ye will hold to it. My father will do so as weel, but only if he can gain from it. If he sees no gain, he willna keep any treaty or honor any bond made. And, if my father believes he canna defeat a mon in a fair fight, he will slip about in the dark and cut the mon's throat or stab him in the back. Ye have been kind and fair, Gabel de Amalville, to me and to mine. 'Tis only fair to tell you the truth about the mon ye will soon be facing."

"I thank you for that. Howbeit, your father must have the wit to see that, if he does not honor this bond, he will bring on the complete destruction of your clan."

"I pray he does. Even my brothers, who arena the best of men, dinna deserve that." She eased his shirt off of his shoulders. "I dinna wish to talk of it or to worry about what is to come. I certainly dinna wish to think of my father."

Gabel closed his eyes and sighed with pleasure as she trailed soft kisses over his chest. She had slowly grown bolder in the week they had been lovers and he reveled in it. He did not want to think of her father either, for it reminded him that, in three very short days, he would lose her. What he wanted to do was spend every moment of those three days making love to her, but he knew he could not do that either. As he threaded his fingers through her hair, releasing it from the loosely tied leather thong she had caught it up in, he felt a surge of angry frustration. He had never considered how much he might have to give up to be lord of Bellefleur.

All thought of what he was forced to do and to forego because of his high birth, faded when Ainslee unlaced his hose. She tugged them off of him, heating his legs with kisses as she did so. He tensed as she crouched between his legs, smiling seductively at him from behind her tousled hair. His breathing grew heavy when she undid his braies and tossed them aside. A soft groan escaped him as she slid her hands up his thighs while she bent towards him and touched a feather-light kiss to his erection. He gently caged her between his legs as she stroked him with her tongue, kissing his length as she smoothed her hands over his hips and thighs. Watching her pleasure him so put him into a sweat, but he grit his teeth and fought to keep his passion under some restraint. He wanted to enjoy her loving for as long as he could. When she answered the request he made with an unmistakable shift of his hips and slowly encased him in the heat of her mouth, he cried out from the strength of the pleasure flooding his body. He could endure it for only a few moments before he caught her up in his arms and pressed her down onto the sheepskin.

Crouching over her, he stared down at her as he fought to rein in his need so that he could repay her for such delight, giving her some before they were forced to answer the urges of their bodies. "Do you think to drive me mad ere you leave Bellefleur?"

Ainslee smiled and trailed her fingers over the front of his muscular thighs, enjoying the way he trembled from the power of the desire she had stirred within him. "I but sought to please you," she murmured.

"Oh, you did that tenfold, and 'tis clear from the cocky look on your lovely face that you know it."

"Ye appear hesitant to act upon it."

"Oh, nay, not hesitant. I but catch my breath so that I may show you that two can play at that game."

Ainslee did not have the time to worry about his passionate threat or ask him what he intended to do. Gabel began his assault upon her senses at once. Although she blushed when he removed her robe, she did not attempt to hide herself from his eyes, despite the bright light from the fire. She found the way he stared at her so hungrily, his appreciation of her form easy to read in his eyes, exciting and the perfect cure to any touch of modesty.

He lowered his body onto hers and kissed her. Ainslee returned his deep kiss with a fierceness to match his, and a touch of desperation. She had very little time left to soak her mind and senses in the feel of him. With a murmur of pleasure, she tilted her head back, allowing him free access to her vulnerable throat, as he began to ease his kisses down her body.

A shudder tore through her when he stopped at her breasts, lathing the tips and suckling as if he had all the time in the world, as if passion was not causing him to tremble and breathe heavily against her skin. Her own passion had been so heightened by making love to him that she was not sure she could endure such a leisurely seduction, but she fought to keep enough of her senses so that she could enjoy his every touch and kiss. She did not know where he found the strength, but she was determined to match it.

He crept his way down her midriff, kissing her, gently nipping her skin and soothing the light sting with strokes of his tongue. When he reached her thighs, she was unable to touch him and she murmured her regret. He chuckled against her inner thigh and proceeded to cover the length of her legs with his caresses. Despite her intention to push aside all modesty, she tensed and gasped in shock when he touched a kiss to the soft curls between her thighs, but this time he ignored her. With one slow stroke of his tongue, he took away all urge to protest the intimacy of his kiss.

Ainslee fell completely beneath the power of the feelings he stirred in her, opening herself to him and moaning her pleasure. The only clear thought she had came when she knew she was too near her crest to wait any longer. She cried out her need and groaned her relief when he forcefully joined their bodies. Wrapped tightly around his strong body, she clung to him as he took them both to the heights they had resisted for so long.

It was not until they lay sated in each other's arms that Ainslee gave any thought to what they had just done. She fought the embarrassment that seeped over her, but was only partially successful. It was not even dark yet, she thought with an inner groan.

"Ainslee," Gabel whispered against her ear as he idly stroked her side. "Cease berating yourself."

"And what makes ye think I was berating myself?" she asked, unable to look at him, and she cursed softly when he laughed.

"For one so bold when she is loving me, you have become quite the blushing maid now that I have served you in kind."

She grimaced and peeked at him through the tangle of her hair. "Weel, there must be something we shouldna be doing, and I but thought that was probably it." She was able to smile a little when he laughed, rolled onto his side, and pulled her into his arms.

"We should not be doing this at all, but I am willing to bear up under the weight of that guilt."

"So gallant of you, sir knight." She trailed her fingers up and down his arm as she stared at the fire. "There shall undoubtedly be years of penance to pay when I finally confess this."

"And will you be thinking that it was worth it?" he asked softly, grimacing at his weakness which prompted him to try and pull some statement of her feelings out of her, even if it meant he must trick her into it.

"Oh, aye. I havena enjoyed the wealth of experience ye have," she drawled, glancing at him briefly, "but I think I will find that such heat canna be matched."

"Nay, *it canna.*" He laughed when she lightly slapped his arm, but then grew serious as he studied her delicate profile. "I swear I do not make it my habit to seduce young virgins into my bed. I am well aware of how important chastity is to wellborn women. Howbeit, I could not turn away from you. I hope that you will be able to forgive me for that weakness."

Ainslee turned and gently touched a kiss to his mouth. "And I hope that ye will cease trying to take the full burden of this upon your shoulders, wide and strong though they are. Ye must ken by now that I am no meek, simpering lass. I have a voice. I could have cried nay, and ye are too honorable to ignore that. I also ken how to fight a mon, something many a young womon is ne'er taught. Aye, I could never beat ye in a fight, but ye ken that I could certainly have freed myself of your lustful grip, and left ye sorely regretting that ye had ever taken me into your arms."

She frowned as she studied him. "Do ye fear that I shall turn on you when I return to Kengarvey, that I shall then cry rape?"

"Nay. I did wonder about it, but only for a moment, as I felt in the very marrow of my bones that you would never do such a thing. 'Tis just that I am the man, I am older than you, and I know more about such things than you do, so I felt it only fair that I accept the responsibility."

"I may not have ever done the deed, but do ye really think a mon like Ronald would allow me to grow to womanhood without kenning all about it, about what men want of a lass, and the tricks they might play to get it?"

"Nay." He laughed and shook his head as she settled back into his arms. "Any man would be delighted to have a lover such as you."

But not a wife, she thought and scolded herself for allowing that bitterness to taint their time together. "I am pleased that, as one of those cowardly MacNairns, I am able to do something worthwhile."

"I suppose Ronald can be blamed for the sharpness of your tongue as well," Gabel murmured.

"Nay, he claims I was born with it."

"And what has he had to say about my becoming your lover?"

"What can he say?"

"A great deal as he is your father in heart and soul, if not in blood. I have looked at him whene'er we meet, but I see no anger, and he has said nothing. Have you even told him?"

"Aye, of course, I have. As Ronald himself said, he is neither deaf nor blind. He would have discovered the truth for himself, and I thought it best if he heard it from me. He has raised me to ken my own mind, and so doesna try to make me do as he pleases or feels is right. All Ronald cares about is if I am happy and if I am safe."

"And are you happy, Ainslee?"

"I wouldna be sprawled here if I wasna." She sighed, deciding that a little truth would not hurt, and said, "I shall have some verra warm and pleasant memories to pull forth when I am back at Kengarvey, and such things can be verra valuable. Kengarvey may be my home, but most times 'tis neither warm nor pleasant."

"I am sorry for that."

"Why? 'Tis none of your doing."

"You have such a clarity of mind, dearling. Nay, 'tis none of my doing, but I can still feel sorry that you must endure it."

"Pity?" She tensed slightly, finding the thought that he might pity her very distasteful. "That neither helps me nor changes what Kengarvey is."

"Not pity, so you may pull in your thorns, my red-haired Scottish thistle. I do not believe anyone could long pity a woman with your strength. Howbeit, I see no harm in a touch of sympathy. You deserve better than you have. Mayhaps this treaty will bring Kengarvey some peace."

"Aye, mayhaps."

"Ainslee, is there anywhere else you may go? Any place you may live beside Kengarvey, if only for the next few months?"

"Do ye think the next few months will be enough to change my life?"

"Nay, but it could greatly change life at Kengarvey."

She sat up, oblivious to her nakedness, her long hair her only covering. "Ye want me away from Kengarvey because ye think there may be a reckoning."

Gabel grimaced and ran his hand through his hair. He wished he could lie to her, but he could not, and she was too clever. She would easily see the lie. The truth was harsh and he regretted it, but he knew she would greet it more favorably than she would any pretty lie.

"Aye, there may well be a reckoning. I have no wish to take up the sword against your kinsmen, loving. 'Tis the very last thing I wish to do, for I know it will hurt you as well."

"Ye have no choice."

"None. If your father does not abide by the treaty we will make, then the king will demand a battle. There will be nothing

I can do to stop it, and I cannot really refuse to join in it. In truth, because he gave me the responsibility of ending your father's bloody tyranny o'er this land, I will be the first man he turns to. I do not wish to think that you are locked inside the walls I must batter down."

"I ken that ye would ne'er harm me, Gabel."

"I would not, but I will not be able to watch every arrow or sword. You are painfully aware of how the innocents can suffer in the heat of battle." He reached out to stroke her hair when she trembled.

"The men of Bellefleur would ne'er act like the Frasers," she protested in a meek voice.

"Nay, they would not, for I would ne'er keep such men in my service. But, Ainslee, the men of Bellefleur may not be the only ones at the walls, clamoring for blood and vengeance. If your father breaks his bond, the king will be so furious he may want Kengarvey razed to the ground. There may well be others sent with me to do the deed. I can swear on my honor that I will not hurt any who do not try to fight me, that I will do my utmost to ensure that the women and children, the innocents of Kengarvey, do not suffer for their lord's foolishness, but I cannot speak for any of the others who may join the battle."

"Ones like the Frasers and the MacFibhs."

"Aye, old and bloodthirsty enemies. Can you promise me that you will leave Kengarvey and go somewhere else for a time? You and Ronald?"

She wanted to, if only because the urgency with which he made the request revealed that his feelings did indeed go deeper than lust alone. What he said distressed her deeply, yet a part of her was elated at this sign of emotion. He asked for such a simple thing, the assurance that when he attacked Kengarvey, he would not risk killing her or Ronald. He did not want their blood on his hands, even if he was forced to spill the blood of the rest of her family.

There was no way she could promise him that, however. There were kinsmen who would take her in. She might even be able to impose upon her sisters. It was her father who could force her to break any promise she might make. There was no way to get out of Kengarvey without him knowing and, after she had just cost him so dearly, she doubted her father would ever let her out again. She would be fortunate not to find herself caged in the dungeons for the rest of her life.

"I wish I could make that promise, but I canna," she said quietly, her voice shaking, for she was on the verge of tears over her inability to give him the ease of mind he needed.

"Why? Are you so enamored of your home that you would die for it? Or is this some strange, useless gesture of loyalty to your father? If so, then you could be throwing your life away for nothing, as he will neither live long enough or have heart enough to appreciate it."

"I ken it," she snapped, resenting his speaking of things she would rather forget. "I dinna mean to stand and die for Kengarvey or my father. Even if there still existed some bond between us other than a few drops of like blood, I have ne'er believed in dying for naught save honor. If I am to die, I am sorry, but I wish it to be for far more than to have people say of me that I died with honor. I canna give ye the promise ye ask, for I canna be sure that I can keep it."

"There is no place you can flee to?"

"Nay, there is a place or two, but I canna be sure I would be allowed to go there. I used to be allowed to come and go from Kengarvey as I pleased, as long as it was kenned where I was going. Howbeit, I feel certain that my being caught and taken for ransom has stolen away that freedom. I dinna believe my father will ever allow me out of the gates again, and escape from Kengarvey is nearly impossible."

Gabel cursed, sat up, and ran his hands through his hair. "Are you certain that escape would be so difficult?"

"Verra certain. Do ye think no one has tried? Prisoners, despondent women, frightened servants, and even cowardly men-at-arms have all tried, and none survived the attempt except for one or two who were worth more alive than dead."

"Yet your father always seems to be able to escape when the battle turns against him." Gabel's eyes widened at the bitterness of the smile she gave him.

"Of course he does. There is certainly a way out, a bolthole, but he and his sons are the only ones who ken where it is. He didna e'en tell my mother so that she could save herself or me. I could try to get the information from my brothers, but I hold out little hope of doing so, as they are terrified of my father. In truth, I think they ken that they would die if they told even me."

"God curse the man's eyes," Gabel muttered.

"I can only promise ye one thing," she said as she reached out to stroke his cheek. "I will promise ye that I will try. 'Tis all I can do. I will tell Ronald what ye have asked of me, and what I have sworn to, and he too will try." She shrugged and gave him a sad smile. "I am sorry."

"You have naught to be sorry for. You are caught up in the quarrels of men and kings through no fault or crime of your own. I fear that, in our eagerness for battle and honor, we often give no thought to any but ourselves and our own grievances."

" 'Tis the way of the world. I can also promise ye one more thing."

"And what is that? That your father will abide by the treaty and I need not worry o'er this?"

"Nay, I fear that is in God's hands, and I sometimes think He must be growing eager to send my father to the devil. Nay, I will promise ye that, if my father forces a battle and anything happens to me or the ones I care about, I willna blame you, Gabel de Amalville."

" 'Tis small comfort."

" 'Tis all I can offer."

"Nay, not all," he said in a roughened voice as he pulled her down into his arms. "You can offer a way for both of us to forget what awaits us. 'Twill be but a momentary blindness to the truth, but 'twill be a most sweet one," he added as he kissed her.

Thirteen

Ainslee shivered as she stood in the bailey of Bellefleur waiting for Gabel to bring out the horses. It was cold, but she knew that was not what made her shiver. A deep chill had set into her heart from the moment she had opened her eyes and realized that she had to leave. For three days she and Gabel had spent every moment they could making love and trying not to think about her leaving. Time could not be halted to satisfy them, however, and the day they had fought so hard to forget had finally dawned. She felt as if her whole body was one tight knot as she struggled against the painful urge to weep and beg him to keep her. Pride did not stop her from doing so, as she was willing to sacrifice that if she could stay with him, but she knew it would change nothing.

"Ainslee," called a sweet voice, and there was a light tug upon her cloak.

Taking a deep breath, Ainslee turned and smiled at Elaine. " 'Tis quite early in the day for you to be about."

"I wished to say farewell to you," Elaine said as she held out a small bundle.

"And what is this?" Ainslee asked as she accepted it.

"Two of the gowns you so liked."

"Nay, I canna take such a rich gift." Ainslee tried to give the gift back, but Elaine just pushed it back into her hands.

"You can and you will. We have more gowns than we need, and you looked far prettier in these than we ever did. My mother and I also wished you to have something to remember us by, for, although I wish it were not the way of it, I fear we may ne'er see each other again."

"Nay, I fear we may not," Ainslee whispered, finding it difficult to speak over the lump in her throat. "I thank ye most kindly and I should like to thank your mother, but I dinna see her about."

"You will not see her either. My mother cannot abide saying farewell. She says she has said far too many in her life."

"I understand. E'en when ye are certain that the ones leaving will return, 'tis still hard."

"Aye. I fear my mother's reluctance arises from the fact that too many of the ones she has watched ride away ne'er rode back." Elaine took a deep unsteady breath, then gave Ainslee a weak smile. "You have been the best prisoner we have ever had."

"And no one could ask for more gracious captors," Ainslee replied, fighting to return Elaine's smile.

"There is one thing I would ask of you."

When Elaine hesitated and lightly chewed on her bottom lip, Ainslee urged, "Ask me what ye will."

"I mean no insult to you," Elaine assured her, reaching out to pat Ainslee's hands. " 'Tis just that I have heard such troubling things about your father—"

"And ye fear that matters may not go along as planned." She touched Elaine's blush-reddened cheek. "I take no insult. I ken what is said about my father, and accept that most of it is true."

"Will you watch out for Gabel and the others?" She glanced toward the men gathering in the bailey and preparing to ride out. "There are so many of my family amongst the men. If there is a betrayal or some treachery—"

"Ye could lose most of your kinsmen. I will watch out for them, Elaine. I ken the tricks my father can play, and I have no intention of allowing him to succeed in any murderous game this time. Some might call me a traitor to my own blood, but, since my father has agreed to a treaty, I see no crime in at least one of the MacNairns trying to hold to the bond."

"Thank you. I feel more at ease knowing that, and I am certain that my mother will as well. Good journey, Ainslee MacNairn," she whispered, and kissed Ainslee on the cheek before hurrying away.

Ainslee touched her cheek and watched the younger girl disappear into the keep. She would miss the kindness shown her at Bellefleur, the air of contentment of its people, and the feeling of safety which surrounded her. Compared to Bellefleur, Kengarvey was a dark, foreboding, and dangerous place. It was not just because she wanted to stay with Gabel that she dreaded going home.

She straightened her shoulders and watched Gabel approach with the horses. In an effort to calm herself and ease the sorrow tearing her apart, she told herself that she would be accomplishing something her clan had needed for many years— peace. Although she had little faith in her father holding to the treaty for very long, she did not want Kengarvey's chance of peace to be lost because she was too selfish to sacrifice anything in gaining it. It proved to be a small comfort, giving her just enough strength to face Gabel with calm as he held out his hand. With a faint smile, she took it and swung up into the saddle behind him.

"Ye mean to ride to the river on Malcolm?" she asked as she stroked her horse's strong flank.

"Aye," replied Gabel as he led his men out of Bellefleur. "I would say I am sorry for taking your horse, but it seems as if I am saying I am sorry each and every hour. I will treat him well."

"I ken it. He will have a better life here. And I dinna believe I will have much need for a horse, so he will be given to my father or one of his men, and they will be cruel to him. Do ye mean to boldly show my father that ye are keeping the one thing he inquired about?"

"I do. We ne'er discussed the horse's price, and I believe

that, if he asks today, I will set it so high he would ne'er agree to it."

"He will be verra angry. Aye, enraged." She frowned as she leaned against his back, resting her cheek against the soft thickness of his cloak. "I canna tell ye what my father will do if he is enraged."

" 'Tis difficult to know what your father will do at any time." He patted one of the small hands clutching at his waist. "Do not concern yourself. My men and I are prepared for most anything."

Ainslee prayed that that was not an idle boast, but she said no more. She had warned Gabel about her father, and she could not force him to heed her warning. All she could do was pray that, whatever treachery her father may have planned, it did not include some immediate threat to Gabel's life or to any of his men. She tightened her grip on Gabel and closed her eyes, weary from their long night of lovemaking, and too despondent to continue any conversation.

Gabel sighed as he felt her grow heavy against him. He was tired as well, but he needed to be alert, and his emotions were in such a turmoil, he doubted he could sleep anyway. The hardest thing he had ever done in his life had been to wake Ainslee this morning, knowing it was the last time she would lie in his arms. Duty forced him, but, like a coward, he had left her alone as quickly as possible, afraid of what he might do or say if he stayed another moment.

What truly angered and dismayed him, was that he could not be sure it would be all over when he reached the river and met with Duggan MacNairn. That man could easily decide he did not like the terms he had agreed to or, worse, try some trick that would even put his own daughter in danger. If he could be sure that giving up Ainslee would solve the problems Duggan MacNairn caused, thus make the king happy, it might be an easier thing to do. At the moment, he could not know whether his sacrifice would gain him anything.

"Ye have left the wee lass exhausted," said Ronald as he rode up alongside Gabel.

Gabel eyed the older man warily, not sure he completely believed in the man's good humor or Ainslee's assurances that Ronald would not fault him in any way for her place in his bed. "She is safe enough. If we need to ride hard or fast, I will place her before me."

"Aye, I ken that ye will look after her."

"I find your manner most confusing," Gabel said, and he shook his head. "Are all Scots thus, or is it just you and Ainslee?"

" 'Tis Ainslee if ye are confused because I am nay crying out for your blood. Aye, ye could have been stronger and left the lass be, but I canna see that any harm has come of it. She was happy. 'Tis all that matters to me."

"And she is not happy at Kengarvey?"

"Nay, but she has ne'er bemoaned her fate. She will survive. 'Tis why I raised her to be strong."

"Oh, she is strong, strong and willful and far too clever for a woman. It must cause her trouble with a father like Duggan MacNairn."

"Aye, it would, if I ever let the bastard get near her, but I do all I can to keep the two apart. He nearly killed her once, and I vowed that he would ne'er set hands on her again, not as long as I lived."

"She told me about that. It appears that at least one of her brothers may have some good in him."

Ronald nodded. "Young Colin. He doesna have much to do with the lass, but he can be trusted to protect her. The other three arena as black of heart as their father, but they are terrified of him, and would ne'er act against him no matter how wrong they thought he was. Colin spent a few years at a monastery, got some learning from the monks, and that is what gives him the strength to step forward, although he does it rarely."

"He must have some wit, for he does it and survives and,

from what I have been told, very few question what MacNairn does and live to tell of it."

"There is a black truth. Howbeit, Colin is a favored son and has a keen eye to his father's moods. He kens how to stay alive." Ronald reached out and adjusted Ainslee's cloak so that it more fully covered her legs. "Ye need not fear for her. I have kept her well these many years and, God willing, I will continue to do so."

"Aye, but she has ne'er cost the mon before."

Gabel was not encouraged by the way Ronald just shrugged and rode away to rejoin Justice and Michael. He had wanted some assurance that Ainslee would not pay too dearly for what he had forced her father to do, but, just as Ainslee had refused to offer him false promises, Ronald simply refused to lie just to soothe him. Gabel prayed that, before he reached the river, some brilliant solution to the problem of gaining a treaty *and* keeping Ainslee safe would occur to him.

Ainslee groaned softly as she was lifted from the saddle. She felt stiff and not as well rested as she thought she ought to be. As Gabel set her on her feet and turned to tend to his horse, she looked around and struggled to shake free of sleep's fog. Her rest had been troubled by bad dreams. She could remember hearing Gabel's deep voice as he spoke to her in soothing tones, so, she suspected that she had cried out at least once.

Seeing Ronald sit down beneath a gnarled, leafless tree, she walked over to sit down next to him. Ronald had protected her for almost her whole life, and she hoped being near him would ease the lingering fear that left a sour taste in her mouth. It was going to be hard enough to return to her father, without going to him shaking in terror of some unknown dangers her frightened mind had conjured up.

"Are ye sickening for something?" Ronald asked as he handed her a wineskin and she took a drink. "Beside that hulking great Norman, that is."

"Nay, I dinna believe I am falling ill," she replied as she leaned against the knotted trunk of the tree and ignored his last remark. "I am just weary."

"Weary? Ye have slept away the whole of the morning."

"I ken it, and I find it most irritating that I am not weel rested. Howbeit, it was a troubled sleep filled with dark dreams and fear of what is to come."

"Mayhaps the dreams about your mother return because ye are drawing near to Kengarvey," he said gently as he put his arm about her shoulders.

"I didna dream about my mother. I dreamt about us, all of us here now. I dreamt of the river," she said in a voice softened by the remembered horror of the scenes in her mind.

"From the pale look upon your face, I guess we werena having a verra good time."

"Oh, nay, we werena. Mayhaps 'tis just my mistrust of my father which causes me to see treachery and death."

"Two things your father has reveled in his whole black life. What did ye see, lassie?"

"We were all there, the men of Bellefleur on one side and my kinsmen on the other. The river that flowed between us was neither gray nor blue, but red. Red with blood."

"And where were you?"

"Standing in the very heart of it, watching it swirl about my knees and trying to stop its flow. 'Twas as if it flowed from me, yet I had no wounds."

"A verra dark dream indeed," Ronald said, and shivered a little. "I pray ye havena become sighted, and that it is some omen."

"Ye canna pray for that any more than I do."

He kissed her cheek as he watched Gabel stride toward them. "Here comes your braw lover, lassie. Go with him. He may weel take that lingering darkness from your mind."

Ainslee allowed Gabel to draw her away from Ronald, but she doubted he could lift her spirits at all. Being with him only reminded her of how few hours they had left together.

She smiled weakly at Justice when he handed them some bread, cheese, and wine, and then she followed Gabel as he led them to a secluded spot away from camp and the curious eyes of his men. He sat down on a mossy spot of ground beneath a large tree and tugged her down beside him.

"You look very tired and mournful for someone who has spent the last few hours snoring quietly against my back," he said as he handed her her share of their light repast.

"I dinna snore," she protested amiably as she began to eat. "Not even quietly."

"Nay, of course not. It must have been the wind."

"Aye, it must have been."

"And was it the wind which cried out in fear several times?" he asked softly, watching her carefully out of the corner of his eye.

Ainslee sighed and took a small drink of the hearty wine in his wineskin. "Nay, I fear that was me and, nay, ere ye ask, I wasna dreaming of my mother again."

"Well, whatever was threading through your mind, it was not pleasant."

She turned to look at him, wondering if he would take her dream as a warning. It had clearly unsettled Ronald almost as much as it had unsettled her. Although she had not seen any sign that Gabel was a man who would believe in dreams or omens, it could do little harm to tell him, she decided and related what she had dreamt about. For a long moment after she had finished, he just stared at her, until she squirmed a little beneath his steady gaze.

"Ye need not swallow your laughter," she finally said. "I ken that some people put verra little value in dreams."

Gabel kissed her cheek and then tugged her up against his side. "I have ne'er changed my plans because of a dream, but I do not discount their value completely. Yours is not a comforting one, but I am not sure how to judge its meaning."

"I judge it to mean that there is danger waiting for us at that river," she said.

"Well, we knew that ere we set out this morning. We have known that for days. Mayhaps that is what preys upon your mind, and puts such darkness in your dreams."

"Aye, mayhaps," she replied, mildly irritated by his response, for it closely matched Ronald's and she wondered if men did not like to think a dream could tell them anything of real importance.

" 'Tis evident that you do not think so. What do you think one ought to do? I mean, do you truly believe you have seen the future, that God or something tries to warn you?"

"I dinna ken. It could even be bad beef."

"We did not have beef last night."

She softly cursed and frowned at him. "I dinna ken what it means. 'Tis why I told ye and Ronald about the dream, and not about what I think must be done now."

"And you clearly do not like that confusion. I wish I could tell you it meant something and what that was, or convince you that it means nothing at all. I cannot. Let us say that it is a warning, and one we should heed. So what must we do? Hie back to Bellefleur and cower behind the walls? Face your father armed and prepared for battle, even if he is doing all he agreed to? Or mayhaps we should betray him, creeping up on your kinsmen from behind and killing the whole lot of them ere they can hold a sword against us?"

"Nay, ye canna do any of that," she grumbled, and tugged fretfully at her braid. "Mayhaps ye are right. I am afraid, I confess it, and that has caused me to see demons and death even when I close my eyes." She looked at him and clutched at his arm. "Howbeit, let us at least take some extra cautions. Mayhaps this dream is but born of my conviction that blood will be spilled between the MacNairns and the de Amalvilles. Can we not do more to insure that at least it isna spilled at the river this afternoon?"

"Aye, that much we can do. I believe that we have already prepared ourselves well, but I will look again to be sure."

"Thank ye, Gabel. I beg your pardon for being such a

trouble, but—" she stopped talking when he touched a kiss against her mouth.

"You are no trouble." He smiled slowly. "Well, at least as concerns this matter."

She playfully struck him on the arm. "Your cousin told me Bellefleur had ne'er had a better behaved prisoner."

"Bellefleur has ne'er had a prisoner at all until I brought you through its gates!"

Ainslee laughed. "I think ye had best keep a close eye on your cousin, Gabel. 'Tis clear that she has a clever way with words."

"I suspected that from the moment she first began to speak." He smiled fondly as he thought on his cousin, but quickly grew somber again. "We will rest here for only an hour, and then continue on to the river. Just before we reach the bank, I will return all of your weapons to you. I trust that you will not then stick a dagger in me?" he asked.

"Nay, I willna, and I thank ye for doing that as I will feel a wee bit less afraid if I am armed."

"Do you think you father would do anything to hurt you?"

She shrugged. "Who can say? And least he would pause a moment, if I had a sword in my hand."

"Only a fool would not at least pause if they faced you when you have a sword in your hand." He held her close and kissed her, trying to comfort her and himself, yet knowing it was not enough. "I pray I am not sending you into danger," he said as he rested his cheek against her hair.

"There is naught ye can do to change that. I must be returned to Kengarvey for your sake and for the sake of my people. This could bring some peace to Kengarvey, and it has been far too long since anyone there has enjoyed a day without fear. I owe Kengarvey's people a chance and, if I dinna go back, I have stolen that away."

"Aye." Gabel stood up and held out his hand. "I think we had best rejoin the others. I cannot be alone with you for too long, or my thoughts turn to shedding our clothes and doing something beside talking about duty."

She stood up and laughed softly, her pleasure over his words briefly cutting through her sorrow. "Ye are a verra greedy mon, Gabel de Amalville."

"I dearly wish I was a great deal greedier," he murmured, and stared at her for a long moment before leading her back to camp.

Ainslee hurried to keep pace with his long strides, and puzzled over what he meant. It sounded like a statement of deep regret over the need to send her away, but she feared she might be allowing her heart to see too much behind his words. She wanted to ask him what he meant, but, before she could think of the appropriate way to word the question, they joined Justice and Michael and the chance was gone. As they talked, all of them pretending they were on some pleasant ride over the countryside, she told herself it did not matter. Even if she was right, and Gabel had just expressed some hint of what he felt for her, it would only reveal to her how much more she would be losing when she had to leave.

As soon as everyone had finished eating and the horses had rested, they started on their way again. Ainslee began to recognize the land they crossed over, and her heart sank. There would be no divine intervention. In but a few hours she would be back with her family, and she dreaded it. Gabel may have been thinking of her safety and his fear of hurting her if the de Amalvilles had to fight her father, but his wish for her to leave Kengarvey had given her food for thought. If she ever had the chance and there was some place she could go, she would leave Kengarvey. Although she loved the land itself and many of the people there, it was no longer a place she wished to live in. Somewhere there had to be a haven for her, and she swore that she would find it.

* * *

"We will be at the river in but moments," Gabel said as he reined in his horse and dismounted.

"Aye, I recognize this place, although I have been this far only a few times," Ainslee replied as he helped her down from the saddle.

"I brought along an old mare for you to ride across the river." He curtly signalled one of his cousins to bring the horse to him. "Your weapons are already packed on her."

Ainslee looked at the horse Justice led over, and smiled crookedly. "I believe my father will ken that I am not riding Malcolm," she murmured, and Justice laughed.

Gabel smiled faintly. "I am hoping that he does. 'Tis a spiteful gesture, but, from the moment he asked about the horse before he asked about you, I decided that he would not get it back. This horse has been a good mount and a fine breeder, but she is far past her good years. I hope she is not treated too poorly, but she is now so aged, she would probably die quickly." He patted the mare's nose.

"I will try to see that she is pastured weel," Ainslee promised.

"Good." Gabel helped her up into the saddle as Justice walked away. Despite his efforts to be calm, he lingered for a moment, his hand stroking Ainslee's stockinged leg. "There may not be time to say farewell when we reach the river—" he began.

Ainslee leaned down and touched a kiss to his mouth, aching for a deeper one, but knowing that it was neither the time nor the place. "So say it now," she whispered.

"Faretheewell, Ainslee MacNairn," he said with an equal softness. "And, for my sake, take care."

"Aye, as I pray ye will, Gabel. Dinna let my father bring about harm to ye or yours."

He nodded, briefly tightened his grip on her leg, and remounted his horse. He had known that it would not be easy, but he was alarmed at how hard it was to say goodbye to her. Gabel fought the nearly overwhelming urge to grab her, toss her over his saddle, and ride to places unknown, cursing the king and all his intrigues.

As they rode to the river, the water slowly becoming visible through the trees, he wondered just how big a mistake he might be making. He repeated all the reasons why he had to do what he was about to do and why it was foolish to even think of keeping Ainslee MacNairn for his own, but they had lost the power to soothe him. When he saw the MacNairns waiting on the opposite bank of the river, he cursed. A few problems would have been solved and he might have been able to steal a few more days with Ainslee, if Duggan MacNairn had simply not shown.

He studied his adversary as they rode to the edge of the river and halted. Duggan MacNairn stood right at the edge of the far bank, a big, solidly built man, his hands on his hips and his stance one of arrogance. The man could goad one simply with a look. Seeing the man made Gabel believe everything that had been said of him, and he realized he had had a few doubts. It seemed impossible that any man could be so steeped in wrongs and survive for so long, but one look at MacNairn answered that puzzle. Gabel also got the sinking feeling that the only way they would stop MacNairn from doing exactly as he wished, was to kill him.

Fourteen

"So, ye Norman interloper, ye have brought my whore of a daughter back," bellowed Duggan MacNairn.

Ainslee rode up next to Gabel just as her father spoke, and quickly reached out to clasp Gabel's hand. "He but tries to goad you."

"I know," Gabel replied between gritted teeth. "I shall ne'er understand him. The way he speaks of you appalls me."

"He kens no other way to speak." She chanced a subtle wave to Colin, who stood just behind her father, and, to her delight, her brother warily and hastily returned it.

"Are you still ready to accept the bargain made and hold to your pledge to our king?" Gabel called.

"I am here, am I not, Norman?" Duggan signaled to a man who rode closer to the riverbank.

"He should address you with more respect than that," Ainslee murmured, but she was no longer paying much heed to her father and his insults.

As Gabel repeated what had been agreed to and Duggan repeated his agreement before witnesses, then repeated his oath to the king, Ainslee studied the area. Her father's presence was enough to make any wise man suspicious, but it was more than that which caused the hairs on her arms to stand up, tingling and irritating her skin. Her father was being too genial. There was no sign of the rage he should have been in. He was being forced to bow before a Norman knight and swear to support a king he despised. That should have had him nearly tearing his hair out in a fit of fury, but he stood there as if he owned the world itself. That made Ainslee very nervous.

"Something is wrong," she muttered as Ronald rode up beside her. She spared him a brief glance before returning to her intense study of every patch of ground on both sides of the river.

"What makes ye think so, Ainslee?" Ronald asked, leaning closer to her so that they could hear each other over the bellowing going on.

"Look at my father, Ronald. Where is his anger? He has been beaten, yet he stands there as if *he* is the victorious one. He should be in such a rage that he needs to be tied to a tree to stop him from lunging across the river in a blind murderous charge at Gabel."

"Aye, old Duggan does look too at ease." Ronald looked around. "I canna see anything."

"Neither can I, and that should make my fears ease some, but they are growing stronger. Curse it, I need to see something, or we shall soon be crossing that river."

She continued to search, but nothing was there. Inwardly she cursed, wishing she had paid more heed to the tales of her father's deeds, but she had quickly grown weary of listening to the boasts of all his crimes. Now she could not be sure she knew all the tricks he might play. She needed to be able to point out a trap and have Gabel see it, if she was to stop the trade of her for the ransom. Once that began, she, Gabel, Ronald, and Justice would be in the midst of the deep, swiftly running river, and there would be no way to protect themselves.

"There, has all been said to your satisfaction, Norman?" said Duggan.

"Aye," replied Gabel, his voice tight with the anger he was struggling to keep in control.

"Then send the little whore to me. I suppose ye mean to return the cripple as weel."

"He is your man."

"Mon isna the right word for the old fool. Now, put her back on her horse and send her, whilst I send my mon to meet you."

"She is riding the horse she is being returned on."

Ainslee winced as her father spat a multitude of blasphemous words at Gabel. Colin stepped forward and spoke to his father, but it was several moments before MacNairn calmed himself. She realized that she was embarrassed by her father's behavior. He was a wellborn laird, a knight, yet he acted like the lowest of thieves. The sympathetic way Gabel's men glanced at her made her cringe with shame.

"I can see nothing," she snapped, her voice low so that only Ronald could hear her.

"Mayhaps there is nothing to see," Ronald replied.

There was such a lack of confidence behind his words that she ignored them. Ronald was just trying to ease her fears. He did not believe what he was saying any more than she did. The memory of her terrifying dream haunted her as she looked around fruitlessly trying to locate the trap she knew her father had set.

"It is time, Ainslee," Gabel said, breaking into her thoughts.

"Nay," she whispered, briefly caught up in a wave of panic.

Gabel reached out to touch her tightly clenched hands. "Are you that afraid of your father?"

After taking several deep breaths to steady herself, Ainslee turned to face Gabel. "Nay, I but had a moment of fright. 'Tis nothing."

"Are you sure? You are quite pale."

"I will be fine."

"Ainslee—" he began.

She touched her fingers to his lips. " 'Tis time for us to do what duty demands."

He pressed his lips tightly together and nodded. Slowly they began to urge their horses across the river. At the same time the MacNairn man started across. They were to meet midstream and trade the ransom for her, then return to their respective sides. Although she prayed that nothing was going to happen, that everything would go as it should, and Gabel would ride safely back to his people and go home, she continued to look for some sign of danger.

The MacNairn man was so close she could see the sweat on his face before she finally saw what she sought. When her father's man cast a nervous glance in the direction she was looking, she knew she was not imagining things. High in a tree on her father's side of the river was a man with a bow. He was aiming straight at Gabel. Although she was sure there were others scattered through the trees, she did not take the time to look for them.

"A trap!" she cried and kicked out at Gabel.

Gabel slipped to the side as he nearly lost his seat. Before he could right himself, he heard the distinct sound of the arrow passing close by. If he had still been sitting upright in the saddle, it would have buried itself in his chest.

When Ainslee cried out he reached for her, terrified that she had been struck by the arrows now filling the air around them. Instead he saw her try and grab a falling Ronald. Ronald disappeared into the rapidly flowing water, his body twisting and bouncing as he was carried downstream. Ainslee sent Ugly after him, then looked at Gabel. Gabel felt his heart clench at the look on her face, and tried again to reach her even as Justice urged him to ride back to their side of the river.

"Flee while ye can, Gabel," she said. "Remember, I willna hold ye to fault for what ye will now be forced to do. Watch your back." She spurred her horse forward, riding straight toward her father.

Gabel yelled after her, but, before he could try and chase her, Justice grabbed the reins of his horse and pulled him back. "Ainslee will get herself killed," he protested as Justice dragged him along.

"She is trying to save your fool life. Do not waste the chance she has given you!" Justice snapped.

It took Gabel a moment to realize what she had done. By riding straight toward her father, she had sent his men into confusion. They ceased to fire their arrows, afraid that they would hit their laird's daughter, and the brief respite was all Gabel needed. Even as he obeyed his cousin's urgings to return to the relative safety of the opposite bank, he heard Duggan MacNairn bellowing at his men to continue shooting their arrows in a blatant disregard for his own daughter's safety.

Gabel was not able to see how Ainslee had fared until he was back with his men and they had retreated far enough to be out of the reach of the MacNairn arrows. Her horse stumbled up onto the opposite bank, and her father was quick to reach her side. He pulled her out of the saddle and threw her to the ground before she had a chance to draw a weapon and defend herself. Gabel's two cousins quickly grabbed his reins to restrain him when Duggan MacNairn yanked Ainslee to her feet again and began to pummel her, beating her until she fell, and then kicking her.

"He will kill her!" Gabel cried, but was unable to pull free of his cousins.

"And if you ride blindly to her rescue, you will be cut down," said Justice. "That will do her no good, and she would not want it. She did this to save you, not to have you charge the whole MacNairn force in a fit of rage and misplaced gallantry."

"Look," said Michael, pointing toward the horrifying scene in the MacNairn camp. "There is at least one of those cowards who will not allow him to kill her."

As he fought to push aside his blind rage, Gabel watched Colin MacNairn grab his father and pull him away. The pair wrestled furiously for a while, the younger man talking all the time. When he finally released Duggan MacNairn, he was struck so hard he fell beside a frighteningly still Ainslee, but Duggan did not return to his brutality. Instead, the laird of Kengarvey turned his attention to the men of Bellefleur.

Both sides glared at each other, but for a while all that was exchanged were a few bellowed insults. Gabel knew his men were eager to fight the MacNairns, furious at the treachery shown them. He hesitated because what had just happened showed him that he did not know what strengths his enemy had, or where all of his men were. There was also Ainslee to consider. If she was still alive, and he forced himself to believe that she was, she would be caught in the middle. The place he had chosen for the meeting had been carefully selected to protect him and his men; but it was not a good place to try and engage an enemy in battle.

"Are we to do nothing?" asked Michael, his handsome face taut with fury.

"I am trying to think of what we can do without risking our slaughter," replied Gabel, his voice hoarse as he tried to control his own rage. "He will not come to us, so we will have to go after him, and that places us in the midst of the river."

"Where his archers can murder us at their leisure," said Justice, pounding his fist against his thigh in a gesture of frustration. "No matter how fast we ride, we will still lose too many of our men."

"Find Ronald," he ordered his cousins. "We must swallow our anger and pride and retreat, unless MacNairn tries to charge us, and I do not believe the man is that great a fool."

"Surely Ronald is dead," protested Michael.

"Then bring me his body so that I might give him the burial he deserves. I cannot aid her now, but at least she can know I cared for her friend."

Gabel sat glaring at MacNairn as his cousins rode away. The man knew he was safe. He knew that Gabel would never risk the slaughter of his men in crossing the river. What galled Gabel even more was the sudden certainty that that was why MacNairn had so readily agreed to the meeting place he had chosen. Gabel had been looking for the safest place, and MacNairn had seen the perfect spot for treachery.

As he watched the MacNairns prepare to leave, their taunts searing his ears, Gabel turned his attention to Ainslee. Her brother Colin was tending to her and, when he saw her move slightly, he breathed a heavy sigh of relief. He had felt certain she was not dead, that Colin had stopped his father in time, but her stillness had troubled him. He felt even more at ease when he watched Colin take her to his horse, set her on his saddle, and mount behind her. For now she was safe from her father, and Gabel felt sure that Ainslee had learned how to stay out of her father's way at Kengarvey. He wished Ronald was with her, but at least now he had proof that someone at Kengarvey was willing to keep her alive.

"Do we chase them, m'lord?" asked one of Gabel's men as the MacNairns began to disappear into the thick wood on the opposite side of the river.

"Nay," Gabel replied through gritted teeth as he fought to restrain his need to go after Duggan MacNairn and cut the man down. "It turns my stomach to but sit here and watch the dogs creep away, but we cannot win against them now. They set the trap and we rode into it. All we can do now is make certain that we do not all die because of my blindness. MacNairn will pay. Sadly, so will all of his people. The arrogant fool thinks he has won, but he has just signed the death warrant for his clan."

Once the MacNairns were gone, Gabel and his men waited for Justice and Michael to return. Gabel sent a few of his men into the surrounding wood to watch for any further sign of treachery from the MacNairns. When he finally saw his cousins riding toward him, a blanket-wrapped form slung over Justice's saddle, he sighed. It seemed most unfair that MacNairn's betrayal should cost Ronald his life. When Ainslee finally learned of her friend's fate, she would be heartbroken, as the old man had truly been her father as well as her companion.

"He is not dead yet," Justice announced as he reached Gabel.

"Nay?" Gabel dismounted and took a closer look at the old man before calling for a litter. "How could he survive?" he muttered as he eased the unconscious Ronald off of the horse. "He has suffered an arrow wound to the chest and is chilled to the bone." As he gently laid Ronald on the ground, he idly patted Ugly's dripping head as the dog sat down next to the Scot.

"We saw the dog first," explained Justice as he dismounted and stood next to Gabel. "The beast had pulled the old man from the river. We assured ourselves that he was still alive, tended the wound as best we could, and brought him back."

Justice shook his head as he studied Ronald. "I am not sure he will live to reach Bellefleur though."

"He will live," Gabel vowed as he helped strip Ronald of his wet clothes and wrap the man in blankets. "I have been naught but trouble and misery for Ainslee MacNairn, and there is more to come. At least I can give her back the one person who truly cares about her."

"Do you really think you will ever see her again?" Justice asked quietly.

"I have to," Gabel replied with an equal softness. "If only to beg her forgiveness for taking everything from her and giving her only heartache."

Ainslee bit back a groan as consciousness returned and pain flooded her battered body. She felt a strong warm body at her back, and briefly hoped it was Gabel. One glance down at the hands on the reins was enough to smother that hope. She peeked over her shoulder and managed a shy smile for her grim-faced brother Colin. Although the memory of her father's furious attack was mostly a blur of terror and pain, she knew it was Colin who had saved her life.

"Thank ye," she whispered, and saw a brief glimpse of softness in his hard blue eyes.

"Ye are my blood. I couldna let my father kill my sister," he replied in a flat voice.

"And the de Amalvilles?" she asked.

"Have returned to Bellefleur, no doubt to plan the best way to slaughter us."

She shuddered, for she knew that was exactly the fate her father had brought down on their heads. "And Ronald?" She tensed for his reply.

"I dinna ken what his fate is," Colin replied, a shadow of regret in his voice. "The last I saw of the mon he was tumbling down the river with that beast of yours racing after him. He took an arrow in the chest." He tightened his grip on her when she swayed.

"He survived a serious wound before."

"Aye, but no doubt he had ye fussing o'er him. He will be alone now."

"Nay," she said with a conviction she felt deep in her heart. "Sir Gabel will care for him."

"For a MacNairn? Ye are mad."

"Nay, Gabel will care for Ronald. He willna leave until he finds Ronald and, if my dear friend lives, Gabel will do all he can to make sure he survives, or he will give him the godly burial he deserves."

"Weel, believe what ye will. I but pray that, in a few weeks time when we are all scattered on the ground in heaps, there is someone who has the kindness to bury us."

Ainslee wished she could reassure her brother that their future was not so black, but she was not a good liar, and he had the wit to know when she did lie. Gabel would be in a rage over this treachery and, even if *he* could find some bloodless way to make her father pay for it, the king would not hear of it. Duggan MacNairn had just thrown away his clan's last chance for survival, and this time he would not even be able to save himself and his precious sons.

"Wake, Ainslee, but dinna move."

The whisper drew Ainslee from the restless sleep she had fallen into. She understood the warning behind Colin's words. Her father was near, and she might draw his attention her way, if she was not careful. Colin might fight to keep her from being murdered, but he could not save her from everything her father might wish to do to her.

As they rode through the heavy gates of Kengarvey, Ainslee was astounded by the work that had been done. With so many enemies surrounding him, her father never had the time to build in stone, even if he had the coin to do so, but it was clear that the battered people of Kengarvey had become very skilled at swiftly enclosing themselves in a wooden keep. The thick stone walls of Kengarvey were still intact, and whatever had survived the latest fire had been put to good use. It did not really matter what her father built his keep of anymore, however, for Ainslee suspected that now even the magnificent Bellefleur could not protect the man.

Once inside the bailey, she caught sight of her father and trembled, hating the fear she felt, but unable to control it. When he dismounted and started to walk toward her, she slumped against Colin and feigned unconsciousness. She had not yet had the time to tend to the injuries he had dealt her, and she could not afford to have anymore added to them.

"So, the little whore is still in a swoon," Duggan said as he stood next to Colin's horse and glared at his youngest daughter.

"I believe it may be more serious than a swoon, Father," Colin murmured. "And why do ye keep calling her a whore?"

"And what do ye think she has been doing with that Norman bastard whilst she has been at Bellefleur?"

"I have no proof that she has been doing anything with him."

"Those monks softened your wits, lad. Of course, the mon had his fill of her and, since she looked quite hale as she rode to us, I believe she didna put up a fight. 'Tis a good thing I had no marriage arranged for her, as it would ne'er be done now, and she has cost me enough."

"I thought we had gained today, for we have Ainslee, and we still hold the ransom ye collected."

"Aye, true enough. I spit squarely in that Norman pig's eye, and he willna soon forget it."

"Nay, he certainly willna," Colin agreed in a heavy voice.

"Weel, toss the stupid lass somewhere, and come and feast with us. 'Tis a day for celebration."

"I will join ye soon," Colin said, but his father was already striding into the keep.

After peeking to be sure that her father had left, Ainslee sat up a little straighter. "He truly believes he has won," she murmured, astounded that her father could be so blind.

"He did win today," Colin said as he dismounted, then reached up to take her into his arms.

"Aye, one could say that, but he lost far more than he gained." She gritted her teeth against the pain in her body as Colin carried her inside and started up the narrow wooden stairs. "He is a dead mon. Ye ken that, dinna ye?"

"Aye, I ken it. Ye will see that the fire hasna destroyed everything. 'Tis charred, but your tiny room is still intact."

"There is a blessing."

It was not until she was tucked up in her small bed, her injuries washed and bandaged, that Ainslee found another chance to speak privately with Colin. He sat on the edge of her bed and helped her drink some mead. She wished he did not look so downcast, but she had nothing to say which might lift his spirits.

"Ye must leave Kengarvey, Colin," she said, and reached out to clutch his thin hand in hers.

"Oh? And where shall I go?"

"Back to the monks?"

"I can ne'er go back there. When our father decided I didna need any more learning, he not only took me out of there, but most all else that was of value."

"He stole from a church? From holy men?"

"Aye, but dinna think all monks are holy men, lass. There were a few there who were weel steeped in sin, and cared little about saving their souls."

"Weel, there fades my faith in the church." Ainslee was a little surprised when Colin gave a short bark of laughter. "Gabel will be back, Colin."

"I ken, and I notice that ye call him Gabel. Mayhaps Father is right."

"That I am a whore?"

"Nay, only in saying that ye were bedded down with the mon."

She blushed and grimaced. "Weel, that doesna matter."

"Not to me, but I shouldna let Father ken that there may have been a softness in that Norman toward you. He would think it something he could use, and ye will find yourself back to standing squarely between the two."

"Never. I shall never go through that again. But, heed me, Colin, for it could save your life. Gabel will come, and he will raze Kengarvey to the ground. He has no choice. The king will command it. What we must pray for is that only the men from Bellefleur will come to kick down our gates."

"I canna see that that is something to pray for. How can it help us?"

"Gabel canna hate a person simply because they carry the name MacNairn. He kens the value of mercy. Aye, I think he now has no choice but to kill our father, or at least deliver him to the king, who will kill him. What I fear is that others will join the battle, ones who dearly wish to see every last MacNairn drown in a pool of his own blood, ones such as the Frasers and the MacFibhs."

Colin sighed and ran his hands through his long, ill-cut auburn hair. "Then we are truly doomed, for they willna cease until naught is left of Kengarvey save blood and ashes."

"I ken it. So, if—nay, *when*—the enemy comes and ye see that the battle is lost, get yourself to a mon from Bellefleur and surrender."

"Why? So that I too may be dragged before the king in chains? I much prefer to die by the sword than meet the gruesome death he will deal out."

"So that ye may have a chance to live. Gabel has sworn that he will do all he can to save all he can. Our father is a dead mon. He died when the first arrow was shot at the river. Ye need not die with him. Nay, not ye or our brothers, if ye can put yourselves in Gabel's hands. Truly, he doesna wish to eradicate the whole clan. He but seeks peace, and he is willing to believe that he could deal with the sons, even if he can ne'er deal with the father."

"And how does he mean to deal with the daughter?" Colin asked quietly.

"He means to keep me alive, but he can do nothing else." She smiled sadly as she relaxed against the hay-stuffed sacks that served as her pillows. "He is too good a mon for a lass like me. Swear to me, Colin, that ye will try to save yourself, and mayhaps one or all of our brothers."

"I have no wish to die, Ainslee."

It was not until he left that Ainslee realized he had not sworn to anything. She sighed, realizing that he probably did not believe her, thought that her talk of Gabel's mercy came from the blindness of a lovesick girl. There was still time to convince him, for she knew it would be weeks before a full battle could be fought. It could even be spring before Duggan MacNairn was forced to pay the full price for his treachery.

She struggled to put aside all her concerns, her fear and grief for Ronald and the pain of leaving Gabel, so that she could rest. It was important that she heal and grow strong again. Before the final battle came to their gates, she was going to have to try and speak to her father, to make him see that he was condemning everyone, and that, even if he could not save himself, he should at least try to save his clan. Such a confrontation could cost her her life and she knew it, but she could not cower in her room without even trying to save her people. At best, she would simply suffer another fierce beating, and she wanted to be strong enough to endure and survive it.

Before she gave in to the urge to sleep, she prayed for Ronald, prayed that he had been found and was alive. If she survived the weeks ahead, she was going to be in need of him, and she did not want him to have paid such a dear price for the treachery of his laird. She also prayed for Gabel. She knew he had seen how her father had greeted her, and his one true concern had been for her safety. He was undoubtedly feeling guilty, and she wanted to survive long enough to relieve him of that burden.

Fifteen

"Ye must speak to the lad," Ronald said, looking at the two forlorn young men sitting on his bed. "He has sulked for a week now, and that isna helping anyone."

Justice exchanged a grimace with Michael, and then looked at Ronald. "I am not sure Gabel can help anyone. He knows, as we all do, that he must now face the king with failure and take up the sword against your clan."

"Aye, for that fool Duggan has given the laddie no choice."

"You are most calm and accepting about the fact that your people are facing destruction."

"My people have been facing destruction for years, since my father's time and, mayhaps, before that. I am nay calm about it for—believe it or not as ye choose—but there are good people there, people who dinna deserve to pay for Duggan's bloody crimes. Howbeit, the sword has been hanging o'er our heads for many a year, and though it grieves me that Sir Gabel will be the one to wield it, I dinna blame him. I think what truly troubles him is that wee Ainslee is trapped inside those walls."

"Aye," agreed Michael. "I think what also deeply troubles him is that he had to sit on that riverbank and watch the girl nearly beaten to death. He could do nothing to help her, and that is a sore blow to a man's pride."

"Weel, 'tis past time that he ceased to nurse his poor wee bruised pride and did something." Ronald smiled when both young men laughed. "I would go and do something meself, at least for my poor lassie, but I need to regain my strength."

"You are very lucky to be alive, you old fool," Justice said, a hint of affection in his voice softening the scold. "You took an arrow in that skinny chest and suffered a long swim in the cold water of that cursed river. And you lost a lot of blood. I grow weary of tracking you by what is leaking out of your old body."

"I swear to keep my body's humors where they belong from now on." He laughed, then grimaced when it made him cough. "Now, one or both of you lads are going to have to gird your wee loins and go and talk to your cousin."

"*Wee* loins?" Michael grumbled, but both Ronald and Justice ignored him.

"Our aunt and cousin have been urging the same," murmured Justice.

"Then why do ye hesitate?" demanded Ronald. "With each day that passes, Duggan is able to strengthen his defense."

"True, but do you think he believes we will attack? He acted so victorious that day. He may believe he has beaten us."

"He will still be strengthening his defenses. The mon and the people of Kengarvey have become verra skilled at rebuilding. True, 'tis with wood, which can be burned, but there is good solid stone there as weel. 'Tisna as easy as ye may think to bring down Kengarvey."

"Alright." Justice stood up and yanked Michael to his feet. "We will go and speak to Gabel. The time has come to face the king and learn just what must be done. If naught else, if Gabel feels a need to aid Ainslee, he cannot do it from his bedchamber."

Gabel stared out of the narrow window in his bedchamber, cursing his inability to act, yet not moving. His mind was filled with the images of Ainslee helpless on the ground as her father kicked her. It was an image that had haunted his dreams. He had failed her. He had failed his king. About the only good that had come out of that day at the river had been that he had managed to save Ronald's life, but the man would not have been injured if he had not been such a fool.

What kept Gabel locked in his thoughts, his black mood of despair deepening every day, was the knowledge that he had made a great error, and not just in his confrontation with Duggan MacNairn. He now knew that he should never have let Ainslee go. At the river that day his mistake had been both strategic and emotional. He had cut out his own heart, and he saw no hope of mending the wound.

He sighed when a soft rap came at his door. His command to go away was ignored, and he turned to scowl at Michael and Justice when they entered the room. Caught up in his own thoughts and misery, he not only found it difficult to deal with anyone, but irritating.

"I will not be good company," he warned as he went to a small table and poured himself a tankard of wine from the jug set there.

"Oh, we are fully aware of that," replied Justice as he moved to do the same. " 'Tis why we have all left you alone for a full week. 'Tis time to set aside our cowardice, however."

"A week?" Gabel asked in a stunned voice, trying to recall how many days had passed and alarmed to find that he had no idea.

"Aye, a week. You came in here to hide the moment we returned to Bellefleur, and no one has seen or heard much from you."

"Aye," agreed Michael. "You bellow for food and drink and have inquired about Ronald a time or two, although even that ceased when you were assured that he would live."

"A week," Gabel muttered and sank down on his bed.

Justice cursed and sat down beside him as Michael helped himself to some wine. "Must I lay hands upon you and shake you to wake you from this moody sleep?"

"Nay." Gabel took a long drink of wine and then looked at his cousin. "I but lost count of the days."

"We began to think you may have lost your mind, but assured ourselves that you would never take a defeat so hard."

Gabel cursed and stood up to pace the room. " 'Twas not the defeat, although that was a fool's errand and a bigger fool's mistake. I was so intent on protecting everyone from any possible treachery that I did not consider how well such a place could also protect MacNairn."

"I should not beat myself too severely about that, as I do not believe there was any other place that would have proven better. They all had weaknesses, and most had ones that could have proven deadly to us. Aye, and MacNairn is an arrogant, treacherous dog who has a skill of making defeat taste as bitter as it can." Justice took a deep breath and ventured, "I do not believe it is the defeat which has cast you into such a dark mood."

"Nay," confessed Gabel as he turned to face his cousin. "Not seeing MacNairn's treachery was not the only mistake I made that day, and I believe it was not the most grievous either."

"Nay, it was sending that poor girl to her father and then having to watch the man murder her," said Michael as he sat down next to Justice.

"She was alive," Gabel snapped.

"Well, aye, I meant to say that he *almost* murdered her."

"I am sorry," Gabel said, smiling weakly at his wary young cousin. "I have spent too many hours fearing that she is dead, that I did see her murdered. Reminding myself that I saw her move no longer holds the ability to ease that fear. Aye, I should ne'er have sent Ainslee back to her father."

"Because you wanted her for yourself," said Justice, watching Gabel closely. "You could not have kept her as your leman forever. Ainslee MacNairn is not a woman to quietly sit in a cottage somewhere and wait for you to tiptoe away from your wife and spend a few hours with her."

The distasteful picture Justice drew made Gabel grimace, and he was ashamed to admit that he had contemplated just such an arrangement a time or two. "Nay, Ainslee would never allow that. She would probably have cut my throat if I had even suggested it." He sprawled in a chair facing the bed and stared into his wine. "Nay, my mistake was in thinking that I could ne'er take a woman like her to wife, that somehow that would hurt Bellefleur."

"Why should you think such a thing?"

"Because she is a MacNairn?" Gabel smiled faintly when Justice grimaced and nodded. "There was also that fact that she could bring nothing to the marriage save herself. I am not a greedy man, but I had everything planned so carefully, from how much coin my bride should have to where her lands should be. I also considered the power and prestige her family should have. As I watched Ainslee ride into her father's brutal grasp just to save my arrogant hide, I realized how useless all of that is, and how little I need it."

"You certainly are not in need of a bride with a heavy purse, and Bellefleur is surrounded by good fields, so, nay, you do not *need* more land. Howbeit, you cannot fault yourself for thinking that that is what one must look for in a bride. 'Tis what we all do. One does not just marry for the begetting of children, but for gain."

Gabel shrugged. "True, but I did not need to be such a slave to my own plans. Nay, each time I thought I was softening, each time the mere thought of keeping her slipped into my mind, I berated myself and convinced myself that I needed that sort of bride for Bellefleur, that I was doing it all for Bellefleur."

"And you were not?" Michael asked.

"Nay, I was not. I was doing it because the bride I had planned to take was one of duty. A man does not take a bride like Ainslee out of duty."

"Ah, I see." Michael nodded. "You love the girl."

"Quick, is he not?" drawled Justice, ignoring Michael's scowl over the insult. "You were not so quick yourself, cousin, if you did not realize what you felt for the girl until she was back in her father's ungentle hands."

"Oh, I believe I suspected what was in my heart from shortly after I brought her to Bellefleur." Gabel shook his head. "I was determined not to let emotion rule me, however, and Ainslee was all emotion."

"Ah, so she loves you as well," said Michael, smiling until Justice patted him on the head.

"Such a sweet, simple lad," Justice murmured, and ducked when Michael tried to hit him.

"Leave him be, Justice," ordered Gabel, although he found he was able to smile at his cousins' antics. "Your goading of Michael is no help at the moment. I do not know if she loves me, Michael. I never asked, and she never said anything."

"She bedded down with you."

"Passion."

"Nay. Well, aye, there had to be that. I meant nay, Ainslee MacNairn is no whore or light-moraled girl. I was her guard for most of her stay. I cannot see her bedding down with you just because you made her feel somewhat lustful. She has far too much pride for that."

"I think the boy has actually spoken with some keenness of wit," Justice said. "Nay, Ainslee MacNairn may not have said anything about what was in her heart, but it had to be more than passion. Mayhaps she felt you did not *want* to know."

For a long moment Gabel just stared at Justice as he mulled that over in his mind, his emotions tumbling around inside of him as he began to see the truth of it. He had not asked Ainslee for anything save her passion, and she gave him that in full measure. In the last few days he had tried to pull some vow from her, but, as he thought over his words, he could see how she simply would not have realized what he was trying to make her say. Since, at that time, he had not wanted to be forced to answer in kind, he had been far too subtle.

"Curse my idiocy," he said after taking a long drink of wine. "Nay, I did not act like a man who had any interest in the true state of her heart. If there was any more to what she felt than the fierce passion neither of us had the strength to resist, I undoubtedly left her afraid to tell me. I certainly gave her no reason to think I was interested."

" 'Tis a common mistake between lovers," Justice reassured him. "After all, who wishes to be the first to bare his heart and soul? Think of the humiliation of doing so, only to find that it is not returned in kind and may never be. And, with Ainslee, she also knew that she would not even be staying here. We never gave her any choice, but to return to Kengarvey."

"Aye," agreed Michael. "That plan never changed, so why should she tell you anything? As far as she knew, how she felt or did not feel about you would make no difference."

"And all of this discussion makes no difference either," Gabel said as he stood up. "I made a mistake—nay, I made two— I was not as wary as I should have been with MacNairn, and I gave him the only thing I value. I must count myself fortunate that he does not know that. And I must cease to sulk in my room and do something."

"That is what Ronald said."

"Is it," Gabel murmured, and then laughed when Justice grinned and nodded. "That old man grows too comfortable."

"He calls you *laddie*," drawled Justice.

"Far too comfortable. Well, the first thing I will do will be to go and assure him that I am no longer gazing blindly at my walls and pitying myself, and that I will do my best to get his *lassie* back. You two can go and make the preparations for a journey. We will ride to the king's court on the morrow. 'Tis past time I cease hiding from him as well."

"I know you are not asleep," Gabel said as he stood by Ronald's bed and stared down at the man.

Ronald warily opened one eye and looked up at Gabel. "Ye are a braw laddie, arenae ye. Ye could cause an old mon to suffer quite a fright by looming o'er his deathbed like that."

"You are not dying." Gabel sat down on the edge of the man's bed. "You sent my cousins to berate me."

"Not to berate you, but to wake ye up, to do something to make ye see that time is slipping by."

"Aye. I had not realized how much time had gone by. I was too soaked in my own self-pity and wounded pride." He shook his head. "There were so many mistakes, I did not know how to atone for them."

"Ye have naught to atone for. Ye certainly arena the only one who has been tricked by that bastard MacNairn. Nay, and ye are certainly not the first mon not to ken what he wants until he has lost it."

"Do you think I have lost Ainslee?" Gabel asked, making no attempt to deny Ronald's assumption or hide his feelings. Hiding his feelings had gained him nothing, and may well have cost him more than he dared consider.

Ronald shook his head. "Nay, laddie. Ye need not worry that being a great fool has cost ye the lass. Weel, if she is still alive."

"She is."

"Young Michael wasna so sure."

"I saw her move as her brother Colin tended to her."

"Ah, so he was in time again. Howbeit, that doesna mean she is safe."

Gabel reached out to pat the man's hands, stilling their fretful movements. "Ainslee has survived in that place for many years. I am sure she can survive for a few weeks longer."

"Do ye think it will be only a few weeks ere ye can go after her? 'Tis a poor time of the year to ride to a battle."

"Only if the weather turns sour. We are being blessed with a mild season. I can but pray that it continues; if it does, we will ride for Kengarvey as soon as we have the king's orders."

Ronald sighed. "He will want the whole clan put to the sword."

"At first, but the king is not a man who craves the blood of all his enemies' kinsmen. He has never held the belief that you must kill everyone to protect yourself. 'Tis Duggan MacNairn he wants. I may not be able to save MacNairn's sons, but I will try, for Ainslee's sake. I am hoping that, since the sons have ne'er been condemned by name, if I bring the king Duggan MacNairn's head, 'twill be enough. I just wish that the head I needed to pacify my liege lord was not the head of Ainslee's father."

"Ye must do as the king wills ye to."

"Aye, I must. I must also try to keep away all the carrion who may wish to ride along, the ones who wish to see no MacNairn live. I do not wish to be part of a bloodbath."

Ronald smiled sadly. "That may weel be impossible. The only thing Duggan has e'er done with any great success, is to make most of Scotland wish to kill him and anyone who fights with him or shares his blood. The mon is verra good at making folk hate him, deeply and lastingly."

Gabel nodded sadly in agreement as he stood up. "I can only promise to do my best to save as many as possible. I thought you should know that, and I did rather hope that you might be able to assure me that Ainslee will be safe. That was foolish."

"I can only remind ye that she is a clever, strong lass. If any can survive there, e'en with Duggan angry at her, she can."

"Rest, Ronald. I pray I can bring you good news shortly."

"Never mind the news—bring me my lassie."

Gabel took a deep breath and walked into the great hall of Edinburgh Castle, where the king awaited him. It had taken three days to reach the king, and then three days before the king had agreed to see him. Gabel prayed that that was not a sign of disfavor. Even though he had to give the man bad news, he needed the king to be in a mood that could allow some mercy.

There was little sign of mercy on the king's face, as Gabel bowed before him. At the man's right stood Fraser, and Gabel was sure the king had been told all about the failure to bring Duggan MacNairn to heel. The look of gloating on Fraser's face warned Gabel that he would have a great many lies to battle, and Fraser was confident that not all of them could be successfully disputed.

"It appears that the outlaw MacNairn has succeeded in making a fool of you, Sir Gabel," the king said, his tone of voice almost pleasant as he watched Gabel closely.

That stung his pride, but Gabel decided that the complete truth would only aid him now. "He did, my liege." He almost smiled at the way the king's brows rose slightly in a gesture of surprise and Fraser scowled. "I planned well to protect my men, but that plan also allowed MacNairn to play his low tricks and flee without penalty. I was well warned about the clever treachery MacNairn is capable of, but I think I did not believe all of the tales."

"And now you do?"

"Aye, my liege. I do learn from my mistakes."

"And so you feel you could face the man again and be victorious?"

"If I must pull Kengarvey down stick by stick and stone by stone, I will either kill the man or capture him and bring him to you to face punishment. I gave him his chance to save himself, and he did not take it."

The king nodded and rubbed his chin. "I want Kengarvey taken down piece by filthy piece, e'en if you have already cut down Duggan MacNairn. I want that thieves' nest razed to the ground."

"And what of the people?" Gabel asked quietly.

"What of them? They are thieves as well."

"I believe they are mostly a people who are so in terror of their laird they will do most anything he asks. 'Tis MacNairn himself and a few of his followers who are the trouble. No one dares to speak against anything the man does, for he becomes so enraged, he murders them. There are few surer ways to insure that no one ever argues with you."

The king smiled faintly. "Nay, 'twould certainly silence a carping tongue. You are asking me to show mercy."

"Aye, my liege, I am."

"Mercy?" bellowed Fraser, taking a step toward Gabel. "How can ye e'en ask for mercy? E'en that whore of a daughter MacNairn left to rot at Bellefleur deserves no mercy. Kengarvey is naught but a nest of vermin and 'tis long past due a thorough cleaning-out."

It was hard, but Gabel fought the urge to strike at Fraser for his insults to Ainslee. The way the king looked from him to Fraser and back again, told him that his sire had guessed at the animosity between them. He had no time to deal with the arrogant, foul-mouthed Fraser, however, for he was desperate to save Ainslee's life and the lives of as many of the innocent people of Kengarvey as he could.

"Not everyone at Kengarvey deserves to be put to the sword, my liege," Gabel said to his king.

"Would you even keep his sons alive?" asked the king.

"If they gave me their word that they will honor the treaty their father treated with such contempt."

"And you have good reason to believe they will? You are not making your judgement upon what some fair lass whispered in your ear as you lay in each other's arms?"

"Nay. I but ask the chance to offer life to any of the people of Kengarvey who do not fight me, and who are willing to swear their allegiance to you."

"And to you," the king murmured, "for I have decided that you deserve the lands. Therefore, any who survive the battle will be your people, and you will carry the weight and responsibility for their deeds." The king waved Gabel away. "I will tell you what I wish this evening. I need to consider the matter."

Gabel was still cursing Fraser when he reached the room he shared with his cousins. He poured himself a tankard of hearty mead and drank most of it down before he felt his fury ease a little. There was still a chance that he could get the promise of mercy he needed, and he gained nothing by ranting about Fraser. He was just glad that Lady Margaret was not at court this time, for he knew he did not have the patience to deal with that woman without saying or doing something that could cause a scandal.

"The meeting did not go well?" asked Justice.

"Nay," grumbled Gabel. "Fraser was there, and had obviously been using his time here at court to fill the king's ears with lies. I should like to believe that they have not all been heeded by our liege, but I cannot be sure. I will not know what has been decided about Kengarvey and its people until this evening."

"You must take hope in the fact that the king was not raging about your failure to get the treaty he sought, nor did he become enraged when you asked him for the right to make merciful choices concerning the people of Kengarvey."

"True, yet I have an ill feeling about all of this."

"What do you mean?"

"I want mercy, and the king wants revenge for the insults MacNairn has dealt him. I have this dull feeling that the king will try to give us both what we want."

"How can he do that?"

"I do not know, but it will bode ill for the MacNairns."

"He wishes me to do *what?*" Gabel bellowed, causing the king's messenger to take several nervous steps backward.

"Ye are to go to Kengarvey and see that MacNairn dies. If the mon survives the battle, then ye are to bring him here."

"That was not what caused me to bellow, young man. 'Tis what else you just said. I am not allowed to do this on my own?"

"Nay, Sir Gabel," the messenger replied, his voice unsteady. "Ye are to allow Sir Fraser and his men to go with you. The MacFibhs are also to be allowed to join the fight. Our liege believes that ye will need the extra armed men if ye are to defeat Duggan MacNairn."

"But to send Fraser and the MacFibhs? They loathe the MacNairns, and would like nothing better than to see even the last and smallest child cut down." He sighed and ran his hand through his hair when the messenger just stared at him. "Go and tell the king that I will ride for Bellefleur in the morning, collect my men, and ride straight for Kengarvey, if the weather continues to remain in my favor."

The moment the king's messenger left, Gabel paced the room and swore vociferously. He stopped only when he noticed how warily Michael and Justice were watching him. Slouching in one of the small, hard chairs in the room, he took several deep breaths as he tried to calm himself. He needed to plan what he would do, for, with the Frasers and MacFibhs also fighting the MacNairns, he had to be sure that he found a way to protect as many of the McNairns as he could.

"I do not understand," said Justice. "How can he grant you the power to give mercy where you will, yet set upon the Mac-Nairns two of their worst enemies? Who does the king think will be left if the Frasers and MacFibhs ride in there with an order of fire and sword against the MacNairns?"

"I think the king knows full well that Fraser and even the MacFibhs are going to do their utmost to cut down every Mac-Nairn they can, from Duggan himself to the tiniest suckling child. My job, if I do crave mercy, will be to run about and see how many I can save from the sword."

"This will not set well with our men. They hate the Frasers," said Michael. "I do not think there is one of your men-at-arms, who would truly wish to ride at the side of the Frasers."

"Well, they shall have to swallow their distaste. I cannot afford any of my men dragging their feet. Come, we had better get some rest, as we will have to leave at dawn. I cannot even allow my men the chance to resign themselves to fighting along-side the Frasers, for I think we must get to Kengarvey as swiftly as possible. I do not want those two bloodthirsty clans clamoring at MacNairn's door before I have even reached the battle-field."

Sixteen

Taking a deep breath to steady herself, Ainslee slipped into the great hall. She grimaced as the smell of filthy rushes and equally filthy bodies assaulted her nose. Although she tried not to, she found herself comparing it to the one at Bellefleur. It was not only the lack of finery or the wooden walls that made Kengarvey's great hall look like a hovel next to Bellefleur's. Even the poorer dress of the people inside and the hearth in the middle of the room sending acrid smoke up through a hole in the roof were not what made the difference. It was the filth, the disarray, and the general squalor. It was also the sullen and fearful moods of the people gathered there.

Ainslee crept along the wall even as she scolded herself for approaching her father so timidly. Her skin was still smeared with livid bruises from the beating he gave her the week before at the river. The thought of enduring another one made her stomach clench from fear. Looking around at the people gathered in the hall, she wondered why she should risk so much for them. They would simply stand by and watch if her father decided to beat her to death, yet she was risking just that in the faint hope of saving some of them. It was loyalty to the clan, to Kengarvey and the few good people still within its walls that pushed her, and she decided that loyalty was not always very sensible.

To her relief the men gathered around her father left before she reached him. Only Colin and her eldest brother George remained. Without his men around, Duggan MacNairn might well be ready to listen to reason, for he would feel no need to display his strength and lack of fear to anyone.

"Father," she said as she stepped up to his scarred and battered chair. Her voice was hoarse and unsteady and she hastily cleared her throat, not wanting him to scent the fear she felt in facing him.

"Where did ye get that gown?" Duggan MacNairn demanded, roughly taking a fold of her skirt between his dirty fingers to fondle the material.

Inwardly cursing her lack of forethought in putting on one of the gowns Elaine and Marie had given her, Ainslee subtly tugged her skirt free of his grasp. "The ladies of Bellefleur gave them to me."

"They didna think what I dressed ye in was fine enough, eh?"

"My clothes had suffered from my capture and the journey to Bellefleur."

"Humph. I suspect it wasna the ladies who dressed ye so fine, but that Norman ye have been rutting in. 'Tis clear ye have no shame, or ye wouldna be flaunting your whore's attire."

It was going to be more difficult than I thought, she mused, as she fought down a brief flare of anger over his insults. The man was blinded by the strength of his own pride, yet had no consideration for the pride of others. She decided that the best thing to do was to ignore his insults, to keep talking as if he had never said such cruel things.

"The laird of Bellefleur is going to come and avenge the treachery at the river."

Duggan shrugged. "Someone is always clamoring at the gates of Kengarvey. We will drive them away as we have always done, and we will rebuild."

"Not this time, Father." She tensed when his eyes narrowed and he leaned closer to her. "The laird of Bellefleur is acting under the king's command. 'Twas at Sir Gabel's urgings that the king allowed him to try and bring about a bloodless peace. He willna give ye a second chance."

"I dinna believe I asked the bastard for one."

There was such a tight coldness in her father's voice that Ainslee almost stopped and fled the room, for she knew his temper was stirring. "Father, 'twill be no small battle ye face this time, no squabble with the MacFibhs or sword-clashing with the Frasers. Ye have signed your death warrant, and that of everyone here."

"I have had the threat of death looming o'er me for years. I am thinking that ye have stayed with those Norman interlopers for too long, for 'tis clear that ye have forgotten who ye speak to, lass."

"Nay, I ken exactly who I speak to—the laird of Kengarvey." His growing anger terrified her, but she felt a flicker of her own temper seep up through her fear. The man was refusing to listen, refusing to see how much danger he had put them all in. " 'Tis time ye acted like the laird and gave some thought to your people." Her voice rose to a startled squeak when he suddenly leapt to his feet and grabbed her by the front of her gown.

"The bruises I gifted ye with before arena even gone, and yet ye stand here and beg for another beating."

"I but try to save some of the people of Kengarvey. The bloodletting that will soon come will leave no mon, womon, or child alive. Canna ye see that?"

She bit back a cry when he slapped her and tossed her to the floor. Shaking with fear, she stood up to face him again. " 'Twill not only be Sir Gabel who rides here, sword raised high, but every other enemy ye have. We shall face a sea of men who hate you, and wish to see every MacNairn rotting on the ground. Do ye care nothing for your own people?" She neatly ducked his swing, but knew she could not avoid his fists for long. "If ye canna save yourself, at least think of the bairns, of your sons."

Before she could say another thing, he set upon her with a

fury she could not evade. She fell beneath the strength of his blows. Curling up, she tried to avoid the full force of his kicks, but the pain he inflicted soon had her reeling close to unconsciousness. When he pulled her to her feet by her hair, she tried to cover her face, and he struck her in the stomach. Then, suddenly, she was free of his grasp. Her eyes already swelling shut, she could not see clearly, but she knew Colin had leapt to her rescue again. To her astonishment, her father immediately stepped back.

"Ye push my love for ye to its verra limits, laddie," Duggan said, his voice hoarse from the fury still possessing him.

"Ye canna kill the lass," said Colin.

"I wasna trying to kill her. I was just beating some respect into her dim-witted head. The lass thinks she is better than she is just because she spread her legs for some laird the king favors."

"She was trying to help Kengarvey. She is afraid. That is all."

"If she wished to help Kengarvey so badly, she should have asked that rutting Norman for a few favors whilst he was spilling his seed into her. Aye, and if there is some bastard growing in her belly, e'en ye willna stop me from beating it out of her."

"Let me take her to her room," Colin said as he picked Ainslee up in his arms. "Then ye dinna need to see her."

"I had better not see the whore for a verra long time," Duggan yelled after his son as Colin began to walk out of the great hall.

"Are ye mad?" snapped Colin as he started up the steps to her bedchamber.

"I wished to try and save Kengarvey, or at least some of it," she replied, slumping against his shoulder and wondering if her words sounded as slurred to him as they did to her.

"Why dinna ye just try and think of keeping *yourself* alive?"

"We will all be slaughtered if our father doesna try to make amends."

"I dinna think he can make amends now. No king can look strong, yet forgive a mon for the many crimes and treachery Father has committed. Our father has made no attempt to hide his scorn of the king. I was surprised when we were offered a chance to make a treaty. We shall ne'er get a second chance."

Ainslee made no reply as Colin called over a timid maid who lurked in the hallway. She helped Colin put her to bed and tend her wounds, then scurried away. Wincing as she did so, Ainslee leaned against her pillow and sipped at the mead Colin served her as he sat on the edge of the bed. It hurt her mouth to drink, and she knew it was bruised, cut, and swollen again.

"Father ne'er will," she agreed. "Gabel is willing to extend the hand of peace to any who wish to lay down their arms."

"Ye sound so certain of that."

"I am. If only Gabel were facing us, I would have no fear for the innocent and helpless ones trapped within the walls of Kengarvey. Gabel would ne'er hurt them. Howbeit, 'twill not be just Gabel."

"I am nay sure I can accept your word that the mon would be so kind to MacNairns. Aye, 'tis clear that he was kind to you and to the old mon, but the mon was sharing your bed, and we all ken that no one can hurt Ronald without ye stepping to his aid."

"Gabel was kind to me ere I even let him kiss me. I wish I could make someone here listen to me," she said, her voice unsteady, shaken by pain and a growing frustration.

"If ye keep trying, ye will be dead, and then ye will ne'er see your fine Norman knight again, nor help anyone when the battle finally commences." He gently patted her on the arm when she looked at him, her annoyance and disappointment clear to read in her expression. "Rest, Ainslee. E'en if the weather holds fine, our doom canna ride to our gates for another fortnight or so, and we may yet have until the spring."

"And ye think that shall change anything?"

It did not really surprise her when Colin just smiled and

then left. She had had very little to do with Colin, and she decided that her brother was very good at not answering questions. As carefully as she could, she eased her body down until she was flat on her back. He was right. There was still time, even if it might only be a fortnight. It was not enough time, however, for her to heal and then try to convince someone at Kengarvey to seek peace, even if only for themselves and their families. She knew she would try at least once more, but then she would start to try and find a way to save her own neck.

Ainslee whispered a curse as she started to slide along the wall. It had only been a week since her father had beaten her for the second time in a fortnight. Gaining the new injuries on top of ones that had not completely healed, had left her still feeling sore and weak. She could no longer stay in bed, however. No one was listening to her, except for the timid little maid who brought her her food and helped her when she was still too weak to get out of bed. Ainslee feared that, although the maid had agreed to go to Gabel or one of his men if the battle turned against the MacNairns, the girl was so scared of everyone and everything that she would probably get herself killed.

"Or try to make a treaty with the wrong people," Ainslee muttered as she crept by the battered doors of the great hall.

It was after her last talk with Colin that she decided she had wasted enough time, and that she now had to consider her own safety. Her brother had actually spent some time with her, either talking or playing chess. At times she thought he was not her companion, but her guard, then she had silently apologized for that mistrust. If Colin was guarding her, it was only to insure that she did not do something foolish, such as trying to talk to Duggan MacNairn again.

The cold slapped her in the face as she eased out of the heavy doors and crept into the bailey. Ainslee shivered, and hugged her small bundle of supplies and clothes a little closer.

It was not a long distance from the door of the keep to the gates of Kengarvey, but, as she stared across it, it looked like miles. The men on the walls were looking for an attack, not for one tiny woman to run away, but she too easily recalled the few who had tried to leave before her and their fates.

Keeping to the shadows and trying not to make a sound, she scurried to the shelter of the high walls next to the gates. Here there was a small thick door, banded in iron and bolted tightly. Once outside of it, Ainslee was sure she could disappear into the night, but it was not going to be easy to open it.

Tiptoeing past the sleeping gatekeeper huddled in his tiny lean-to, she set down her pack and inched the bar out of its slots, wincing at every tiny sound it made. She took a long time to lay the heavy wooden bar down on the frozen ground, breathing a hearty but silent sigh of relief when she was able to do so without making a sound. Collecting her precious supplies, she eased the door open and slipped out.

Nearly giddy with her success, she had to fight the urge to run straight across the open land and into the wood encircling Kengarvey. Her heart pounding, she stayed to the shadows as much as she could, and made her cautious walk to the wood. She had until morning to put as much distance between herself and Kengarvey as possible and, the moment she reached the shelter of the woods, she walked with a surer and much faster pace.

There was barely an hour left before dawn when she finally gave up her fight against exhaustion and all the pain in her battered body. Finding what she hoped was a suitable hiding place amongst some thick hedges, she spread one blanket on the ground, used the second to wrap herself in, and laid down to get some rest.

A murmur of annoyance escaped Ainslee as a sound pulled her from her deep sleep. She then remembered where she was and, more importantly, why she was there, and clapped a hand over her mouth. Even the smallest of noises could easily give away her hiding place. Fighting to wake up, she lay as flat on her belly as she was able. A cold knot formed low in her stomach when she saw the men peering around the small clearing. Her father's men had found her.

When she espied Colin walking side by side with George, both of her brothers closely studying the ground as they tried to find some trail, Ainslee fought the deep feeling of betrayal that gripped her. Her brothers were her father's pawns. They would do as Duggan MacNairn told them to, and even the risk to their own sister's life would not make them hesitate. Ainslee realized that, except for Colin, she was not sure if her father's men would kill her or just capture her. Duggan MacNairn treated all attempts to escape as a serious crime, as serious as betrayal.

Watching a frowning Colin search for her made her also feel a little guilty. It was clear that Colin would not kill her or allow their father to, but it could cost Colin dearly if she *did* escape. Their father would blame him for that error, and the punishment would be brutal. Colin might well be Duggan MacNairn's favored son, but that would never stop the man from giving his son a painful beating.

She fought down her sympathy for the brother who had helped to keep her alive. It was a weakness that could make her do something extremely foolish, such as allowing him to capture her in the mistaken belief that he could continue to protect her and that it would save him from their father's anger. Ainslee knew she had to think of herself now.

Holding her breath, she carefully inched back, away from the men searching for her. Her hiding place would not be safe for very much longer, and she had to find another. One of the men would soon see what a perfect hiding place it was. She nervously rolled up her blankets, hating to take the time, but knowing she was going to need them. Crouched as low as she could get while still being able to move with stealth and speed, she slipped out of the hedges and crept away.

A sense of panic began to choke her as she frantically searched for another hiding place or a way to elude all the men looking for her. Somewhere she had made a mistake, left some hint of a trail that one of the men had seen. As she approached a tiny clearing, she saw that across it lay wood so thick it would be easy to lose herself within it and leave no trail. She looked all around to be sure none of the men were at hand, that she had some small chance of making it across the clearing without being seen. Taking a deep breath to strengthen her wavering courage, she bolted toward the wood.

It did not really surprise her when a cry went up from the men. From the moment they had appeared to thrash the brush all around her, she had anticipated capture. Ainslee still cursed the fates which seemed determined to keep her from saving anyone at Kengarvey, including herself. She kept running, darting from side to side in an effort to elude the hands trying to grab her. Suddenly a horse loomed up in front of her, and she stumbled to a halt. When she saw her father glaring down at her, she panicked and ran, not caring where she was going, just that she escape her father.

She cursed when one of the men tackled her to the ground. It knocked all of the air from her lungs, stealing her ability to fight his hold. As he dragged her to her feet she caught a glimpse of Colin and George running her way, but she feared that this time Colin would be too late. Her father was riding her way, and he had his sword in his hand. She heard the man holding her whisper a curse, and realized that she was not the only one who believed her father was about to cut her down.

"Ye filthy little whore," her father snarled as he reined in before her. "Did ye think to run back to your Norman stallion and tell him all he needed to ken so that he could destroy me?"

A courage born of a resignation to her fate made Ainslee say, "Fool! If I was going to my Norman, why have I run north? Canna ye open your drunken eyes enough to see where ye are?"

A soft cry of surprise escaped her when she was suddenly released and pushed away from the man holding her. She barely escaped the full blow of her father's sword, and realized her captor had merely been trying to elude the murderous rage her father was in. Fighting to avoid the hooves of her father's massive horse, Ainslee tensed for his next strike. The second one came so swiftly that she nearly fell, she had to move so fast to avoid it. The sound of her cape and dress ripping, the feel of the steel grazing her skin beneath the tears, told her how close death had come. She could hear her brothers shouting, but dared not take her eyes from her father. Her only hope of staying alive was to be quicker than his sword.

Even as she leapt to elude yet another swing of his sword, she was astonished to see all four of her brothers attack her father. They pulled the ranting man off of his horse, and, as George and Martin tried to hold the man down, Colin and William moved to flank her. Panting from fear and the efforts of staying alive, Ainslee was only able to stare at them all in stunned silence, tensely awaiting what would happen next.

"Bastards!" screamed Duggan as he thrust off his sons and stood up, his sword still in his hand. In a dangerous rage, he swung it at George and Martin, who danced out of its reach, then looked at Ainslee. "Ye are all traitorous bastards!"

"Ye canna kill your own flesh and blood, your own daughter, for sweet Jesu's sake," Colin yelled back, and he held his sword at the ready when his father took a threatening step toward him.

"And when did all of ye become so enamored of this stupid lass?" Duggan demanded, glaring at all of his sons.

"Whate'er we think of the lass doesna matter," said Martin, his deep voice tight with fear and anger. "Ye canna kill her."

"The laws of God and this land say I can do whate'er I wish to with the whore," said Duggan, but he sheathed his sword. "She was trying to betray me."

"I have spent a long time with the monks, Father, and no-where was it written or said that ye have the right to murder your own child," Colin said in a cold, calm voice. "If such a sin could be yours alone, I dinna believe we would all have the courage to stop you, but the blood would cling to our hands as weel, simply because we could have stopped it and did not. Ye may do as ye wish with your immortal soul, but we canna allow your fury to blacken ours as weel."

Ainslee watched as her father fought back the fury that had inspired him to try and murder her in cold blood. She suddenly realized that it was not only Colin's being a favored son which gave her brother that tiny bit of power over her father, but the fact that Colin had been with the monks and had been educated by them. Despite the multitude of sins her father had commit-ted, despite the fact that he had little chance of salvation, Dug-gan MacNairn still held all the deep fears of the church and damnation so many others did.

"I want the lass locked up," Duggan said in a cold voice.

"I will see that she is weel secured in her bedchambers," Colin vowed.

"Nay," snapped Duggan. "Throw the traitorous whore into the dungeons."

"But, Father—"

"Ye heard me, son. Throw her in the dungeon. I willna have her creeping back to her Norman lover to betray all of us."

Ainslee opened her mouth to defend herself yet again against the charge of treason to the clan, but Colin tightened his grip on her arm until she gasped. Despite her need to prove her innocence, if not to her father, at least to the others gath-ered around, she fell silent. Colin was right. It would set her father's temper afire again, and this time she had come far too close to death to challenge that opinion.

Her other three brothers dared to cast her a sympathetic look as Colin dragged her to his horse. She thought crossly that, although they had stopped her father from cutting her down on the spot, they would do no more to aid her, so what good was their sympathy? It would not surprise her if they thought she had brought this down on her own head, and that they had done her a great service by keeping her alive. Rotting away in her father's dungeons was not what she considered life.

To her relief Colin rode behind the others, despite her father's constant glares. She did not wish to be in the midst of the men or very close to her father. Slowly, as they rode back to Kengarvey, despair and a deep pain began to seep through her fear and anger. It was hard to accept that her own father, the man whose seed had made her, would try to murder her. All the beatings had not brought that realization into her heart and mind as clearly as his attacking her with his sword.

"I always kenned that my father had no love for me, mayhaps for any of us, despite his claims that he loves you and his other sons," she said to Colin as she slumped against him, her gaze fixed upon her father's broad back. "I just ne'er realized that he hates me."

"Nay—" Colin began.

"Aye. Dinna try to soothe my feelings with lies. The times he nearly killed me with a beating, one could at least assume that his fury made him blind to how badly he was beating me. When the mon is trying to take my head from my shoulders with a sword and needs to be held back by his own kinsmen, 'tis clear that he loathes me. I canna ignore it, yet I canna think why he should have such hate for me. I have done naught to the mon. Most of the time I have been alive, I have done my best to stay out of his way."

"Ye ken that father has little use for women."

"Aye, save to make more sons and he has e'en given that up, believing women canna e'en do that chore correctly. 'Tis not enough to explain it. His hasna gone about killing women, not that I ken anyway."

Colin laughed, but it was not a pleasant sound. "Nay, although he has beaten a few near to death. I am sorry, Ainslee, but I long ago came to believe that your crime—the reason our father loathes you—is because ye are alive."

She frowned as she glanced over her shoulder at him. "I dinna understand. I may have been but a bairn e'er our mother died, but I canna remember this hatred. I believe I was alive then, too," she drawled, and Colin smiled crookedly.

"Aye, ye were, and so was our mother," he added solemnly.

"He canna blame me for our mother's death," she whispered, shock and disbelief robbing her of her voice.

"Nay. The only thing our father loved about our mother was that she had a skill at producing live sons. That was shown when he fled Kengarvey and left her to face the Frasers. He kenned what fate that would mean for her."

"So, if his hate comes from that black day, why was it born?"

"Because ye didna have the grace to die with your mother. Every time he looks at you, he hears the whispered condemnation of his cowardly desertion of her. He may not have loved her, but many another did. Any who hear how she died wonder how he could have left his wife and child to face the Frasers, who are weel kenned for their brutality and the way they kill everyone in a battle, warrior and bairn alike. Ye are a walking reminder of his shame."

"I didna think our father felt any shame."

"Nay, and I am not sure he actually feels he is responsible in any way for our mother's death. Howbeit, the one thing he is feverishly protective of is his reputation for courage. There was no courage shown when he left her behind. If he could save himself, then he should have been able to save his wife and little daughter. Mother saved you." Colin sighed. "When we returned to Kengarvey and he found you sitting amongst the ashes, he almost cut you down then and there, but Ronald and I stopped him. Ronald and I have continued to stop him. I had hoped that his hate would fade, but it has only deepened."

"And one day neither ye nor Ronald will be around to stop

him," she murmured, and shivered when Colin offered her no reassurance of continued protection. "If I remain at Kengarvey, I am dead. Didna our sisters ken this?"

"Aye, they have always kenned that father loathes you, although they have never asked why."

"Yet they have ne'er offered to take me into their homes, where I would be safe."

"Aye, ye would be safe, but our sisters dinna think they would be, or rather that their men would be."

"They canna think that I would try and steal their men or, weel, cuckold them?"

"Aye, they can and they do. Ainslee, ye understand honor and trust and all of that, for Ronald has taught it to ye. I only learned what little I ken from the monastery. Our sisters may not be as steeped in crime and sin as our father, but they have his heart and mind. They would rather ye die at our father's hands than chance their husbands eyeing ye with lust." He shrugged. "I am sorry, for I ken that this must hurt you, but mayhaps 'tis past time that ye knew a few truths."

"All of ye have kenned this for all of these years, and yet I am still here? I can understand Ronald not taking me away, yet could none of ye help me flee? Unlike Ronald, ye have the freedom to go where ye please, and ye ken the safest way out of Kengarvey."

"And that would be the surest way to cut our own throats. We may stop our father from killing you, Ainslee, but more than that and we truly risk our own lives. Aye, we may all be cowards, but the one lesson anyone learns weel at Kengarvey is how to stay alive."

She fell silent, knowing that she could never convince him to help her escape. He had to make the hard choice of saving her or himself, and she could understand his decision to just try and keep them both alive. It terrified her though, for she knew now that no one would help her get out of the dungeon. She could not even hope for her father to have a change of mind, as the man obviously hoped that she would die in the dungeons, as so many others had.

It was almost sunset when they finally returned to Kengarvey. Ainslee was surprised at how far she had managed to travel in the dark and cold. Now, however, she knew that she would have failed, even if she had managed to reach her sisters. If everything Colin had said was true, and she had no reason to doubt him, then her sisters would have handed her back to her father. Steeped in sadness and a sense of hopelessness, she suspected that any of her kinsmen would have done the same. They may have turned their backs on Duggan MacNairn, but she was sure they still feared him.

When she was taken from Colin's horse and dragged into Kengarvey, she fought to hide her fear. It did not help her when she was separated from Colin. He would still have put her in the dungeons as her father had ordered, but his presence would have given her some strength. If nothing else, she might have deluded herself into thinking that someone would remember her and, even if they would not free her, would keep her from dying in the damp bowels of the keep. The cold-eyed, barrel-chested man dragging her down to the dungeons would forget her the moment he shut the heavy iron door.

Despite all her efforts to show courage, Ainslee gave a soft cry of terror when the man shoved her into a damp cell and slammed the door. The musky air, the dark, and the damp chill all terrified her. From the earliest days of her childhood, she had understood that the dungeons of Kengarvey were where people were sent to die. She winced as her jailer turned the key in the lock, then closed her eyes and shuddered as she listened to him walk away.

Slowly she walked to the tiny board bed in the corner, and warily sat down on the rat-gnawed mattress. Ainslee fought the blind terror that tried to possess her heart and mind. She should at least wait a while before she went mad, she thought a little bitterly. Glancing around, the light from one torch in the wall too dim to allow her a clear view of anything, she could feel the ghosts of the poor souls who had been there before her, and wondered just how real they might soon become to her.

A tall, thin man entered the dungeons and sat on a hard stool opposite her cell. He said nothing to her, so she ignored him. She could not understand how her father could still be so concerned about her escaping that he would put a guard on her, for no one had left the cells beneath Kengarvey except to be carried to the graveyard. Ainslee also knew that the squint-eyed man watching her would do absolutely nothing to help her. He might well have been set there just to see how long it would take her to starve to death.

Ainslee shook away that dark thought, for it stirred up the terror she barely held in check. She had to fix her mind on something else, no matter how impossible that something was. If God would heed her prayers, she might survive, she might even escape, and this time she would head back to Bellefleur, and she might still be able to save some of her clan. And Gabel would soon come to Kengarvey, there was no doubt in her mind about that. She could only pray that he would come in time.

Seventeen

"There has been yet another fight between one of our men and one of the Frasers," announced Justice as he strode into Ronald's room without knocking, knowing that Gabel would be there.

Gabel cursed, rose from where he sat on the edge of Ronald's bed, and began to angrily pace the room. Only a week had passed since he had spoken with the king and received his liege's unsatisfactory command. He had barely dismounted in the bailey of Bellefleur three days later when the Frasers had begun to arrive. From the first moment Fraser's hirelings and kinsmen had begun to gather, there had been trouble. One of his men had even been murdered, and his swift hanging of the guilty man, a distant cousin of Lord Fraser, had only made matters worse. Gabel dreaded the battle ahead, yet also ached to ride to Kengarvey. It would at least put an end to the turmoil and danger of having Bellefleur swarming with Frasers.

"Was anyone hurt?" he asked as he paused by Ronald's bedside table and helped himself to some mead.

"Nay," replied Justice, waving aside Gabel's silent offer of a drink. "A few bruises. Some of our men put an end to it just as the Fraser man drew a knife."

"Ye have to get these mad dogs out of Bellefleur," Ronald said as he eased himself up into a sitting position, wincing a little, but shaking his head when Gabel tried to assist him. "I dinna need help, laddie. It pains me some, but I can do it without hurting meself, and, if I dinna make meself move now and again, I will rot in this bed." He sighed as he sank back against his pillows. "Those Frasers have been naught but trouble since the first one slithered through the gates three days ago."

"I know," agreed Gabel, sitting back down on the edge of Ronald's bed. "I should have made them camp outside the walls, but I never thought they would cause this much trouble."

"Ye arena witless, but too often ye do put too much trust in others, expecting them all to act as ye would. Canna ye throw them outside the walls now?"

"Nay, not without causing a grievous insult to Sir Fraser, and I dare not do that, not until I have settled the matter of Kengarvey to the king's satisfaction."

"Ye really believe that the king is displeased with you?"

"Not as deeply as I feared he would be, but, aye, he is displeased. His offer to give me Kengarvey and whomever I am able to save was not the gracious gift some might think it to be. He feels that all of the MacNairns are a curse, and that I will be sadly beset in trying to rule them. He also knows that both the Frasers and the MacFibhs covet the lands there. They are unhappy that I will gain Kengarvey, and they will cause me some difficulty. And let us not forget that there are other kinsmen to Duggan MacNairn besides the ones the king considers outlaws. They too will think I have usurped what is rightfully theirs. Aye, 'tis a reward, but one carrying a few hard curses with it."

"There will be few at Kengarvey who will fight your rule when Duggan is finally dead."

"Not even his sons?" asked Justice.

"Nay," replied Ronald. "The one thing those lads have learned is how to survive. They will have the wit to ken that, under you, they can do that with more comfort and more ease than they have e'er done beneath the fists of their father."

"And they will not feel a need for vengeance for the death of their father?"

"Nay, I think not. Aye, most children love their parents no

matter how foolish those parents are, but Duggan MacNairn has beaten all the love out of his children. They are terrified of the mon, no more. If they obey, 'tis out of fear. They dinna leave him, for they love Kengarvey, although Duggan has made it little better than a hovel with all his fighting. Nay, those sons willna seek to make anyone pay for their father's death; they may even be more loyal to the mon who kills him, for they will finally be free. The only thing I fear is that they will allow Duggan to take them to their deaths."

"I will do my best to save them," Gabel said.

"I ken it. I have had little to do with Martin, George, and William, but I canna believe I am wrong to say that they dinna carry their father's taint. Colin has little of his father in him, and he is the one I will grieve for if Duggan gets him killed. Howbeit, I realize that ye canna save all of the fools, laddie."

"At the moment I seem incapable of even helping my own men who are so sorely beset by those cursed Frasers." Gabel frowned when Michael suddenly burst into the room. "Does no one knock anymore?"

"My pardons, cousin, but I bring good news," Michael said as he fought to catch his breath. "The laird of the MacFibhs is here."

"The laird himself?"

"Aye," Michael said, but before he could say any more a huge, black-haired man marched into the room.

Gabel immediately recognized the lord of the MacFibhs, even though he had only met the man once. Angus MacFibh was hard to forget. The man stood head and shoulders over most men, was built as strong as the finest destrier, and had a huge red scar marring his square, homely face. He wore mostly rough peasant attire and a thick cape made of wolf's fur. Sir Angus started toward him, but as Gabel stood to greet the man, the Scot stopped abruptly and stared at Ronald.

"Ye treat the enemy verra kindly," Angus said, eyeing Gabel warily, his hand on his sword.

"I do not consider this man an enemy," Gabel replied in a

calm and courteous voice, but he was angered by the look of mistrust on Angus's face.

"He is one of those cursed MacNairns, isna he? Didna our king say that the whole nest of them needed to be cleared out?"

"Our king also said that I may save any of them I wish to, except for Duggan MacNairn. I am of a mind to save Ronald."

"And I am of a mind to make Kengarvey bleed. Are we to be working against each other, my laird?"

"I think not, not if you do not try to stop me. After all, what good is Kengarvey to me if I have no one to work its lands?"

"There are a lot of MacFibhs who would do that for you."

"I am sure, and I shall remember that they are there if I have need of them. May I ask why you have come to Bellefleur? I expected a mere messenger to come and tell me that you were ready to attack, not the laird himself."

"I felt this battle was important enough to tell ye meself that I am ready." Angus scratched his belly and spared another glare for Ronald. "I am eager to ride beside ye as we set upon those MacNairn swine."

Gabel sent Ronald one sharp look when the man began to speak, eager to answer MacFibh's insults with a few of his own, and, although he grumbled and scowled, Ronald obeyed the silent command to be quiet. After a few moments of polite murmurings between him and Angus, Gabel had Michael take Lord MacFibh to his chambers, where he could rest after his hard ride. The moment the door closed behind the man, Gabel cursed and poured himself another tankard of mead.

"The arrogance of that man is nearly choking," grumbled Justice as he too helped himself to a drink.

"The smell of him isna too healthy either," muttered Ronald, but he managed a smile when both Justice and Gabel grinned.

Gabel frowned as he sat at the end of Ronald's bed, leaned against the bedpost, and took a long drink of his mead. "I do not see it as a compliment that MacFibh himself has come to tell me that all his men are gathered. I also find the man's eagerness to kill MacNairns a little chilling."

Ronald nodded then shrugged. "I can understand his hatred, even though I think it most unfair that he feels it for all Mac-Nairns. Duggan has a lot of MacFibh blood on his hands. He has killed a fair number of Angus's close kin, and sometimes left the MacFibh lands so battered and burnt that people starved ere things could be put aright again."

"So, even if I do not have trouble from him about the lands themselves, I may well have trouble protecting MacNairns."

"Aye. He willna stop hating us simply because we have a new laird."

"And we have already had a taste of what treachery the Frasers are capable of."

"Mayhaps you can be rid of the place after the king's temper has cooled, and he is feeling more generous toward you," said Justice.

"Nay," Gabel answered, and he shook his head. "I am the one who will be taking the laird of MacNairn's life. 'Tis my duty to try and help the people who are left leaderless. And who would take the lands then? MacFibh? Fraser? If I give up the lands, the ones who will greedily take them up are men who will treat the people as poorly as their laird did. In truth, I would be handing Ainslee's people o'er to their executioners. 'Twould not be a very welcome wedding gift. I think I may have enough trouble explaining how 'tis not only her father's life I have taken, but her lands."

Ronald smiled crookedly. "She may be a wee bit angry, but I dinna think ye need to fear any great trouble from her o'er who rules Kengarvey."

"Nay? You do not think she will feel that one of her brothers ought to be made laird, and not me?"

"She kens that her brothers will be lucky to be alive. She also kens what a poor choice of lairds there is out there. Nay, she may feel angry with the king that her brothers are losing their birthright, when the crimes were of their father's making and not theirs, but she will nay fault ye."

Gabel wished he had Ronald's confidence, but did not argue with the man. "Well, I had best go and be courteous to my unwelcome guests. Fraser skulking about has been hard enough upon my poor aunt. I fear she may have to take to her bed after she meets that brutish Angus MacFibh."

"They willna all be here for verra long, will they?" asked Ronald.

"Nay. Now that the MacFibhs are prepared for the battle, we need not linger here any longer. If all of the Frasers are not here, that is their loss. I mean for us to ride to Kengarvey on the morrow."

"I will tell the men," said Justice even as he headed out of the door. "This is the news they have waited for."

As Gabel stood up, he glanced at Ronald. "I do not believe I have ever been so reluctant to go to battle."

"I ken it. Ye must do as the king commands and, although my heart sorely aches for my people, if any mon must be sent to end the troubles at Kengarvey, I am glad it will be you. I can rest easy kenning that, if God wills that any of my people survive, ye will treat them weel."

He nodded to Ronald, silently thanking him for his trust, but Gabel's heart was heavy as he left the room. The allies the king had sent him could neither be trusted nor liked. Bellefleur was crowded with brutish men who made no attempt to ally themselves with the men they would soon have to fight side by side with. Even his plans to show some mercy would be disobeyed, and he would not only have to fight for his life and those of his men, but for the people of Kengarvey who were willing to surrender to him. And, somewhere in the midst of all the duplicity and bloodshed, he had to try and find Ainslee before a Fraser or a MacFibh did.

Gabel knew that the next few days would be one of the worst ordeals he had ever had to suffer. He could only pray that he had the strength and wits to survive it, and to gain all he sought.

Ainslee blinked, her eyes hurt by the light of the extra torch Colin set into the wall. She had been in the dungeons for five long days, and this was only the second time Colin had come to see her. All the rest of the time she was virtually alone, her guards acting as if they sat before an empty cell. She was rather surprised that her father even bothered with the guards anymore. As she stood up and walked to the bars, she also wondered how Colin could get rid of the guards without bringing her father's wrath down on his head. She did notice that Colin was never left with the key.

A little embarrassed by her own greed, she snatched the bread and cheese he pushed through the bars. The meager offerings Colin had slipped her before were all she had had to eat since her imprisonment. Her father saw to it that she had water and nothing else. It was very clear that he intended to starve her to death. Her guards probably had to report on how sickly she had grown. That would soon cause trouble for Colin, however, for her father would become suspicious if she lingered too long.

"Are ye not afraid that the guards will tell our father what ye do?" she asked as she forced herself to slowly chew on a thin slice of the loaf of bread he had handed her.

"They willna tell him about my visits," Colin replied as he leaned against the bars.

"How can ye be so certain of that?"

"Because no one here ever tells our father what I am doing. In truth, only one or two of his hirelings would report on someone, but everyone is verra careful not to let them find out anything."

" 'Tis odd for I would have thought that they would seek his favor."

"Most all ken that our father's favor doesna last from one

hour to the next. They gain more by keeping their own counsel. It means that, every once in awhile, one can do as one pleases, and not fear that they face a beating or worse."

"How have I missed this?"

"Because ye didna need to join the conspiracy. Ye had Ronald." He frowned when she carefully placed the rest of the cheese and bread beneath her thin, worn blanket. "Why dinna ye finish that?"

"If I eat it all now, what shall I do about tomorrow or the next day?"

"Eat whate'er slop they are serving you," Colin replied, but he spoke with a slow wariness, tensing against the bars as he watched her.

"There is no slop, Colin," she said quietly, and watched a hint of color flood his high-boned cheeks. "I am given only water." She winced a little when he spat out a foul oath and slammed his fist against the bars, apparently oblivious to the pain that had to cause him.

"I begin to understand why it was so easy to get the guards to allow me down here with my meager offerings. Everyone kens that our father has ordered that no one be allowed to see you, and he promised a fierce punishment for anyone disobeying that command. I had expected to have to argue with the guards."

Ainslee smiled faintly. "I am also surprised the guards would allow it. They show no signs of their sympathies. They sit there and act as if I am but one of the many sad ghosts haunting this place."

"Father means to kill you—slowly."

"I ken it."

"Ye should have said something."

"I didna really accept that that was his intention until yestereve. I thought I was suffering through an added punishment, but that he would soon send me something. Ye have stopped him from beating me to death, and stopped him from cutting me down with his sword, so now he tries to quietly starve me. After all, who would question it if I died down here? People die in such places all the time. And, although some might frown upon putting one's own child in the dungeons, 'twill not cause him the troubles that simply murdering me would."

Colin dragged over the guard's stool and sat down, his hands clasped so tightly in his lap that they shone white in the flicker of the torches. "Mayhaps I can get the key."

"Nay." She rose, walked to the bars, and reached through to clasp his hand. "That wouldna be allowed by the guards, for my escape would cost them their lives. Worse, it could easily cost ye yours. We both ken that there is only one way for me to flee Kengarvey without risk of capture, and, if ye tell me how to go that way, ye will do so at the risk of your own life."

"So I am to sit here and watch our father starve ye to death?"

"Aye, although I dinna think it will come to that."

"Nay? He will soon realize that ye are living too long when fed only water every day. I am certain that I shall be the first one he turns to when he suspects that someone has been feeding you, and he will do whate'er he must to see that it stops."

"Then mayhaps ye should cease to help me."

"Oh, aye? And lie comfortable in my bed, my belly full, while ye slowly die down here? Do ye think me completely without conscience?"

"I think that mayhaps ye have more than is safe for life inside Kengarvey." She smiled faintly when he grimaced. "The threat of damnation ye keep hurling at Father will soon cease to intimidate him."

"Ah, ye guessed my game. Ye always were the most clever one of us."

"Ye are not without wit."

"Mayhaps. I ken that I grow verra weary of using it simply to keep people alive. Kengarvey could be nearly as grand as

Bellefleur if Father would cease to waste its strength and wealth in battles and warring with all about us."

" 'Tis the way life has gone on here for many years. One does what one must to survive." She met his gaze and tried to be stern, knowing she could be risking her own life if she made him see sense. "Ye must protect yourself. Father forces everyone to that with his furies and cruelties. Ye may not wish to carry my death on your conscience, but neither do I wish to be the cause of yours."

"I begin to think that there is no answer to this dilemma. If I help you, I do so at risk to myself. If I protect myself and dinna help, then ye slowly die. No one should be given such a choice. Nay, especially by one's own father."

"Then we must pray that the king decides he has had a stomach full of our father's insults, and sends an army here."

"Oh, aye, and then we both die."

Ainslee laughed, surprised that she could find any humor in such a desperate situation. "Ye should be trying to cheer me, Colin."

Colin smiled crookedly. "I canna cheer myself from hour to hour. Ye expect a great deal from a mere mon." He quickly grew somber again. "I suppose one can only laugh when there is nowhere to turn and little hope. Howbeit, someone coming to end our father's tyranny doesna seem to me to be a thing to hope for. Whichever one of our enemies is sent, he will be determined to see all of us pay for Duggan MacNairn's sins and arrogance."

"Nay, not Gabel."

"Ye see with the clouded eyes of a lass in love."

"Mayhaps a wee bit, but I am not completely blind. Gabel doesna wish to wipe Kengarvey from the earth. Aye, he will kill our father now, but the laird of Bellefleur isna a mon who will make every mon, woman, and bairn pay for the wrongs of the laird. I can think of no way to make ye believe me, except to keep saying this. Howbeit, repeating myself doesna make ye heed me, does it?"

"Nay, and I am sorry for that. I should like to believe it, for it would give me hope, but I have learned that hope isna such a good thing at Kengarvey either. 'Tis too often crushed, and one gets weary of it, thus ceases to hope." He stood up and briefly clasped her hands through the bars. "I will do what I can to aid you." He touched a finger to her lips when she started to speak. "Nay, there is no use in warnings and protestations. I do what I must. And I shall pray that ye are right, and that the laird of Bellefleur truly does have mercy in his soul. I will also pray that, when the king sends an army against us, 'tis lead by de Amalville."

She grimaced as she watched him leave. Gabel had lost his wager that he could make the laird of Kengarvey accept a truce and hold to a vow. That may well have cost him the king's confidence. As she went back to her bed and lethargically watched her silent guard return, she decided she had best do a little praying as well. She would ask God to give the people of Kengarvey one last chance, and let Gabel lead the army that would soon come clamoring at the walls.

It was the only hope any of them had for survival.

Gabel kissed his aunt and young Elaine farewell, smiling kindly at their commands that he protect himself. They were not good at hiding their fears each time he had to ride off to battle, but they did not beleaguer him with them. This time he knew they had good reason to fear for him. Not only was he riding off to fight an enemy, but the men the king had forced him to accept as allies were little more than enemies themselves. This time he not only rode toward danger, he rode with it.

Mounting his horse, he smiled faintly and patted Malcolm's strong neck. He had put the animal through many a test to judge his worthiness as a war-horse, and the animal had passed each and every one with admirable skill. Someone had taught the animal well. It did strike him as a little ironic to ride a

MacNairn horse to a battle with the people of Kengarvey, but he could not set aside such a battle-worthy animal just because it used to be Ainslee's mount.

As he rode through the gates of Bellefleur, Michael and Justice quickly moving up to flank him, he glanced back at the men crowding behind him, some on horseback, some on foot. The bloodthirsty eagerness of the Frasers and the Mac-Fibhs still chilled him. What troubled him more at the moment, however, was the way the two had joined forces. He knew that he and his men were alone in the fight ahead. Their allies would help in that they would kill the men they had to fight, but he knew that not one of the MacFibhs or the Frasers could be trusted to watch his back or those of his men. A chill went down his spine when he caught Fraser staring at him. In truth, he began to suspect that he would have to carefully watch his own back against a traitorous attack by his allies.

"I had prayed that the king would have a change of heart and call back these dogs," murmured Justice.

Gabel smiled faintly as he turned his attention to the road they had to travel. "That would have eased my mind, but I do not believe our king realizes that he might well have put all of us in danger. He wants Duggan MacNairn dead, and he knows that the Frasers and MacFibhs will do it. I fear our king is no longer so certain that I will accomplish the task."

"He cannot believe that you would betray him with Mac-Nairn," Michael whispered in shock and outrage.

"Nay, but he no longer wishes to show mercy, and I think he feels I am too endowed with that quality. MacNairn is a traitor, and the penalty a traitor must pay by law is a long and gruesome death. It is intended to make all others obey the king out of a fearful loyalty. I think our king would not be pleased if my sense of mercy forced him to execute MacNairn himself. He wants the man killed in battle."

"He fears how his other lairds will act if he must brutally kill one of their number, no matter how wrong the man is," said Justice.

"Aye. He is surrounded by a troublesome lot and, although none act as brazenly as MacNairn, the king must tread warily, carefully weighing every action and word. This is not an easy kingdom to rule."

"Well, we cannot smooth the way for him except in this small corner."

"And that we will do on the morrow."

"You do not think we will reach Kengarvey today?"

"Nay. If we march too swiftly, we will tire the men who are afoot, and they will not be able to fight their best. We would also arrive near nightfall or even in the dark, and I do not wish to camp within sight of the MacNairns. Nay, we will camp at least an hour's ride from Kengarvey, and finish the journey on the morrow."

When the sun began to set and Gabel ordered a halt, he was met with an immediate argument from Fraser and MacFibh. Nearly an hour was lost as the pair bellowed their disapproval, and threatened to continue on without him. The fact that they knew that would sit ill with the king was the only thing that stopped them from splitting the army, riding straight for Kengarvey, and putting every plan in jeopardy. When Gabel was finally able to sit with his cousins and eat, he was so furious that he barely tasted the food his page served him.

"Arrogant bastards," muttered Justice as he watched the Frasers and the MacFibhs, who had camped at a small distance from the men of Bellefleur.

"They have scented my weakness," murmured Gabel as he tossed aside his empty plate and took a long drink of wine.

"What do you mean—your weakness? I see none."

"Look more closely, cousin. The king's disapproval may be small, but I am still marked by it. That 'tis only slight is all that keeps that rabble from rushing off, from completely ignoring any command I may utter. Howbeit, Fraser and MacFibh see a chance to pull me down lower in the king's esteem and, if they can find a way to do it, they will act upon it without compunction."

"So, you believe it may not only be the MacNairns we must watch, that we may have to protect ourselves—and especially you—from the conspiracies of Fraser and his new lacky MacFibh."

"I am certain of it. Each time I look toward Fraser, I find the man glaring at me. He is my enemy as much as MacNairn is. Aye, I must watch the man closely, or he may well try to use the battle to be rid of me."

"You mean you think he may try to murder you?"

" 'Tis what the man does to those he feels are in his way or have done him some wrong. He has gone without punishment for so long because he plays his deadly games with a subtlety MacNairn lacks, and because, as of yet, he has not killed anyone the king holds in high esteem. There is something that troubles me far more than Fraser's possible plots to kill me or dishonor me."

Justice shook his head. "What could trouble you more than that?"

"Fraser knows that Ainslee was my lover. I suspect he also knows that she is the one I was thinking of when I asked to be allowed to show some mercy to any of the MacNairns, save Duggan, who request it. What I fear is that he will seek to reach Ainslee first and kill her, if only to strike at me."

"I begin to dread this battle more and more," muttered Michael. " 'Tis not a comfort to know that we ride to fight one enemy whilst surrounded by others. In battle you want men who will watch your back. Now you tell me we shall have to watch our own against our *allies*, as well as against the MacNairns."

Gabel smiled crookedly and shrugged, detesting the situation, but knowing it could not be changed. "Then we shall fight alone. It should not be difficult, as the armies are already separated. Thus they shall remain. It will ne'er come to an open battle between us, so keeping our distance from our untrustworthy companions ought to serve well enough."

"You expect a great deal from all of us," said Justice.

"Ah, but 'tis naught which you cannot do with ease, such is your wit and skill."

Justice snorted with amused disgust over Gabel's effusive flattery. "When you try to use sweet words and guile to soothe our fears, I know we are in for trouble."

Gabel laughed with his cousins, but his good humor was fleeting. He wanted the battle over. He wanted the Frasers and the MacFibhs to slither back from whence they came. Most of all, he wanted Ainslee back in his bed, safe and unharmed. It was a lot to hope for, and all he could do was pray that God felt kindly enough to grant his wishes.

Eighteen

"There lies Kengarvey," murmured Justice as he reined in his horse next to Gabel.

"Aye, there it lies," Gabel agreed absently, his gaze fixed upon the newly rebuilt keep, but his mind fixed upon what he would be forced to do next.

Justice glanced over his shoulder at the men gathered behind them and waiting to start the battle. They all waited within the thick wood, using the trees to hide their approach. If any of them moved forward more than a few yards, they would be in the expansive clearing surrounding Kengarvey, and the men stationed upon the high walls of Kengarvey would see them, unless they were blind or asleep. Justice was sure that their army thought that Gabel was making some important last judgement upon Kengarvey's strengths and weaknesses, but the Frasers and the MacFibhs would not be able to sit still for very much longer.

"Cousin, our allies begin to grow restless," he said, leaning closer to Gabel and hoping to shake the man free of his reverie.

Gabel briefly glanced back at the men and noticed how the Frasers and the MacFibhs were edging ever forward, each trying to stay but one step ahead of the other. "Each of them is so busy trying to insure that he and not the other man is in the lead, that they will soon creep out from the cover of the trees."

"I understand what makes you hesitate, Gabel, but, if you

mean to save any of the MacNairns on this day, it might be best if you did not linger here for too long."

"Nay, for, if I do, I am sure to be trampled into the dust by MacFibhs and Frasers, eager to begin their slaughter."

"They have been eager for that since the king told them that they could join us. Do you make new plans, or do you sit there hoping that some sorcery will allow you to see through those thick walls and find Ainslee before the battle even begins?"

A faint smile curved Gabel's mouth. "That would suffice to comfort me somewhat. And, nay, I do not make any new plans for the battle ahead. Tell our archers to be ready to do what is expected of them. Our charge will pull all eyes at Kengarvey our way, but only for a short while."

"I wish you well, cousin. Every Bellefleur man knows that they must try to find her before the others do. With so many eyes searching for her, I am certain that she will be found."

Gabel nodded, wanting to believe Justice's assurances, but unable to do so. He knew how a battle brought nothing but chaos and destruction. It could easily prove impossible to find Ainslee amongst all of the people who would be fighting, trying to flee for their lives or hiding from their enemies. Far too often he had been forced to wait until a battle was over before he could discover the fate of his own kinsmen, even when the de Amalvilles had been one of the victorious army. As he signaled his men, Gabel prayed that Ainslee had found some way to flee Kengarvey.

Ainslee frowned, an odd sound pulling her from her lethargy. She rose from her meager bed, and cursed under her breath when her first steps toward the bars were unsteady ones. The beatings she had endured while at Kengarvey, the cold damp of the dungeon, and the lack of food, all conspired to sap her strength. Her constant hunger slowed her healing, and made it hard to fight the ill effects of her dark prison.

Gripping the chill, slick bars, she looked over at her thin, narrow-eyed guard. In the week he had sat there staring at her, all she had been able to learn about him was that his name was Robert. That tiny scrap of information had come her way only because the other guard had once greeted him by name. After only two days she had ceased trying to end his silence, and had accepted his mute presence. The very evident uneasiness Robert was now revealing told Ainslee that her ears had not deceived her. She listened intently for a moment, and suddenly recognized what she heard. A chill snaked down her spine.

"We are under attack," she cried, torn between fear for herself, her brothers, and all the people of Kengarvey—and elation. A battle meant danger for them all, but it also meant that Gabel was close at hand.

"Nay," protested Robert, but there was little conviction in his voice, a voice amazingly deep for a man with such a slender chest. "Mayhaps your father is simply in one of his tempers."

"Weel, my father can have some gloriously loud and deadly rages, but ye must ken that we arena hearing the frightening sounds of his temper now. The battle has begun." When he still said nothing, she cursed softly and viciously. "Come, ye are one of my father's hirelings, and ye must have sold your sword to others ere ye came here. If I can recognize the sounds as those of a battle, then ye must as weel."

"Aye, ye may be right," he snapped, his inability to decide what to do next fraying his temper, "but I was told to stay here and guard you."

"And so ye want us to both sit here and merely wait for the enemy?"

"The enemy may ne'er get this far into Kengarvey."

"We could die here, fool."

"Mayhaps, but that isna certain, is it? 'Tis certain that, if I release you and we have misjudged what is happening above us, I *will* die, for your father will kill me for my failure without any hesitation."

There was no argument Ainslee could make to that, for it was the cold hard truth. She clutched the iron bars tightly as she fought her fear and rising temper, stirred by the man's inability to think for himself. She studied him closely for a moment as he paced, pausing only to scowl up the narrow stone steps leading up to the keep. It might serve her purpose better, she mused, if she played upon the man's deep desire to survive, as that appeared to concern him the most.

"Just heed me for a wee moment," she said, speaking in as calm and as pleasant a voice as she could muster, so that she did not anger or offend him. "What good will it do my father if we are both killed down here, or if I am snatched from his grasp once again, thus costing him more of his precious and scarce coin?" Seeing that her guard was mulling that over, she pressed on. "Mayhaps my father is right, and I am the laird of Bellefleur's lover. This could easily be him, coming to take me back to his bed. There can be no real harm done if ye simply go and try to discover what is wrong. If we are being attacked and, if Kengarvey is about to fall into the hands of our enemies, 'twould be wise to release me. My father would prefer me running free than to have me taken for ransom once again. After all, if I am alive and free, he can capture me later and kill me in his own cruel way, something we both ken he is trying to do."

"Aye, he does want ye dead, and so he may not care if ye are slain in battle."

"Oh, aye, he will mind, and ye ken it weel. My father appears to loathe me, and we both ken that he willna appreciate it if another mon's sword steals away his sport."

"Be still," Robert yelled as he dragged his fingers through his filthy black hair. "Aye, ye are right. 'Twould be best to discover exactly what is happening above our heads. I will return in but a few moments."

The moment he disappeared up the narrow, littered stairs,

Ainslee wanted him to come back. She knew that she was allowing her fears to make her foolish. There was only the smallest of chances that the man would protect her, and he was not the sort of companion who would do anything to help ease her fears as the battle raged around them. Her guard's only real concern in life was to stay alive, and she suspected that he would readily sacrifice her to accomplish that. All she could pray for was that he would return and let her know what she might have to face.

"Not that I may do anything about the danger hieing my way," she grumbled, and struck the bars with one small clenched fist. "I can do nothing else but sit here and await my fate."

She closed her eyes and took several deep breaths to try and calm herself. A full sense of calm and hope was impossible, but she was finally able to hold back the crippling sense of panic threatening to choke her. Ainslee knew that, as long as she remained locked in the dungeons, the best thing she could hope for was that the ones who were attacking her home contained some mercy in their souls. She tried to ignore that cold disheartening fact, but found it very hard to deceive herself.

As time crept slowly by, she grew more and more agitated. There was no doubt in her mind that a battle was raging over her head. The sounds grew more distinct with every passing moment. She paced her tiny damp cell, cursing her captivity, her father, her weakened state, and her lack of weapons.

Finally, she stopped, pressed against the bars, and closed her eyes. She tried to concentrate on the muffled noises that caused her to feel such alarm, praying that some noise would penetrate the thick stone surrounding her so clearly that she would learn what was going on. So intent was she on listening that, when the door at the head of the stairs was banged open, she jumped in alarm. The sounds that, for one brief moment, came distinctly through the open door, confirmed all of her fears. Kengarvey was in the midst of a fierce battle.

Her heart skipped with hope when she recognized the man running down the stairs. Colin himself was all that inspired that heady feeling, however, for his appearance justified all the dark terrors that had been preying upon her mind. He wore his padded jupon, his mail shirt, and his helmet. All were smeared with blood. What little she could see of his drawn face beneath his helmet was streaked with sweat, dirt, and blood. Even the sword he still held in his hand was badly bloodstained. Kengarvey must be falling to the enemy, for Colin would never have left the battle he had so clearly been in the midst of just to have a talk with her.

"Our enemies have come," he announced as he slumped against the bars and fought to catch his breath.

"And they are winning the battle," Ainslee said, only the slightest hint of a question in her voice.

"They are but a wee splinter or two away from breaking through our gates. They will also soon swarm o'er our walls. More men now slip o'er the parapets to fight us sword to sword than we are able to push back."

"Ye havena told me which of our enemies is attacking us." She tried to keep all of her hope out of her voice, but Colin's weary glance of irritation told her that she had failed.

"Your fine laird of Bellefleur is there, fighting to be the first mon through our gates!"

Ainslee was prepared to argue the insulting tone weighing Colin's words, then paused, frowning as she rethought his words. "What do ye mean by the *first* mon to get through our gates?"

"He hasna come to Kengarvey alone. Those two dogs Fraser and MacFibh are yapping at his heels."

"Nay!" Ainslee was appalled, certain that Gabel would never deal with such men, yet unable to doubt her brother's assertion. "Gabel sent Fraser from Bellefleur because the mon tried to kill me twice. He ached to do more, but couldna punish the mon for his crimes against me as I am proclaimed an outlaw."

"Weel, ye can ask your lover why he is cheek to jowl with

those men—if ye live long enough." Colin moved to where the guard usually sat, sheathed his sword, and took the key from the hook on the wall. "I didna come here to talk about de Amalville, what he allies himself with, or e'en if he chose the men himself." He fumbled with the key as he struggled to fit it into the lock of her cell door. "I came here to set ye free, so that ye may have some chance to save yourself."

The moment Colin opened the door, Ainslee fought the urge to collapse at his feet with relief and gratitude. She hugged him, easily ignoring the stench of battle he carried. Now she might be able to save at least a few of the Kengarvey people.

"Save yourself as weel, Colin," she said as she pulled away enough to look him full in the face. "Dinna let our father take ye or our brothers into the grave with him."

"Dinna start telling me how de Amalville will help us," Colin snapped as he started to drag her up the stairs.

"He swore to me that he would try to save all he could."

"The mon is beating down the last vestiges of our gates with his own hands. He is as eager to cut our throats as his hellborn allies are."

"Or, mayhaps, he but tries to reach us ere the Frasers and the MacFibhs do so, for he kens that those men will slaughter us and show us no mercy."

Colin stopped once they reached the upper hall, cursed, and then pushed her toward the stairs leading to the bedchambers. 'Go, get your weapons so that ye might fight, or supplies so that ye may flee this blood-soaked place, but cease trying to lull my wits with talk of old promises made."

Ainslee started to argue, but Colin was already running back out of the keep into the very heart of the battle. She felt like weeping, certain that she had failed to convince Colin to trust in Gabel and thus save his life, but she fought that urge. There would be time enough to grieve later, if she could stay alive long enough to learn the fate of her kinsmen. As she raced up the stairs to her bedchamber, she decided to gather her weapons as well as some supplies. There was little doubt in her mind that she would have to fight, even if she decided to try and flee her home. Ainslee prayed that the fates and God would deliver her into Gabel's hands before she had to do either.

Gabel cursed as he watched the Frasers and the MacFibhs scramble over the walls. He still faced a doorway he could not break through. The battle had become a race. His treacherous allies intended to beat him to the MacNairns, planning to kill as many as they could before he could begin to save any. He also suspected that Fraser and MacFibh each ached to be the man to kill the laird of Kengarvey. That was not an honor Gabel really wished to fight them for, even though he knew it could greatly enhance his favor with the king. All he cared about was getting inside Kengarvey before every MacNairn was cruelly slaughtered, before Ainslee could be found by men who only wished her dead.

The MacNairns had fought hard to hold the king's army back, and Gabel had to admire them for that. He was also glad that, of all the bodies littering the ground outside of Kengarvey's walls, only a few were men of Bellefleur. The way Fraser and MacFibh had hurled their men against the high thick walls with little regard for the men's lives had sickened Gabel. It had eventually worked to overwhelm the MacNairns but the cost had been too high to justify such tactics. Instead of seeing how badly they had erred, Fraser and MacFibh loudly blamed every death on the MacNairns. Gabel swore to himself that, even if the king himself ordered it, he would never fight with such men again.

"We are almost through the door, m'lord, and the MacNairns begin to retreat from the other side," cried one of the men from Bellefleur, who was helping to batter down the thick door.

Before Gabel could reply, another man cried out for his attention, pushing his way through the men gathered at the gate with such vigor that he stumbled into Gabel. "Look to the north, m'lord. Someone comes."

With Justice close at his side, Gabel moved to the rear of his men and looked at the small knot of men to the north of Kengarvey. The group waited at the edges of the tiny village, which still lay in ruins from the last attack upon MacNairn's lands. One man broke free and rode toward them, gaining confidence when he realized he did not need to fear any deadly arrow fired from the walls.

"You are a MacNairn?" Gabel questioned as the man reined to a halt in front of him.

Something about the man made Gabel uneasy. He needed no more of MacNairn's enemies joining in the fray. The man had to be forty years of age or older, for there was a great deal of dull white streaking his long fair hair. He was slender and elegantly dressed, looking completely unsuited for the battle he coolly watched.

"Nay," the man replied. "I am married to Elspeth, Mac-Nairns's eldest daughter." He bowed slightly, barely tipping more than his head and shoulders. "I am Donald Livingstone." He lifted one elegant hand when Gabel started to introduce himself. "I ken who ye are, Sir de Amalville."

"Why have you come to Kengarvey on this of all days?"

"To watch, no more. I willna join with ye against my kinsmen by marriage, and I dinna plan to join with my wife's father either."

"Then what reason do you have to be here at all?" snapped Gabel, in no mood for the man's courtly manners.

"I heard that the king had ordered this final battle, and felt it was my duty to come and observe the outcome. I refuse to join MacNairn in his traitorous games, but ye must also see why I canna join with ye either. I do, howbeit, wish to ask one gracious favor of ye, m'laird."

"If you would but look about you, sir, you would see that I am in the midst of a bloody fight. I have neither the time nor the inclination to be gracious."

"This willna impede you, sir. I wish that Ainslee MacNairn be allowed to live."

"Why?" Gabel demanded, instinct telling him that he was not going to like the man's reply at all.

"I have found a mon who is willing to wed with the disobedient girl."

"You come to me to speak of this *now?* Begone, if you do not mean to aid us or ask to surrender your sword to me. If any of us survive this slaughter, you may seek me out, but later, much, much later."

Gabel turned his back on the man and pushed his way through his soldiers to get back to the gates. "The man has to be completely, utterly mad," he complained to Justice, who struggled to remain close by his side.

"He but seeks to insure that whatever plots he has devised are not ruined by MacNairn's death."

"And so he rides into the midst of a bloody battle, calmly watches his wife's kinsmen being cut down, and asks that I try and spare the life of but one? He did not even ask that any of the brothers be saved."

"He can gain naught from them except more mouths to feed. Nay, he has a plan, and this battle could easily destroy it."

"Well, he shall soon discover that all of his clever plans are for naught. E'en if I did not plan to keep Ainslee for my own, I would ne'er send her to that man."

"Nay, I think she could fare just as poorly beneath his rule, or that of any man he might choose, as she does beneath her brutal father. Look there, Gabel, they have finally broken through those twice-cursed gates."

Gabel quickly found himself caught up in the surge of men pushing through the shattered gate. One look around the bailey as he stumbled into it stole away all thought of Donald Livingstone from his mind. The people of Kengarvey were still fighting fiercely, but the MacFibhs and the Frasers were exacting a bloody toll. The allies he had come to detest were caught up in a wild-eyed frenzy of bloodletting, offering no quarter.

"Sweet Jesu," murmured a wide-eyed, pale Michael. " 'Tis as if they are all maddened with hate and the scent of blood. I think they may turn on us if we try to put a halt to their murdering rampage."

"Aye," agreed Gabel, "so we must herd what few souls we can gather into a safe place, and then guard them well."

Selecting two archers and three swordsmen from his force, Gabel led them to a corner, carefully placing the still sturdy wall of Kengarvey at their back. Within the semicircle of armed men he created, some of Kengarvey's terrified people could find protection. He gave them stern instructions that any MacNairn who sought it should be given shelter, and that only one man at a time could leave to try and rescue someone. Assured that his men understood what he wanted, Gabel then strode toward the keep itself. He was not surprised when, a moment later, Michael and Justice hurried to his side.

"Do we go and search for Lady Ainslee?" Michael asked.

"Nay—her father," Gabel replied. "I saw him run in here, leaving his sons to fend for themselves." He shrugged. "At least I assume that the four young men he deserted were his sons. Fraser's men were keeping them hard-pressed." He nodded his approval when, just before they entered the keep itself, Michael signalled a few of Bellefleur's men to go and try to help the MacNairn sons. "Many will think me raving mad to hope that the sons survive, but Ronald swore to me that the sons are not like their father, and I would prefer to meet Ainslee with the assurance that we had done all we could to try and save her brothers."

"Are you sure you wish to confront her father then?" Justice frowned as they entered the great hall to find Duggan Mac-Nairn facing three of MacFibh's men-at-arms. "It does not look to me as if the man has any intention of surrendering to us, and that means that you must kill him, or step aside and let another do the deed for you."

"Nay," Gabel said, smiling briefly at his cousin, understanding Justice's silent offer to do the deed. "I will have no difficulty in killing Duggan MacNairn, if only because of the beating he gave Ainslee. That sight has burned in my mind and my innards since the day we lost her at the river. My only hesitation comes from having to face Ainslee later with her father's blood upon my hands. Howbeit, she has adamantly claimed that she understands that her father has brought this fate upon himself. 'Tis time to push aside MacFibh's dogs."

While he kept a close watch upon Duggan MacNairn, Justice and Michael dismissed the MacFibhs. The three men loudly protested the loss of what they considered to be a very valuable prize. When Michael and Justice nearly came to blows with the MacFibhs, Gabel curtly ordered his allies' men-at-arms to back away. After a moment of tense, belligerent hesitation, the three men did move away, but only for a short distance. Gabel did not like the three men lurking at his back, angry and feeling cheated, but he forced all thought of that possible threat from his mind. Justice and Michael would guard his back. He needed to keep all of his attention fixed upon Duggan MacNairn, for he knew that the man would be willing to try and use any treacherous trick he knew to save himself.

"You still have a chance to save yourself," Gabel told Duggan MacNairn.

"Do ye really think me so dull of wit that I dinna ken exactly what the king wishes to do to me?"

"You must have a clever tongue, or you would have tripped o'er all the lies you have told over the years. Why not face the king like a man and, if you cannot save yourself, at least you could try to save your sons, Kengarvey, and your people."

"They can save themselves. I have my own life to attend to, and if ye think ye can take it, Norman, come ahead," Duggan said, his voice and his arrogant stance heightening the taunt behind his words.

Gabel was certain that he would not get the truth out of MacNairn, but he decided to ask after Ainslee. If Duggan gave him a true reply it could save him time, as well as save Ainslee's life. He found that he needed to dredge up the strength to ask the question, for, if Duggan had hurt Ainslee, the man would savor the chance to taunt him with the fact.

"Where is your daughter Ainslee?" he demanded.

"Did ye think to have yourself a wee bit more of the dull slut then?"

This is going to be far more difficult than I thought, Gabel mused, as he fought against the urge to immediately strike out at the man who insulted Ainslee. "What I mean to do with her will cease to be your concern if you do not soon surrender your sword to me."

"The fool lass tried to flee Kengarvey. She should have kenned that no one escapes this place."

"You have killed her?"

"Might have done so by now." Duggan MacNairn shrugged. "I dinna ken."

"Ere ye die, MacNairn, you had best tell me where she is. If you do not, your death here, at my hands, could easily be as painful as the traitor's death the king plans for you."

"The whore rests in the dungeons and has done so for a week, mayhaps more. And, she may truly *rest,* for she has had naught but water to drink for the whole time she has been caged down there."

Gabel was so angry he trembled from the force of it. He struggled to bring it under control, for it could cause him to strike out blindly, and that was just what Duggan MacNairn wanted him to do. It would give the man a dangerous advantage over him. MacNairn spoke of his cruelty to Ainslee, his own daughter, and of his attempt to murder her through starvation, with such gloating that it churned Gabel's stomach. It was now easy to push aside the concern he felt over how Ainslee might feel if he had to kill her father. Gabel did not think he had ever faced a man who deserved to die more than Mac-Nairn did.

"Honor forces me to ask you one more time—do you yield?" Gabel asked, his voice hoarse with rage.

"Nay, ye rutting interloper. If ye are too much the coward to fight me, then bring on another. I shall bathe the great hall in my enemy's blood."

"I think not, you arrogant bastard. 'Tis only your blood which will stain these filthy rushes."

The moment his sword struck against MacNairn's, Gabel felt almost invigorated. He realized that he had been aching to fight the man since that day by the river, when he had been forced to watch helplessly as MacNairn nearly beat his own daughter to death. MacNairn had lived too long and, even if it caused him some trouble with Ainslee later, Gabel knew he wanted to be the one to put an end to the man's brutal reign.

He was not surprised when MacNairn proved to be an able fighter. The man had to have skill to have stayed alive for so long. Neither was he surprised when twice he had to fend off an attempted sly, murderous trick by MacNairn, for he had not expected Duggan MacNairn to fight with any honor. What did astound him was the older man's strength. From the blood and filth smeared all over MacNairn's padded jupon and mail, it was evident that he had already fought a battle or two, yet, except for a fine sheen of sweat appearing on his brow, MacNairn showed very little sign of tiring.

It was one slight misstep that ended the battle. MacNairn stumbled, and Gabel took swift advantage of the opening that afforded him, plunging his blade deep into MacNairn's heart. As he withdrew his sword and watched MacNairn slump lifelessly to the floor, Gabel fought back a brief pang of disappointment. MacNairn had not earned such a quick, clean death. He shrugged, cleaned his blade off on the dead man's jupon, and resheathed his sword as he turned to face the others.

"Where have the MacFibhs fled to?" he asked when he saw that Justice and Michael were alone.

"The moment your sword entered that bastard's chest, those three men raced out of here," replied Justice. "They are probably hieing back to their laird to tell him what you have just done." Justice walked over to MacNairn and roughly nudged him with his boot. "Are you certain that this beast is dead?"

"You saw my blade point pierce his heart."

"Aye, but a man like this often makes one wonder if he even has a heart you can pierce."

Gabel's smile was weak and fleeting, for his next thought was of Ainslee. The mere thought of what her own father had done to her made him shudder. He wondered why he was not racing down into the bowels of Kengarvey. It was a moment before he admitted to himself that fear of what he might find was what held him back. The thought of finding Ainslee dead or dying, starved past redemption, and undoubtedly covered with the bruises and swellings raised by her father's ready fists, was almost more than he could stomach. The thought which hastily followed that one was that, if she was still alive, she might need his help. It finally gave him the strength to move.

Justice and Michael were close on his heels as he strode into the hall, grabbed one terrified girl by the arm before she could flee, and demanded that she tell him the way to the dungeons. She fled the moment she told him what he needed to know, and Gabel eased his grip on her arm just enough so that she could wriggle free. As he drew near to the door hiding the stairs which led down into the underbelly of the keep, Gabel's pace increased, and he began to suffer a few doubts. Finding Ainslee simply could not be this easy.

The darkness and the damp chill he felt as he descended the stairs added to Gabel's fears for her safety, as well as his fury at MacNairn. Ainslee had never done anything to deserve such a punishment. Disappointment stabbed sharply at his heart when he found the dungeons empty, but he was not really surprised. There had to be someone at Kengarvey with the kindness to set her free once the battle had turned against the MacNairns and the chances of MacNairn remaining the laird were very slim.

"But now I must find the wench ere her enemies do so," he muttered, and lightly slammed his fist against the iron bars.

"She is a clever woman, Gabel," Justice said. "She must have fled the keep."

"She is also afraid for her people and, despite how little they have done to help her through the years, she will do her best to try and help them."

"Then she would make her way to the bailey, for she would be seeking you out, knowing that you will hold to your promise to save as many of her people as you are able to."

"And she will be walking into the midst of a battle, chaos, and within the reach of dozens of men eager to kill her," Gabel said as he started back up the stairs.

"Remember the woman you seek, cousin." Justice followed Gabel and paused only to glare at Michael, whose ascent up the stairs was dangerously loud. "Ainslee MacNairn would have gotten her weapons together the moment she was free to do so, and she knows well how to use them."

Gabel laughed shortly and harshly, little humor in the sound. "Aye, but even that skilled little girl cannot fight all of the Frasers and the MacFibhs who will be trying to spill her blood."

As Gabel raced through the hall of Kengarvey, he saw the fleeting shadows of the terrified people trying to hide within a keep that had now begun to burn. He called out to them, telling everyone who might hear him, that they would be treated fairly and mercifully, if they surrendered themselves to the men of Bellefleur. Realizing that some of the people hiding there might not know which of the enemy swarming over Kengarvey was from Bellefleur, he told them what badge his men wore. Since there was little else he could do beside chase down each man, woman, and child, he turned his full attention to the matter of finding Ainslee. If he could reach her before his blood-crazed allies did, he might yet save her life.

Nineteen

The moment Ainslee buckled on her sword, sheathed her daggers, and took up her bow and arrows, she felt a little more at ease. She was still weakened by a lack of food, the appalling conditions of the dungeons, and the beatings she had endured, but she was no longer helpless, no longer trapped and completely at the mercy of whichever one of the enemy happened to stumble upon her. With her poor health and lingering injuries, she would have little chance of winning a fight, but she swore that she would cost the Frasers and the MacFibhs dearly if they tried to kill her.

Into a small bag she stuffed what little she could find that would be useful if she was forced to flee the keep. Slinging the sack over her shoulder, she cautiously left her tiny chilled bedchamber, watching intently for some sign of the enemy as she crept her way toward the stairs. The only times she hesitated was to briefly search for some of her father's people so that she could urge them to seek out a Bellefleur man and surrender to him. She only found a few in the upper chambers, and decided that another thing the people of Kengarvey had learned to do with great skill was hide.

As she reached the bottom of the stairs, she caught a glimpse of the young maid who had helped Colin tend to her injuries after the beatings. The young girl was visibly trembling, clutching a small, wide-eyed boy in her arms, as she tried to press deeper into a tiny niche in the wall near the stairs. Although the girl squeaked in alarm when Ainslee approached her, she still clung to enough of her wits to recognize a friend and not try to run away. There was such a wild look of panic in the maid's eyes, however, that Ainslee feared she would never be able to talk sense to the girl.

"Morag, is it?" she asked in a soothing, friendly voice as she crouched next to the girl, positioning herself so that she could still keep a close watch out for the enemy.

"Aye, mistress," the maid replied, her voice high and strained. "I thank God that someone let ye out, but now ye must flee whilst ye can. We are all doomed here. The Frasers and the MacFibhs are putting everyone to the sword."

"Hush, lass, dinna let your fears cause ye to be careless and thus bring those filthy cowards hunting us." Ainslee gently grasped the girl by the arm, holding her in case she tried to bolt, but also trying to soothe her. "Is this your bairn?" The girl nodded. "A fine, handsome lad."

"He is your father's bastard."

That did not really surprise Ainslee, for she had already noticed something painfully familiar about the child's eyes and hair. Ronald had tried to keep that part of life at Kengarvey a secret from her, but it had proven impossible. She had barely become a woman herself when she had discovered that her father made free use of all the women and young girls at his keep, girls barely past their first flux. Ainslee sighed and lightly ruffled the child's soft auburn curls.

"I am sorry for that, Morag," she murmured.

"Why? Ye did naught to me. Ye werena treated much better than me either. Nay, my mother hoped to get me to my cousins in Edinburgh ere I passed my first flux, but there was no way out of this accursed place. I tried to stay hidden in the shadows, but he found me. 'Tis my good fortune that he found me too timid, too cold, and too thin, so he rarely dragged me into his bed." The expression on her small face hardened for one brief moment. "I am glad he is dead."

"My father is dead?" Ainslee was a little surprised at how much that shocked her, for it was the fate her father had been assiduously courting for years. "Come, child," she ordered the girl, knowing she had to be forceful. There was no time to continue to cajole the girl. "Ye and my wee bastard brother are coming with me." She started to pull the maid toward the door leading to the bailey.

"Nay," cried Morag, her terror swiftly returning in full strength, and she tried to pull free of Ainslee's tight grasp. "We will all die."

"Not if we can reach the men of Bellefleur."

" 'Twas the laird of Bellefleur himself who killed our laird. Cut him down in the great hall. He is as great an enemy of the MacNairns as the others are."

"Nay, he isna," snapped Ainslee, her temper fraying as the girl's nearly palpable terror began to strengthen her own fears. "If I ever hear ye compare Sir de Amalville to those other swine again, I shall strike ye soundly." The maid's eyes were so wide, Ainslee was sure they had to be stinging. Since the girl was so stunned by her mistress's show of temper she had grown quite still, Ainslee took swift advantage of it and dragged her to the doors of the great hall. "Ye say that my father was slain in here?"

"Aye, but I swear that I had naught to do with it, and I beg your forgiveness for saying that I was glad your father was dead."

"If ye would cease to allow yourself to be so blinded by your own fears, ye would see that I am neither grieved nor angry o'er his death. Ye would also see that none of the enemy are in the halls of this keep. We have neither heard nor glimpsed them since I pulled ye from your hiding place." Ainslee found that a little strange, but decided it would be wise not to say so aloud, for the girl was still trembling. "I canna see my father's body," Ainslee muttered as she looked into the great hall, seeing all the signs of a fight, but no body.

For one brief moment her gaze became fixed upon the bloodstained rushes where she was sure her father had fallen. A touch of grief came and went, leaving only disappointment.

After a minute of confusion, she realized that her disappointment came from knowing what her father might have been and, although it would have taken a miracle to change the man, what he would never become.

"They took the body away, mistress," Morag said, breaking into Ainslee's sad musings.

"Took it away? Why should they take the time from slaughtering us to drag a dead mon away?"

"I was hiding, mistress. I but saw them and was too far away to hear what they were saying. They were some of Fraser's men; that I can swear to."

"Curse them. Weel, there is nothing here worth lingering over. We shall go out into the bailey." She cursed under her breath when the maid whimpered and tried to pull away from her. "I will see that ye and your son are safely placed in the hands of the men from Bellefleur."

"Oh, sweet Mary, we are soon to die."

"Hold your judgement until ye actually see such a threat."

Ainslee ceased trying to be gentle and understanding, dragging the girl along as she pushed her way through the heavy, partly splintered door leading out of the keep. The sharp scent of smoke had already begun to sting her nose and eyes, so she knew the keep had been fired, but her first sight of the bailey nearly caused her to echo Morag's whimper. The ground was strewn with bodies, the smoke from the slowly burning keep swirling around the twisted corpses. There was a number of Frasers and MacFibhs scattered amongst the dead, but that gave Ainslee little comfort. The toll amongst her own people had been appallingly high.

A sharp cry of horror from Morag and the maid's renewed attempts to pull away, yanked Ainslee from her dark thoughts. She turned to scold the girl, only to frown when she saw that Morag was not looking at the corpse-cluttered ground, but upwards. Ainslee warily followed the direction of the maid's stare and heard herself cry out in shock. Now she knew why the men had taken the time to move her father's corpse. Their enemies had separated her father's head from his body, and were displaying it on the end of a spike placed high up on the walls of Kengarvey. Although she felt no real grief over her father's death, she found this barbaric display enough to churn her stomach. She fought the urge to simply turn and flee, to run from the gruesome sight of her father's dismemberment, from the stench of blood, smoke, and death, and from the purposeful destruction of the only home she had ever known.

One glance at Morag and her baby helped Ainslee subdue that urge. The child clung to his mother, but stared at Ainslee with fear and confusion. Ainslee knew that she did not have enough supplies to care for the mother and child as well as herself if she fled Kengarvey. She also knew that, if she did not lead Morag to safety, the maid would rush back to her inadequate hiding place and get herself and her child murdered.

"Come along, Morag, and I will lead you to Gabel's people," Ainslee said, her weariness weighting her voice.

"We dinna need to go now." Morag pointed a shaky finger at Duggan MacNairn's head. "The battle has clearly been lost. The fighting will soon cease as weel. We but need to hide—"

Ainslee cursed and gave the maid a brief hard shaking. "Ye will do exactly as I say, and cease this endless whining."

When Morag immediately grew quiet and obedient, Ainslee wished she had been so fierce from the moment she had discovered the girl. She did feel a little guilty about treating Morag so, as it was the constant brutality of life in Kengarvey that had made the girl such a coward. Sympathy and kindness would not save the girl's life now, however.

As she searched for some sign of a Bellefleur man who could help them, Ainslee stayed close to the keep. Sparks from the burning building fell dangerously close to them, but Ainslee felt that the Frasers and the MacFibhs were far more dangerous. There was still a lot of fighting going on, for the MacNairns knew that the Frasers and the MacFibhs were offering no chance of mercy, and her father's hirelings never expected any, so entered each battle as if it were one to the death. In the midst of all that confusion, men busily robbed the dead and looted the outer buildings before setting them afire as well, squabbling amongst themselves over what few spoils they could find.

She stumbled against a body slumped next to the wall. When she glanced down even as she and Morag stepped over it, Ainslee whispered a curse. Her guard stared into the emptiness of death, a look of surprise on his face. Ainslee felt the usual horror she did when looking upon a violent death, as well as a twinge of regret. By allowing Colin to visit her and sneak her a few morsels of food, the man had revealed a hint of goodness.

Distracted by finding Robert's body, Ainslee did not see the Fraser man until it was almost too late. Morag screamed softly and sank to the ground, sheltering her child with her own body. Ainslee cursed, raising her sword just in time to successfully block the man's deadly blow. The painful way her arm shook from the force of the blow confirmed her fears that her captivity had weakened her. She would have to resort to some trickery or deception if she was to win the fight, and she prayed that some opportunity would present itself quickly, before what little strength she still had was all used up.

"Ye are MacNairn's youngest whelp, arena ye? The one that crippled fool raised up," the man said.

That Fraser's hireling would talk to her as they fought revealed how confident he was that he could beat her, and Ainslee wondered if she would be able to take advantage of that. "Aye, and that cripple is more of a mon than ye can e'er hope to be."

"Aye? Put down your sword, lass, and I will show ye just how much of a mon I be."

"Ah, so the Frasers still indulge in the crime of raping and murdering women."

"I ne'er said I would murder you."

"Ye ne'er offered me a chance to live either."

"Nay, if ye seek to live, ye had best go to one of those tenderhearted men of Bellefleur."

She neatly eluded his lunge, but he was quick to recover. His next strike came so close that it sliced into her skirts, and Ainslee knew that she could not fight him for very much longer. All of the deprivations she had suffered through since returning to Kengarvey had left her too weak, and that weakness robbed her of much needed skill and speed. She wished Morag was not so afraid and would notice that she could use some help, but knew she would have to depend upon her wits alone.

The next blow that came too close cut through the bodice of her gown and scored her side. Ainslee felt the warm dampness of her blood begin to soak her clothes, and had to fight her own swiftly rising fears. The man's insulting reference to the tenderhearted men of Bellefleur told her that Gabel was keeping his promise to try and save as many of her people as he could. With safety so close at hand, she could not die now. It would be so unfair. It would also lead to the death of Morag and her child, for Ainslee knew that, once she fell, the man would immediately turn his murderous attentions upon the terrified maid and her helpless baby.

Just as Ainslee began to think that the opportunity she so badly needed would not come until she was too exhausted to take advantage of it, Morag leapt up and grabbed Fraser's man by the arm. "Ye shouldna try and kill a woman, ye stinking coward," Morag screamed as she repeatedly kicked the man in the legs.

When the man turned to shake off Morag, Ainslee did not hesitate. Even as she drove the sharp point of her sword deep into his chest, he had begun to turn back to her, his expression revealing that he had suddenly realized what a fatal mistake he had made. As he slumped to the ground at her feet, Ainslee heard Morag whimper in horror, and watched the girl hastily retrieve her child from where she had set the boy down.

"Thank ye, Morag," she said, as the trembling girl returned to her side "Ye have just saved my life."

"Oh, I have?" Morag blinked in surprise and calmed down a little. "I fear I didna really think about what I was doing. I just wanted the fighting to stop," she added in an unsteady whisper.

"Weel, this ugly cur will ne'er bother us again," Ainslee said as she nudged the man's body with her boot to reassure herself that he was truly dead.

"I canna believe ye have just killed that mon." Morag stared at Ainslee with a mixture of horror and deep admiration.

" 'Tis not something I take any pleasure in, but I prefer to fight and kill than stand and die."

"That must be a verra hard choice for a woman to make."

"Aye, it is," Ainslee replied in a soft, somber voice. "Now, we must move on ere we are seen by one of his companions, and they decide to take up his sword and face me. I am too weak to fend off another of these murderers."

Ainslee saw the fear rush back into Morag's expression and inwardly cursed her too free tongue. She had spoken the simple truth, but it was not a truth Morag was in any condition to hear. The girl had just begun to calm herself with the thought that her mistress could fight off the enemy, only to have her mistress reveal her own weakness and doubts.

"Come, Morag, let us hurry and find some place where ye can cease to be so afraid," Ainslee murmured as she urged the girl along.

"M'lady," Morag whispered in a thin, shaking voice a few moments later. "Is that not one of the Bellefleur men ye seek?"

Ainslee looked in the direction Morag pointed, and her heart skipped with a heady mixture of hope and joy. She was certain Gabel was only yards away from her now, the clutter of fighting men and the helmet the man wore causing her only a moment of confusion. What stole away all her pleasure as swiftly as it had come was the sight of Fraser confronting Gabel. Every inch of Fraser's burly frame bristled with fury, and Ainslee could sense the danger of the moment even from where she stood. Suddenly, all of her concern about getting to safety, even about saving Morag and her child, was pushed aside. Instinct kept her wary of the dangers all around her, but she began to move faster, desperate to reach Gabel before the argument between him and Fraser resulted in drawn swords.

Gabel scowled at Fraser as he and MacFibh strode over to face him. It was easy to see that the men were furious, and Gabel had no trouble in figuring out what stirred their rage. None of the Frasers or the MacFibhs were happy about the number of MacNairns he had placed under his protection. The fact that all four of Ainslee's brothers now stood with him had obviously been more than either of his contentious allies could bear. Gabel had feared that this moment of confrontation would come, but, this once, he would have been pleased to have been proven wrong.

He resented the constant bickering and this delay. Gabel did not feel that he should have to constantly explain himself to his allies, nor should he have to spend so much of his time trying to keep innocent people from being murdered. Because of the constant discord and other problems, he had still not found Ainslee. His ability to search for her had been severely curtailed during the battle itself and now, when he could even afford to employ some of his men in the task, Fraser appeared to hinder him yet again. Gabel realized that he had come to loathe the man.

The MacFibhs had been easier to bear, which had surprised Gabel a little. Lord MacFibh was an unwashed uncouth man, who had some cold bloodthirsty ideas on how to conduct a battle and treat one's enemies. Yet the man also had a firm sense of what was right and what was wrong, and could be counted on not to change his opinions just to please others or to accomplish his own gains. Fraser was the worst sort of courtier and, in comparison, MacFibh had begun to look almost likeable. MacFibh still believed that the only way to end the troubles caused by the MacNairns was to kill every last one of them, but he had finally—grudgingly—conceded to allowing the women and female children a chance to surrender. There was a hint of mercy in the MacFibhs, however, for some had allowed a male MacNairn to surrender as well, and even MacFibh himself had tossed a small boy into Gabel's arms in the heat of the battle, saying only that his sword arm had grown tired by the time he had reached the child.

MacFibh now stood with Fraser, however, and Gabel could not be sure how firmly he did so. There was too little of the man's face visible beneath his helmet, his wild hair, and the filth of battle. In the man's eyes was a cool look of consideration, nothing more. Gabel did not even want to try and guess at what the man was considering. His only concern at the moment was what Fraser planned to do, and if MacFibh— who had displayed a tendency to argue, complain, and do exactly as he pleased—would now cross the line into treachery.

"What game do ye play, de Amalville?" Fraser demanded as he faced Gabel, sparing only one hate-filled glance for the MacNairn brothers.

"I play no game."

"Nay? We are here to crush the MacNairns, yet ye gather them to your breast like long-lost, weel-loved kinsmen."

"I do not believe I was clutching them that closely." When Fraser's face reddened and his expression grew almost feral, Gabel tensed, sensing the danger of the moment. "I am doing exactly what I told the king I would do—saving as many of the MacNairns as I can." When Michael and Justice moved to silently flank him, Gabel relaxed a little.

"The king wished Duggan MacNairn and all of his spawn dead."

"Nay, the king wanted only the laird's head. Mayhaps he believes as I do, that one should not set the burden of a father's guilt upon his children's shoulders. These young men have expressed a willingness to swear an oath to the king, and have already sworn one to me. I believe that a living, strong ally is of a greater worth than any dead enemy."

"Ye canna trust these MacNairns any more than ye could trust their father," Fraser bellowed.

"I have had no proof of that as yet. I have shown them that I have the strength and the skill to punish the men who betray me. If they choose to follow their father's treacherous path, then I will deal with them as I have dealt with their father." He cast one brief glance at the gruesome trophy upon the castle walls. "Well, almost. I believe I would at least return them to their king in one piece, so that he could dispense with their corpses as he saw fit to."

"Weel, if ye dinna have the stomach to do what must be done—I will."

Fraser drew his sword, but took only one step toward the huddled group of MacNairns. All four MacNairn brothers reached for their swords, and cursed when they grasped only an empty sheath. Fraser advanced no further, however, for he met the drawn swords of Gabel, Justice, and Michael. MacFibh stood firm for a moment, scowling in confusion, then stepped back, silently distancing himself from Fraser and the man's challenge.

"Coward," Fraser snarled at MacFibh, but his former ally just shrugged.

"I am nay one of the king's favored laddies," MacFibh said. "I would lose more than ye would if I drew a sword on the Norman. Aye, and though I dinna agree with his need to show such mercy, I came under oath as his ally. Ye may keep this squabble atween yourselves."

"Ye must live near these bastards. How can ye stomach any of the MacNairns remaining here, especially the mon's own heirs?"

"I will deal with them as I must. A ruined keep with no one to guard the lands doesna do me much good either."

When Fraser turned back to him, Gabel smiled coldly. "And are you sure you wish to fight o'er this?"

"These men are as guilty as their father, and they will plague this land as sorely as he did. I demand that ye punish them. If ye dinna, ye are as great a traitor as they are."

When Justice and Michael moved as if to attack the man, Gabel halted them with one sharp movement of his hand. Their job was to protect his back and help him guard against treachery, not to fight his battles for him. This time Gabel knew there had to be a battle. Such insults could not go unpunished, and Fraser would have to nearly grovel in apology to make any attempt at forgiveness become acceptable to his men and the others who watched them. And Fraser would never debase himself to apologize, no matter how rash the words. Gabel just hoped they could solve the matter without a killing.

"In but moments you have accused me of cowardice and of being a traitor," Gabel said, his voice cold as he stared steadily at Fraser. "You go too far, Fraser. Your insults to me began months ago within Bellefleur itself, and have continued unrelentingly. I expect the most profuse of apologies, or I will put a swift end to your sly ways here and now."

"Apologize!? For what? I but tried to kill a MacNairn at Bellefleur. 'Tis no crime. And I willna take back one other word." He assumed a fighting stance and sneered at Gabel. "Prove yourself, Norman. Show us that ye can do more than speak prettily and beg for truces from bastards and outlaws."

"You may well have just talked yourself into your grave, Fraser."

Gabel had barely finished speaking when Fraser attacked, the resounding clang of their swords silencing everyone around them. He did not need to look at the MacNairns sheltered behind his men to know that they were dismayed. A soft groan arose from them the moment the battle was begun. They knew as well as he did that it was not only for his honor that he fought, but for their lives. If Fraser succeeded in killing Gabel, the man would feel no compunction about cutting down the men of Bellefleur to reach the MacNairns, and MacFibh would probably join in the slaughter. After promising the terrified remnants of the MacNairn clan that they would be safe with him, Gabel could not allow his stung pride and Fraser's blood lust to tear away that safety.

Fraser had skill, but Gabel quickly recognized how the man allowed his own anger to diminish it. The man did not even have to be taunted openly to grow angry. Gabel knew that the cool demeanor he struggled to hold onto infuriated the man. The angrier Fraser grew, the calmer Gabel forced himself to appear, even beginning to smile faintly. Fraser's temperament made it easy to deceive the man into believing he was just being toyed with. That proved to be Fraser's downfall, causing the man to lose the last few vestiges of skill he had managed to cling to in the midst of his rage.

As Fraser panted and began to weaken, fighting Gabel as much as he was fighting against his own fury, Gabel found the chance he waited for. In a few swift clean moves, he knocked Fraser's sword from his hand, and then knocked the man to the ground. Before Fraser could regain his footing, Gabel pinned him to the ground by placing one booted foot on the man's heaving chest and holding his sword point against his throat.

"I would advise you to yield," Gabel said with cool politeness, aching to kill the man, but knowing it would be wiser to accept a bloodless victory for now.

Fraser's muttered *yield* was completely unsatisfactory, but Gabel slowly released him. The man snatched up his sword, glared at them all, and strode away, roughly pushing his way through the men who had gathered to watch the battle. Gabel shook his head as he resheathed his sword. Nothing had been solved, and Fraser's hatred of him had only been irrevocably deepened.

"That mon will do his utmost to see that ye pay dearly for his shame," Colin MacNairn said.

Gabel turned to look at Ainslee's brother, noticing how the other three now gathered around him, silently choosing him as their leader. "I realize that I have just made an enemy for life."

"Aye, and he will try to make that life as short a one as possible."

"Ye should have cut the bastard's throat. Ye had that right," muttered George, who then cursed softly when Colin cuffed him offside the head.

"Pardon, m'lord," Colin said. "He forgets whom he speaks to. Although, there is a cold truth to his blunt words."

"I know, but I cannot treat Fraser as I might treat some other foe, at least not until I have had a chance to speak to the king about the man's crimes and insults. Fraser sits high in the king's favor. To kill him and then try to explain why I did so could damage my own prestige, and I need it. I am still seen as an interloper, e'en as a thief who takes the land some Scot could rule in my stead. Nay, it seers my innards to allow that cur to live another moment, but, for now, I gain more by doing so."

Colin shrugged, then frowned as he looked over Gabel's shoulder. "I told that child to flee this place," he muttered and shook his head. "It doesna soothe my pride much to ken that, out of all of our father's children, 'tis the youngest girl who holds most tightly to her spirit and honor, whilst the rest of us followed like lambs to the slaughter pens, too terrified to do aught else."

It took Gabel only a moment to comprehend who Colin spoke of. He spun around and searched the still crowded bailey, finally espying Ainslee stepping clear of the smoke and shadow-shrouded walls of Kengarvey. Elated to see her on her feet, alive and carrying no visibly serious wounds, Gabel smiled at her. He started to walk toward her, intending to meet her halfway, and waved aside Justice's and Michael's attempts to accompany him.

Ainslee sheathed her sword, certain that she would no longer need it. She quickened her pace even as she glanced around to reassure herself that the battle was really over. A man on the wall behind Gabel caught her attention, and she came to an abrupt halt. One of Fraser's men was notching an arrow in his bow, and it was aimed at Gabel. She frantically looked around for Lord Fraser and found the man off to her right. His attention was fixed upon his archer, and Ainslee's blood froze when he gave the man an abrupt signal. Ainslee looked up at the archer again and saw him pull back on his bow. This time there could be no doubt about his target—Gabel's unprotected back.

"Look out, Gabel!" she screamed, but he only stared at her in confusion.

Hiking up her skirts even as she began to run, Ainslee raced toward Gabel. As she neared him, she lowered her head, butting him in the stomach like a goat. Gabel groaned and cursed as he stumbled backward. He hit the ground hard, panting as he struggled to reclaim all the air she had knocked out of him.

Ainslee straightened up to look at Gabel, reassuring herself that she had not really hurt him, then felt something slam into her shoulder. She stared down at the arrow protruding from her body, even as she staggered backward from the force of the blow. Then the pain came. Crying out and trying to grab the shaft of the arrow in a vain attempt to remove the source of her pain, Ainslee slumped to the ground. As the thick blackness of unconsciousness began to creep over her, she hoped that bellow of raw pain had not come out of her.

Twenty

Gabel stumbled to his knees, half-crawling over to Ainslee. His throat was raw from screaming her name as she fell. Out of the corner of his eye, he saw his men scramble to protect him from any further attack. Just as he reached Ainslee's side, he heard a scream and looked up to see the man who had tried to murder him tumble from the walls, several arrows protruding from his chest. His hand shaking, Gabel reached out to search for some sign of life in Ainslee. He shuddered with relief when he felt her heartbeat. The young maid Ainslee had brought with her fell to her knees at Ainslee's side, an older woman quickly joining her.

"I am Morag, m'laird," the maid announced as she tore open Ainslee's bodice to survey the wound. "This is my mother. Ye go and do what ye must do. We can tend to the mistress."

"But—" Gabel protested even as he began to get to his feet.

"Go, m'laird. 'Tis most clear that ye have some verra deadly enemies. 'Tis best to be rid of them ere they really do kill someone."

Although he ached to stay at Ainslee's side, terrified that she might slip away from him while he was not watching, Gabel knew that the maid was right. The assassin had been a Fraser man. Gabel turned to look for the man who had given the order to the archer.

Fraser stood but a few yards away to Gabel's left. He was flanked by a half-dozen armed men, and faced twice that number of well-armed Bellefleur men. Knowing that none of his men would act without his command unless Fraser made another attempt to kill him, Gabel walked over to stand next to Justice and Michael. He wanted Fraser for himself, and this time he did not intend to give the man any chance to yield.

"You tried to murder me, to cut me down from behind like some low stinking coward," Gabel charged as he took a step toward Fraser, his sword in his hand and his whole body tensed and ready for battle.

"Nay, I didna. I thought that MacNairn lass meant to do ye some harm," Fraser replied.

Gabel watched the man look around nervously, clearly trying to discover some route of escape. This time, however, there was no way for Fraser to flee, not from him nor from the punishment rightfully due a murderer. In one ill-thought-out attempt to cut down his rival, Fraser had lost all he had achieved over the years, especially the hard-won and highly coveted favor of their king. There were too many witnesses to his devious attempt to kill a king's man. Fraser could not successfully lie his way out of trouble this time.

"You cannot expect us to believe that, Fraser," Gabel said. "Nay, not even the king, who has been blind to your sly ways and deadly games for many years, will believe that lie. If naught else, you insult me and my men by implying that we need your help to fend off one tiny Scottish woman."

"Woman? 'Tis no mere woman we speak of, but one of the devil's own spawn."

"Ware, Fraser. Do not make the mistake of adding insult to the injury you have caused."

"I have done naught but cut down a MacNairn. There is no crime in that."

"There is when she is under my protection, a protection the king himself allowed me to offer to anyone of my choosing. And not when the arrow was intended to sit in my back. Nay, cease trying to lie your way free of this cowardly act, and prepare to try and save yourself."

"Ye canna cut me down, de Amalville. I too am one of the king's own men. Ye will have to answer for my death."

"I have no doubt that I can easily justify what I am about to do."

Before Gabel could act, however, Fraser and his men attempted to flee. They started to back away, warily watching him and his men as they did so. Behind them stood MacFibh and several of his men. If the MacFibhs sided with the Frasers, Gabel knew the fight could be very costly. He was debating within himself whether or not to stand and fight, chancing a deadly battle with the combined forces of the Frasers and the MacFibhs, or move to pull his men and the MacNairns out of Fraser's reach, when the need for any decision on the matter was ripped from his hands.

MacFibh struck with no warning, startling both Gabel and the vulnerable Fraser. Even as Fraser's expression revealed his horrified realization that his allies had deserted him, MacFibh neatly severed his head from his shoulders. Fraser's men were dispatched with an equal brutality by MacFibh's men. Throughout the bailey, Frasers fled or fought and died at the hands of the MacFibhs. Gabel realized that, as he and Fraser had confronted each other, MacFibh had quietly placed his men so that they could end the threat before it really began. After staring at his dead enemy for several moments, speechless with surprise over this turn of events, Gabel looked at MacFibh. The man finished cleaning his sword off on Fraser's jupon, stood up, resheathed the weapon, and then met Gabel's look.

"I had planned to kill him myself," Gabel said, disappointed that he had not been able to personally avenge the harm the man had done Ainslee, and not exactly sure that he could trust MacFibh yet.

"I ken it, Sir de Amalville, but I had my own reasons to want the mon dead," MacFibh replied.

"He was your ally. The two of you have stood shoulder to shoulder against me ever since we began this venture."

"That mon was ne'er anyone's ally save his own. He would

have cut his own mother's throat, if he had thought it would bring him any gain. But one year past he cost my cousin his lands and his life. I now must house and feed his widow and her bairns, their name left so badly stained that they might ne'er retrieve it."

"Yet you joined forces with him?"

"The king ordered it, and I had a wee urge to spill some Mac-Nairn blood." MacFibh stared down at Fraser's body for a moment, then spat on it. "I could speak upon this mon's crimes until the sun has set and risen again, but I suspect that ye ken what he was."

"Did you come to this battle intending to exact revenge upon Fraser, as well as upon the MacNairns?"

"Nay, but I did come intending to keep a close watch for any chance to cut him down. His jealousy of you gave me that much longed-for chance. I suspected that he would use this battle to try and murder you."

As Gabel resheathed his sword, he eyed MacFibh with an increasing cynicism. "You did not think that I or even one of my men ought to be informed of your suspicions?"

"I saw no need to trouble ye with them," MacFibh drawled, then smiled faintly, his own cynicism plain to read upon his harsh features. "And, Sir de Amalville, why should one king's mon heed an old minor laird's suspicions about another of the king's men?"

Gabel almost laughed, but his concern about Ainslee's health was already pulling his thoughts away from Fraser and MacFibh. "I truly had wished to kill him myself."

"And for stealing your chance to seek the revenge ye wanted, I do beg your gracious pardon." MacFibh winked. "There will be others, m'laird, and I swear that I willna intrude in the killing of them."

Gabel shook his head and moved to find Ainslee. He knew that later he would find some dark source of humor in the situation and in MacFibh's ingenuity. The man was barbarous, unclean, and unmannered, but was also a great deal more clever than Gabel had first judged him to be. MacFibh had watched for a chance to cut down his old enemy without cost or retribution, and had not only seen that chance the moment it had arisen, but had acted with a swift deadly cunning to grasp that chance without seriously endangering himself or his men. It was devious, yet the man was blunt about what he had planned and what he had done. Gabel decided that he would have to keep a very close eye on MacFibh, and try to find the time to learn all he could about the man. At the moment, however, all he had time for and interest in was Ainslee.

He found Ainslee inside of a small shelter constructed of sticks and dirty sheepskins. The little maid and her mother had already removed the arrow and bandaged the wound. Gabel took one look at the strips of cloth wrapped around Ainslee's slender shoulder, and felt a chill slide up his spine. They were gray with filth, nearly as filthy as the furs Ainslee lay upon and as the hands of the maid and her mother. Although he did not know if Ainslee's insistence upon cleanliness while treating a wound was based upon any facts or reason, and had even found it endearingly amusing, he did know one thing— the wounds Ainslee had treated, Justice's and Ronald's, had healed perfectly.

Careful to speak gently to the timid women, thanking them for their help, Gabel ushered them out of the lean-to. The moment they were back with the other MacNairns, he signalled to Justice. Gabel prayed that, if Ainslee was correct about dirt being a real danger to any wound, he was still in time to correct any damage the well meaning women had wrought.

"She has not woken up?" Justice asked as he looked at Ainslee. "Ah, well, 'tis not really a bad sign," he added in a quiet belated attempt to soothe Gabel's obvious agitation.

"Do you remember what Ainslee did when she treated your wound?" Gabel demanded as he knelt by Ainslee's side.

Justice shrugged. "She smeared a few salves o'er it and bandaged it. It looks as if those women tended her well enough."

"Look closer and think harder, friend. Do you not recall Ainslee's insistence upon cleanliness, of the wound and of herself as she treated it?"

"Oh, aye." Justice grimaced. " 'Tis clear that cleanliness is not a concern of the MacNairns."

"Nay. Come, help me take these filthy rags off of her."

"I will fetch some clean blankets and water first. And, mayhaps, I can find some of the foul brew these people drink. I now recall that she poured some of it o'er my wound."

As soon as Justice left, Gabel turned all of his attention to Ainslee. Her pale color and her stillness worried him. When he finally got the bloodied strips of cloth off of her wound, the sight of the jagged hole in her soft flesh made him sick with fear. She was so small, so delicate, that such a wound could prove to be a dangerous one, could even prove to be fatal. Her lithe body was covered with bruises, and she had lost some weight. Gabel knew that both of those things were the results of her father's brutality, and could easily steal away the strength she would need to heal. He wished he could make her father pay all over again for his mistreatment of his own child.

The moment Justice returned with the water, clean rags, and clean blankets, Gabel stripped and bathed Ainslee. He fleetingly begged Ainslee's forgiveness for slighting her modesty. Justice held Ainslee still as Gabel cleaned and stitched her wound, for, even in the depths of unconsciousness, she felt the pain and cried out, trying to twist away from him. When he was done, he splashed some of the clean water on his face as Justice covered her limp form with blankets, and even took a hearty swallow of the strong brew.

"I cannot believe anyone actually drinks this," he said, his eyes watering a little as he set the jug aside.

"I tasted it once and found it very strong," Justice murmured.

"Aye, it fair burns its way to your belly." He sighed and gently brushed the hair from Ainslee's ashen face. " 'Tis a deep, bloody wound, and her father's cruelty has ensured that she is not at her full strength to fight off all the threats of such a wound."

"Even like this, bruised and half-starved, Ainslee MacNairn is stronger than most women we know or have ever known. If any woman can survive such a wound, she can."

"I pray that you are right, Cousin, for I will ne'er forgive myself if my weakness causes her death."

"Your weakness?" Justice looked at his cousin in surprise and confusion. "What are you saying? Even if I could think of some weakness, how could it be blamed for this tragedy?"

"My weakness is my hesitancy to treat my enemies as they deserve. I show mercy to those who deserve none. I try to make peace with men who have no honor. My reluctance to spill the blood of others has brought Ainslee to this. I should have cut Fraser down the first time he tried to kill her, back at Belle-fleur."

"Mercy and a reluctance to slay all who stand against you is not a weakness. If you had killed Fraser at Bellefleur, you may well have angered the king so deeply that he would not have allowed you to lead this fight, or even to join in it. That would assuredly have cost Ainslee her life and the lives of all of her people as well."

"I should have seen Fraser's treachery ere it cut her down."

"You are an honorable man, Gabel. Sometimes 'tis hard for an honorable man to see treachery, or guess what trick a dis-honorable man might play. Aye, mayhaps you need to look at other men with a far more distrustful eye, but 'tis no true weakness or fault.

"You fought Fraser fairly, man to man. You won and he yielded." Justice shook his head. "I myself thought that that would be the end of it, and I am the one who should be more cautious for 'tis my place to watch your back. Nay, Gabel, you cannot blame yourself for not seeing what a low cowardly trick Fraser was about to play."

"MacFibh saw it," Gabel said quietly, his gaze fixed upon

Ainslee's face as he tried to will her to wake up and look at him.

"MacFibh is but a breath away from dishonor himself."

Gabel smiled fleetingly. "The man does bear close watching. He wanted Fraser dead, yet was willing to bide his time until he could wreak the revenge he sought without any fear of retribution. I believe the wrong Fraser did MacFibh's cousin is but one of many crimes and insults he dealt the man, yet MacFibh waited, patiently, coldly, until the perfect moment to strike. I thought the way MacFibh acted toward the MacNairns revealed the full true nature of the man."

"Ah, but the MacNairns have long been declared outlaws, thus MacFibh could deal with them however he pleased," Justice said as he carefully folded the cleanest of the animal skins and slid it beneath Ainslee's head.

"Aye, so I must now study the man." Gabel cursed softly. "Why does she not wake, if only for a moment?"

" 'Tis clear that her time at Kengarvey has not been an easy one. Mayhaps that takes its toll now, forcing her to sleep so deeply. With MacNairn lurking about at every turning, she may have slept very little."

"I should never have let her return to this accursed place."

"You had no choice, cousin."

Before Gabel could argue that, Michael arrived, saying, "That simpleton who came to speak to you outside of the gates has returned. He is demanding to speak with you again."

"Does the fool not know what has happened?" Gabel snapped as he stepped outside of the tiny shelter to stand next to Michael.

"Now he does, for Lady Ainslee's brothers loudly informed him. 'Tis clear that there is no love lost between the brothers and their sister's husband. The news that Lady Ainslee has been wounded only appeared to irritate Livingstone. I think you had better come and speak with him, ere there is trouble between him and his kinsmen."

Gabel cursed softly. He wanted to stay by Ainslee's side, to encourage her to wake and to be there when she did. The last thing he wished to do was to deal with a man who clearly wanted to gain hold of Ainslee for his own selfish reasons. There was one way to be rid of Livingstone, and that was to tell the man that he intended to marry Ainslee himself. Gabel did not wish to tell anyone outside of Bellefleur about those plans, however, until he had had the chance to talk to Ainslee.

"Stay with her, Justice," he ordered his cousin. "I will send that maid to help you. Try to get the girl to clean herself, or at least wash her hands, without insulting her. If Ainslee stirs, I wish to be told immediately."

After Justice assured him that he would and that Ainslee would be well cared for, Gabel went to confront Livingstone. He saw the man pacing angrily in front of the MacNairns, and had to fight to constrain his own anger. This was just more proof that Ainslee had been surrounded by uncaring people, people who just wished to use her to gain what they wanted or to vent their fury on her. He guiltily admitted that he was not much better, that he too had used her to try and gain what he wanted. Peace without bloodshed may be an honorable goal to reach for, but it did not completely excuse his actions. Gabel was determined, however, that it would all end now. From now on, Ainslee would have the freedom to do as she wished.

"Lord de Amalville," Livingstone said in cold greeting, his bow so small as to be an insult. "I hear that my wee sister by marriage has been severely injured."

When Michael softly cursed and grew tense, Gabel knew he was not allowing his own guilt to make him hear the sharp accusation behind those words. "Lord Fraser attempted to kill me, and Lady Ainslee courageously placed herself between me and the arrow aimed at my heart."

"Why was she running about in the midst of a battle?"

"Have you ne'er fought a battle, sir? 'Tis nigh to impossible to place all the innocents in some safe haven, wrapped in eiderdown, whilst we men cut and slash at each other. You try to place blame for something that could not be prevented, and you edge ever closer to uttering a grave insult." Gabel was pleased when his cold warning caused Livingstone to visibly compose himself. He had no wish to fight with even more of Ainslee's kinsmen.

"I was but unsettled by such grave news," Livingstone said in a soft conciliatory voice. "If her wound has been tended to, I can take her with me now. Her sister Elspeth can nurse her. There is no need to trouble yourself."

"But there is. I owe the girl my life."

"Surely, sir, 'twould be best if her own kinsmen care for her now."

"From what I have seen, Ainslee will fare far better at Bellefleur than in the hands of her kinsmen."

"My laird—" Livingstone began in protest.

"Enough. She will return to Bellefleur with me. If naught else, because her man Ronald is there, and he has shown a true skill in the healing arts."

Livingstone tried to change Gabel's mind, but soon realized that it was hopeless. The man did not hide his frustration and anger well as he promised to come to Bellefleur in a fortnight's time, weather permitting. He left without asking what the fate of Kengarvey was to be, and it was one small thing Gabel could be grateful for. He did not wish to get into an argument over that at the moment.

As Gabel watched Livingstone ride away, he swore that, even if Ainslee would not accept him as her husband—a possibility he found painful to consider—he would never allow Livingstone to gain hold of her. He had not discovered the name of the man Livingstone wished to sell her to in marriage, but he was sure that her well-being and her wishes had not once been considered. It was far past time that they were.

"That bastard has ne'er given Ainslee a thought until now," muttered Colin, glaring after his departing brother-in-law.

"Have any of the MacNairns ever done so?" Gabel asked in a voice cold and tight with anger as he recalled the many bruises marring Ainslee's slim form.

Colin flushed and nodded. "Few and rarely," he agreed. "Howbeit, Sir de Amalville, ye should be careful about condemning what ye canna fully understand, as I am certain that ye have ne'er lived the sort of life we all have in this thrice-cursed place. Until ye have seen hell, ye can fear it, but ye can ne'er truly ken its torments."

"Nay, I cannot know what life at Kengarvey was like for all of you. Yet, you are her brothers, her closest kin, and good strong young men. How could you continue to just stand by and allow your father to nearly kill her?"

"She isna dead though, is she?" muttered George, clamping his lips together tightly when Colin signalled him to be quiet.

"Every bruise she bears has added to the burden of guilt I will carry to my grave," Colin said in a voice softened and weighted by sorrow. "I canna explain why we did as little for her as we did. From the moment we left the warmth of our mother's womb, we have learned only brutality from our father. From the cradle we learned survival, learned how to avoid the beatings and all the other cruelties he inflicted upon us and others under his care. Aye, we are strong, and we can face most any mon, sword to sword, without flinching. Howbeit, we all lived in mortal terror of Duggan MacNairn, and that fear is a deep old one, fed to us with our mother's milk."

Gabel shook his head and dragged his fingers through his hair. "I am sorry. You are correct. I cannot understand such a life, or how it must affect a man. I respond to what is before my eyes—that a tiny, delicate woman was treated savagely by her own father, and no one raised a hand in her defense."

"I understand and take no insult, but, George, inelegant as his muttering was, is also correct. Ainslee isna dead, and she could weel have been, many times over. 'Tis all we could do. We kept her alive, and e'en that was at great risk to ourselves."

"But why would a father wish to kill his own child?"

"He loathed her. She should have died with our mother. Our father saw his own shame and cowardice each time he looked at Ainslee. He could have saved our mother and Ainslee, but he fled the battle that day, and ne'er once tried to help them. Ainslee was a living, breathing reminder of that cowardly desertion, and of the fact that he wouldna have changed that day e'en if given the chance. He would have still run to save his own wretched neck. 'Twas something he did often. He would have fled today, leaving all of us to die, except that he was trapped within the great hall and couldna reach the bolt hole."

Colin shrugged. "I truly didna see how he wished her death, not clearly, until she returned from Bellefleur. Ainslee tried to escape from here and, when we found her, our father would have cut her down on the spot if we hadna stopped him. Then he tried to starve her to death in his dungeons. I couldna ignore the dark truth any longer. Ye arrived at our gates ere I could think of a way to help her escape without costing too many lives."

"Weel, it looks as if our old enemy, Fraser, has finally succeeded in doing what our father couldna," said George.

"Your sister will *not* die," Gabel snapped, knowing that he tried to convince himself of that, as well as her brothers.

"Did ye say that Ronald still lives?" asked Colin.

"Aye. He was gravely wounded that day at the river's edge, but he is strong. He even wished to hobble along with me today, but I would not allow it. He will be able to care for Ainslee."

"Are ye sure ye should be moving her before she has recovered?"

"There is no place left here to shelter her adequately. E'en if you build something, 'twill take more time than it will for me to get her to Bellefleur. There she will have people to tend to her needs, a warm, soft bed, and plenty to eat. Nay, 'tis best to take her to Bellefleur. My men and I will ride out at dawn."

"Even if she takes a fever?"

Colin's soft words chilled Gabel to the bone, but he struggled to hide and subdue his fears. He did not wish to alarm Colin and his brothers, nor did he wish to stir up his own fears. A fever could be deadly. Even in the short time he had sat by Ainslee's side, he had constantly touched her face, searching for any sign of fever, yet dreading the possibility that it might appear. It was foolish, but he wanted to banish all thought of it from his mind. He wanted to wait and confront that demon only when and if it appeared.

"No matter what state she is in," he replied. "Now, there is something I have not yet told you—the king has granted Kengarvey and all of its lands to me."

"I had guessed that, sir. Why else should ye be asking us to swear an allegiance to you?"

"So that you would no longer trouble me, my people, or my lands. 'Tis reason enough."

"And, mayhaps ye wanted our vows ere ye told us just how much we have lost this day."

"Mayhaps," Gabel admitted reluctantly, for the thought had crossed his mind as he had accepted the oaths of each Mac-Nairn he took under his protection.

"And ye are willing to trust in the word of a MacNairn?" Colin asked, watching Gabel closely as he waited for an answer.

"Although all that has happened here today has shown me that I am often too trusting—aye—I will accept your oaths as they were spoken. I will watch closely, though, for any sign that treachery was another thing you learned from your father. Trusting your father's word cost me dearly, and may yet cost me more than I care to think on. Howbeit, I do not believe one should hold what a father does against his children. I am not the only one you must prove yourselves to, you realize."

"Aye, I ken that most every mon, woman, and bairn in Scotland has become our enemy o'er the years. I dinna consider a wary attitude an insult or a problem. We intend to try and wash away some of the stain our father—and his father before him—have so thoroughly smeared our name with." Colin glanced in the direction his brother-in-law had ridden, and grimaced. "There is one who willna take the news that ye now hold Kengarvey weel. 'Tis not only our wee sister he seeks. Livingstone truly believes that he has a right to gain from our loss."

"Yet he did not wish to lift his sword in the king's name."

"Livingstone rarely lifts his sword at all. When he married our sister, he was expected to stand with us in our battles, but he simply didna stand against us. He took our sister's dowry, fled to his keep, and was rarely seen again. The mon is here, because he seeks some gain from all of this. Aye, and 'tis certain that Elspeth was the one shoving him out the gates. She has always had a keen eye for gain, no matter whose hands she must snatch it from," Colin added bitterly. "That is one of my father's children who learned all of our father's ways. 'Tis nay good to speak ill of one's own kin, but Elspeth spits upon her kinship with us. Did ye hear any offer made of shelter or aid in rebuilding?"

"Why, nay," Gabel replied, unable to hide his surprise. "But, surely, if these lands were given to Livingstone, you and your people would be allowed to remain here."

"Nay, Sir de Amalville," replied Colin. "Mayhaps the maids and some others who work the lands and clean the stables, but none of *us* would be allowed to remain here. And what do ye plan, m'laird? Ye asked for our oaths yet, e'en now, ye dinna say whether we are to stay here or must set out to wander the land."

"You may remain here. If you hold true to the oaths you have given me, I see no reason to cast you out."

"I thank ye for that, Sir de Amalville. And who shall ye put o'er us?"

"I am not yet sure." Gabel looked around at the destruction wreaked by the Frasers, the MacFibhs, and by his own men. "There is not much left."

"We shall rebuild," Colin assured him, and his brothers nodded in agreement. "We have done so many times o'er the years, and we have become quite good at it."

" 'Tis late in the year. The weather has been most kind, but that could change at any moment. It could prove to be quite difficult for you and all of these people." Gabel frowned, not wishing to leave the MacNairns without adequate shelter and with few supplies, yet he did not think he could shelter so many people at Bellefleur without causing his own people some hardship.

"Dinna fear for us, m'laird. We will soon have shelters readied and, whene'er the weather allows, we will rebuild the keep. Mayhaps now we may enjoy a long enough time of peace and prosperity that we may finally add the stronger stone, but I shall leave such hopes and plans in yours and God's hands."

Gabel just smiled, and then ordered his men to give the Mac-Nairns what aid they would need to find themselves some shelter for the swiftly approaching night. Although the MacFibhs were departing, it was too late in the day for him to try and return to Bellefleur. There was no sign of an impending storm, and Gabel felt it was safe enough to wait until dawn before leaving. On his way back to the lean-to Ainslee sheltered in, Gabel paused only long enough to say farewell to the MacFibhs.

When Gabel reached the place where he had left Justice and Ainslee, he barely recognized it. Justice had clearly gathered some men to enlarge the shelter, make a fire pit, gather some supplies, and even lay out bedding with plenty of blankets. Ainslee now lay near a gentle fire on several layers of pelts. Gabel knew he would have appreciated it all the more if Ainslee had been awake. He slipped into the shelter and sat down on the blanket-covered straw bed Justice had arranged next to Ainslee. The maid hurried away before Gabel had a chance to thank her for her help.

"Before you ask—nay—I did not insult the girl," said Justice. "She is a very timid girl. Since she has a child, I thought her husband may have been killed in the battle, but it appears that her babe is Duggan MacNairn's bastard."

"She was his leman?" Gabel did not think it could be safe to have MacNairn's mistress tending to Ainslee.

"Nay, just another of his victims. MacNairn was one of those lairds who felt it was his God-given right to bed any maid he pleased, even if she said no."

"These lands will be the better for his leaving of them."

When Gabel idly brushed his hand over Ainslee's forehead, he tensed and held his hand in place on her brow. The skin beneath his hand was dry and hot. Ainslee had slipped from the unsettling grip of unconsciousness into the terrifying grasp of fever.

"Fever?" Justice whispered when he saw the look of horror on Gabel's face.

"Aye."

"We will return to Bellefleur on the morrow, and Ronald will soon restore her health."

Gabel said nothing, simply began to bathe Ainslee's face with cool water and fervently prayed that his cousin was right.

Twenty-one

"You have paused to touch her face at nearly every mile," Justice murmured as he watched Gabel lean over the cart to lightly brush his fingers over Ainslee's fever-flushed cheeks.

Gabel grimaced, ignored the young maid Morag's sympathetic smile, and moved away from the cart. The day was clear enough, but to the north there were some very ominous clouds forming. Although he had been able to make the feverish Ainslee comfortable in a cart, he had not been able to find any covered vehicle, and that troubled him. Ainslee was wrapped securely against the chill in the air, but she had no protection against the rain or the snow. If the storm caught up with them within the next hour or so, before they could reach Bellefleur, they would have to seek some shelter, and Gabel could see little of that in the land they traveled over.

Even as dawn had brightened the skies over the battered Kengarvey, Gabel had felt torn about the journey he was about to make. Because Ainslee was wracked with fever and delirium, he had wanted to stay where he was, nursing her until she was well enough for a long journey. He had also felt a strong need to get her to the comfort of Bellefleur and into Ronald's care. It had been the thought of Ronald's skills which had decided him. The moment they had all ridden away from Kengarvey, however, Gabel had begun to be plagued by doubts about his decision to move her. He had to continuously remind himself that Ronald could well be Ainslee's best chance for survival.

"I but reassure myself that she has not worsened," he explained to Justice as the two of them rode side by side behind the small cart which held Ainslee.

"Within the hour we can give her o'er into Ronald's care," Justice said.

" 'Tis my hope that he will agree with my decision to move her."

"She is no colder bundled in that cart than she would have been in that shelter at Kengarvey. And cease looking at those storm clouds at our backs. I do not believe they can catch us ere we reach Bellefleur's gates, but, even if the weather begins to turn against us, we are close enough now that we will not have to suffer it for long."

"Aye, I know it. In truth, I know that all you say is the truth—in my head. 'Tis the rest of me which frets like some old woman." He exchanged a brief grin with Justice.

"Well, tell that old woman that Lady Ainslee has not worsened, and will soon be lodged in a place where she will have all she needs to heal."

Gabel nodded, but he did not fully share Justice's confidence. Ronald was skilled, but was he skilled enough? Bellefleur had every comfort Ainslee could need or want, yet people could still die even when surrounded by the greatest of luxuries. He knew it was the presence of the fever that scared him. Too often he had watched it burn away the strength and the life of a fully grown, strong man. Knowing that, it was hard to find faith in everyone's assertions that the tiny Ainslee could successfully fight it off.

When Bellefleur finally came into view, Gabel felt a sense of nearly heady relief. The chill and damp of approaching night and the storm lurking to the north had rapidly increased in the past hour. Soon even the heavy wrappings they had sheltered Ainslee in would not be enough protection.

The moment Gabel and his entourage rode through the gates, Elaine and Lady Marie hurried out to greet them. Gabel was pleased that, despite their shock and upset over Ainslee's wound, his aunt and cousin accepted his assurances that he would explain everything as soon as Ainslee was taken care of. They helped to get Ainslee to her bedchamber, while he hurried to find Ronald. He left the old man with the women to tend to Ainslee, while he went to clean up from his journey.

By the time Gabel returned to Ainslee's bedchamber, Ronald had done his work, shooed the women away, and was seated at Ainslee's bedside. "How is she?" Gabel asked as he moved to the other side of her bed, tentatively reaching out to touch her forehead and silently cursing the heat he felt beneath his hand.

"Weak, battered, and feverish," Ronald answered bluntly. "No need to keep touching her head. I have a fine skill at healing but even I canna wipe away a fever in but a few moments."

Gabel smiled faintly at Ronald's ill humor. "It would not have surprised me if you had done just that." He sat down on the edge of Ainslee's bed and took her hand in his. "A part of me rather hoped that you could," he said quietly.

"Weel, laddie, I wish I could too, but I canna. The wound looks clean, she hasna lost any more blood since it was last tended to, and I find no signs of the wound turning poisonous."

"All good things and, yet, I hear a strange hesitancy in your voice, as if you do not wish to tell me everything"

Ronald shrugged. "I dinna, for 'tis clear that ye have a fear of such things, and I dinna wish to be adding to that."

"Any man with a few wits scattered in his head would fear the deadly touch of fever."

"Aye. Weel, the truth then. I would feel more confident about her chances for recovery if that bastard Duggan, her blood-drenched swine of a father, hadna done her such harm already, ere she was even wounded by the arrow. He beat her savagely at least twice."

"How can you tell how often he did it?"

"The color of the lassie's bruises tell me. Some are fainter than the others. There are two different sets of bruises. I am fair certain of that. And the poor lass has lost weight, which she didna have too much of to begin with. The time she spent at Kengarvey stole away a lot of her strength. Howbeit, the lass is a good wee fighter."

"That she is, but this time she may face too great a challenge."

" 'Tis in God's hands."

"Aye, and may He forgive if I touch upon blasphemy, but I wish He would at least let us know His plans and spare us this gut-wrenching fear, or leave it in our hands." He fleetingly smiled when Ronald chuckled. "And what of you? Are you strong enough to tend to her?"

"Aye, although I confess that I am not as strong as I would like to be or need to be. I will have to allow others to help, so that I might rest from time to time. I ken that I will do the child no good if I make myself ill and weak ere she has begun to heal. Now, if ye wouldst be so kind, would ye tell me how she came to be wounded, and how Kengarvey fares?"

Gabel took a deep breath and reluctantly told Ronald everything, pausing in his tale only to answer Ronald's few sharp questions. He sensed no blame behind Ronald's quiet grief over those who had died, forced to pay the highest price for all of Duggan MacNairn's follies. When he told Ronald how the brothers had reacted to the news that he was now the lord of Kengarvey, Gabel waited to see what the older man thought. He also wondered if Ronald would have any opinion on Donald Livingstone.

"I am pleased to hear that the laddies have survived and have accepted their loss," Ronald finally said.

"Do you really believe that they have?" Gabel asked, needlessly readjusting the blankets over Ainslee.

"Aye. In truth, I dinna think any of them believed that they would live long enough to rule there anyway, or that there would be anything left of Kengarvey. The lads have their faults. Who wouldna, after being raised by Duggan MacNairn? Howbeit, Duggan didna have the full raising of them, and their mother left a strong mark upon their hearts and souls. Ye need not worry that another Duggan MacNairn lurks there."

"Colin seems to believe that his sister Elspeth is the one who has their father's nature."

"A mean-spirited, heartless lass. Aye, had she been born a mon or wed a husband with the stomach for battle, she could have been another Duggan."

"She could yet prod her husband to take up the fight on her behalf."

"Only if he doesna have to go to war o'er it. Livingstone may do a lot to try and get what he wants, but he will ne'er do anything to bring an army to his gates or go to battle himself. 'Tis our good fortune that Elspeth wasna married off to a warrior. Livingstone will come, and he will argue for what he wants. He may even take his claims to the king. But ye can refuse the oaf without fear that ye will soon be riding off to battle Ainslee's kinsmen yet again."

"Good. Now, all I need to worry o'er is Ainslee. There is a lot I must tell her and ask of her when she recovers."

Ronald said nothing, and Gabel found the man's lack of assurances unsettling. He ordered Ronald back to his bed for a few hours, since Ainslee was resting as comfortably as she ever would while held so tightly in the fever's grip. He wanted someone to tell him that Ainslee would be well again, yet, when they did, he found little comfort for he could not believe the reassurances. As he took Ronald's seat in a chair by the bed, Gabel had to smile over his own vagaries. The only one who could convince him that she would heal was Ainslee herself, and she had yet to give him any comforting signs. He prayed that he would see one soon, for the longer the fever possessed her, the less were her chances of recovery.

Gabel stretched and moved to splash some cold water on his face. It had been three long days since he had brought Ainslee back to Bellefleur, and he had spent a great deal of that time at her side. He had bathed her with cool water, seen to her needs, tried to force some hearty broth down her throat whenever she was aware enough to swallow, and tried to comfort her when she was caught in the terrors the fever produced in her mind. Only once had she recovered enough to recognize him, calling him by name and reaching out to touch his face. He had been unable to take much comfort in that, for she had quickly revealed that she did not know she was ill, where she was, or even what day it was.

He poured himself a tankard of wine and returned to his seat by her bedside. Even when he left her side to tend to what little work he still did, or to seek out his own bed, he got little rest from his vigil. Leaving her side did not stop him from worrying or wondering if there had been any change in her condition. Ronald's increasing ill humor told him that the man was also getting very concerned.

Deciding that it was time he took yet another useless break from watching at her bedside, Gabel leaned forward and placed his hand on her forehead. It had become a habit, an act he repeated with almost embarrassing frequency, but this time he froze. He lifted his hand and gaped at it, the dampness on his palm glistening brightly in the light from the candles by the bed. Numbly, he replaced his hand on her forehead. Suddenly he leapt to his feet and proceeded to feel her whole body. Ainslee was drenched in her own sweat from head to toe. Gabel stood by the bed, torn by all the things he wanted to do, from hugging her to racing through the halls of Bellefleur screaming the news that her fever had finally broken.

He took several deep breaths to try and calm himself, succeeding only enough to stop himself from acting like a complete madman. Although he hated to leave her alone in case she woke, he knew he had to fetch Ronald. As a compromise he went to the door and told a passing maid to fetch the older man. He then returned to Ainslee and sat down on the edge of the bed. Gabel took her hand in his, stared at her face, and tried to will her eyes open. He wanted to see that her eyes were clear of the clouds of delirium that had darkened them for days.

* * *

Ainslee inwardly grimaced and shifted slightly. She felt weak, battered, and uncomfortably damp. When she realized that someone was holding her hand almost too tightly, she opened her eyes, a little startled at the effort it took to do so. When she was finally able to see Gabel clearly, she tried to smile, and winced when she discovered that her lips were too dry and cracked for her to do so comfortably.

Gabel pressed her hand to his lips, not meeting her gaze for a moment, and she studied him. He did not look very well. There was a wan look to his dark skin and a look of great weariness lining his face and darkening his eyes. When she tried to reach out to touch the bristle of beard on his face, she cursed. She was too weak to do more than lightly brush her fingers over his cheek, before she had to drop her arm back down on the bed.

"I was thinking that ye looked most poorly, Gabel," she said, surprised at how hoarse her voice was and how it hurt to speak. "Howbeit, I begin to think that I must look a great deal worse. Have I been ill?"

Gabel laughed shakily, amazed and a little embarrassed by the emotion choking him. "Aye, you have. This is the first time you have said anything sensible since that arrow buried itself in your flesh."

For a moment Ainslee did not know what he was talking about, then memory flooded her. She tried to reach up to touch her shoulder, then decided there was no need. She could feel the wound. The fact that it was not as painful as it ought to be told her that she had been out of her senses for some time.

"How long have I been ill?"

"Four days." Gabel decided to keep his answers short for fear that he would begin to babble and tell her far more than she was ready to hear.

"I am back at Bellefleur?"

"Aye. I brought you here for you could be better cared for, Kengarvey had little shelter and few supplies."

"Kengarvey," she whispered. "How are my brothers? How many died? Does the keep——" Her eyes widened when he placed a finger on her lips to silence her. "Do ye fear to tell me? Is the news so bad that ye think I shall fall back under a fever again?"

"Nay. I but want you to be quiet. You have lain abed wracked with a fever for four days, near to five, if one counts the day you were wounded. You should not use up what little strength you have regained in asking a lot of questions. Ah, Ronald," he said when the older man hurried into the room.

To his relief Ronald took over, hushing Ainslee, cleaning her, and dressing her in a clean gown. Gabel used the time to compose himself. One of the things he had grieved over as she had lain so ill, was the possibility that he had lost all chance of telling what was in his heart. The words had swirled in his head every minute she had been ill, and they now sat on the end of his tongue, fighting to be said. He knew he was close to giving into the urge to tell her everything he felt, but now was not the time. If nothing else, she might accept his words and reply in kind out of gratitude for all he had done, or she could be too weak to refuse him. He dreaded the thought that she might not return his feelings, but the idea that she would accept him without really wanting to, out of gratitude and mayhaps even pity, was even harder to bear.

When Ronald stepped up to him and helped himself to some wine, Gabel glanced back at the bed and saw that Ainslee's eyes were closed again. "She has not fallen back into a fever, has she?"

"Nay," Ronald replied. "The lass is just weak, and my attentions wearied her. 'Tis just as weel that ye werena at her bedside, for the lass can have a foul blasphemous tongue at times."

Gabel grinned, knowing that Ainslee's ill temper was a good

sign. She might be weak in body, but her spirit was still strong. He was sure that was what had helped her fight off the fever.

"Do you believe she will now begin to truly recover?"

"Aye. The wound has been healing weel despite her fever, and her eyes and mind are clear. She will be verra weak for a while, and we shall have to bear the bite of her tongue, for she will try to do more than she ought, sooner than she ought."

"She will stay in her bed until you say otherwise. Aye, even if I must bind her to it."

Ronald laughed and finished off his wine. "The evening meal is being set out. Do ye wish to go to the hall? I can sit with her."

"Nay. You go and have a page bring some food up here, enough for me and for Ainslee. She may not be able to eat much yet, but her appetite will soon return."

"Aye, and 'twould be best if she ate hearty for a while, to regain her lost strength and some of that lost weight. The lass is naught but skin and bone."

"Ah, but 'tis most fair skin and bone."

Gabel laughed at Ronald's look of disgust. When the man left a moment later, after one final look at his patient, Gabel returned to his seat by the bed. He discovered himself constantly brushing his hand over Ainslee's forehead and cheeks, and smiled at his own foolishness. When she had been ill, he had been constantly looking for a sign that the fever had lessened or left, and now that it had, he kept looking for its return. He knew, however, that he also sought reassurance that she really was on the path to recovery.

It was late before Gabel finally sought his own bed and left Ainslee in the care of Morag. She had only woken up once more, but her eyes had still been clear, and she had eaten some solid food. As Gabel settled himself in his bed, he knew he would be able to sleep soundly for the first time since she had been sent back to Kengarvey.

* * *

Gabel met Ainslee's glare calmly. In the four days since her fever had broken, she had become more and more belligerent, fighting everyone's commands even though they were in her own best interest, her good health all that concerned people. He decided that she needed to be told just how badly she was behaving and, if she had not thrown him from the room, he would then have a more serious talk with her. The temper and spirit she was showing told him that she could hear his proposal and reply to it honestly. He no longer feared that weakness or gratitude could force her to agree when she did not really wish to. She was showing very little of either at the moment.

"Do you doubt Ronald's knowledge of the healing arts?" he asked her as he helped her settle herself against the pillows Morag had plumped up before she had fled the room.

"Nay, of course not," Ainslee said, crossing her arms over her chest and glaring down at her blanket-covered toes.

"Yet you question everything he says you must do to recover."

"He kens how to heal people, but he can also be a fretful old woman."

"Considering how ill-tempered you are, I really do not think he would want to keep you abed any longer than he needed to. You make life most unpleasant, and any sane man would wish to see an end to that." He met her angry look with perfect calm and a hint of condemnation.

"I havena been quite so bad," she muttered.

"You have been almost intolerable. 'Tis only the understanding of those who tend to you that keeps you from being left completely alone." He sat down on the edge of the bed, and took her hand in his when she flushed and would not look at him again. "I understand how infuriating illness can be to one who is unaccustomed to being abed and unable to do much of anything. Did you think I had passed so many years as a knight without getting a scratch?"

Ainslee sighed, slumped back against her pillows, and gave

him a crooked apologetic smile. "Nay. Have I outdone ye in ill humor and ingratitude?"

"I should like to say aye, but I suspect there are those here who would be quick to argue that."

"I am sorry, and I shall apologize to the others when they dare to draw near me again." She shook her head. "My wound doesna trouble me much and I feel hale enough, yet the fever robbed me of most of my strength. My mind and heart say that I am weel enough to get up and to do something, yet my body shakes and trembles from weakness and willna allow me to move. 'Tis maddening and, since I canna thrash myself, I take my temper out on others. I dinna try to excuse my poor manners, just to try and tell ye where they spring from."

He brushed a kiss over her lips, laughing softly when she curled her arm around his neck and stole a deeper kiss from him. When he pulled away a little, forcing his passion aside, he shook his head as he grinned at her. "You are certainly not strong enough for that yet."

" 'Twould nicely pass the time. After all, if I must lie abed all the day—"

"Do not try to tempt me," he admonished genially as he pulled away.

Ainslee sighed. "Ye need not keep me company if ye have work to do."

"I have a great deal of work to do, but I have decided that you have recovered enough for one thing."

"And what is that?" she pressed when he just looked at her, saying nothing and his expression unsettlingly somber.

"We must talk, and I have thought o'er this moment for days, weeks even, yet suddenly I found it hard to speak."

"Now ye are truly making me uneasy."

Ainslee tried not to let her fears show. Was he about to tell her that she would be returned to Kengarvey as soon as she was well enough to travel? He was her laird now. Perhaps he had even arranged a suitable marriage for her. She cursed herself for a fool for thinking that his bringing her back to Bellefleur meant anything more than a kind concern for her well-being. She had been injured and had even saved his life, so he had brought her to the one place where he had known she could get the best care. Although she had told herself that time and time again, she now realized that she had not really listened to herself.

" 'Tis nothing so ominous." He stared at her hand, idly running his thumb over her knuckles. "I have not treated you well, Ainslee."

"What nonsense." She pressed her lips together when he gave her a quelling glance.

"This will not go smoothly if you insist upon interrupting me."

"I will be quiet."

"Good. Now, I have treated you poorly. I bedded you, yet continued to search elsewhere for a wife. In that I insulted you, treating you like some whore. Although, I swear to you that I ne'er once thought of you in such a denigrating way." He grimaced and shook his head. "I am doing this poorly."

"Then mayhaps ye should cease trying to explain so much, and just say what ye wish to."

"Aye, although I did feel that I had a lot to atone for ere I asked you the question that appears to be stuck in my throat."

She reached out to caress his cheek and smiled faintly. "I can think of nothing ye need to atone for, but, if it will make ye feel better, then I forgive ye for all those little wrongs ye have convinced yourself ye committed."

"Thank you—I think." He took both of her hands between his and looked at her. "What I wish to ask is—will you be my wife?"

Ainslee stared at him. She had heard the words, but doubted her own ears. There had been no preamble of love words, no talk of how he had decided he could not live without her, simply the blunt question. She could not even read what emotions he felt in his expression, which was one of tense waiting.

"Ye dinna need to wed me just because ye have taken my

maidenhead," she said carefully, afraid he was acting out of a sense of honor. "And ye certainly dinna need to do this because I took the arrow that was meant for you."

"I do it for none of those reasons. I want you to be my wife. I would have asked you the moment you awoke from your fever, except that I was afraid you would say aye for all of the wrong reasons. I wanted your mind clear, your spirit back, and some of your strength back as well. Ainslee, I had some very strange ideas of what I needed in a wife, and I had clung to them for so long that I was unable to accept any change in my plans. It was not until I thought I had put you out of my reach that I realized I wanted you, that you would make me a very fine wife."

"And what does your family think of this?"

"Everyone at Bellefleur is pleased, and most wonder why I took so long." When she said nothing, he touched a kiss to her frowning mouth and asked, "If you do not wish me for a husband, you need but say nay."

"I dinna want to say nay." She grimaced. "I fear ye have taken me so by surprise that I canna think of what I wish to say. My only clear thought is that ye might be wedding me out of a sense of honor, and that is an arrangement I would say nay to."

"Nay, I am not wedding you out of any sense of honor."

Before he could say anything else, a young page stumbled into the room and said, "There is a man demanding to see you, m'lord." He flushed and backed toward the door. "Oh, I should have knocked and begged entrance," he mumbled.

"Aye, you should have. Just recall your manners next time. Who demands to speak to me?" Gabel asked when the boy shifted from one foot to the other and chewed on his bottom lip.

"A Sir Donald Livingstone. He is most persistent."

"I know," Gabel muttered, then cursed. "Tell him I will be down in but a moment." As soon as the little page hurried away, Gabel stood and looked down at Ainslee. "I will take heart in the fact that you have not refused me. While I speak to Livingstone, mayhaps you can consider my offer and we can speak on it again." He frowned. "I had not expected the man so soon. He had said a fortnight."

"If he seeks some gain, then 'tis my sister who has sent him early. She probably drove him from his keep with her demands."

He brushed a kiss over her lips and started toward the door. "Well, he shall soon discover that his journey is for nothing. He will get neither you nor Kengarvey."

Before Ainslee could ask what he meant, he was gone. Soon after she had recovered, Gabel had told her of the fate of Kengarvey, and she had assured him that she felt no anger toward him. After the crimes her father had committed, only a fool would think that the lands would stay with the family. All she cared about was that many of her people and all four of her brothers had survived, although it had taken some time to convince Gabel of that. She was not surprised that Elspeth would try to lay claim to the lands. What troubled her was Gabel's implication that Livingstone wanted *her* as well.

"Curse the mon," she grumbled as she carefully sat up, going cautiously so that she did not bring on the dizziness that still affected her from time to time. "He tells me to stay abed and rest, then leaves me with words that will prey upon my mind."

As she carefully slid out of bed and reached for a gown, she decided she could not wait. Now that she considered it, there was only one reason for her sister to want her, and that was to marry her off for gain. The thought of such a thing sent chills down her spine. Gabel had not spoken of love or even uttered any sweet words when he had asked for her hand. She had hesitated because of that, and now regretted it. If she had left Gabel with the idea that she might not accept his proposal, he could easily consider some match that Livingstone put forward.

It took her far longer than she liked to slip on her gown,

and she knew she looked a tousled mess, but she began to feel a strong sense of urgency. As far as she knew, Gabel had no reason to refuse her kinsman's proposal of a match, and she was desperate to give him one. Ainslee knew that marriage to Gabel—if he did not return the love she felt for him in full—could prove painful at times, but it was far preferable to anything else she could think of. It was certainly far preferable to being sold to some man of her sister's choosing. She would tell Gabel she accepted his proposal, even if she had to crawl to the great hall to do it. All the problems she could foresee could be sorted out later.

Gabel sipped at his wine and studied the man who cautiously sat down next to him. It was evident that Livingstone did not really want to be at Bellefleur, did not wish to chance that he would anger Gabel, but did not have the stomach to refuse his wife. There was probably some of the man's own greed prompting his actions, but Gabel felt more at ease. He had no intention of giving Livingstone Ainslee or Kengarvey, and now he could see that Ronald was right, that he could refuse the man everything he asked for and not risk more battles.

"You said you would come in a fortnight's time," he murmured. "I had not realized that a fortnight had come and gone already."

"I beg your gracious pardon for my inability to wait, but I began to fear that the weather would soon worsen, and thus keep us from settling these matters until spring," Livingstone said.

"I am not sure what matters you think we have to settle."

"Why the matter of Kengarvey and of Ainslee, of course."

"Kengarvey is mine."

"Yours? Not all of the MacNairns were traitors to the king. Surely the land should go to those of the family who remained loyal."

"The king felt I should hold the lands. You may go to him with your claims, if you so wish. I will not attempt to stop you. I am a king's man and will follow his wishes in this matter. His wishes at this time are that I hold Kengarvey."

"And who shall be its castelean? Ye canna rule this keep and that at the same time."

"I have placed a good man there, and with the help of the MacNairns who survived, I believe I can bring Kengarvey back. Aye, and make it even better than Duggan MacNairn ever allowed it to be."

Livingstone took a long drink as he visibly tried to control himself, then slowly asked, "And what of Ainslee MacNairn? Has she recovered from her injuries?"

"She is slowly recovering."

"When she is well, m'lord, my wife and I will take her into our care."

"Nay, I think not." Gabel smiled faintly when Livingstone gaped at him.

"The king didna give ye her as weel, did he?"

"Nay, but I see no reason to hand her over to you."

"I am her kinsmon," Livingstone said in a tight voice as he struggled to hold onto his temper.

"You have ne'er had an interest in her before, so why should you want her so badly now?"

"My wife and I have been fortunate enough to find her a husband. I believe I mentioned that back at Kengarvey. It was not easy, for she is already eighteen and has no dowry. Howbeit, we chanced upon a mon who badly wishes a wife, and is willing to make a settlement. It would be a most advantageous arrangement."

"Aye, for you."

"And for Ainslee. She canna wish to become a spinster, doomed to be no more than a nursemaid to whatever children her brothers might spawn."

"I do not believe she will suffer such a fate."

"This is a good marriage I offer her."

"Well, I believe I might have a better one—me."

Livingstone gaped at him again, and set his goblet down with visibly unsteady hands. "Ye wish to wed her?"

"Aye. I have asked for her hand this very day."

"And what was her reply?" asked Livingstone, watching Gabel closely when he hesitated to reply.

"Her reply was aye," said Ainslee, entering the great hall in time to hear the exchange.

Gabel did not know whether to be overjoyed or furious when he turned to see Ainslee slowly walking to the head table. She was pale and looked badly tousled, as if she had just thrown her gown on over her nightrail and run out the door. Watching her every measured step, he glanced down at her feet, saw that she had no slippers on, and knew that that was exactly what she had done. What occupied his thoughts far more than her foolish, and possibly dangerous, walk to the great hall, was that she had just accepted his proposal.

As he helped her sit down on his right and silently handed her a linen square to mop the beads of sweat from her pale brow, he thought over what that acceptance had been prompted by. She had guessed Livingstone's plans for her, and had come down to put a stop to them in the surest way she could. It was not the reason he wanted her to have for accepting his proposal, but he decided he would not argue. He might have doubts about how much of her mind and heart he could claim, but he knew they shared a fierce passion. It was a start.

Even as he kept a close watch on her, Gabel talked to Livingstone. The man tried to argue, but he had to give up at last. Gabel offered him a bed for the night, but, after a curt farewell to Ainslee, Livingstone left. Confident that he would have little further trouble from the man, Gabel turned to look at Ainslee.

"I believe I told you to cease trying to get out of bed. That did not mean rise, dress, and stroll down to the great hall," he drawled.

"I didna stroll," she said, wondering if her voice was trembling as much as her legs were.

"Nay?"

"Nay, I staggered. I thought ye would like to hear my answer."

"I did." He leaned forward and gave her a gentle kiss. "It could have waited."

"Nay. Weel, mayhaps, but I decided I didna want ye to change your mind."

"There was no danger of that. Now, I should heartily scold you for using what little strength you have regained to come down here."

"Mayhaps that could wait." She smiled crookedly. "I think I had best return to my bed."

When she did not move, he frowned slightly. "Are you intending to dine first?"

"Nay, I am trying to think of a way to tell ye that I canna move another step, and that ye will have to carry me back."

Gabel laughed softly and stood up. "You are not going to be a very obedient wife, are you?" he asked as he picked her up in his arms.

Ainslee curled her arms around his neck and rested her head on his shoulders. "I fear not, Sir de Amalville. There is still time to change your mind," she said, praying that no such thing would happen.

"There is little chance of that. As you well know, I can cling to a plan with great tenacity. I have but one question—do you say aye simply to chase away Livingstone?"

"Nay, I simply said aye a little faster than I might have," she replied sleepily.

"Then, 'tis settled. As soon as you have the strength to stand before a priest, we shall be married."

Twenty-two

"Will you cease your wriggling?" Marie demanded in affectionate aggravation.

Ainslee grimaced and forced herself to stand as still as she could. It had been three long weeks since she had accepted Gabel's proposal. Everyone was pleased, and had spent the whole time preparing for the wedding. Ainslee began to think that she was the only one who was not completely delighted.

Not once in all that time had Gabel spoken of love. She had told herself that it did not matter, that she had enough love for both of them, and that he could grow to love her. It was all nonsense and she knew it. Such sentiments did not still the fears gnawing at her heart, and she could not make herself believe them, not even a little. She was also badly torn between what she wanted and what she would accept. She desperately wanted Gabel to marry her because he loved her, yet, even knowing she could suffer from that lack, she could not bring herself to stop the marriage. She wanted to be Gabel's wife too badly.

The hardest thing she knew she would face was that she would still not be able to love Gabel freely and openly. From what little she knew, men who did not love, did not wish to have love thrust upon them. It made them uncomfortable when the woman showered them in a love they could not return. So, even though she would be his wife, she would still have to be careful to hide all she felt. That she feared could become a torture to her.

"At last, you are ready to face the priest," Marie announced as she stepped back.

Ainslee looked at herself in the tall looking glass hanging in her bedchamber. The blue gown the women of Bellefleur had made for her was lovely. Although she had not regained all the weight she had lost at Kengarvey, she filled it out nicely enough. She did not think she had ever looked so good, and she smiled at Marie and Elaine in thanks. Despite all the doubts and fears plaguing her, she could not help but feel pleased that she would be dressed suitably for the wedding. Gabel was forfeiting a lot to marry her, every advantage a man usually sought in marriage, and she at least wanted to look as though she could serve as the lady of Bellefleur.

"You do not look as happy as I think you ought," said Elaine, and then quickly eluded her mother's light slap. "Well, she does not."

"Marriage is a verra important step in any woman's life," Ainslee began, struggling to think of some way to explain the sadness Elaine had sensed in her, and ease the worry both of Gabel's kinswomen could not hide. "I am but uncertain, Elaine. Within a verra short time, I will take a step that I can ne'er turn back from."

Marie briefly hugged her. "I know the fear you speak of, child, but you are the most fortunate of women. So many of us must marry the men chosen for us by others. Some of us do not even have the chance to come to know our husbands ere we must marry them. I would think that you must know Gabel very well by now. You were given a choice, and can wed a man you know loves you."

"Does he?" Ainslee asked, then cursed softly, angry with herself for her inability to hide her own doubts.

"Ah, I see what the problem is," murmured Elaine. "My stupid cousin has not spoken of love, has he?"

"He has asked me to be his wife. 'Tis a great honor, and I am being most ungrateful to complain."

"Nay, you are not. He could at least have muttered a few

pretty words, and I wager he did not even do that. Men can be so stupid."

"My sharp-tongued daughter has the right of it," agreed Marie as she idly smoothed Ainslee's hair, which had been left to hang free and was decorated with blue and white ribbons. "Put aside your worries, Ainslee. I will not try and convince you that Gabel loves you, for only he can do that, but I assure you that he is not without some deep feeling for you. I saw it when he returned from the river that day. He realized he had erred in giving you back to your father, and he was sadly tormented by that mistake. I saw it while he nursed you. The man spent hours at your bedside. Even when he left your side to work or rest, all could see that his mind and his heart were still with you, still praying for your recovery. Nay, he cares, child. Mayhaps he just needs you to pull the words from him."

As Ainslee entered the great hall a few moments later and saw Gabel waiting there with the priest, she prayed that Marie knew what she was talking about. She desperately wanted Gabel's love, but she could find some satisfaction if he at least cared deeply about her. Everything Marie had said indicated that he did have some strength of feeling for her. At times she had glimpsed it in him, but, since she so desperately wanted his love, she had not dared to trust in her own conclusions. Ainslee just wished she had more faith in what other people seemed to see so clearly.

"Have heart, lassie," Ronald murmured as he stepped up to kiss her cheek.

"I am trying, Ronald."

"Good lass. Ye are doing the right thing, though I am thinking it may take ye both a wee bit of time to see how right this is."

She gave Ronald a weak smile as she walked to Gabel and let him take her by the hand. He was looking very much the lord of Bellefleur in his elegant black tunic trimmed with delicate silver embroidery. Ainslee suddenly felt very inadequate.

Gabel deserved so much more than a penniless, landless girl with a name that drew only scorn and hatred from others. Some day he had to realize that, and what would happen to their marriage then?

When she met his gaze, she caught a brief glimpse of uncertainty in his dark eyes. It amused her a little that she should find that comforting. As they knelt before the priest, she prayed that she could learn to be happy with whatever Gabel had to offer her.

Gabel drank his wine and watched Ainslee closely. She laughed and talked freely with everyone, but he sensed a reticence in her. When she had joined him by the priest, he had seen a hint of fear and sadness in her eyes, and it made him uneasy. He was willing to try and live with the fact that she might never love him as deeply as he loved her, but if she began to think she had erred in marrying him, he dared not consider how much that would cut him.

"We will try and slip away soon," he murmured as he took her hand in his and kissed her palm.

" 'Twill require great skill to leave this crowded hall unseen," she said, smiling faintly as she looked around.

"Then we shall just leave it swiftly."

Ainslee laughed when Gabel suddenly stood up, picked her up in his arms, and bolted for the door. Only a few of the people in the hall recovered from their surprise fast enough to make a few ribald comments. She clung to his neck as he bounded up the stairs.

"They will be talking about this for days to come," she said.

"Ah, well, one likes one's wedding to be memorable."

"That escape has assured that."

She laughed again when Gabel entered the bedchamber they would now share, kicked the door shut behind him, walked over to the bed, and dropped her onto the soft coverlet. Her humor swiftly vanished, replaced by passion when he started to shed his clothes. For a moment she just laid there and watched him undress, his clothes tossed haphazardly around the room. There was an expression of deep hunger tightening his features, and she was quickly infected by his urgency. She rose to her knees and began to take off her own clothes.

Just as she began to undo her chemise, he fell upon her. Ainslee made no protest as he roughly removed the last of her clothes. When their flesh finally met for the first time in far too long she echoed his groan of satisfaction. Their lovemaking quickly became fierce, as they hurriedly tried to satisfy their need to touch and kiss each part of each other. When he finally joined their bodies, she clung to him, easily matching the ferocity of his movements, her passion as hot and wild as his. Their cries of ecstasy blended as they found the release they sought as one.

Ainslee was still panting from the strength and speed of their lovemaking when Gabel rose from the bed. She blushed slightly as he cleaned them both off, then hurriedly curled up in his arms when he returned to their bed. It felt so good to be back in his arms. Even though she had been healed enough for lovemaking before the wedding, he had stayed out of her bed, stealing only the occasional passionate kiss. She snuggled closer to him and decided that, for a little while, she would not think about anything else.

Gabel smoothed his hand over her tousled hair and said quietly, "I had planned to make love to you slowly, with all my meager skills, so as to chase away your doubts with the passion we can share. I thought that, if I could remind you of how special and strong that passion is, you would cease to question how right our marriage is—for both of us."

"Doubts?" Ainslee cautiously looked up at him. "Why would ye think I had any doubts?" She decided that, since she had chosen to wed a man she loved almost beyond reason but who did not love her, she needed to learn how to keep her innermost thoughts from showing themselves in her face.

"I saw them. Every so often, when I would look in your

·yes, I would see, well, an uncertainty, almost a fear. It was here when you took my hand and we knelt before the priest."

"Marriage is a grave and important step," she murmured, inwardly grimacing over the inadequacy of her words. It had not been a good enough answer to silence young Elaine, so why should it work to silence Gabel's questions?

"I know. I suffered from that hesitation as well. 'Tis one that every man and woman must feel when the moment comes to actually say the vows before the priest and before God. What I saw in your eyes was more than that. I cannot believe I am being fanciful."

Ainslee sighed and flopped onto her back at his side. "Nay, we are not. 'Twas there," she admitted, deciding that she simply could not lie to him on their wedding night, the night which began the whole rest of their lives together.

Gabel turned on his side and looked down at her. "Why were they there?"

"Why? Gabel, I have just married a mon who can sit higher at the table than I, and have brought him no lands and no dowry, as weel as a name most people in Scotland consider only good enough to spit on. Ye did look so verra fine, high-born and wealthy, in your wedding finery, and I suddenly felt so verra unworthy, as I have brought ye nothing to repay you for this honor."

He smiled and brushed a kiss over her mouth. "I need only you."

Her heart skipped a little, for there was definite feeling behind those words. "Ye might have eased some of my fears and doubts if ye had said a few such pretty words when ye asked me to marry you."

"They are more than just pretty words, Ainslee. I would not try to beguile you with empty flatteries," he said as he slid his hand down to her stomach and lightly caressed her. "I am not very good at flattery anyway. 'Tis odd, but I feel as if you want something, and I am failing to give it to you. You must know that I will give you most anything you want."

"Ask and I shall receive?"

He shrugged. "Aye, within reason."

"Then I want ye to love me."

"That is no challenge, for I do already."

The tension that had knotted Ainslee's stomach as she ha
made her demand left her so swiftly, she needed a minute t
regain her breath. She felt as if someone had just punched he
in the stomach, very hard, and wondered how mere word
could hold such power. "What did ye just say?"

Gabel eyed her warily as she sat up. "I said that your reque
was easy to meet, for I do love you."

Ainslee cursed and shoved him down on the bed. Still curs
ing softly about the idiocy of men, she straddled his body an
stared at him. It surprised her a little that the words she ha
waited so long to hear, had so wanted to hear, should mak
her so angry. The confusion of emotion she labored under als
tied her tongue. There was a great deal she wished to say, b
she found herself unable to speak.

"When I finally got the courage to speak my heart, I di
not expect you to look as if you want to throttle me," Gabe
said, his uneasiness growing when she just stared at him with
out speaking for several minutes.

"Actually, I was wondering if I really want to put the pillo
o'er your head until ye cease to breathe. Howbeit, I migh
enjoy it now, but I think I would regret it later."

"That is a comfort to know. Why have I made you angry?

Placing her hands on either side of his head, she leane
down to look him straight in the eye. Slowly, her thought
were becoming clearer, and she felt she could speak coherentl
not simply babble about how stupid and inconsiderate me
could be. Since she knew that Gabel was neither, she was gla
she had been briefly shocked into silence. She certainly di
not wish to reply to his unadorned declaration of love wit
insults.

"How long have ye kenned that ye loved me?" she asked
Tentatively, unsure of just how angry she was, he lifted hi

hands and began to smooth them up and down her slim back. "Since I saw you cross the river that day."

"And yet ye have ne'er considered the possibility that I might wish to ken this wee bit of information?"

"Ah, I should have told you sooner." Gabel felt his spirits rise as he realized what had angered her. Ainslee would not be so furious about his lengthy silence unless he had been holding back words she had been hungry to hear.

"That would have been nice. It may have saved me many long weeks of wondering how big an idiot I am. It may have saved me the turmoil of trying to decide if I should risk all and wed a mon who might ne'er love me as I wanted him to. It may have e'en saved me a great deal of lost sleep as I struggled to convince myself that the love I had for you would be enough to make our marriage a good and happy one." She cursed softly with surprise when he suddenly pulled her tight into his arms and kissed her.

"And mayhaps," he murmured against her lips, "I would have been saved from a few doubts and fears myself if *you* had been more forthcoming."

She raised herself up enough to look him in the eye. "Ye had doubts and fears?"

"When a man finally accepts that he is in love, did you think he just calmly believes his feelings are returned, and that all is right with the world?"

"I ne'er gave that much thought, since I didna ken that ye felt such things for me." She met his disgusted look with a brief grin, then grew serious as she gently traced the lines of his face with her fingertips. "I can see that we both suffered. Mayhaps we should learn to speak more openly with each other. Surely whatever we might say canna cause us as much pain as we have just suffered."

"Agreed. And I give you leave to remind me of this bargain, if you think I am being too reticent."

"Fair enough." She wriggled against him, smiling when she

felt him harden with interest. "I think I have loved you from the first moment I saw you."

"Aye? You have a very strange way of showing affection then, for, if I recall correctly, you were trying to stick your sword in my chest."

"Mayhaps I was but trying to catch your eye?" She giggled when he cursed softly. "I knew it when we became lovers. Oh, I tried to be practical, but I failed quite miserably. I was sick with jealousy when ye were courting Margaret Fraser."

"I realize now how I must have hurt you. I can only ask your forgiveness. I often felt guilty about it all, yet I refused to see what was in my own heart, and talked away any doubt I had that I was doing what was right for me and for Bellefleur. I also wished to avoid emotion, for I feel one should always use only one's wits, and emotion can sometimes make clear thought difficult. You stirred up such emotion within me, it was almost frightening. Nay, I confess, it did frighten me and I ran from it, claiming a need to let only cool reason rule my life.

"It was not until I thought you were forever beyond my reach that I realized I did not want to be a man of only reason, that it would leave me only half a man. Dangerous and maddening as it can be, I realized I wanted all of those feelings you can so easily rouse within me."

"Ye made me no promises and spoke no pretty lies. I wasna forced into your bed; I came willingly. There is naught ye have to ask forgiveness for."

"You are far kinder than I think I could have been had the situations been the other way round."

"Nay, I am simply too happy to moan and complain about what is past and done. As I said, ye ne'er lied to me, Gabel, and that honesty can only be praised. At times I deceived myself, but ye canna be faulted for my own foolishness." She touched a kiss to his mouth, and then began to lightly trace the shape of his face with soft quick kisses. "I do so love ye Gabel de Amalville."

"And I you, Ainslee."

"E'en though I am as prickly as a thistle?"

"Aye, for I have found all the softness that lurks within."

"I shall be a verra good wife to you," she whispered.

"Just be as you are, Ainslee. I ask for no more. 'Tis that which I have come to love, even though, in my blindness, I fought that love as hard as I would fight any of my enemies. If you wish to stand at my side, sword in hand, then do so. If you wish to spend your days making Bellefleur so clean a man can eat off of the stable floor, then do so. You do what you wish. My happiness will come from seeing you happy. Sweet Mary, no one deserves happiness more than you, not after all the years you have suffered at Kengarvey."

"Oh, they werena all so bad," she said, her voice thick as she fought the emotion stirred by his words. "I had Ronald, and I begin to believe that my brothers werena as cold and as heartlessly blind to my troubles as I had thought them to be." She studied him for a moment, before saying quietly, "When I was young and being punished by my father or simply feeling very much alone, do ye ken what I used to do?"

"Nay. What?" he asked as he held her in his arms and turned so that she was beneath him. "Plan how many ways you might find to repay your father for all of his cruelties?"

"Weel, aye. I did do that a time a two and, I confess, I could devise some verra blood curdling punishments in my mind. Howbeit, what I refer to is the wee dream I had from time to time. I would think of myself as a beautiful woman instead of the wee skinny bairn I was."

"That part of your dream has certainly come true."

She lightly kissed him to reward his flattery, and then continued, "And one day, as I feared I could endure no more, out of the mists rode a mon." When Gabel started to grin, she scowled at him. "Ye had best not laugh."

"Nay, I would ne'er be so rude."

Since his voice was shaking with laughter, Ainslee ignored him. "That mon was tall and dark and ever so handsome, and he took me up on his horse. We rode away from Kengarvey to places I had ne'er seen, and places where there were no battles and no brutal men, and as much food as any person could e'er want. And he loved me. 'Twas odd that such a silly dream should bring me any comfort, but it did."

"Nay, 'tis not odd." He gently kissed her. "I fear I cannot promise that there will be no battles, no deaths, or even that you shall always have all the food you could want. Such things are not always in my hands, but in God's."

"Weel, it doesna matter. All ye have to do is promise that ye will do your best to love me," she said softly. "Aye, love me as hard and for as long as I will love you."

"That, *my bonnie wee lassie,* is one of the easiest promises I have ever been asked to make, and I make it now, with all my heart."

About the Author

Born and raised in Massachusetts, her family's home since the 1630s, Hannah Howell is the author of thirteen historical romances, including *Only For You,* which is available from Zebra Books. Her love of history prompts the choice of venue, and also has her dragging her sons, Samuel and Keir, and husband Stephen to every historical site she can get to. Her fascination with the past makes research as much a pleasure as a necessity. It was a thrill for her to be able to turn her love of history and writing into a career, one that allows her to share those loves with others. Hannah is currently working on her next historical romance, which Zebra Books will be publishing in September 1996. Hannah loves hearing from her readers, and you may write to her c/o Zebra Books. Please include a self-addressed stamped envelope, if you wish a response.

Please turn the page for an exciting sneak peek of
Hannah Howell's newest historical romance
HIGHLAND CHAMPION
coming soon!

Scotland, Spring 1475

What was an angel doing standing next to Brother Matthew? Liam thought as he peered through his lashes at the couple frowning down at him. And why could he not fully open his eyes? Then the pain hit and he groaned. Brother Matthew and the angel bent closer.

"Do ye think he will live?" asked Brother Matthew.

"Aye," replied the angel, "though I suspicion he will wish he hadnae for a wee while."

Strange that an angel should possess a voice that made a man think of firelit bedchambers, soft unclothed skin, and thick furs, Liam mused. He tried to lift his hand, but the pain of even the smallest movement proved too much to bear. He felt as if he had been trampled by a horse. Mayhap several horses. Very large horses.

"He is a bonnie lad," said the angel as she gently smoothed one small, soft hand over Liam's forehead.

"How can ye tell that he is bonnie? He looks as if someone staked him to the ground and rode over him with a herd of horses."

Brother Matthew and he had always thought alike in many

ways, Liam recalled. He was one of the few men Liam had missed after leaving the monastery. He now missed the touch of the angel's soft hand. For the brief time it had brushed against his forehead, it had felt as if that light touch had smoothed away some of his pain.

"Aye, he does that," replied the angel. "And, yet, one can still see that he is tall, lean, and weel formed."

"Ye shouldnae be noticing such things!"

"Wheesht, Cousin, I am nay blind."

"Mayhap not, but 'tis still wrong. And he isnae at his best now, ye ken."

"Och, nay, that is for certain. Howbeit, I am thinking that his best is verra good, aye? Mayhap as good as our cousin Payton, do ye think?"

Brother Matthew made a very scornful noise. "Better. Truth tell, 'tis why I ne'er believed he would stay with us."

Why should his appearance make someone think him a bad choice for the religious life? Liam did not think that was a particularly fair judgment, but could not seem to give voice to that opinion. Despite the pain he was in, his thoughts were clear enough. He just seemed to be unable to voice them, or make any movement to indicate that he heard these figures discussing him. Even though he could look at them through his lashes, his eyes were obviously not opening enough to let them know he was awake.

"Ye dinnae think he had a true calling?" asked the angel.

"Nay," Brother Matthew replied. "Oh, he liked the learning weel enough, was verra quick and bright, but we could only teach him so much here. We are but a small monastery, nay a rich one, and nay a great teaching place. I think, too, that he found this place too quiet, too peaceful. He missed his family. I have met his kinsmen and I can understand. A large, loud, somewhat, weel, untamed lot of men they are. The learning offered to him eased that restlessness in Liam for a while, but it wasnae enough in the end. The quiet routine, the sameness of the days began to wear upon his spirit, I think."

Liam was a little surprised at how well his old friend knew and understood him. He had been restless, still was in some ways. The quiet of the monastery, the rigid schedule of the monastic life had begun to press in upon him and feel more smothering than comforting. He had missed his family. For a moment he was actually glad that he seemed unable to speak for he feared he would be asking for them now like some forlorn child.

"'Tis hard," said the angel. "I was most surprised that ye settled into the life so verra weel. But ye have a true, deep calling, dinnae ye?"

"Aye, I do," Brother Matthew replied softly. "I did e'en as a child. But ne'er think I dinnae miss all of ye, Keira. I did and do most painfully at times, but there is a brotherhood here, a family of sorts. Yet I will probably visit again soon. I have begun to spend a great deal of time wondering how the bairns have grown, if everyone is still hale and strong, and many another such thing. Letters dinnae tell all."

"Nay, they dinnae." Keira sighed. "I have missed them all, too, and I have been gone for but a sixmonth."

Keira, Liam repeated the name in his mind. A fine name. He tried to move his arm despite the pain and felt a twinge of panic when it would not respond to his command. When he realized he was bound to the bed, his unease grew even stronger. Why would they do that to him? Why did they not wish him to move? Were his injuries so dire? Was he wrong to think he had been given aid? Had he actually been made a prisoner? Even as those questions spun through his mind, he fought past his pain enough to tug against his bonds. A groan escaped him as that pain quickly and fiercely swept through his body from head to toe. He stilled when a pair of small, soft hands touched him, one upon his forehead and one upon his chest.

"I think he begins to wake, Cousin," Keira said. "Hush, sir. Be at peace."

"Tied," Liam hissed the word out from between tightly

gritted teeth, the pain caused by speaking that one small word telling him that his face had undoubtedly taken a severe beating.

"Why?"

"To keep ye still, Liam," Brother Matthew replied. "Keira doesnae think anything is broken save for your right leg, but ye were thrashing about so much it worried us some."

"Aye," agreed Keira. "Ye were beat near to death, sir. 'Tis best if ye remain verra still so as not to add to your injuries or pain. Are ye in much pain?"

Liam muttered a fierce curse at what he considered a very stupid question. He heard Brother Matthew gasp in shock. To his surprise, he heard Keira laugh softly.

"'Twas indeed a foolish question," she said, laughter still tinting her sultry voice. "Ye dinnae seem to have a spot upon ye that isnae brilliant with bruising. Aye, and your right leg was broken. 'Tis a verra clean break and I have set it. After three days there is still no sign of poison in the wound or in the blood, so it should heal verra weel."

"Liam, 'tis Brother Matthew. Keira and I have brought ye to the wee cottage at the edge of the monastery's lands. The brothers wouldnae allow her to tend to your wounds within the monastery, I fear." He sighed. "They werenae too happy with her presence e'en though she was weel hidden away in the guest quarters. Brother Paul was particularly agitated."

"Agitated?" muttered Keira. "Cousin Elspeth would say he—"

"Aye," Brother Matthew hastily interrupted, "I ken what our cousin Elspeth would say. I think she has lived too long amongst those unruly Armstrongs. She has gained far too free a tongue for a proper lady."

Keira made a rude noise. "My, but ye have become verra pious, Cousin."

"Of course I have. I am a monk. We are trained to be pious. Now I can help ye give Liam some potion or change his bandages, if ye wish, but then I must return to the monastery."

"Ah, weel then, best see if he needs to relieve himself,"

Keira said. "I will just step outside so that ye can see to that. Now that he is waking, 'tis best, I think. I shall just run up to the monastery's garden and collect a few herbs. I shall be but a few moments."

"What do ye mean now that he is waking?" demanded Brother Matthew, but then he grunted with irritation when the only reply he got was the door closing behind Keira as she hurried away. "Wretched wee lass."

"Cousin?" Liam asked, realizing that not only was his throat injured, but his jaw and mouth as well.

"Cousin? Oh, aye, the lass is my cousin. One of a vast horde of cousins, if truth be told. A Murray, ye ken."

"Kirkcaldy?"

"'Tis what I am, aye. Her grandmother was one, too. Now I do fear that nay matter how gentle I am, this is going to hurt."

It did. Liam was sure he screamed at one point, and that only increased his pain. He welcomed the blackness when it swept over him, as he suspected the continuously apologizing Brother Matthew did.

"Oh dear, he looks a wee bit paler," Keira said as she set the herbs she had collected down on a table and moved to stand at the side of the small bed Liam was tied to.

"He still suffers a great deal of pain, and I fear I added to it," said Brother Matthew.

"Ye couldnae help it, Cousin. He is better, nay doubt about it, but such injuries will be slow to heal. There truly isnae a part of this mon that isnae hurt. 'Tis a true miracle that only his leg was broken."

"Are ye certain that he was only beaten? Or that he was e'en beaten at all?"

"Aye, Cousin, he was beaten. I have nay doubt about that, but he could have been tossed off that hill, too. Some of these injuries could be from the rocky slope his body would have fallen down and the equally rocky ground he landed on.

I dinnae suppose he was able to tell ye what happened to him, was he?"

"Och, nay. Nay. He spoke but a word or two, then made a pitiful cry and has been like this e'er since." Brother Matthew shook his head. "I wish I could understand this. Who would do such a terrible thing to the mon? I ken I havenae seen that much of the mon o'er the years since he left here, but he really wasnae the sort of mon to make enemies. Certainly nay such vicious ones."

Keira idly tested the strength of the bonds that held Liam still upon the bed and carefully studied the man. "I suspect jealousy is a problem he must often deal with."

Brother Matthew frowned at his cousin. She seemed far too interested in Liam Cameron, revealing more than just a healer's interest in a patient. A healer surely did not need to touch her patient's hair as often as Keira did Liam's thick, dark copper hair. Liam was certainly not looking his best, might well have lost a little of his beauty due to this vicious beating, but there was clearly enough allure left in his battered body and face to draw Keira's interest.

He tried to see Keira as a woman grown, not simply as a cousin he had played with as a child. His eyes widened slightly as he began to see that his cousin was no teasing child now, but a very attractive woman. She was small and slight, yet womanly, for her breasts were well shaped and full and her hips were pleasingly curved. Her hair was a rich, shining black and hung in a thick braid to well past her tiny waist. That hair made her fair skin look even purer, a soft milk white with the blush of good health. Keira's oval face held a delicate beauty, her nose being small and straight, a hint of strength revealed in her small chin, and her cheekbones being high and finely shaped. What caught everyone's interest was her eyes. Set beneath gently arced black brows, and trimmed with thick, long lashes, were a pair of deep green eyes. Those wide eyes bespoke innocence, but their depths held all the womanly mystery that could so intrigue a man. He was a little startled to realize that her mouth, slightly wide and full of lip, held the same contradictions. Her smile could be the epitome of sweet innocence, but Brother Matthew suddenly knew men of the world would quickly see the sensuality there as well. He suddenly feared it had been a serious error in judgment on his part to allow her to tend to a man like Liam Cameron.

"Ye have a rather fierce look upon your face, Cousin," Keira said as she moved to begin preparing more salve for Liam's injuries. "He willnae die, I promise ye. He will just be a verra long time in healing."

"I believe ye. 'Tis just that, weel, one thing Liam did find hard to abide about the monastic life was, weel, was . . ."

"No lasses to smile at." She grinned at the severe frown he gave her for it sat so ill upon his boyishly handsome face.

"I think, just as with our cousin Payton, this mon has a way with the lasses. Aye, and he need do nay more than smile at them."

"I dinnae think he e'en needs to smile," grumbled Brother Matthew.

"Nay, probably not. Come, Cousin, dinnae look so troubled. He is no danger to me now, is he? Aye, and e'en when he is healed enough to smile again, he can only be a danger to me if I wish him to be. Ye cannae think that, with the kinsmen I have, I havenae been verra weel taught in the ways of men." She glanced toward Liam. "Is he a bad mon, then? A vile, heartless seducer of innocents?"

Brother Matthew sighed. "Nay, I would ne'er believe such a thing of him."

"Then there is naught to fret o'er, is there. 'Tis best if we worry o'er our many other troubles. They are of more importance than whether or nay I can resist the sweet smiles of a bonnie lad. I have been here nigh on two months now, Cousin. There has been nary a sign of my enemy so I think, soon, I must try to get home to Donncoill."

"I ken it. I am fair surprised none of your kinsmen have

come round. 'Tis odd that they wouldnae start to wonder on how long ye have stayed at a monastery, or e'en why the monks would allow it."

"'Tisnae so verra unusual for guests, male or female, to linger in the guest quarters, and I paid weel for the privilege."

She smiled and patted his arm when he flushed with embarrassment over that hard truth. "It has been worth it. I needed to hide and mend my wounds, needed to o'ercome my grief and fear, and needed to be certain that, when I did go home, I wasnae leading that murderous bastard Rauf to the gates of Donncoill."

"Your family would protect ye, Keira. They would feel it their duty, their right, and willnae be pleased that ye denied them."

Keira winced. "I ken it, but I will deal with it. I also had to decide what to do. Duncan pulled a vow from me and I had to think hard on how to fulfill it, and how much it might cost me to do so."

"I ken it willnae be easy. Rauf is cunning and vicious. Yet ye swore to your husband ye would see to it that his people didnae suffer under Rauf's rule if he failed to win the battle that night. He failed. He died that night, Keira, so your vow is much akin to one made at a mon's deathbed. Ye have to do all ye can to fulfill it." He kissed her cheek and started for the door. "I will see ye in the morning. Sleep weel."

"Ye, too, Cousin."

The moment he was gone, Keira sighed and sat down in the little chair next to Liam Cameron's bed. Her cousin made it all sound so simple. She dearly wished it was. The vow she had made to her poor, ill-fated husband weighed heavily on her mind and heart. So did the fates of the people of Ardgleann. Duncan had cared deeply for his people, a mixed lot of gentle and somewhat odd souls. It distressed her to think of how they must be suffering under Rauf's rule. She prayed for them every night, but she could not fully dispel the guilt she felt over running away. Although some of what Duncan had asked of her did not seem right, the people of Ardgleann could no longer wait for her to debate the moral complexities of it all, however. It was time, far past time, to do something.

She idly bathed Liam with a soft cloth and cool water. He did not really have a fever, but it seemed to make him rest more quietly. He was a strong man and she felt certain he would continue to recover. When he would be able to tend to himself, she had better have decided what to do about Ardgleann and Rauf. Once she knew why Liam had been hurt and was certain that no enemy hunted him still, she would leave him in the care of the monks and face her own destiny.

Keira felt an immediate pang at the thought of leaving the man and almost laughed at the absurdity of it. He was a mass of bruises and had barely said three words in as many days. She supposed that she felt some odd bond with him because she had been the one to find him. In truth, she had been drawn to him by a strange blend of dreams and compulsion. It had been a little frightening for, although similar experiences had occurred in the past, she had never seen things so clearly or felt as strongly. Even now she could not shake the feeling that there was more to it all than helping him recover from his injuries.

"Foolishness," she muttered and shook her head as she patted him dry with a soft rag.

Perhaps she should send word to his people, she thought as she began to make a hearty broth to feed him when he woke again. From what her cousin had told her, Sir Liam's kinsmen were more than capable of protecting him. Keira quickly discarded the idea for the same reason she had given her cousin when he had suggested sending for the Camerons. Sir Liam might not want that, might be reluctant to pull his family into whatever trouble he had gotten himself into. She could sympathize for, she, too, hesitated to involve her family in her own troubles.

That, too, was foolish, she suspected. She had done nothing wrong, had not caused the trouble or invited the danger.

If one of her family was in such trouble, she would be ready and eager to ride to their side. Which is why they would hesitate to tell her about it, she suddenly thought and briefly grinned. It was instinctive to try to keep a loved one safe, she decided. When her family found out the truth, they would be angry, perhaps a little offended or hurt, but they would understand for they would know in their hearts that they would have done the very same thing.

And, she told herself as she sat down at the small table near the fire, if this man was as close to his family as her cousin implied, he would do the same. The last time she had seen her cousin Gillyanne, she had heard a few tales about the Camerons. Even though the tales had been told to amuse everyone, they had revealed that the Camerons were probably as close a family as her own. There was also Sir Liam's manly pride to consider. It would undoubtedly bristle at the implication that he could not take care of himself. No, Keira decided, it was not a good idea to send for his people without his permission.

After a meal of bread, cheese, and cold venison, Keira took a hasty bath. She then settled herself upon a pallet made up near the fire. Keira stared into the flames and waited for sleep to come. She hated this time of the night—hated the silence, hated the fact that sleep was so slow to come, leaving her alone in the silence with her memories. Try as she might, she could not shake free of the grip of those dark memories. She could only suppress them for a while.

Duncan had been a good man, passingly handsome, and gentle. She had not loved him and she still felt guilty about that, even though it was hardly her fault. At nearly two-and-twenty, however, she had decided she could wait no longer for some great, passionate love to stroll her way. She had wanted children and a home of her own. Although she loved her family deeply, she had begun to feel an increasing need to spread her wings, to walk her own path. Marriage did not usually free a woman, but all her instincts had told her that Duncan would never try to master her. He had wanted a true partner and, knowing how rare that was, she had accepted him when he had asked her to be his bride.

She could still recall the doubts of her family, especially those of her grandmother Lady Maldie and her cousin Gillyanne. Their special gifts had told them that she did not love the man she was about to marry. They had sensed her unease, one she could not explain even to herself. Keira was not sure it was a good thing that they had not pressed her on that, then roundly scolded herself. They had respected her choice, and it had been her choice.

Why she had felt uneasy from the moment she had accepted Duncan's proposal of marriage was still a puzzle to her. Keira had smothered that unease and married him. Within hours of marrying him, the first hint of trouble between them had begun and within days of reaching Ardgleann, the trouble with Rauf had begun. She had thought that explained all those odd feelings she had suffered, the reluctance and the wariness, but now she was not so sure. Every instinct she had told her that the puzzle was not solved yet.

Just as she began to relax, welcoming the comfort of sleep, a harsh cry from Sir Liam startled her. Keira hurried to his side to find him straining against his bonds, muttering furious curses at enemies only he could see. She stroked his forehead and spoke softly to him, telling him over and over where he was, who cared for him now, and that he was safe. It surprised her a little when he quickly grew calm again.

"Jolene?" he whispered.

Keira wondered why hearing him speak another woman's name should irritate her as much as it did. "Nay, Keira," she said as she placed her hand over his to try to stop him from tugging against his bonds.

"Keira," he repeated and grasped her hand in his. "Aye. Keira. Black hair. Confused me. Thought I was home. At Dubheidland."

"Ah. She is your healer?" Keira tried to wriggle her hand free of his grasp, but he would not release her, so she sat down in the chair at his bedside.

"Sig'mor's wife. Lady of Dubheidland. Thought I was home."

"So ye said. I can give ye something to ease the pain, if ye wish it."

"Nay. Thought I was caught again."

She could see that it pained him to speak, but could not resist asking, "Do ye remember what happened to you?"

"Caught. Beaten. Thrown away. Ye found me?"

"Aye, me and my cousin Brother Matthew."

"Good. Safe here."

"Aye, ye will be." She tried yet again to wriggle her hand free of his, but failed.

"Stay." He heaved a sigh. "Please. Stay."

Keira inwardly cursed the weakness that caused her to heed that plea. She carefully shifted her seat closer to the bed so that she could sit more comfortably as she waited for him to release her hand. After a few moments of silence, she wondered if he had gone back to sleep, but his grip upon her hand remained firm. To her surprise, he began to stroke the back of her hand with his thumb. The warmth that gesture stirred within her was a little alarming, but she could not bring herself to stop him.

This was not good, Keira thought. The light brush of a man's thumb over her hand should not make her feel warm. True, it was a very nice hand, the fingers long and elegant, but it was too benign a caress to stir any interest. Or it should be. She looked at his battered face and sighed. To all the troubles she already had, she realized she now had to add one more. A man she did not know, a man whose face was so bruised and swollen it would probably give a child the night terrors, could stir her blood with the simple stroke of his thumb.

<u>BOOK YOUR PLACE ON OUR WEBSITE</u>
<u>AND MAKE THE</u>
<u>READING CONNECTION!</u>

We've created a customized website just for our very special readers, where you can get the inside scoop on everything that's going on with Zebra, Pinnacle and Kensington books.

When you come online, you'll have the exciting opportunity to:

- View covers of upcoming books
- Read sample chapters
- Learn about our future publishing schedule (listed by publication month *and author*)
- Find out when your favorite authors will be visiting a city near you
- Search for and order backlist books from our online catalog
- Check out author bios and background information
- Send e-mail to your favorite authors
- Meet the Kensington staff online
- Join us in weekly chats with authors, readers and other guests
- Get writing guidelines
- AND MUCH MORE!

Visit our website at
http://www.kensingtonbooks.com